Beyond the Ashes

To Ariel
Fear Not!
Karen
Barnett

Other Books by Karen Barnett

Mistaken

The Golden Gate Chronicles
Out of the Ruins
Beyond the Ashes

Beyond the Ashes

The Golden Gate Chronicles

Book 2

Karen Barnett

Abingdon Press

Nashville

Beyond the Ashes

Copyright © 2015 by Karen Barnett

ISBN-13: 978-1-4267-8141-4

Published by Abingdon Press, P.O. Box 801, Nashville, TN 37202

www.abingdonpress.com

Macro Editor: Teri Wilhelms

Published in association with the Books & Such Literary Agency

Library of Congress Cataloging-in-Publication Data

Barnett, Karen, 1969-
 Beyond the ashes / Karen Barnett.
    pages ; cm. — (The golden gate chronicles ; book 2)
 ISBN 978-1-4267-8141-4 (binding: soft back : alk. paper)
 I. Title.
 PS3602.A77584B49 2015
 813'.6—dc23

2015004760

Printed in the United States of America

1 2 3 4 5 6 7 8 9 10 / 20 19 18 17 16 15

To my husband, Steve.
Every fictional hero pales in comparison.

Acknowledgments

Thank you to . . .

- My dear family for allowing me to pursue this crazy dream called writing, even though it means a messy house and a wife/mom who continually talks to imaginary people. I appreciate your support and your sacrifices.
- Critique partners: Tammy Bowers, Heidi Gaul, Patricia Lee, and Marilyn Rhoads for friendship, laughter, and for being the iron that sharpens iron (Proverbs 27:17).
- Amber Nealy for her radiology advice.
- Life-long friend, Autumn Zimmerman, for advice on all things San Francisco.
- Rachel Kent, my patient and understanding agent.
- Ramona Richards, Cat Hoort, Teri Wilhelms, and everyone at Abingdon Press Fiction. You are a joy and a delight!
- The Christian writing community, especially the "Bookies" of Books & Such Literary, Oregon Christian Writers (OCW), American Christian Fiction Writers (ACFW), and the Mount Hermon Christian Writers Conference.

I know the plans I have in mind for you,
declares the LORD;
they are plans for peace, not disaster, to give you a
future filled with hope.
Jeremiah 29:11 CEB

. . . To give them a crown in place of ashes,
oil of joy in place of mourning,
a mantle of praise in place of discouragement.
Isaiah 61:3b CEB

1

I refuse to attend another wedding. I'm through." Ruby King Marshall juggled two glasses of punch in her gloved hand as she shepherded her blind cousin through the overcrowded ballroom. Each doting couple waltzing around the polished floor reminded Ruby of her loss, like a needle thrust into her heart. *Widows and weddings— shouldn't it be bad luck?*

Miriam gripped Ruby's elbow, leaning forward to be heard over the dozens of nearby conversations. "Then I'm relieved mine was last December. I'd have been sad if you'd missed it. And don't forget Anne Marie's next month." A tiny smile flirted at the corner of her lips.

Ruby glanced out the ornate windows, the quiet evening beckoning. Only her cousin—and best friend—would have the audacity to make light of the situation. Newspaper stories of San Francisco's earthquake refugees weighed on Ruby's heart. "With everything that's happened this year, it seems inappropriate to turn a simple wedding into a grand social occasion."

Miriam adjusted her smoky-hued spectacles. "We're not suffering here in Sacramento, Ruby. Besides, love is always worth celebrating. Our hurts remind us to delight in life's joys."

Ruby focused on the sparkling ring on Miriam's finger to prevent her gaze from wandering to her cousin's thickening waistline. She must be at least four months along. Ruby drew up her shoulders, pulling her elbows close to her body. *What have I become?*

Miriam leaned close to Ruby's ear, squeezing her arm. "Elizabeth told me you received a letter from your brother. How is he?"

Ruby escorted Miriam to a corner table and waited as she took a seat. "He sounded rather discouraged. He'd lost another cancer patient." Ruby sat, scooting her chair closer to her cousin's so she could be heard. "With all he suffered after the earthquake and fires, I thought he might come home and set up practice here."

"You just want him where you can keep your eye on him."

"Is it so wrong? He must be lonely, working long hours at the hospital and coming home to a bachelor apartment." Ruby's gaze wandered back to the bride, the gown heavy with Irish lace and ivory buttons—a near duplicate of the dress Ruby had sewn for Miriam last year. "He mentioned having some good news, but you know Robert—he insisted on remaining vague about the topic."

"With six sisters, I imagine he clings to his privacy."

Two gray-haired matrons approached the table, smiles brightening their faces. Mrs. Frederick Compton's lemony-yellow silk gown shimmered in the glow of the hall's electrified chandeliers, her sister's mauve dress fading in comparison. Mrs. Compton's gaze flitted over Miriam and settled on Ruby. She clucked her tongue. "Oh, Ruby, dear. We're so pleased you chose to attend. How are you?"

Ruby clenched her hands in her lap. "I'm fine, Mrs. Compton. How kind of you to inquire."

The woman waved her handkerchief at someone across the hall and turned to her sister. "There's Reverend Greene, Claudia. We must speak to him about the library benefit." She nodded to Ruby. "Please excuse us, dear."

The second woman ignored Ruby and Miriam, apparently content to be pulled along in Mrs. Compton's wake, a peacock feather bobbing atop her silver curls. A high-pitched voice floated back to the table. "Poor child. So young to be widowed."

Miriam pressed a handkerchief to her nose. "Someone needs to speak to Mrs. Compton about her cologne." She muttered the words under her breath. "Worse than smelling salts."

A warm flush crept up under Ruby's collar. "I dislike coming to these functions. This is the fourth wedding in as many months and at every one, I'm petted and cooed over like a child with a skinned knee. I'm tired of being the center of everyone's pity." Ruby thumped the cup down, punch sloshing over the edge and onto her gloves. "Oh!"

Miriam lifted her shoulders. "At least women speak to you. It's as if they believe I don't hear, either."

"I wish they'd ignore me as well." As soon as the careless thought passed her lips, Ruby winced. She placed a hand on her cousin's wrist. "That was thoughtless of me. I apologize."

"Please don't guard your words around me, Ruby. I know you better than that." Miriam flicked her fingers through the air dismissively. "Why would I care if some stranger speaks to me, anyway? I'd rather listen to you—even if you're being ridiculous."

Ruby's skin crawled. Her cousin had an uncanny habit of seeing right through people. "What do you mean?"

"With the exception of gossips like those, most people aren't fussing over you. Hardly anyone gives a thought to the accident any more. You're the one who's stuck fast."

Ruby swallowed against the lump rising in her throat. Who'd have expected the mere thought of Charlie's death would bring tears, two years later?

"It's good you came tonight. You're alone too often." Miriam touched Ruby's sleeve.

"I'm not alone. I have Otto." The little black and tan dachshund sported tiny gray hairs on his muzzle. How many more years before she lost him, as well? Ruby tightened her fingers around the cup's delicate handle. "And if you say you've found the perfect man for me, I'm going to march out the door." In her haste, she splashed punch onto the white tablecloth for a second time. "Drat! I'm going to need another napkin."

Miriam's gentle laugh trilled. "You wouldn't walk out on me. We promised as girls to always speak the truth to each other." She passed a linen square to Ruby and gestured toward the refreshment table.

"Now, would you like a refill? Or have you spilled enough for one evening?"

"I think I'll pass for now."

"I do know some nice fellows, but I wouldn't dream of trying to match you up."

Ruby pushed back the cup. "Everyone keeps telling me to move on, and I'm too young not to marry again. I don't feel young. I feel like I'm a hundred years old and my life is over. I can't even look at another man without seeing Charlie's face." She stared down at her hands.

Miriam spoke, her voice hesitant. "You're only twenty-seven, Ruby. If you won't marry again, then it's time to decide what you *will* do."

"What do you mean?" Ruby lifted her head.

"You were always the one with the plans and dreams. You arranged every step of our lives when we were children." Miriam's hand settled on the bump in her midsection.

"Exploring haunted attics and searching for lost Indian camps?" Ruby fingered her lace cravat. "Most of my schemes led to disaster, or have you forgotten? I got us into some pretty good scrapes."

"And then you planned a way out."

I never planned a way out of widowhood. A familiar ache twisted in her stomach. According to her early dreams, she should be the one expecting the baby. "I think God laughs at my schemes."

"Perhaps. But it never stopped you from making them."

Ruby's throat squeezed as she stared at the centerpiece, the riotous flowers overflowing with ridiculous joy. "I gave up dreaming when Charlie died."

"Then maybe it's time you started seeking God's plan for your life. Find a new sense of purpose for yourself." Ruby's cousin landed her cup squarely in front of her. "It doesn't have to be marriage. It's the twentieth century, not the Middle Ages. You're free to make your own choices."

Shivers ran down Ruby's arms. The thought had been close to her heart as well. "I keep reflecting on the situation in San Francisco. I saw an article in the *Evening Bee* stating the need for aid workers.

Thousands are still homeless. Robert mentioned they were short-staffed at the hospital, too. I suppose many of the nurses fled the city after the disaster." She closed her eyes and pictured her own nurse's cap gathering dust on the upper shelf of the wardrobe. How would it feel to pin it on again? To bring hope to the sick and the dying? Her heart fluttered, like the wings of her mother's peach-faced canary beating against its wire cage.

Miriam placed her hand atop Ruby's. "Perhaps God is calling you back into nursing."

God calling? Ruby pushed the difficult thought away. She made her own decisions, she didn't require divine guidance. "It isn't the dream I had for my life."

"God has a plan for you, Ruby—but it might be profoundly different than your own."

Ruby sighed. Her cousin would not by swayed once she'd taken to an idea. It explained why she'd always been such an excellent conspirator. "I'll think on it, I promise."

"I'll pray God provides you swift counsel."

Elizabeth, Ruby's seventeen-year-old sister, wove through the crowd, a smile dancing across her face. She hurried to the table, clasping her fingers in front of her. "Have you heard? Hattie and Ernest are engaged. Ruby, Hattie hopes you will help with the gown."

Not again. Ruby grabbed for the cup, desperate to distract her nerves. It clattered across the table and dumped the remainder of its contents on the linen cloth.

Miriam giggled, pressing a hand to her mouth. "Ask and ye shall receive."

Ruby blew a long breath through her gritted teeth and shook her head. "Please give Hattie my regrets, Elizabeth. I'm going to San Francisco."

2

San Francisco, California
July 23, 1906

A beam of sunlight pierced the stained glass window in Dr. Gerald Larkspur's study, casting a rosy glow on the stationery in his hand. He eyed the dainty feminine script marching across the page in ordered lines. Gerald lowered the letter, staring at Dr. Robert King over the stacks of medical files littering his desk blotter. "Your sister wants to come to San Francisco now? Does she understand the city is in shambles?"

His friend leaned on the oak desk. "Ruby wants to help with the relief work. She's had extensive nursing training. My sister even assisted our father in surgeries, back when we were children." Robert frowned. "Never seemed fair, since he wouldn't let me step foot over the threshold. Sure, she was six years older, but I was a boy. If anyone should be man enough to handle the sight of blood, you'd think it would have been me."

Gerald passed the letter back to Robert as he fought a smirk, picturing his young medical partner as a petulant child. "Sounds like she was 'man enough.'"

The paper crinkled as Robert tucked it into his inside pocket. "Trust me, Ruby has a strong spirit. She put up with my antics, after all."

"I can imagine."

Robert leaned forward, placing both palms against Gerald's desk. "I know it's asking a lot. With your mother living here, and your cousin's family, and me—maybe I should put Ruby off the idea."

Gerald rested his chin on his palm, the paper's rosewater scent lingering on his skin. Another woman in the house? So much for the quiet bachelor life. "I can't see why not. What's one more?"

Robert grinned. "Abby's already set up an extra bed in her room."

"I see." Gerald opened the nearest file, and flipped through the pages. "You two were so confident I'd say yes?"

His young partner straightened, tugging on the hem of his gray vest. "Not confident, just optimistic. You're always reaching out to help others. You've taken the rest of us in, after all."

The chair squeaked as Gerald rose to his feet. The scent of vegetable stew scented the air, his stomach rumbling in response. The noon meal must be nearly ready, one advantage of having three women—soon to be four—in his house. "Does your sister know about Abby?"

Robert's gaze lowered. "I haven't informed my family, yet. I'm certain Ruby will be pleased."

A chuckle rose in Gerald's chest. He clasped Robert's shoulder with a firm hand. "In the same way you were sure I'd consent? Your understanding of human nature never fails to amaze me."

San Francisco, California
August 1, 1906

I hope Robert received my telegram. Ruby clutched her wrap with one hand and the ferry rail with the other, stunned at the sight before her. She thought the newspaper stories had prepared her for the devastation, but as the boat pulled up to the dock, prickles crawled across her arms. Even three months after the earthquake and subsequent firestorm, San Francisco looked like the parlor stereoscope images of Pompeii. Skeletal buildings dominated the skyline, either half-destroyed or half-built—Ruby couldn't decide. Stacks of building supplies lined the piers.

The ferry eased to a stop, the passengers collecting their belongings. Ruby lifted her bag and clumsy wicker basket and clutched the items before her as she joined the stream of passengers jostling their way to the front. At the plank, a porter reached for the basket.

"No, I'll hold this. Thank you." She offered the carpetbag instead, and the man grasped it with a nod before assisting her to the dock.

Ruby froze as the crowd pushed past her. The stench of ashes lingered in the air. Beyond the hundreds of voices, she could hear a cacophony of hammers and saws.

"Miss?" The porter held the bag toward her, a frown dragging down his bushy moustache.

Ruby transferred the awkward container to her left hand and reached for the bag with her right, trying not to stare at the man whose face resembled a walrus minus tusks. She stumbled a few steps forward before lowering the rectangular carton to the ground and grappling with her wrap, pulling it tight around her shoulders. She swiveled her gaze from side to side, overcome with the image of the city as a giant anthill, carelessly kicked over by a mischievous child.

She didn't belong here. A wave of emotion swept over her. *Charlie, why'd you have to buy the fool horse, anyway?* Ruby stepped close to the basket, brushing it with her shoe tips. She shouldn't have allowed Miriam to bully her into making new plans. It wasn't her place to save the world. She should be home where life remained predictable and secure. And boring.

Ruby tucked a stray curl under her hat before grasping the wicker handle and hoisting it up over her arm. She straightened her posture, willing confidence into her steps. She'd come to help the people of San Francisco. And poor Robert, slaving away in this broken carcass of a city. *No more talk of weddings and babies.* Robert was clearly too immersed in his work for such nonsense. It still seemed remarkable her impish baby brother would grow up to be a doctor like their father. If only she'd been a boy.

A shout from the distance drew her attention.

"Ruby!" Robert pushed through the crowd, arms extended.

Ruby dropped the bags and fell into his arms. "I am so relieved to see you. This place is such a mess."

He laughed. "This is nothing, Sis. You should have seen it a month ago." He pulled her into an embrace so tight it lifted her off her feet.

Robert's touch crumbled the last of her resolve and tears stung at her eyes. "It's a joy to see your face." She squeezed his arm. "I can't believe I'm actually here. We've been so worried about you. It's been months since we received your last letter. Mother is irate." A shiver rushed through her and her voice trembled. "Why haven't you written, you lout?" She dug into her pocket for a handkerchief.

Her brother laughed, pressing a silk square into her hand. "I'm fine, Ruby. I've been a little busy." His face lit up in a huge boyish smile. "Just wait until you hear all my news. You'll forgive me in a heartbeat."

"Never. There can be no excuse for keeping us all wondering. I'm sure you're not at the hospital every hour of the day. Certainly you could have spared a moment to write."

He pushed his chocolate-brown derby to the back of his head, a familiar puckish grin lighting his face.

She took a step back and studied him. Shadows under Robert's eyes showed the effects of the disaster and his difficult work—these she'd expected—but his expression also contained a spark of unspoken delight. He didn't look the part of a lonely, overworked bachelor.

Robert stepped to one side, revealing a well-dressed man and woman standing directly behind him.

Ruby dabbed at her reddened eyes, a wave of heat crawling up her neckline beneath the collar of her traveling jacket.

The man flashed a disarming smile, his Bristol-blue eyes causing Ruby's breath to leak from her chest. Fine lines around his mouth spoke of a life filled with either worry or laughter.

Ruby glanced down, awash with emotions after the long, exhausting trip. She certainly wasn't going to swoon over a man, even if his eyes were a dead-ringer for her Charlie. *Especially because of that.*

Robert clasped a hand on the man's shoulder. "Ruby, this is Dr. Gerald Larkspur, my mentor and friend. I've written to you about him, right?" He turned his attention toward Dr. Larkspur. "Gerald, may I present my sister, Mrs. Ruby Marshall?"

Ruby reached her hand out to the doctor, noticing too late she still clutched the damp handkerchief.

Dr. Larkspur took her fingers, with only a quick glance at the fabric crushed between their palms. With his other hand, he touched the brim of his black hat. "It is an honor to meet you, Mrs. Marshall. But your brother does himself a disservice. I can't be called a mentor any longer. He's left me in the dust, I'm afraid. I keep reminding him, we're partners now."

Ruby bobbed her head, giving herself a second to string words together into a polite greeting. "Dr. Larkspur—the honor is mine. My brother has spoken most highly of you." She retrieved her hand and tucked the handkerchief into her sleeve, casting a final glance at the man's eyes. *Not exactly like Charlie's. A tad darker.* She pushed the memory from her mind.

Ruby directed her gaze at the young woman hovering near her brother's other arm. *Mrs. Larkspur, perhaps?* The woman glanced up at Robert, her sweetly freckled cheeks sporting a light blush. Ruby's stomach crawled up into her throat. *Oh, no. Please, no.*

"Ruby," her brother turned back to her. "I'd like to introduce you to someone very special."

Ruby fought the urge to cover her ears and run screaming back to the ferry.

Robert cleared his throat, his eyes warming as he gazed at the young woman. "This is Miss Abby Fischer. Abby is Dr. Larkspur's cousin . . ." his words rushed toward her like an engine roaring down the track, ". . . and my fiancée."

3

Gerald toyed with the watch chain hidden in his pocket as he studied the young woman standing on the dock. As a confirmed bachelor, he never considered himself a good judge of female emotions, but the woman's pinched brows and puckered lips suggested Robert's announcement was something akin to the taste of quinine.

Mrs. Marshall clutched her bag against her midsection, her pale blue eyes growing wider by the second. "Your—your fiancée?"

Robert darted a quick glance at Abby before focusing on his sister. "I'm sorry to spring this on you, Ruby. I only received your letter a few days ago, so I didn't have time to write. I had hoped to bring Abby home to meet everyone."

Gerald's cousin took a step backward, bumping into his elbow. "I shouldn't have come. I ought to have let Robert get you settled in first."

Gerald brushed his hand against Abby's back. Since her family had moved to San Francisco, he'd stepped into the role of protective older sibling. If Robert's sister dared say one unkind word to Abby, she'd have to deal with him.

Robert latched onto his fiancée's arm. "It was my idea. I couldn't wait to introduce you." He cleared his throat. "Abby, may I present my sister, Mrs. Ruby Marshall?"

Mrs. Marshall's mouth opened and closed like a fish in a glass bowl. She reached up and tucked a curling wisp of red hair behind her ear.

Gerald's eyes traveled down to her other hand, clenching the folds of her blue skirt just below her tiny waist. He forced his gaze upward in time to spot the color draining from her heart-shaped face. *She's going to faint.*

Gerald took a swift step forward and put a hand on the woman's arm. "Mrs. Marshall—"

Robert had also spotted the sudden shift in his sister's demeanor and caught her other elbow. "Ruby?"

"Robert, there's a bench behind you." Gerald gripped Mrs. Marshall's hand and motioned with his head. "Let's sit her down. Shall we?"

Mrs. Marshall's arm stiffened, resisting his attempt to steer her to the seat. "No, thank you, Dr. Larkspur. I feel . . . it's been a long . . ." her voice faltered. "I'm fine now, thank you." She turned to her brother. "I'm sorry, Robert. I'm a bit overwrought from the trip." She pulled her fingers from Gerald's grasp and clamped her mouth into a tight-lipped smile, directing her gaze back to her brother. "You're getting married? Why it's—it's wonderful news. I am so pleased."

Gerald fought off a smirk, amused to witness his cocky partner rendered into a wide-eyed silence.

Mrs. Marshall stepped forward to Abby. "Miss Fischer, was it?"

"Please, call me Abby." His cousin fingered the locket she always wore.

Gerald winced at the quaver in Abby's voice. The poor girl had been through so much in the past year, the last thing she needed was a meddling older sister.

Mrs. Marshall's lips turned downward. "You agreed to marry my kid brother?"

Abby's freckles stood in sharp contrast to her pale face. "Yes."

The woman reached out gloved hands to grasp Abby's elbows. "I hope you know what you're in for, Abby, because he's a handful." A bright smile replaced her frown, like warm sunshine breaking through the fog. With a shrug, she tipped her head in Robert's direction. "And any woman capable of taming Robert's heart, I'd be honored to call a sister."

Gerald pushed his hat back. Ruby King Marshall was clearly made out of stouter material than he'd given her credit for.

Abby released a sudden laugh, her expression brightening.

Gerald let his attention flicker back and forth between the two women. Though smiling, his cousin appeared on the verge of collapse, her face blotchy. Mrs. Marshall's eyes shone, but he couldn't ignore her shallow, rapid breathing. He shook his head. He'd never figure out why women acted the way they did. Probably why he was still unmarried.

Abby ran fingers down Robert's sleeve. "If anyone did the 'taming,' it was your brother, Mrs. Marshall. He has the patience of a saint."

Mrs. Marshall laughed. "Patient? Are you sure we are talking about the same Robert King—the boy so eager to practice medicine that at fourteen, he sneaked into our father's office and pretended to be the physician? He had at least half of the patients completely hoodwinked." She shook her head. "I don't think he knows the meaning of the word patience. Outside of medical patients."

Abby brightened. "Tell me more."

Robert's sister linked arms with Abby as the two walked toward the Ferry Building. "I have many such tales. Where shall I start? First, you must begin by calling me Ruby."

Robert grasped the handle of the wicker basket. "Ruby, no stories. Please."

His sister shot a smirk over her shoulder, eyes flashing.

Gerald chuckled. Obviously, Robert was not going to get off scotfree for this little escapade.

Robert grunted as he hoisted the wicker container in the air. "Ruby, what have you got in here?"

His sister smiled. "Otto, of course."

Gerald froze, staring at the hamper now jostling in Robert's hands. "Otto?"

Robert's jaw hung open. "Ruby, you didn't."

The basket growled in reply.

"You didn't expect me to leave him in Sacramento with Mother, did you?" Mrs. Marshall cocked her head to one side, her elbow linked with Abby's.

Gerald's stomach dropped. Not only a meddling sister, but a yapping dog, too?

Robert gripped the container under his arm, reaching for the carpetbag with his other hand. He glanced up at Gerald, the corner of his mouth rising. "It won't be a problem. Right, Gerald?"

❧

Robert is getting married.

Ruby walked down the cobblestone street, arm in arm with the stranger, soon to be a sister. She lifted her chin, pressing away the thought. She'd squashed her own feelings, put Robert on the defensive, and pulled Abby close. Next on the agenda—inform Robert she'd decided on a brief visit.

Coming to San Francisco had been a mistake. As usual, she had blundered ahead with her plans, not bothering to consult anyone. She shook her head and glanced heavenward. *God laughs at my schemes, right, Miriam?*

Ruby's mind wandered, barely registering the landmarks Abby pointed out as they walked along Market Street. Once they reached Robert's apartment, he and Ruby would have a long talk. They would chart out her short stay and buy a ticket for the return journey. She wasn't staying around to help plan a wedding. *When our mother and sisters hear the news, they'll be on the next ferry.*

The two men followed, Robert occasionally putting in a word or two. Dr. Larkspur remained silent. Back at the Ferry Building, his probing eyes had caught her unprepared—as if the stranger could read her thoughts as clearly as her sightless cousin. If she had Robert and Abby convinced of her sincerity, why would someone like Dr. Larkspur believe any different? And why should she care what he thought?

The group stopped beside a gleaming red automobile.

Ruby stepped back, a cold chill washing over her. "I thought we were walking to Robert's apartment. You don't live far, do you?"

Robert tucked her luggage and Otto's basket into the rear seat. "My apartment building was destroyed in the fires. I wrote and told you. Remember?"

"Where are you staying?" The street noise multiplied, as if pounding its way inside her brain. She'd arrived with no thought to accommodations.

"It's not a problem, Sis. I talked to Gerald about it, and he doesn't mind. We'll just shuffle around a bit. Everyone in the city is getting used to tight quarters."

"I thought I was coming to help, but I'm just going to be in the way." Ruby covered her burning cheeks with her hands.

A huge smile danced across Abby's face. "Don't feel bad, please! We'll all make space. It will be fun."

Ruby's stomach jolted. "Am I staying with you?" She turned to Robert. "You haven't answered my question. Where are you living?"

Her brother's face split into an annoying grin. "I'm staying with Gerald—Dr. Larkspur. And so is Abby's family. And Gerald's mother, Mae Larkspur. But it's a large house. There's plenty of room, really."

"You're—you're all living . . ." Ruby's idea of coming to the city to console her lonely brother crumbled, replaced by the reality of being trapped in a houseful of strangers.

Dr. Larkspur swung open the vehicle's rear door. "If you will just step in, Mrs. Marshall, I'm sure we can explain everything on the way."

Ruby grabbed the edge of her coat and twisted, glancing from one face to another and then at the automobile. The door yawned open like a mouth preparing to devour her. Scurrying backward, she stumbled on a loose cobble, nearly landing on her backside.

Robert reached out and caught her elbow. "Ruby, what's gotten into you?"

She leaned heavily on Robert's arm as her stomach churned. Beads of sweat broke out between her shoulder blades. *Get in the car, you silly goose.* Panting, she heard her own words as if from a distance.

"I—I can't. I'm sorry!" Pulling away from Robert's grip she retreated toward the Ferry Building.

❧

Gerald released the door handle as Mrs. Marshall fled, her brother trailing behind. "What is wrong with her?"

Abby's chin trembled. "It's me. She doesn't approve of me, and now she thinks Robert and I are . . . are . . ." She drew her hands up to cover her eyes. "This is a disaster."

"She thinks what?" Why was he always two steps behind the conversation when speaking with women? And Abby always seemed one of the sensible ones.

She shot him a withering look. "Robert and I are living in the same household, Gerald."

"Don't be ridiculous. She couldn't possibly think you two have done anything improper."

"Then why would she rush off?"

Gerald glanced toward the siblings. Robert had caught up to his sister, and they were talking in hushed tones. Gerald laid a hand on his cousin's shoulder. "Well, whatever has put her out of sorts, Robert will straighten it out. She does seem a little flighty, don't you think?"

Abby frowned. "Robert said she was quite levelheaded before her husband died."

Gerald swiped a palm across the back of his collar. "She's young to be a widow. Do you know what happened to her husband?"

Abby raised an eyebrow at him. "Don't you men ever talk about anything but medicine?"

A rumbling growl drew his attention to the back seat. Gerald shoved his hands in his pockets and scowled at the pile of luggage. *Lord, you told us to take care of widows and orphans. You said nothing about widows with dogs.* He turned his gaze back to Robert and his sister, arguing just out of earshot. Mrs. Marshall's hat hung slightly askew.

Gerald leaned closer to Abby. "How did he die?"

"Mr. Marshall's horse was spooked by an automobile. He broke his neck in the fall." Abby sighed. "Robert was apparently away in medical school when it happened."

The sound of hooves clattering across the stones obscured the rest of his cousin's words. Spooked by an automobile? Gerald ran his hand along the car's frame, the metal growing warm in the sunlight. "Wait here, Abby." He strode toward his friend.

Robert's voice carried on the breeze. "Ruby, you just arrived. You can't return home today. Be reasonable."

Mrs. Marshall's gaze fluttered over her brother's shoulder, widening as Gerald approached.

Gerald pulled a watch from his vest pocket and clicked open the cover, glancing down at the Roman numerals. "Robert, you wanted to get back to the hospital this afternoon, right? I know Mrs. Meier needs another treatment. She favors you over me." He leaned toward Mrs. Marshall, cupping a hand about the corner of his mouth. "I believe Mrs. Meier is a little sweet on your brother. In fact, most of our female patients seem to prefer his attention. I can't understand why, myself." He snapped the lid closed.

Mrs. Marshall's eyes softened.

"You would think they would fancy someone wiser and more mature." He cocked his head to one side, appreciating the flush springing to his partner's face. "But apparently not."

Robert frowned. "Yes, I did want to get back, but I couldn't abandon my sister on her first day."

Gerald turned to the young widow and tipped his hat. "Mrs. Marshall, have you had the pleasure of riding one of San Francisco's famous cable cars?"

Her countenance brightened, her lips parting. "No, I haven't."

"Perfect. The cable line is running again, as of a few days ago." Gerald turned to Robert. "You and Abby take my car over to the hospital and meet with Mrs. Meier. I'll escort Mrs. Marshall to the house and help her get settled into Abby's room."

Robert huffed. "The cable car would take—"

"Robert," Mrs. Marshall grasped his sleeve, "I would prefer to take the cable car if it isn't an inconvenience for Dr. Larkspur."

Gerald's chest swelled. He'd called that one exactly right. Maybe there was hope for him, yet.

Robert pulled off his derby and scratched his head. "Well, if you're certain."

She smiled, looking from her brother to Gerald and back, cheeks pink. "I am. I don't want your work to suffer during my visit."

Gerald presented his arm to Mrs. Marshall, rewarded by a smile and the touch of her hand.

Robert raked fingers through his dark hair. With a shrug, he assisted Abby up into a seat. "I'll retrieve your trunk and bring it to the house when we're done at the hospital."

Perhaps Robert's ability to understand the female species didn't apply to his own sister. Gerald studied the graceful curve of Mrs. Marshall's fingers resting against his coat sleeve. And perhaps having one more woman under his roof wouldn't be such a bother after all. It might be entertaining to watch her keep Robert on his toes.

Ruby gripped Dr. Larkspur's arm as they strode down the sidewalk. She hoped she hadn't given the man the wrong impression. She stopped in her tracks. "Robert and Abby took my luggage."

"Is it a problem?"

"Otto's still in his basket. He doesn't much like Robert."

The man chuckled. "How dangerous could the dog be if it's small enough to fit in a picnic basket?" He paused, his voice lowering. "I assume you don't approve of automobiles?"

Ruby bit her lip. Did this man miss nothing? "Actually, I've never ridden in one. And I don't want to. Not now. Not ever." First, she falls apart on the ferry dock, and then she runs from the vehicle like a frightened child—what must he think of her? Ruby tugged at her lace collar. "Of course, I could if I wanted to. I'm not afraid of them." She cast a quick glance at his face.

The corner of his mouth curved upward. "If you say so."

"I'm not." A wave of heat crept up her back.

"Of course."

She cleared her throat. "Or rather, I wouldn't be, if I could be in the driver's seat."

Dr. Larkspur stopped, his brows nearly disappearing under the brim of his hat. "You can't be serious. You want to drive my automobile?"

"Not yours in particular." The intense blue of his eyes sent a tingle across her skin. "I'm sure it sounds outlandish. I just thought if I were driving, it might not be so fearsome." Ruby thrust her shoulders back. "Things we can't control are frightening. Things that control us are truly terrifying. But things we control are—" she lifted her hands, palms up, "—well, if you shrink from them, I suppose you don't have much faith in yourself."

Dr. Larkspur rubbed a hand across his chin. "I suppose there's truth to what you say. And yet, I think you might be missing a part of the puzzle."

"What?"

"We're never really in control."

She laughed, the sound bubbling from deep in her chest. "Are you a philosopher?"

He smiled. "Hardly. But I am an observer of life. One who just rode out a major earthquake." Dr. Larkspur rubbed a finger across his chin while he spoke.

An endearing gesture. She remembered the feel of Charlie's face— the bristly stubble when he rose in the morning, the freshly shaven silkiness of his cheek against hers when he kissed her goodbye. She pulled her gaze away and blinked rapidly.

"In my field, I've learned there are few events over which we have power. People become ill. They attempt to regain some authority over their bodies by coming to me. I do what I can," he cast his eyes downward, "but too often it's out of my hands. I can do everything right and still lose the patient." Dr. Larkspur pressed his lips into a thin line. "You can't always be the one in charge, Mrs. Marshall."

Her throat tightened as she studied the man's drawn expression. He must have a grief story of his own.

A shadow passed over his face as he shrugged one shoulder. "Sometimes you have to trust someone else to drive the car."

4

$\mathcal{T}$he mahogany-paneled dining room echoed with the sounds of voices and the clatter of silverware. Gerald leaned back in his chair and gazed around the table. Five years ago, when he'd bought this house, he'd hoped to fill it with family. He'd dreamed of an adoring wife and a collection of bright-eyed children. Instead he got his mother, his cousin and her family, his best friend, and his friend's widowed sister. Even so, warmth crept into his chest as he enjoyed the presence of the people he loved. The beautiful guest added an extra sweetness to the blend.

His mother lowered a chicken-laden platter to the tablecloth. Gerald took a deep whiff as fragrant steam rose from the serving dishes, the scents of roasting meat mingling with rosemary and cornbread. His stomach grumbled in response.

Gerald's cousin, Clara Fischer, added a dish of creamed peas before taking her place next to her husband, Herman. She smiled as her daughter Abby helped four-year-old Davy draw his seat up to the table.

A German accent colored Herman's words. "Clara, Aunt Mae—everything smells wonderful."

Clara smiled as she touched her husband's shoulder, the evening light glinting off her blonde hair.

Gerald pulled his gaze away. Every time he noticed Clara's resemblance to Cecelia—her daughter, Abby's older sister—a new thorn embedded in his heart. The family had come to San Francisco last year seeking treatment for Cecelia's leukemia. She'd improved under his and Robert's care, but the cancer had been far too advanced. She passed away a few months before the big quake.

Losing a patient was always difficult—losing a member of his own family left a scar on his soul.

Robert cleared his throat. "Yes, you've outdone yourselves. Dinner looks delicious."

At least one good thing came out of our tragedy. Robert and Abby. What a perfect combination.

"Gerald, would you ask the blessing for our meal?" His mother sat in a chair at the corner of the table, between him and Abby, and reached for their hands.

Gerald nodded, clasping her palm and extending his other hand to Mrs. Marshall.

Her crystal blue eyes widened, but she didn't pull away as his fingers settled over hers.

"I hope you don't mind." He squeezed her small hand. "It's a family tradition."

"Of course." Her fingers were icy cold.

Gerald nodded and bowed his head, forcing his eyes closed, trying to direct his mind away from the gentle touch of her skin against his own. "Father, we thank You for this glorious day and for Your many blessings, especially another guest at our table. Lord, bless this food and the loving hands which prepared it. Amen."

Ruby tugged her hand free, a flush brightening her cheeks all the way to the tip of her nose.

His mother's silvery brows drew low over her eyes. "Gerald, what's this on your palm?"

His throat tightened as he pulled away from her grip. "It's nothing, Mother, just a burn from the machinery."

She frowned, lines deepening around her mouth. "Another? Or the same burn you had last month? Hasn't it healed?"

Gerald pulled his arms under the table. The glow of being head of a large household fizzled under the scrutiny of an overanxious mother. Suddenly, he felt about eight years old. "I'm the doctor here, remember?"

"And sometimes doctors are so busy caring for others, they neglect themselves." She reached for the platter of chicken and passed it to him.

Robert placed a spoonful of vegetables on his plate. "Do you want me to look at it, Gerald?"

"It's nothing." He lifted the platter from his mother's grip, grasping the dish from underneath to obscure his palm from her inquisitive gaze.

Clara placed a piece of buttered cornbread on her young son's plate, smiling as little Davy licked his lips. "Ruby, it was brave of you to travel all the way to San Francisco by yourself at such a time. Was your mother concerned for your safety?"

The young woman took a sip from her water glass. "She was concerned, but I assured her Robert would be here to greet me."

Abby, sitting on the child's far side, placed a napkin on Davy's lap. "We're glad you decided to come. Robert's spoken so lovingly of his sisters."

Ruby glanced at her brother with a smile. "We've missed him very much. Even though he wrote us after the disaster, it was a relief to actually set eyes on him. His letters had been a bit vague." Her eyes darted toward Abby.

Herman ran a hand over his whiskers. "Your Robert has been a wonderful help to our family. First, with Cecelia," his voice faltered, "and then with *meine* Abigail during the earthquake. He has earned a place of honor in this family. Even if Abby hadn't accepted his proposal."

Abby smiled and ducked her head, freckled cheeks glowing.

Clara reached over and squeezed Robert's arm before turning to Ruby. "I know your family has missed him, but Herman and I already think of him as our son."

Gerald swiped a second helping of mashed potatoes, wincing as the serving spoon brushed against his sore hand. He gripped the silver handle with his fingertips, guiding the steaming food to his plate. How long had it been since he'd seared himself with the X-ray machine? Two months? Three? His mother was right—it should have healed long before now. The sound of laughter echoed off the walls, scattering Gerald's thoughts. He frowned, attempting to concentrate on Robert's story. His friend held the table enthralled.

"She insisted the X-rays had improved her skin. She sidled right up to me. 'Dr. King, don't you think I look beautiful?'" Robert shook his head. "I thought you were exaggerating, Gerald. But every time I see her, she flutters her eyelashes a little more. She's starting to make me nervous."

Mrs. Pembroke. Of course. "I've been telling you for months, Robert. She's clearly sweet on you." Gerald leaned toward his cousin. "You should keep a close eye on this one, Abby. She might steal him from you."

Abby's laugh made his heart swell. Her sister's death had taken a toll. *It's good to see Abby smile again.*

Ruby's nose wrinkled. "Robert, have you informed this woman you are engaged to be married?"

Gerald finished chewing, the buttered cornbread practically melting in his mouth. "I don't think she cares."

"Perhaps you should insist she see Dr. Larkspur, instead."

Gerald snorted. "Oh, no you don't. I was more than happy to turn her attentions over to Robert. I've dealt with her for five years now. I think it's his turn."

Ruby's intense stare caught him off guard. Gerald swiped the napkin across his chin in case he'd somehow smeared crumbs on his face.

"But if she's your patient, why don't you speak to her about this inappropriate behavior?"

"She's not my patient anymore. She requested Robert." Gerald nodded toward her brother.

"What exactly am I supposed to say?" Robert smirked, leaning back in his chair.

Ruby tucked a loose curl into place, sending an onyx earbob swinging. "You could politely inform her you're not interested in her advances. It would be the most respectful way to handle the lady's feelings. It is discourteous to allow this young woman to continue and for you two to make sport of it behind her back."

Gerald fought to keep the smile from his face. He pointed an authoritative finger toward his partner. "You heard your sister, Robert. You'd best inform the 'young lady' her amorous attentions are unseemly."

Ruby's glance darted between the two men. "I recognize Robert's mischievous expression. What am I missing here?"

Gerald's mother huffed, setting her fork on her plate. "You boys are insufferable." She leaned toward Ruby. "Mrs. Pembroke is ninety, if she's a day. Honestly. One would think you'd have a little more respect for your patients. And your elders."

"Mother, if you could see the way she behaves, you would understand."

His mother touched her silver hair and frowned. "Ruby is correct in accusing you of being disrespectful."

Gerald sobered. "You're right, of course." He glared at his friend. "You will show Mrs. Pembroke the ultimate respect, Robert. Even when she's trying to steal a kiss in the exam room."

Ruby gasped. "She didn't. Now you're just being ridiculous!"

He reached for the water glass. "Nope. It's the God's-honest truth. Isn't it Robert?"

Robert rubbed a hand through his hair. "Yes, well, sort of."

She twisted in her seat to stare at her brother. "But, why would she?"

He took another forkful of mashed potatoes and shrugged his shoulders. "Overwhelmed by my staggering good looks?"

The room dissolved into laughter. Even Ruby smiled, rolling her eyes at her brother's attempt at humor.

Robert swallowed. "No, I think it was just a thank-you kiss—a peck on the cheek. I'd finally agreed to give her more of the liver medicine she swears by." He pushed the food around his plate. "Of course, the stuff is primarily alcohol with a hint of opium. I hate giving it to her."

Abby added an extra spoonful of applesauce onto her little brother's plate. "So why do you?"

"Would you want to tell a ninety-year-old woman the medicine she's been taking for forty-odd years is nothing but spirits? She believes it's why she's lived so long." He shrugged. "And who knows? Maybe she's right." He smiled at Abby. "And it makes her happy."

Gerald snorted. "Really, *really* happy."

"Besides," Robert continued. "It's nice to have one content and relatively healthy patient—even if she is overly affectionate."

Gerald offered the dish of creamed peas to Ruby. "Focusing on research was your idea, Robert. I was satisfied treating fevers and broken bones. You couldn't resist the glory of X-rays."

Ruby passed the dish on to her brother. "So, you two are primarily treating cancer patients now?"

Robert nodded. "We still have a few of Gerald's older patients, but we are trying to concentrate our efforts on research. And we're making good progress, too. But it's a long process." He glanced about the table as his voice quieted. "We've lost several patients."

Abby lowered her gaze to her plate.

Clara jumped to her feet and began clearing dishes. "I hope everyone saved room. I baked lemon pie for dessert."

As his mother and Abby rose to join her, Ruby slid her chair back.

Gerald's mother waved her away. "Sit still and enjoy your visit. Who would like coffee?"

Gerald sighed, pushing away from the table. "I would love some, but I'm afraid I must head to the hospital."

His mother set a dish down with a clatter. "Gerald, no! At this hour?"

"Healing doesn't wait, Mother." He dropped his napkin beside his plate.

"I thought when you and Robert decided to focus on research, you would keep more regular hours."

"Someone forgot to inform our patients. One of us needs to check on Mr. Michaels, and I assumed Robert would be helping his sister get settled."

Clara reentered the room with a meringue-topped pie balanced in one hand, a pie server in the other.

Gerald gripped the back of his chair. "I sure hate to miss dessert." He raised a brow at his cousin. "Perhaps you could save me a slice?"

Clara smiled as she slipped a large serving of pie onto her husband's plate. "Well, aren't you fortunate? I baked two."

Gerald squeezed Clara's shoulder as he walked past. "I knew I was making the right decision when I invited your family to stay."

Herman frowned, removing a pipe from his pocket and clamping it between his jaws. "It's only until we find our own place. Don't you be worrying about it."

"Who's worried? When has a bachelor like me ever been this well fed? With Mother and Clara competing to see who can make the finest desserts, I've put on almost five pounds. I'm going to need a new belt soon." Gerald tugged on his waistband.

His mother entered the dining room with the coffeepot. "Sheer nonsense." Her gray eyes sparked. "We aren't competing."

"Of course not!" Clara echoed. "How can you say such a thing?"

Gerald chuckled. "Whatever you say."

Ruby smiled as Clara handed her a dish with a sliver of pie. "This looks delicious, thank you, Mrs. Fischer."

Clara set the pie plate in the center of the table. "Please, Ruby, we're going to be family, you must call us by our given names."

Gerald rubbed the back of his neck, remembering the patient waiting at the hospital. He forced himself out of the pleasant room, voices trailing after him into the hall.

Was there anything better than a home overflowing with family?

He glanced down at his hand, closing his fist over the open sore on his palm. Now, if only God would see about providing the adoring wife to go with it.

&

Ruby opened her eyes to the morning sun already pouring through the bedroom windows. She rolled to her back, glancing across at the other bed. It lay empty and already made up for the day. Ruby leaned back against the pillows, fighting the urge to pull the covers over her head.

She threw an arm across her eyes as her thoughts galloped off. She had obviously misjudged the situation here in San Francisco. Robert seemed happy and content. He had a new family. He didn't need her. *Did I come here for him or for myself?*

Ruby climbed out of bed and walked to the wardrobe, stretching her stiff muscles.

Otto jumped up from his makeshift pallet and padded over to sit at Ruby's feet, his tail thumping a steady rhythm against her ankle. Ruby leaned down to scratch her dog's ears, noting the gray hairs sprouting along the little dachshund's forehead. "Poor boy—you're feeling your age, too, aren't you?"

The dog yawned in response, stretching his long back and bowing his front end toward the floor at her feet.

She opened the wardrobe and pushed aside the russet-brown day dress, a navy suit, and her rose-colored skirt, settling instead for the black silk with the leg-of-mutton sleeves. Ruby turned the dress around and held it before the tall Cheval glass, tilting the mirror's frame so she could see her whole length.

"What do you think, Otto? Does it say, 'Robert, I mean business' or 'look at the poor, miserable widow?'" Ruby frowned at her reflection as the dog offered a noncommittal tail wag. Apparently even her dresses couldn't make up their minds.

She returned the dress to the wardrobe. Puffy sleeves were falling from fashion, anyway. Ruby fingered the walking skirt. Paired with the lace blouse, it would create a softer look. She reached for a pin-striped vest—the tailored shape would add the strength she needed for the day.

Ruby slid the skirt over her petticoats and corset. Wandering over to the window, she fastened the long row of buttons along her wrist, staring out the window.

The homes lined up along the street with barely a breath of space between each structure. *They look like a line of children marching off to school.* She studied the tidy, peaceful neighborhood, standing in stark contrast to many other areas of the city. So many homes had been lost. Dr. Larkspur had been fortunate.

Reaching up, she touched her hair, the curls popping loose from their restraints. If only she had glossy brown hair like Robert's fiancée. Ruby sat down at the dressing table.

The dog plopped on the rug at her feet. He whined, the sound morphing into a yawn before his jaws closed with a snap.

"In a moment, Otto." She removed the ribbon securing her braid and ran fingers through the strands. She shook her head, the curls bouncing free, bushing out like a ruddy crown. Her hair didn't behave any better than her late husband's wild horse. Opening a bottle of Macassar oil, she allowed a few drops of the precious liquid to drip into her palm.

She could still remember Charlie running his fingers through her loose hair. *"I love it like this. Wild and wooly."*

Ruby smoothed the oil through her curls. A woman's hair, like so many other things in life, needed to be carefully controlled and trained. She settled the padded pompadour roll onto her head like a crown and with quick fingers, tucked each curl up over the support and added several hairpins to keep it in place. Turning from side to side, she examined her handiwork in the looking glass. Perfect—for a few minutes, anyway.

Otto trailed at her heels as she hurried down the stairs. The dog halted halfway down, his front feet on the lower step, a growl emanating from his barrel chest.

Robert stood in the front hall, pushing his arms into the sleeves of his gray coat.

Ruby joined him. "You're leaving already? What about your breakfast?"

"I've already had a quick meal. I need to get to work." He retrieved his hat from the rack and cast a glare at the bristling dog.

Ruby bit her lip. She'd barely had two minutes alone with him. "I need to talk to you. Must you leave so soon?"

Robert buttoned his coat, sliding his palms over it to remove any wrinkles. "Why don't you come with me? The hospital ward might not be terribly exciting, but I could show you a bit of the city afterward. We could have lunch downtown."

"I wouldn't be in the way?"

He laughed. "Of course not. And I promise not to put you to work on your first day." His brows pinched together. "But I planned to drive Gerald's automobile."

Moisture gathered under Ruby's lace collar. "Can't we take the cable car to the hospital?"

"Normally, yes. But Gerald ended up staying with a patient all night. He has a meeting across town this afternoon and will need the car. He telephoned this morning and asked me to bring it."

Ruby pulled an arm tight around her midsection to quell the fluttering. "I don't know."

"Come on, Ruby. This isn't like you. You were never afraid of anything when we were children. Was it Charlie's accident?"

Lacing her fingers together, Ruby cleared her throat. "I am not afraid—not exactly."

Robert rolled his hat around his fingertips. His eyebrows drew downward. "I understand now better than I used to. It's been three months since the earthquake, but at night if the house so much as creaks," his voice softened, "I leap out of the bed, anticipating another disaster. I still haven't gotten a full night's sleep."

She reached out and touched her brother's sleeve. "It must have been terrifying." Did she have more to fear than Robert who had lived through such a horrible nightmare?

A squeak from the stairs made them both jump. Otto yipped as he spun around to stand guard at Ruby's toes, paws sliding on the wood floor.

Abby paused on the steps. "Am I interrupting?"

Ruby touched her chest to slow her thudding heartbeat.

Robert chuckled, leaning close to Ruby's ear. "Do you see what I mean?" He reached for Abby's hands, drawing her to his side and brushing a kiss across her cheek. "What perfect timing you have. I was trying to convince my sister to drive in to the hospital with me." Robert's gaze returned to Ruby.

Abby's eyes lit up. "Ruby is going, too?"

Ruby's stomach tightened. Would she never get a moment alone with her brother? "I'm considering it. Are you coming along?"

"No. I—" A shadow crossed the young woman's face. "I don't like to spend much time at the hospital."

Robert shrugged. "I suppose most folks don't."

"Besides, I am going down to Golden Gate Park this morning. There are still refugees living in the camp there, and the Red Cross has a kitchen. I like to help out whenever I can."

Ruby straightened. "I'd like to see the camps, too."

Robert stood up tall and gave her a curt nod. "Everyone's pulling together to make this city strong. Abby, we could drive you to the park on our way to the hospital. Then you can show her the camp, if you'd like."

Ruby swallowed. She had yet to agree to this driving business.

"It's such a nice day, I'd prefer to walk. Ruby, you can volunteer with me tomorrow, if you're interested. I'd love for you to join me." Abby started toward the kitchen. "Aunt Mae is going to be disappointed we are all running off today. I'll go talk to her." Abby disappeared into the other room.

"So? What's your decision?" Robert buttoned his jacket. "Are you ready to brave the new world of automobile travel? I'm a careful driver, I promise." He pushed the hat over his dark hair.

I cannot continue to let this fear control me. "All right. But you better steer clear of any horses."

5

$\mathscr{G}$erald turned his back on the large window overlooking the new waiting room and focused his attention on the woman slumped in the corner seat. He placed a hand on her shoulder. "I'm so sorry for your loss, Mrs. Michaels." The words tasted like dust in his mouth.

What else could he say to a woman who just lost her husband and the father of her four children? His stomach churned as he perched on the chair beside her. The children huddled with their grandmother at the far end of the hall.

"I should have been here, Dr. Larkspur. I should have been with my Leo when he passed." Tears spilled down her flushed cheeks.

Gerald swallowed against the lump in his throat. He sat back, his neck and shoulders aching from the long night's vigil. "There's nothing you could have done. He never woke. You were present when he was last conscious."

She grasped Gerald's hands and pressed them between her own.

He scoured his mind for an appropriate expression of comfort, but as his gaze settled on the golden band glinting on her finger, his words dissolved. *What will she do now?*

"Leo said good-bye to me." She accepted his handkerchief and dabbed at her nose. "He knew, didn't he?"

"Perhaps."

Mrs. Michaels lowered her chin and pressed white knuckles against her lips. "He did—he knew." She straightened her shoulders. "Thank you, Dr. Larkspur."

"I'm sorry we were unable to save him."

A tear rolled down her cheeks, and she wiped it away with the tip of a finger. "You gave us more time."

Gerald nodded. At least they'd done that.

"I know Leo was a tough man—a drinker and a brawler. He hurt everyone he loved." She gazed down at her hands and twisted her wedding band. "Everyone." She glanced over her shoulder to where her mother and children waited. "We'd been apart for a year before he got sick. Nothing brought him to his knees—not even the earthquake. Until this." She took a shaky breath, as if drawing strength from the dry hospital air. "Leo couldn't brawl his way out of the cancer."

Gerald pressed fingertips against his temple. He'd mourn the patient later, in his own way—and find some way to relieve the tightness in his chest.

"You gave him more time, Doctor. And you encouraged him along the way. It's because of your advice he got right with me, with his children, with himself." She patted Gerald's hand. "And he made peace with God. There's no gift more precious." She stood and gestured to her children. The kids broke free from their grandmother's hold and pelted down the hall toward their mother. She gathered them all into a crushing embrace.

The family walked off down the corridor, clustered together for strength.

Gerald slumped in the chair and pressed both palms to his face before raking fingers through his hair. *God, I want to do more than give people time. I want to give them back their lives.*

"Gerald?"

The voice startled Gerald out of his prayer. He opened his eyes and straightened.

Robert stood beside him, his sister Ruby lingering a few steps behind.

Gerald pushed up to his feet. "I, uh . . ." His voice cracked, as if the vocal chords were lined with sand. "I just informed Mrs. Michaels."

Robert nodded. "We saw her leaving."

Ruby's eyes rounded. "Are you all right?" She stepped closer.

Gerald's pulse accelerated. He reversed a step, ramming the back of his leg against the chair. "Yes." He gritted his teeth against the jab of pain. "I'm fine. It's all part of the job, after all."

She placed a hand on his arm. "I can't imagine what it must be like to work with these patients when you know they are going to die."

The shadows around the young widow's eyes tore at his already raw soul. Gerald dropped his gaze to the slender fingers brushing his sleeve, the clean, round tips of her nails evident against his dark coat.

Robert frowned. "We don't allow ourselves to believe cancer is a death sentence. The X-ray radiation is already extending lives." His eyes brightened. "We're on the cusp of a grand discovery. Gerald and I may well be remembered as the doctors who cured cancer."

Acid crept up Gerald's throat. His gaze wandered back to Ruby, the blue of the woman's eyes reminiscent of a pale morning sky, before the sun had fully risen. The idea pulled at him. Maybe it's what he needed—a walk out under God's brilliant heavens, a subtle reminder life could be good again. He sighed and pulled his gaze away before he embarrassed the lady.

Ruby's fingers traced the buttons lining her snug gray vest. She cleared her throat. "Robert had offered to let me view the X-ray laboratory. Perhaps you would join us?"

A smile brightened Robert's face. "Come with us, Gerald. Let's show Ruby what we do."

Head aching, Gerald waved them off. "You two go ahead." He needed a moment to gather himself. One more compassionate glance from Ruby, and he might lose the tenuous grip he had on his emotions.

Robert nodded and offered an arm to his sister. "You know where we will be if you change your mind."

Ruby paused, catching Gerald with a long look. "Are you certain you're all right?"

He swallowed and nodded. "Yes. Fine. Thank you for your concern."

A faint smile crossed her lips before she turned and followed her brother.

He couldn't help but stare at her retreating figure. She moved like thistledown on the breeze.

❧

A gas lamp burned in the corner, eerie shadows creeping across the tile floor. Ruby shivered, pulling her wool wrap close as she gazed about the basement room. "This is where you spend all your time?"

He grinned like a schoolboy. "Isn't it amazing? Our lab was destroyed in the quake, but we were fortunate to salvage most of the equipment. We only had to replace the tubes and the glass plates. We should have electric lights by early next week."

A confusing hodgepodge of machinery stood in front of her. The only piece she recognized was a simple canvas stretcher supported by two wooden sawhorses. Strange apparatus and wires suspended above the stretcher on metal rods seemed reminiscent of an H. G. Wells novel. Other appliances tucked below and behind the stretcher spoke of unusual experiments and medical wonders. Ruby shook her head. "This looks like a machine shop."

Robert laughed. "Well, I suppose in a sense it is. What is the human body, but a complex piece of equipment? We use these tools to peer inside and to improve the way it functions."

She strolled around a wheeled cart. "How does it all work?"

Her brother's eyes danced like a child showing off his latest school project. "In order to make X-ray portraits, we direct the Röntgen rays—X-rays—from this glass tube," he pointed to a long cylinder, " . . . through the person's body and into the plate on the reverse side." He strode over to a desk sitting at the far end of the laboratory and lifted a sheet of glass, carrying it back to where Ruby stood. "The emulsion on the plate captures the image."

She peered at the ghostly outline on the smooth surface.

"The bones and other dense objects in our bodies absorb the rays, so those areas appear lighter on the plate. Let me show you." He held the sheet of glass up to the light.

Ruby's mouth opened. She could see the various bones composing the ribcage, shoulders, and arms. "Father would be so proud." She gazed at the image, a fractured rib evident on the left side. "What about everything else? Their skin, their clothes?"

"The rays pass through them."

She tapped fingers against the table. "Do they feel anything?"

"No, they barely know it's happening. It's like taking a photograph. No sensation at all."

"The radiation is safe?"

Robert placed the plate back on the table. "Of course. They've done thousands of X-rays across the country with no ill effects. In fact, it's quite the contrary. Patients report feeling quite rejuvenated, skin diseases improve, and countless maladies are being cured."

She turned pinning him with her gaze. "How does it do that?"

"Well, we're still working that part out."

Dr. Larkspur appeared in the doorway, a stack of papers clutched under an arm. "I assume he's informing you about the wonders of this great new science?" His voice cracked, as if the dry tone taxed his throat.

Ruby moistened her lips. "It's quite an extraordinary invention."

"Yes, we do seem to be making progress." The doctor's eyes narrowed. He crossed the room and deposited the papers on the desk.

She tilted her head. His dour expression didn't match his optimistic words. "But not enough?"

Dr. Larkspur's chin jerked upward. "I didn't say that. Robert's theories are sound. You should be proud of him." The man's gaze faltered, a hand pressed against his temple.

A sudden longing to rub her fingers along the back of the doctor's neck, as she had done for Charlie when he was troubled, made Ruby tremble. What was it about this man? He summoned her husband's memory like a ghost.

Robert stepped to his side. "Gerald, you've been here all night. Why don't you go home and get some rest before you meet with the board?"

Dr. Larkspur shook his head, lowering the hand and thrusting it into a trouser pocket. "There's not enough time. I need to look over my notes beforehand."

The redness around his eyes cut at Ruby's heart. Clearly, Dr. Larkspur was exhausted and distraught over losing his patient. "Can't you telephone them? Postpone the meeting? Or perhaps Robert could go in your place?"

"We cannot postpone. The meeting has been pushed back three times already. The board's prepared to cut funding to our project." He gestured to the equipment. "If only this apparatus weren't so blasted expensive. The board is already overwhelmed with all the needed repairs from the quake—it's ridiculous to ask them for more."

Robert huffed. "We need the money if we're to continue."

"Almost every hospital in San Francisco sustained damage in the earthquake. Research is not the top priority, and we both know it. The funds are bleeding out, and the board is trying to save what they can. Our experiments will be the first to go."

Ruby sank into a swivel chair near the door. "What will you do?"

Robert sighed, pushing a hand against his forehead. "We've come so far. You must convince them to carry on. We're so close."

Dr. Larkspur swung around, venom spilling out in his words. "Close to what, Robert? Close to a cure? Tell it to Leo Michaels's widow and children. Tell it to the five patients we lost over the last three weeks. Tell it to Abby." He plowed out of the room, the door swinging closed behind him.

Ruby swallowed. She rose, gripping the back of the chair. "What did he mean, tell Abby?" She pressed a hand against her stomach. "Robert, she's not sick, is she?"

He turned away, laying both hands on the table. "No." Robert's tensed shoulders showed through his shirt as he leaned over the X-ray plates. He faced Ruby, eyes dark. "Abby's sister was our first cancer patient."

Ruby took a step back, a metallic taste rising on her tongue. "Abby's sister? When was this?"

His voice remained low. "Months before the quake."

"Is it how you and Abby met?"

He nodded.

Ruby gazed at the canvas stretcher, a lump rising in her throat. "Dr. Larkspur—did he begin this research for her sake?"

Robert sighed. "Yes."

She closed her eyes. What a burden these men carried.

"She improved—for a time. But, like all the others . . ." his voice trailed off.

Ruby ran fingers along her sleeve before turning and facing her brother. "So why are you still trying?"

"Pardon?"

"Why are you still conducting X-ray research? You couldn't save your fiancée's sister, your mentor's cousin." She gestured to the equipment. "Maybe it's time to let someone else take over the project. Obviously, this is causing your friend pain—not to mention what Abby must be feeling. Have you thought about what this must be doing to her?"

His brows crumpled. "You don't understand."

Ruby crossed her arms. "Perhaps not, but I do know you. When you become fixed on a puzzle, you're like Otto defending a bone."

"I'm trying to save lives." He rapped the table with his knuckles. "I couldn't save Cecelia. I saw what her death did to Abby and to her family." His eyes narrowed. "If we give up now, her suffering will mean nothing. We must eradicate this disease. Nothing else matters."

Ruby stepped up to him. "Even if it costs someone you love?"

Robert didn't flinch. "God has called me to this, Ruby. I have no choice."

6

*G*erald closed the door and leaned against it. The office remained in shambles, cluttered with stacks of files and records salvaged from the ruins of his downtown office, not to mention miscellaneous pieces of medical equipment—mostly outdated castoffs—donated by hospitals around the country.

His throbbing temples accused him with every beat. He'd come down too hard on Robert, and his friend deserved an apology. Gerald flopped onto the creaky wooden chair and propped his elbows on the desk. With a sigh, he let his head fall forward into his hands. Their work had never been about gaining prestige; the goal had always been to help patients. They still hadn't saved a single one, and the memory of each loss clawed at his soul like skeletal fingers reaching back from the grave. *Cecelia. My own cousin.*

He pressed cool fingers against his eyes. Sometimes the halls of the hospital seemed to whisper her name. And her parents and siblings living under his roof served as reminders of his failure. After the disaster, he'd considered starting over, leaving this broken city behind. Chicago, Boston, New York . . . But what would it remedy? Could he walk away from his family?

Gerald drew in a deep breath. Grief and the exhaustion drove him today. He mustn't let emotions overtake common sense. He lowered his hand to the desk and opened the curled fingers. The burn scar mocked him, defeat etched into his skin. A simple case of X-ray dermatitis shouldn't continue this long, but there were no signs of infection.

Gathering up the stacks of papers strewn across the desk, Gerald slipped them into a valise and headed for the door. The idea of begging the stolid-faced board for funds wrenched his gut. Perhaps it would be better if the board said no. He could return to patching up broken bones and handing out rheumatism powders. *Let someone else cure cancer.*

He reached for the door and pulled it open, the metal knob icy against his sore palm.

Robert stood in the hall. "We need to talk."

Gerald tucked the valise under his arm. "I know. I'm sorry for the way I spoke to you. It was out of line."

Robert darted a glance back to his sister, waiting at the end of the hall. "No, you were right. I'm passionate about this research. But not for fame or recognition—for Leo and his family and all the others like him. I want to get rid of this disease so no other family suffers like yours and Abby's."

Gerald wished he could crawl under the floor tiles. Instead, he forced his eyes upward, meeting Robert's earnest gaze.

His friend lowered his voice. "I understand you're hurting. We both thought Leo might be the first . . ." Robert ran a hand across his chin, frowning. "Who am I kidding? We've thought each of them would be the first to survive. Otherwise, we wouldn't be in this business. Would we?"

"No." Gerald sighed. The young man leaning against the doorframe had come so far from the naïve student prodigy Gerald had taken under his wing five years ago. And yet, he hadn't lost an iota of his zeal. *What happened to mine?*

Robert cleared his throat. "I'm coming with you."

Gerald stepped back. "To speak to the board? Why?"

"There's no need for you to face them alone."

"You don't think I can handle them?" Gerald pulled the watch from his vest pocket, checking the time.

"Don't choose words for me."

"You think you could do better? Impress them with fancy research papers? Robert, we've got nothing. No clear-cut results, no hard data to support our claims. Do you think you're going to march in there and woo the money from their pockets? This is about medicine, not slick talk."

Robert's face darkened. "Which is exactly why I need to go. You're ready to give up. If you go see the board like this, we're finished."

Gerald shouldered his way past, clutching the leather case to his chest. "Don't forget who's in charge of this project."

Ruby Marshall met them halfway, her rose-colored skirt a welcome bit of color in the drab hospital hallway. She held a straw hat in her hands, draped with dried flowers.

In his weary state, Gerald could no longer keep his gaze—or his focus—where it belonged. Her smile fractured his thoughts.

"Did Robert tell you? We're coming along."

Gerald's throat tightened. "Both of you?" He'd liked Robert better as the malleable young student. He'd grown confident over the past year, the quake and its aftermath giving him freedom to practice his skills unsupervised. Now with a sister to impress, he was proving insufferable. Maybe this would be an opportunity to show Robert he still had a few things to learn. Gerald forced a smile as he faced his partner. "You may come." The inkling of a plan grew in the back of his mind. "But only as observers. You will not speak."

Robert stopped midstride. "Then what's the point?"

"Your choice." Gerald shrugged.

"You're being unreasonable."

"That makes two of us." He turned to Ruby. "Do you see why we make such a good team?"

She placed both hands on her hips, cocking her head to one side as if conducting a careful examination. "Because you're both stubborn and pigheaded?"

"Precisely." Gerald gripped his partner's shoulder. "Curing cancer demands dogged determination, right?"

The look of confusion in Robert's eyes was worth losing a few more hours of sleep.

Gerald surveyed the group of bristly old men surrounding the long, glossy mahogany table, the room reeking of cigar smoke and money. Sweat broke out between his shoulder blades and he swallowed, the cool air reminding him of the hospital morgue.

Robert took the seat beside him, a tad green around the gills. Ruby perched on a chair beside the door, hands folded in her lap.

Gerald glanced down at his reflection in the tabletop in lieu of closing his eyes and breathed a desperate prayer for wisdom. He flexed his fingers and released them, willing away the tension that would cause him to fidget while speaking. "Gentlemen, you remember my partner, Dr. King?"

Robert bobbed his head at the stony-looking men and wiped a finger along his brow, his color fading until you could barely identify where the celluloid collar ended on his neck.

At least I won't have to worry about him wanting to speak.

Gerald adjusted his tie. "Distinguished board of directors, you know why we're here. I've been called upon to give an accounting of our research to date." He cleared his throat and reached for the glass of water. *Confidence.*

"In front of you, you have the details of our findings thus far." He paused as the men shuffled the papers. "Dr. King and I wish to express our gratitude to the board for their abundant generosity and confidence in us during the previous year. As you can see from our results, we have seen astounding success with the X-ray treatments in improving our patient's health and, in the case of two patients, actually sending their cancer into remission."

Dr. Emil Dawson, seated at the far end of the table, pulled a gold watch from his pocket and flipped it open while clearing his throat. "Temporary remission, wasn't it, Dr. Larkspur?"

Gerald paused, waiting for the men's gazes to shift back in his direction. "Yes, Dr. Dawson. You are correct. Temporary remission."

Emil tapped the watch on the table lightly, drawing his bushy gray eyebrows together. "In other words, you haven't actually healed anyone, have you?"

Robert shifted in his chair. The grizzled old doctor taught at the medical college, striking terror into students for decades. Undoubtedly, the unpleasant scrutiny brought back disagreeable memories.

Setting his jaw, Gerald folded his hands. Time to show Robert how one dealt with bullies like Dawson. "We have seen remarkable improvement in almost every case."

Emil sighed. "You said yourself, Dr. Larkspur, this board has been *abundantly* generous. We have funded your research—your grand X-ray experiment—" he dragged out the words like a hissing cat. "But in reality, you don't have any clear results to show for it, now, do you?"

Gerald leaned back in his chair, letting the doctor's words float in the air alongside the cigar smoke. Emil baited him, and Gerald could not afford to take the hook. Instead, he let his attention wander the room, as though the man's assertions were the least of his worries. He paused when his eyes reached Ruby Marshall, leaning forward in her chair.

She met his gaze with bright eyes and a curt nod.

The tension dissolved from Gerald's shoulders as if her faith had crossed the space between them. He took a deep breath, directing his focus back to the men. "Our results are clearly stated in the report."

"And how much money has the board committed to your little sideshow?" Dr. Dawson continued his tirade. "We've all heard the stories—X-rays will cure psoriasis, pneumonia, depression, hysteria . . ." He tapped the watchcase against the table a second time. "I ask you, Dr. Larkspur—where is the proof? It's just more poppycock. Treat cancer by beaming harmless little rays of light at a patient's body? It's ludicrous." Emil's face and scalp flushed, white whiskers standing brilliant against his red face. "Before the earthquake, Lane Hospital was one of the finest in the country. Now look at it. Every department is in shambles!"

The man raised a meaty finger and pointed it at the other board members. "If you vote to support the shenanigans these shysters are passing off as research, we will become the laughingstock of the nation."

Muttering broke out around the table as Emil sat back, mopping his brow with a silk handkerchief.

Gerald clamped a hand on Robert's arm before the younger man could spring from his chair. Gerald leaned close, allowing the hum of conversation to hide his words. "Keep silent. Don't play his game."

Robert's brow furrowed. "How can you just sit there?"

Gerald waited for the room to quiet. As the murmuring subsided, he lifted his chin. "Are you finished, Dr. Dawson?"

A half-smile crossed his accuser's face. "I believe *you* are, Dr. Larkspur."

A low chuckle spread through the assembly.

Gerald gathered the papers, lifting them on edge to straighten the stack against the dark tabletop. Pushing his chair back, he stood.

Robert's jaw dropped. "Gerald, where are—"

Gerald lifted a hand to stop his friend's words. "Yes, Dr. Dawson. I am finished." He slipped the papers into the valise. The silence expanded until it seemed to press against the wine-colored wallpaper.

Robert leaned forward. "What Dr. Larkspur means—"

"No, Dr. King. Our distinguished colleague is correct." Gerald snapped the valise shut and set it on the table. He gestured to the men sitting in the high-backed chairs. "This board has been generous. In the past. But since the earthquake, the organization has been in disarray. Obviously, the board needs to reconsider whether or not Lane Hospital can maintain its revered status as a premier research facility, prepared to compete in the national theater of medicine." He gazed around the room. He raised his voice. "If you have chosen to take a step back, return to the safety of the 1800s—" he shrugged his shoulders, letting his hand fall back upon the leather bag, "—then my partner and I will assume our services are no longer needed. In fact, we were just discussing the X-ray research programs being developed in Chicago, weren't we, Dr. King?"

Robert's Adam's apple dipped. He gave a sharp nod. "Um, yes. Chicago—and Boston, too."

Gerald looked back at the circle of dark suits. "Several cities offer significantly better funded programs and superior facilities. Our research would progress toward a viable treatment rapidly in an environment more conducive to the appropriate levels of financial support."

He glanced across the room at Ruby. A smile teased at the corners of her lips.

"I find it a shame, though." Gerald lifted the bag from the table-top. "After all, you gentlemen worked so hard to make this facility successful and to see our hospital become a leader in medicine and research, only to have it decimated by the earthquake. And now, with the entire nation's newspapers focused on our city—we have an opportunity to show the world San Francisco remains strong."

Gerald folded his coat over his arm and slipped on his derby before strolling toward the doorway. "It's such a pity for you to be left behind. But I'm sure Dr. King and I will be well received in Chicago. Have any of you heard what they are paying doctors in the East?" He lifted an eyebrow and touched the brim of his hat in farewell.

Uproar broke out in the room. The loud voices echoed down the hall as Gerald stepped out, Robert and Ruby on his heels.

A young clerk sitting behind a large oak desk glanced up in con-cern. "What's going on?" He scurried over to the doorway.

Robert turned on Gerald, eyes blazing. "This is a dangerous game you're playing. And it's my future you're betting with."

"Your future couldn't be brighter if it were lit with electric lights." Gerald straightened his tie.

Ruby beamed, clutching her hat between her fingers. "I think Dr. Larkspur is correct, Robert. Did you see their faces?"

Robert swayed, eyes as round as an intern at his first surgery. "What do we do now? Go back to the hospital and start packing our office while the board decides our fate?"

Gerald pulled the watch from his pocket and leaned against the corner of the clerk's desk. "No, this should only take a few minutes."

Robert stared at Gerald as if he had lost all grip on his senses, but the longer the confusion in the room lasted, the more Gerald felt like celebrating. He crossed his arms and waited.

Dr. Hiram Lawrence, the youngest member of the board, slipped from the room with a grin. He grabbed Gerald's hand and pumped it. "Well played, Dr. Larkspur. The board's with you." He shook Robert's hand and glanced back over his shoulder at the doorway. "But stay on your toes. Emil Dawson will see you both in tar and feathers if he has his way."

"Let him try." Gerald chuckled and turned to Robert. "I think we've assured ourselves of some long hours in the months ahead. I hope you're prepared."

A grin spread across Robert's face. "Always."

Gerald clapped a hand on his partner's shoulder and guided him toward the exit. *There goes my dream of bidding farewell to research.* "I think a celebration is in order."

7

A smile crept across Gerald's face as he walked to the car. Nothing made a man feel alive like a battle well planned and fought. He'd bested his competition, put an upstart partner in his place, and impressed an interesting young woman, all in the course of one morning. Gerald lifted his chin to the sunshine and pulled in a deep breath of the fresh air. *Now, that's how one turns around a day.*

Robert trailed behind, Ruby by his side. "How did you accomplish it?" His voice rose two notches above normal timbre. "This morning we stood on the verge of economic ruin, and you marched in and beguiled the board into doubling our funding!"

Gerald reached the automobile and held out an arm to assist Ruby to her seat. "Robert, how can you have so little faith in me? Have I taught you nothing?"

The woman paused, eyeing the vehicle for a long moment before taking Gerald's offered hand and stepping up into the vehicle.

Gerald released her fingers as she settled onto the cushion. Ruby performed an admirable feat, considering her fear of machines.

Robert blocked Gerald from circling around to the driver's seat. "You were prepared to wash your hands of this entire project. I thought you were sending our research to the chopping block." He leaned against the car, brow furrowed. "Were you playing me for a fool?"

Gerald crossed both arms over his chest. "I did it for Leo. And Cecelia. And all the others."

"Gerald, you're swinging like a pendulum. One moment you support the research and the next, you're ready to push me in front of the streetcar. Now, you're on board again? What am I supposed to believe?"

Acid burned in Gerald's throat. He glanced over at Ruby, her face a fairer mirror to her brother's. Gerald laced fingers under his lapels and snapped the jacket smooth before turning to his partner. "I am not a researcher, nor will I ever be. I can play the game with the board, but I'll only go so far. You're the young genius bound to find the answers. Consequently, you'd better get busy." He glanced away, avoiding his friend's eyes. "We may be running out of time."

❧

Ruby gripped the edge of the seat as the car sped down the road. The men's voices rattled in her ears as Robert leaned forward from the rear compartment, his arms braced on the seatback between Gerald and Ruby. She squeezed her eyes shut, regretting her decision not to insist on sitting in the back. With Robert and Gerald posturing like two roosters prepared for battle, it had seemed imprudent to interrupt. She never understood why men felt this constant need to intimidate one another.

Her brother had always described Dr. Larkspur as a glorious benefactor, determined to guide Robert to success. From what she had observed, Gerald Larkspur was a moody, arrogant man with a lofty opinion of himself. She glanced at him, hunched over the wheel, sending the automobile lurching around a cable car on one of San Francisco's never-ending hills.

"Do you think you could slow down a little?" Ruby gritted her teeth. The breeze pulled at her hat, yanking against the pins securing the chapeau to the pompadour frame and threatening to dislodge the whole conglomeration. She sacrificed one of her grips on the upholstery to clasp the brim, but jammed a foot against the floor for extra security.

Gerald glanced over, his pinched brows relaxing and lifting, almost as if he'd forgotten she sat beside him. His face softened.

The tension in her limbs unraveled as she gazed into the man's ghostly blue eyes. *Why is he staring at me?*

"Watch out!" Robert yelped.

Ruby's gaze snapped forward in time to witness the young paperboy bound across their path.

Gerald yanked on the brake, and the car skidded to a halt.

The momentum carried her off the seat cushion and onto the floor, her head cracking against the low brass rail in the process. Blinking away stinging tears, Ruby pressed a palm to her chest, her heart thudding in time with the motor.

"Ruby!" Her brother jumped to his feet. "Are you all right?"

Gerald's eyes widened. "I am so, so sorry. I don't know what happened. Here, let me help you up." He reached out his hand. "Your head is bleeding."

She knocked it away. "You weren't watching the road, is what happened." The bitter sound of her own voice rang in her ears. "Why must men drive so recklessly? You think you are invincible and nothing can happen. You're all alike." She slithered back onto the seat. "I'm done with automobiles, and . . . and horses, and—" she flung her hands skyward. "And anything else driven by men."

Ruby stood and moved to step down to the street as an ear-splitting bell sounded directly behind her.

"Gerald, we're on the rails!" Robert thumped a palm on the seatback.

Ruby glanced back, one foot on the step plate. A cable car rattled toward them, looming up at a frightening clip. She swallowed, grateful for a second time she'd used the facilities at the hospital.

Gerald clamped onto her wrist and yanked, dragging Ruby into the car as he hit the accelerator. The tires screeched as the automobile lurched forward, Ruby's tailbone smacking atop the cushion. They careened to the curb as the long vehicle clattered past, riders hanging from its sides, pointing and waving.

The noise faded until only the rumble of the motor and the sound of her own gasping breaths filled Ruby's head. She turned and glared at the two men. Her brother leaned forward and buried his face in his hands. Gerald stared straight ahead, watching the public conveyance glide down the hill. Ruby clambered to the cobblestones and stood, swaying, on rubbery legs.

"Where are you going?" Gerald's voice quivered.

"Home." She braced one hand on the automobile to gather her wits and determine the direction of the Ferry Building.

Gerald jumped to the ground, hurrying to her side. "Ruby, I am sorry. I was distracted for a moment. Thankfully those boys know how to get out of the way." The man had the audacity to smile.

She fought an urge to kick him, reaching up to straighten her hat instead.

It was gone. Ruby clutched at her hair, the curls slipping and loosening by the second. "My hat—where is it?"

Gerald glanced around the vehicle. "Perhaps it blew away?"

Ruby flushed, several unladylike words springing to her tongue. "Well, find it! You made this mess with your awful driving. I need my hat." *You clod.*

Robert appeared at her arm as Gerald hurried off. "Don't be too hard on him, Ruby. He hasn't slept and then the board—"

"You forced me to ride in this contraption." She sank her elbow into her brother's ribs.

He grunted and stepped out of range. "And no one was hurt."

"Tell it to my head." She touched the goose egg on her forehead with a grimace, a smear of blood coming away on her fingers.

"Doesn't look serious." He pulled a handkerchief out of his vest pocket and pressed it to the wound. "Come on Ruby, no harm done."

Gerald approached. "About the hat . . ." He withdrew the mangled wreckage from behind his back. The boater had been returned to its original elements—wisps of straw, feathers and shredded ribbon. "It may have gone under the cable car."

Gerald fingered the mutilated hat. It didn't seem appropriate to offer the soiled item to the lady, but he would be amiss to leave it in the street.

Ruby slapped the automobile's hood with a grimace. "What is wrong with you two?" Her eyes flashed, her cheeks radiating a rosy glow. She snatched the remains from his grip. "We might have been crushed. Like this . . . this—"

"Hat?" Gerald furnished the word, biting his lip to hide a smile. Her elaborate hairstyle had shifted, reminiscent of the Tower of Pisa. One more stamp of her foot and it might give way completely.

"Yes." She flicked fingers across the brim, as if to brush away some of the dust, only to have the brim detach and fall to the ground at her feet.

"Ruby, get back in the car. Let us take you home." Robert touched his sister's elbow.

"No." She threw the rest of the hat down. "Never. I won't ride in an automobile again. You promised we would be safe."

Robert raised his hands. "To be completely truthful, I said I was a careful driver. I said nothing about Gerald." He hooked a thumb Gerald's direction.

Heat rushed to Gerald's face. "If the newspaper boy hadn't run out in front of me, we'd have been home by now."

Ruby swung around and shot him a glare that made him step back. "Well, then, you can drive your prized automobile anyplace you choose. I'm walking." She leaned down, reaching for the discarded hat. Her coiffure followed, cascading forward and sliding to the side. She straightened up with a gasp, both hands flying to her head. "Oh!" Her eyes glistened.

Gerald pressed a fist against his mouth. The woman's fear and pain were palpable. Laughter would not help things.

Ruby turned her back, pushing the mass of curls upward.

Gerald averted his gaze, turning to face his friend. "We can't permit her to walk home in this state. It's almost four miles."

"What do you suggest? Strong-arm her into the car?" Robert hooked a thumb in his suspenders.

Ruby spun around, curls jutting out at every angle, like Medusa's snakes.

Gerald forced his eyes down from her wild hair only to have the sight of the bleeding scratch above her left eyebrow sting his conscience. His gaze dropped further, focusing instead on her quivering chin.

He pushed fingers through his own hair. *I'm such an idiot.* Scooping up the hat scraps, Gerald tossed them into the back seat. "Ruby," he kept his voice gentle. "You must know how remorseful I am about all of this. For what it's worth, I promise to replace the bonnet." He pointed to the scrape. "But we must get you home and cleaned up."

She sucked in her cheeks as if pondering his words, her gaze darting between him and the automobile.

He patted the passenger seat and reached for her arm. "I'll be extra cautious. No more paperboys—I give you my word."

Robert stood silent, hands thrust in his pockets.

Ruby stared at her shoes. "Fine. I'll get in, but I'm sitting in the back." She ignored Gerald's offered hand and moved toward the rear.

Robert helped her up. "Do you want me to ride with you?"

She settled herself on the cushion. "Absolutely not. You sit up front." She gestured with shaking fingers. "And make sure your partner watches the road."

Robert smirked at Gerald. "You heard the lady. Eyes front."

Gerald pushed past him, grinding his teeth. *As if I desired to gawk at her.* He clambered behind the wheel with a huff. *How do I get into these situations?*

Ruby leaned forward, placing her face between them for a brief moment. "And if I'm to stay in San Francisco," she gripped the seat back, "you two must teach me to drive."

8

*R*uby sat back, stomach churning. Her mother would be aghast. She'd spent years training her daughters to be demure. *Mother never dealt with bullheaded men and their automobiles.* She blew a curl off her forehead and glanced out at the road. They bounced over another set of rails threading their way down the center of the wide street.

On each side of the street, buildings sprouted like seedlings, stretching upward toward the sky. Ruby shook her head in wonder. Only a few months since the disaster and already the new city took shape, the mythological phoenix rising from the ashes of its predecessor.

In less than ten minutes, Gerald guided the automobile into the alley behind his house, the tires crunching on loose gravel.

Ruby catapulted from the vehicle before either man could open the rear door for her. Her knees wobbled as her toes touched the solid ground.

Otto came dashing to the gate, barking and wiggling his long body in a dance of joy. As Gerald approached, the dog stiffened, rumpling his snout and growling at the house's owner.

Ruby crouched down and ran a hand along the dog's spine, carefully smoothing his hackles. "Otto, we're guests here. Be polite." *A lesson I need, as well.*

With little more than a disinterested glance toward the dog, Gerald slung his jacket over one drooping shoulder and gestured for Ruby to enter the house before him. Within moments, he disappeared up the back stairs.

A hundred-pound weight descended on Ruby's frame. The poor man had been awake all night, lost a patient, and had done battle with the medical board for her brother's sake—and she had the gall to yell at him and make senseless demands. And on her first full day in San Francisco. She pushed the door shut behind her, leaning against it as her regrets stacked up.

Mrs. Larkspur hurried down the hall to greet them, her tiny form like a welcoming angel at heaven's gates. Giving Robert a quick peck on the cheek, she turned to Ruby, eyes wide. "Oh, my dear, what has happened to you?" She tugged Ruby into the better light of the sunny kitchen.

Ruby dragged her feet, Otto padding behind. "It's nothing serious."

Robert followed, slipped out of his jacket, and scooped up an apple from a basket on the counter. "We had a little mishap on the way home, but everything turned out fine."

Mrs. Larkspur shot him a glance, a crease forming between her brows. "The poor girl doesn't appear fine to me. Come sit down, Ruby, and I'll get you some tea. You look like you've been through a war zone."

Ruby sank into the kitchen chair, her insides quivering as if she were still bouncing along the roadway.

Robert chuckled. "I'll leave you in Mrs. Larkspur's capable hands. I'm going to get cleaned up, and then I need to head back to the hospital."

Gerald's mother poured tea into a pink-flowered cup. "Now, tell me what happened."

Ruby filled her in on the morning's events, lingering over her son's remarkable performance at the board meeting before launching into the story of the eventful drive home. Her muscles unwound, thanks to the tea or to Mrs. Larkspur's mothering—she wasn't certain.

The older woman clucked her tongue. "The automobile makes me nervous, too. I wasn't pleased when Gerald bought the thing. I'd rather have a simple horse and buggy, myself. But, times are changing. You have to change along with them or get left behind." She patted her silver hair, pinned up in a tight bun instead of rounded out like everyone else's. "Gerald has neither the time nor the inclination to care for a horse." She sipped her tea. "He works entirely too hard. No one to come home to, I suppose, except for all of us. But a young man needs more."

Ruby stretched, her neck and shoulders protesting the sudden movement.

Mrs. Larkspur frowned, her wrinkles squeezing together. "You poor thing. All this way on the train and the ferry—and on your first day in the city, this happens." She stood up and headed for the washbasin. "We must get the cut cleaned up straight away."

"Please, don't trouble yourself. I can go upstairs and do it. I need to fix my hair, anyway. I know it's a disaster." Ruby turned toward the sound of footsteps on the back stairs, a sudden pinch jerking her shoulder. She winced.

Gerald's voice came from behind. "Is your neck bothering you?" He walked into Ruby's field of vision and slid into the seat his mother had abandoned. He sat sideways, his knees brushing against the side of Ruby's skirt.

Otto crept out from under the table, licked a few stray crumbs off the floor, and plopped at the man's feet.

The twinge in her spine increased with Gerald's proximity. "I'm a bit stiff." Ruby reached for the teacup, nearly knocking it from the saucer.

His forehead creased. "You must know how guilt-ridden I am about today's events."

With some effort, she turned and faced him. "Please stop. I forgive you." She set the cup down so as not to spill on the lace cloth. "I'm prone to overreacting, I'm afraid. I haven't been very gracious."

He drummed his fingers on the table. "You showed a great deal of courage climbing into the automobile in the first place. I hope you'll give me a chance to rectify the situation." He leaned in, his face earnest. "Let me take you driving outside of the city. How about Sunday, after church? You will see how fun it can be. And if you still want to learn, well—I'll teach you."

A chill rushed across her skin. "You will?"

Mrs. Larkspur walked back to the table, a bowl of water and a cloth in her hands. "What do you mean, Gerald?"

He grinned. "The young lady wants to learn to drive an automobile."

She plunked the bowl down. "Drive? Are you serious?"

Ruby managed a final sip of tea, the cup trembling in her fingers. "It's as you said." She smiled at Gerald's mother. "You either change with the times, or you get left behind. I'm planning to control the changes in my life. Besides . . ." She cocked an eyebrow. "I think women would probably make safer drivers than men. Don't you agree?"

"You might be right." Mrs. Larkspur chuckled. She dipped the corner of the cloth into the water.

Gerald reached over and stopped her hand. "Allow me, Mother. I am the doctor after all. And the one responsible for this lady's injuries."

Ruby slid her chair backward. "I think I'll take care of it myself."

"Please, let me take a look at it. If you get an infection because of my carelessness, you can be sure I will never forgive myself."

The intensity of the man's eyes melted her resistance. "If you insist."

He smiled and took the rag in his fingers. Drawing closer, he lifted the loose hair on her forehead and dabbed at the scratch with the wet cloth.

Otto sat up and growled, the soft sound rippling through the room.

Ruby shushed the dog. She squeezed her eyes shut, her back stiff as an iron rod. No one had fussed over her like this in ages.

"Doesn't look too bad. It won't need any stitches." His breath stirred the hair near her ear, raising gooseflesh across her skin. She opened her eyes.

Gerald's face hovered only an inch or two from her own, his warm fingers a featherlike touch on her skin, his gaze fixed on the wound.

She stared at his eyes, the blue catching reflections of the sunlight from the window. Tiny lines hovered at their outer corners, as if he'd spent too many nights toiling at his patients' bedside with too little to show for it.

His gaze flickered down to her eyes and remained locked there.

Ruby shoved her chair backward along the kitchen floor until it bumped against the wall. "I told you, I'm fine." His touch made it difficult to concentrate. She pushed his hand away. "I think that'll do. I need to freshen up, anyway."

He nodded and pulled back, lips puckered in a frown.

Ruby stumbled to her feet and thanked Mrs. Larkspur for the tea before escaping to the solitude of her bedroom.

Gerald laid the damp cloth on the table, the hairs lifting along his arms. What was it about this woman? She was demanding, rude, controlling—and completely hypnotizing.

His mother laid a hand on his back. "Rough day?"

Gerald let his head drop back against his shoulders as he stared up at the ceiling. "Rough day. Rough night. Rough couple of months."

She set a teacup in front of him and reached for the pot. "You know what they say. 'Sunshine always comes after the storm.'" His mother poured the tea, the fragrant scent of chamomile wafting upward on the cloud of steam. "And we've had a doozy of a storm this year."

Gerald closed his fingers around the cup, the warmth soaking into his skin. If only it could ease the chill that had locked onto his heart.

The afternoon light glinted off his mother's silver hair. "Ruby will be a pleasant addition, I think." A smile toyed at the corners of her lips, softening the lines around her mouth.

He lifted the cup to his mouth, the hot liquid scalding his tongue. "She's a lovely girl. Don't you agree?"

Gerald swallowed, the tea burning its way down his throat. "I suppose." His mother referred to every woman under the age of thirty as a *lovely girl*. Trouble was, this time she echoed his own thoughts.

"Intelligent, compassionate, thoughtful." She ticked off a few more compliments before leaning forward and squeezing his arm. "And she needs a good man."

"Don't start, Mother. Please." Gerald pushed up from the chair. "I won't have any of your matchmaking."

"A mother's prerogative." Her gray eyes twinkled. "I've been praying for the perfect woman for you since you were a tyke. I was starting to wonder if God had forgotten."

He headed for the stairs, feet dragging with exhaustion. "The perfect woman? I highly doubt such a female exists. And if she did, I'm not sure I would desire to be around her."

᠗

Ruby leaned against the closed bedroom door, chilled by the intensity of the man's gaze. It had been some time since she'd been the subject of such a bold stare. *I didn't come to San Francisco seeking romance.*

Hurrying over to the dressing table, she collapsed onto the stool. The mirrored reflection revealed the truth. Her hair, springing loose from the cock-eyed pompadour frame, resembled an abandoned bird nest after a windstorm—the perfect complement to the flaming-red scratch outlining her brow. Ruby buried her face in her arms. Gerald hadn't been gazing in admiration. It must have been something more akin to horror.

9

*S*tanding before the nurses' mirror, Ruby tied the massive apron over her green skirt and pinned on the crisp white cap. She ran a finger along the cap's steep edge. It had been five years since she'd last worn it. Hopefully, it didn't look outdated compared to the smart ones sported by the nursing students from Cooper College. Ruby turned her chin to the side, surveying her reflection. A week into her stay, Ruby's heart still trembled at every new experience. She ran a quick hand over the apron, smoothing away the last wrinkle.

Ruby hurried down the hospital corridor, her high-button shoes tapping against the sparkling tile floor. She entered the cancer wing and caught Gerald's gaze as he spoke with a patient at the far end of the room. He raised his hand in greeting.

Seven of the eight narrow beds were occupied. The pungent odors of ammonia and iodine tickled her nose, carrying her back to days long past. *Days before Charlie.* She made a quick survey of each patient she passed, stopping just short of where Gerald was speaking with a middle-aged woman. Ruby hung back, not wishing to interrupt and taking the moment to observe the doctor at work.

He leaned over the bed, talking to the woman in soft tones, a smile lifting the corners of his lips. Gerald's clenched hand and squared shoulders contradicted his otherwise calm demeanor. After several moments, he stood upright and gestured for her to join him at the bedside. "It's all right, Ruby—Nurse Marshall. Come meet one of my favorite patients."

Bright eyes stared up at her from a sunken, pale face. She struggled to sit upright. "You're Ruby? Dr. King's sister?"

Ruby drew close. "Yes. I'm going to be assisting for a time."

Gerald stepped back, scribbling on a clipboard. "Nurse, this is Miss Delia Feinstein."

The dark-haired woman pulled the sheets high up over her slight frame. "Call me Dee, honey. Everyone does." She glanced over at Gerald. "Everyone except the doctors, anyway. They insist on this ridiculous formality. I think they're afraid of getting attached."

Gerald tucked the clipboard under his arm and frowned. "Miss Feinstein, you know better."

Dee pulled at her long black braid, twiddling it between her fingers, as she smiled up at Ruby. "Nah, it's because they're bachelors, right, Nurse? If one of them called me by my first name, they might fall in love and have to marry me." She chortled, lifting a hand to cover her lips. "And no one would marry someone with cancer, after all."

Gerald shook his head. "You'd want to snare a better man than me. Ask Nurse Marshall here—she all but called me a scoundrel two days ago after a little misunderstanding with a cable car." He grinned, stepping away to check on a patient two beds further down the row.

Dee's giggles gave way to a couple of wheezing coughs.

Ruby fought the urge to explain the doctor's comments. With a sigh, she stepped to the woman's side and adjusted the pillows to better support her fragile frame.

"Ah, so much better. Thank you, Nurse Marshall."

Ruby touched her shoulder. "If we're going to be on a first-name basis, I think you should call me Ruby."

Dee's smile widened. "Now this is what I mean. I need friends about me, not professionals who hold me at an arm's length because I'm ill." Her rheumy eyes followed the doctor around the room. "He's a pleasant fellow. I wouldn't tease him so badly if he weren't such a nice man."

"Yes, he is."

Dee cackled her way into another coughing spasm. "Oh, so that's how it is?"

Ruby drew back. "No, I—"

"Oh, don't worry, honey. I'm just joshing you. Though I wouldn't blame you if you had eyes for him." The woman shook her head slowly. "He and Dr. King are such handsome gentlemen. Almost makes it worth the relapse, just to come in here to see them."

Ruby's gaze drifted back to Gerald. She lifted a hand to her face, to cool the flush creeping across her cheeks. "My brother would be embarrassed to hear you speak of him in this fashion."

Shifting in the bed, Dee grunted. "Dr. King? Ah, he's used to me. Besides, he's off the auction block now." She heaved another sigh. "A shame."

Ruby scrambled for another subject, anything to return them to safe ground. "How long have you been ill, Dee?"

"Off and on for several months now. Usually I come in for a treatment and head home." She grimaced and touched her belly through the blanket. "Dr. King says I might be in for good, this time. It's just my elderly mama and me at home, and it's hard for her to play nurse." She looked down at her hands, her voice growing low. "And the treatments aren't working like they did at first."

Ruby pulled a chair by the bedside. "I'm sorry to hear it."

A gleam crept into Dee's dark eyes. "No, don't be. Those X-rays are like magic. I was so sick when I first got here, my ma was sure I was dying. But Dr. King and Dr. Larkspur, they started putting me under the X-ray machine, and—" She leaned back against the bed. "Well, it's my own little miracle. In a couple of weeks, I was feeling like myself again. Went back to work, even, and taking care of my nieces and nephew. It was so good to feel alive again."

Ruby tucked her fingers under her legs and relaxed against the chair as she listened to the woman talk. Until she familiarized herself with the hospital routines, a listening ear might be the best medicine she could provide.

"They'll lick this cancer thing. You watch. They already got it on the run." Dee turned toward the window and stared out at the gray fog settling over the city. "But I don't think I can hold out long enough for it." Her gaze lowered. "Time is a precious gift. Don't ever forget, honey."

༄

Gerald strolled back to the office, two clipboards clamped under his arm. Dee Feinstein's bawdy sense of humor usually brought a smile to his face, but today he wanted nothing of it. After a short remission, she'd shown up at the hospital last week in worse condition than he'd ever seen her. An aching hole grew in his chest, and he pressed knuckles against his sternum to ease the pressure.

Ruby's presence in the wing only made the situation more difficult to bear. How would this bright-eyed young woman handle dying patients? Hadn't she experienced enough loss in her life?

Over the past few days, he'd found his mind wandering back to the outspoken redhead more often than he cared to admit. Every time he turned around at home, she was there. And now they had a date to go driving on Sunday. *Not a date. An appointment.*

He rounded the corner and let himself into the office only to discover Robert reclining in the chair with his feet propped on the desk, a half-dozen open books scattered haphazardly across the blotter.

A cloud descended on Gerald as he pulled the door shut. He needed five minutes alone to gather his thoughts. "What are you working on?"

Robert lifted his head, dark circles framing his eyes. "And a good morning to you, too."

Gerald took a deep breath. "Sorry. Good morning."

"You've been as uptight as a cornered skunk the past few weeks." He set the book on his lap. "Is it getting to be too much for you?"

"What exactly—the long hours, the limited funds, or the dying patients?" The sour note in his voice sent a quiver through his stomach. When had he become such a fatalist?

Robert lowered his feet to the floor. "Actually, I meant the extra houseguests."

Gerald sank onto the corner of the desk. "Oh."

His friend shook his head. "Maybe you need to take a day off. Get out of the city for a while."

"Sunday." Gerald placed the clipboards on top of Robert's books.

"Oh, yes. About that . . ." Robert stood and gathered the books into a stack, clearing the desk. "I can't understand why you offered yourself up for the gallows."

Gerald claimed the chair. "What do you mean?"

Robert crossed both arms across his chest. "Teaching my sister how to drive? You've met Ruby. It'll be a nightmare."

"I've spent the last two years with you. I think I can handle her." Gerald ran his hands down his lab coat to smooth the wrinkles, grimacing as his sore palm brushed the buttons.

His partner frowned. "The burn still bothering you?"

"Not much." Gerald tucked it under his opposite arm.

"Let's see." Robert held out a hand, palm up.

Gerald scooted the chair back, imagining other quiet nooks in the hospital where he could find peace. Like the chapel, perhaps. "It's unnecessary. I don't need a consult, thank you."

"Give it here." Robert tapped his foot.

Gerald stood with a sigh. Uncurling his fingers, he extended his hand. Sweat broke out under his collar.

"You're worse than a child waiting for a smallpox jab." His friend gripped his hand and stared down at it, his brows pinching together. "How long has it been like this?"

A chill washed over Gerald's skin. *Longer than it should.* "A few months."

Robert's brown-eyed gaze swept upward as his grasp tightened. "Have you shown anyone else?"

"Perhaps I should have Lawrence look at it."

"You should. But you won't. So we're going to do this now. Sit."

Gerald sank into the chair with a grunt. "When did you get so demanding?"

"I learned from the best." Robert moved the lamp to the edge of the table and retrieved a magnifier and a pair of forceps from the cabinet on the wall. He gestured for Gerald to lay his palm on the desk. Gazing through the magnifier, he probed at the wound. "Does it hurt much?"

"Not really. It itches sometimes."

"Have you taken a sample? Run it under the microscope?"

Gerald shook his head.

Robert perched on the edge of the desk with a set jaw. "You know better than to ignore this. We've seen too much in our business to stick our heads in the sand when something's going haywire. It might be a nagging infection. Contact dermatitis, psoriasis, scabies . . ." Robert ran a hand across his eyes. "Dyshidrotic eczema. Cellulitis. Granuloma annulare. Tinea corporis."

"Ringworm?" Gerald snorted. "I don't think so. You're grasping."

Robert shoved the lamp back to its original position. "Yes, and I'll continue until I find a satisfactory answer. Because I don't like the alternatives, and neither do you."

Gerald glanced at the stack of books on the desk, eyeing the black cover emblazoned with gold letters, *Cancer and Cancer Symptoms*. "If it's not gone in a week, I'll run some tests. Likely as not, it's simple X-ray dermatitis."

His partner nodded. "You're probably right. I'm surprised we haven't seen more of it, as often as we're exposed. I've heard methylene blue in an alkaline solution is a good treatment."

Gerald stared down at the stubborn lesion. *Blue hands. Just what I need.*

10

*R*uby positioned the new narrow-brimmed hat over her hair and inserted three hatpins to ensure it would remain fastened. With a nod to her reflection, she rose from the dressing table and retrieved a pink-flowered scarf from the bureau. A perfect match to her skirt, she wound the sheath of silk over the hat twice before securing it under her chin with a tight knot, the free ends draping down the front of her lace blouse. She could almost hear her mother's voice, *"Redheads shouldn't wear pink, dear."*

Abby ducked her head inside the bedroom. "Are you ready? The men are waiting downstairs." The younger woman's freckled cheeks flushed bright with excitement. "Can you believe this beautiful weather?"

"I'm coming." Ruby reached for a monogrammed handkerchief and tucked the tiny square into the top edge of her skirt. She tugged at the waistband, frowning as the fabric puckered. Abby had helped with her corset laces, but the girl refused to pull the garment as snug as Ruby desired. Ruby ran gloved hands over her hips to smooth the wrinkles.

A lump rose in her throat as she imagined climbing into the waiting automobile. Why had she agreed to this outing? She fiddled with the scarf as her stomach churned. "I'll be right down." She opened the small jewelry box she kept on the dresser. Perhaps a necklace would provide the courage she lacked.

Abby stepped into the room, smile fading. "You don't need to do this. If you're frightened of automobiles, why would you learn to drive?"

Ruby swallowed hard and straightened her shoulders, snapping the box closed. "It's not automobiles I fear. It's the men who control them." She turned to face her brother's fiancée. "I'm ready."

❧

Gerald brushed the powdered sugar from his fingers to hide the evidence. The undeclared culinary contest raging in his home was having unintended consequences. Etiquette demanded he consume copious amounts of baked goods in order to keep both his mother and his cousin Clara contented, and Gerald was never one to bypass good manners. Especially when they involved dessert.

Ruby's dachshund whined, placing his stubby front legs against the cabinet and pushing his long snout up toward the wooden countertop.

"Don't give me away." Gerald nudged the dog back to the floor with the toe of his shoe. "And shouldn't you be outside like a normal dog?"

The pup dropped back to all four paws, staring up at him with chocolate-brown eyes.

"You wouldn't like it anyway." Gerald broke off a small scrap of bacon left from breakfast. "Here, try this."

The dog gulped it down without bothering to chew, turning its nose upward as if in search of more.

Robert strode in to the kitchen, settling a charcoal-colored derby on his head. "Have you seen Abby or Ruby?"

Gerald brushed knuckles over his lip to remove any hint of lingering sugar. "Abby went up a moment ago to retrieve your sister."

"Could be a while, then." His friend lifted the edge of the cake cover. "Is this tonight's *pièce de résistance*?"

"Last night's. You missed it. Lemon cake with whipped cream à la Clara."

Robert swiped a crumbling corner and guided the morsel to his mouth. "I think she's winning."

"Don't let my mother hear you say that. She's already baked a German chocolate cake for this evening. She thinks she's appealing to Herman's heritage."

Gerald turned as the two women entered the room, little Davy clinging to his sister's hand. After a quick glance, Gerald guided his gaze back to the floor. He must learn not to stare like a schoolboy.

The dog ran over and danced around their feet. Davy dropped to the floor and pulled the dog into his lap.

With a laugh, Abby hurried to Robert's side. "You shouldn't ruin your appetite. Mama packed a picnic for our adventure."

Gerald chuckled. "And my mother added a few items."

Robert patted his stomach. "I love this family."

"And they adore you." Abby squeezed Robert's arm.

Gerald turned his attention to Ruby. "Are you ready for your first lesson? Looks as if you're prepared for an expedition."

Skin pale, Ruby nodded. "I'm quite looking forward to it. Though I didn't expect an audience for my little escapade."

Davy jumped up. "I'm coming too, right?"

Robert laughed, lifting the boy and hoisting him onto his back. "Of course you are. We need someone to help us eat all those cookies." He headed toward the door. "Don't worry, Sis. Abby, Davy, and I will stay out of the way. We'll find a scenic meadow for our picnic and then turn you and Gerald loose."

Ruby frowned. "Is it appropriate? I mean, for the two of you to be . . ." She blushed. "Without a chaperone? I'm not sure a little boy qualifies for such a task."

Gerald fought to keep from smiling. For such a young widow, Ruby Marshall clucked like a mother hen. Too bad she didn't have children of her own to fuss over.

"I don't wish to create difficulties, but one cannot be too careful about appearances." Ruby folded her hands.

Gerald buttoned his coat. "Considering Robert and Abby live in the same household, if tongues were going to wag, they'd have begun long before now."

Abby nodded. "And since the quake—most of that nonsense has been overlooked."

Ruby straightened, her head drawn back. "Nonsense?"

"I think it's time we were on our way." Gerald cleared his throat. He leaned toward Ruby. "We'll stay close at hand, I promise. I don't intend to leave the pair of them alone for long." *Then we'd be alone, as well.*

The young woman pressed her lips into a line and followed Abby out the kitchen door.

Gerald hefted the basket onto his arm, catching a whiff of the delectable fragrances emanating from its depths.

~

Ruby folded her knees under her skirt, fiddling with the tassels on the red woolen picnic blanket. The bright sunshine warmed her shoulders and arms and she drew in a shaky breath, filling her lungs with the sweet fragrance of grass and trees. The idyllic meadow reminded her of a scene from a storybook, complete with a tiny brook splashing over a series of small stones on its way down the gentle slope.

Davy cavorted in the trickling water, stomping his bare feet through the water to send it splashing onto the rocks.

Gerald lay sprawled on his back, hat shielding his eyes from the sunshine as he dozed. His lanky legs bent at the knees, feet resting flat on the ground and one arm draped over his stomach. The man could sleep anywhere, it seemed. Likely due to his odd hours. What must he think of her—arriving uninvited in his home, forcing her way into his medical practice, demanding to drive his vehicle? Was this the woman she aspired to be?

She turned her head, glancing down the slope to where Robert strolled along the creek with Abby, his attention never wandering from the young woman's face. The quiet, unassuming girl had clearly stolen her brother's heart. And why not? She was thoughtful and gentle. Abby's beauty turned heads, even though she didn't seem to care about fashion and did little with her hair beyond twisting the long brown locks into a simple knot.

Nothing came so easy to Ruby. She twirled a grass blade between her fingers, her muscles tense with nervous energy. Why did men prefer soft-spoken women? Charlie had never minded her ways. At least he'd never said so. *Then again, he never said much of anything.*

The couple's laughter drifted on the warm breeze. Robert took Abby's hand as she hopped over the small brook, her hat dangling from her fingers. Davy splashed water at them, earning a shriek from his sister.

Had she and Charlie ever been so in love? Ruby brushed away the uncomfortable thought and glanced back at Gerald. His chest rose and fell in an easy cadence, the gentle lines of his arm and shoulder beckoning her to curl up at his side. A shiver raced across her skin. *Mustn't think like that.*

She reached up and checked her hat. It hadn't moved an inch. Her fingers itched to loosen the pins, feel the sunshine on her hair. Of course, the result would be a new crop of freckles. She cast a glance over at the automobile. The drive had been blessedly uneventful. But she hadn't gotten behind the wheel yet.

Ruby pushed up to her feet and strolled over to the vehicle. With everyone else otherwise occupied, it would be a good time to sit at the controls. If she closed her eyes and imagined driving, perhaps the fluttering sensation in her chest would ease.

She ran a hand along the red frame as if it were the flank of a skittish mare. "There, it's not so bad." The sun-touched metal warmed her fingertips. She stroked the brass side lamp. "You're merely a contraption. An invention. You won't hurt me. Right?" Ruby cast a quick glance over her shoulder before placing a foot on the step and plopping into the driver's seat. Touching the wooden wheel, Ruby closed her fingers around it as she glanced over the controls. Levers, foot pedals, and switches surrounded her. What made her think she'd be able to learn all this? Her throat tightened.

"You must be pretty eager."

Ruby jumped, her knee bumping against one of the levers.

Gerald's hand closed around the long handle. "Whoa, there. Let's save this one until we get started, shall we?"

Ruby gripped the steering wheel, her heart racing. "You shouldn't have startled me. Who knows what might have happened?"

The corner of his mouth turned upward. "The engine is off and the tires are resting on flat ground. What on earth could have happened?"

"It might have run off or something." A wave of prickly heat crept up her neck. Ruby released the wheel and straightened her collar.

He chuckled. "It's not a horse. The motor only does what it's told."

"Then perhaps you should demonstrate how I give it orders."

Gerald laid his hand on the seat rail. "You begin by turning on the ignition switch." He gestured to a switch just behind her knee.

She reached out trembling fingers. "Now?"

"Whenever you are ready."

She withdrew her hand. "Perhaps you should go over the entire process step by step before we begin."

Gerald huffed. "We would be here all day. It's not a snake, it won't bite."

Ruby placed her feet firm against the floor. She grasped the device and clicked into place, gritting her teeth in the process.

"That's it. Now, the spark lever on the steering column needs to be like so." He pushed it into position. "I'll go ahead and crank it. We can show you the starter another time." He bent down beside the vehicle and inserted the metal hand crank.

Ruby's arm muscles knotted. She glanced down at the controls. There were three pedals on the floor. Gerald hadn't bothered to explain them. She took one hand off the wheel and wrapped it around the steering column, bending down for a closer look. "What does this—" The engine's roar startled her, and Ruby grabbed for a new handhold, knocking into the lever beside her. The auto lurched.

Gerald popped up like a jackrabbit before tumbling out of the way.

Ruby squealed as the car surged forward. She locked both hands on the steering wheel.

Breath exploded from Gerald's lungs as he collided with the ground. Rolling to his knees, he sprang up and dashed after the car as it trundled away, its occupant shrieking. His heart hammered in his chest.

The car bumped down the gentle slope toward the creek. Davy splashed well out of the path, laughing.

Gerald put on a burst of speed and leaped onto the step, pushing the gear lever and jamming down on the brake with one foot.

As the auto shuddered to a halt, Ruby's shrieks faded to ragged, gasping cries.

She placed both hands on her cheeks. "You said it wouldn't do that."

Robert's laughter carried across the open field. "Good try, Ruby!"

Fire crept up Gerald's throat. "It doesn't, unless someone fiddles with the levers while I am cranking the engine. Why didn't you press the brake pedal?"

Ruby glared. "You never told me which one was the brake."

He hopped down, knees rubbery. "It's on the left. Haven't you been watching as I drove around town?"

"Of course I have, but I couldn't see what your feet were doing." Her cheeks flamed. "Maybe this was a bad idea."

Yes, indeed. Gerald placed a foot on the step. "Scoot over. I'll demonstrate."

She shifted across the upholstered seat, creating room behind the wheel.

Gerald sat down. Drawing a deep breath, he explained each step in detail, as if describing a complicated surgery to a first-year medical student.

Ruby leaned forward, focusing on each item in turn.

The pressure of Ruby's shoulder against his arm nearly drove him to distraction. He swallowed hard. If she sat any closer, she'd be on his lap. Pulling his mind back to the matter at hand, Gerald put the automobile in gear. He kept the pace slow, easing the tires across the meadow grass. He pointed out the reverse gear, the timing lever, the throttle, and most importantly—the brake. *No more surprises.*

She peppered him with questions, pointing at each lever and pedal and demanding succinct answers. After a few more turns around the grassy pasture, she leaned back against the cushion and fell silent.

He shot a covert glance at her face. Ruby's pale eyes sparkled in the sunshine, her pink cheeks framed by the flapping scarf. He increased their speed, enjoying the feel of the tires bumping over the uneven ground.

Ruby's hand shot up to touch her hat, but a second later a smile crossed her lips. "This is actually sort of enjoyable—when there are no streetcars and newsboys about."

"Are you ready to take the wheel?" Gerald backed off the throttle.

"I believe I am."

"Any questions?" he asked.

"Why is your hand blue?"

"I meant questions about the automobile." He stopped the vehicle and climbed out. Careful to walk behind the car, he took his seat on the opposite side as she slid back into the driver's seat.

She smiled. "You didn't specify."

Gerald opened his hand. "It's methylene blue. Your brother thinks it will help with the dermatitis on my palm. Or perhaps he thinks it amusing for me to appear as if I've been squeezing blueberries with my bare hands."

Ruby gripped the wheel with white knuckles, but she flashed him a rare smile. "This is exceedingly gracious of you, Gerald. I appreciate you taking a day away from the hospital to teach me."

Gerald leaned back, a rush of warmth spreading through his chest. "I think it demonstrates great courage on your part. You're the only woman I've met who has shown the least interest in driving. I respect your determination."

She laughed. "Determination is one thing I have in abundance. But I think you're the one showing courage." She faced the front, one corner of her mouth lifting into a smirk. "After all . . . you're putting your life in my hands. Aren't you?"

"I suppose I am. But I think you can be trusted."

She gripped the gear handle as she opened the throttle. The automobile pitched forward.

Gerald braced a foot against the front rail as his black derby hat went sailing.

11

*R*uby dipped a foot into the steaming water, the warmth sending ripples of pleasure up her skin. She sank into the bath with a sigh. After the long drive home—Gerald back at the wheel—her thoughts had been consumed with the idea of an extended soak. The muscles along her spine unknotted, the day's tension seeping out into the water with the road dust.

She relaxed against the back of the tub, trying to push away her niggling worries, but images continued to motor through her mind. The memory of Gerald's ruffled hair at the end of their lesson made her smile. The man deserved a little fright after the ordeal he had put her through earlier in the week.

Ruby hated to admit it, but after today's expedition, she felt a tad of sympathy for the doctor. Evidently controlling an automobile was not for the simple-minded. At least with a horse's intelligence to assist you, one could be relatively confident of not driving off into a creek as Ruby had nearly accomplished. With so many pedals and levers, all designed to manage the mysterious workings of the vehicle's innards, how did one observe the road as well?

She scrunched down in the water, sending wavelets lapping against her chin. She'd been quite unfair by lumping him together with other drivers. Ruby closed her eyes, allowing the water's heat to penetrate into her bones. Occasional droplets plopped from the tap, echoing through the otherwise silent room.

Her heart fluttered as she remembered guiding the vehicle around the meadow, its tires bumping over the grassy hillocks. Gerald kept one hand on the frame, the other gripping the seatback just shy of her shoulder, his face stretched in an unreadable expression—terror, most likely. Had she ever experienced such a heady power? Such control? Life had ruled over her for too long as she had allowed it to carry her places she didn't wish to go. A laugh bubbled up from somewhere deep in Ruby's chest. *Now I'm in the driver's seat.*

A gentle tapping sounded on the door.

Ruby straightened, the water cascading off her skin in rivulets, cold air rushing to take its place. "Yes?"

Her brother's voice wafted in, muffled by the wooden door. "Ruby? Don't forget there are seven other people living in the house. Don't stay in the bath all evening."

"I'm sorry. I'll hurry." She reached for the rose-scented soap. *Funny how he sounds more like Father with every passing year.*

His voice sounded again. "I'm going to retire for the night. I'll see you in the morning. Are you driving to the hospital with me?"

The bar escaped her fingers and slipped under the surface. The auto, again? "Abby asked me to join her at the refugee camp. Gerald said I could work the afternoon rounds. I'll meet you there."

Her brother's footsteps receded down the hall, and Ruby turned her attention to the task at hand. After a quick wash, she pinched her nose and slid backward until her head plunged under the water. A blessed stillness filled her ears and for a moment she floated in a world of her own making. When her lungs complained, she broke the surface and sat up, water streaming down her face like a waterfall. Blinking the droplets from her eyelashes, Ruby reached for a towel. She stepped out of the bath, tiny hairs rising along her arms and legs as the cold air chased away her peaceful mood. She toweled off quickly, imagining Gerald or Mr. Fischer hovering in the hall in wait.

Ruby secured the dressing gown's belt snug at her waist. As the drain gurgled, she opened the bathroom door a tiny slit and peeked into the dark hallway before tiptoeing down the quiet passage.

In the shadows, a door creaked. Gerald stepped into the gloom, a book clamped under one arm, gold-framed reading glasses perched on his nose.

Ruby froze, one hand clutching her dressing gown, the other steadying the towel covering her damp, unruly hair.

His eyes widened. "Oh, I'm sorry. I thought everyone had gone to bed."

She plastered on a smile, hoping to distract him from her unkempt appearance. "Um, no. I'm on my way there now."

He glanced up at her headdress. "So I see."

She nodded, cautious not to let the towel tumble. Bad enough to be seen in her gown, but to display her wet locks would be a disaster. Ruby edged past, escaping to her room.

❧

Gerald sniffed the air, the scent of roses lingering as the young woman hurried down the hall. A rush of heat stampeded over his good sense for a moment as he imagined touching the single corkscrew curl dangling by the woman's milky white ear lobe. Gerald shook himself. Perhaps sharing his home with an unmarried woman was not such a wise idea. When Robert had proposed the situation, Gerald had pictured someone more like Abby or Clara. Someone sisterly. Gerald headed to the back stairway and trudged down, clutching a worn copy of *Radiotherapy and Phototherapy* to his chest. After a day like today, his strained nerves wouldn't permit sleep. He clicked on the electric lamp in the study and settled into the leather armchair. Propping his feet on the padded ottoman, Gerald laid the book on his lap, without bothering to open it.

He stared at the cover, his imagination fixated on the dripping redhead in the hall. Since Robert and Abby had eyes only for one another, Gerald had been thrown together with the young widow on multiple occasions now—an experience simultaneously pleasing and infuriating. Never had he struggled with being so dual-minded. He certainly didn't need another complication in his life, and Ruby Marshall appeared to be the personification of the word.

He flipped open the text, tipping it to catch the glow from the lamp. Squinting in the darkness, he focused on a chapter discussing the deleterious effects of the X-ray. Gerald's stomach churned after reading a few pages of case studies. His hand itched like mad, and he scrubbed it across his knee in an attempt not to dig his fingernails into the irritated skin.

Gerald's thoughts wandered back to Ruby's face as she drove his automobile today, brows scrunched over her fixed eyes, shoulders back, a tip of a pink tongue touching her upper lip.

How quickly she'd mastered the basics. Did many women face their fears in such a manner? He couldn't remember having encountered one before. Not once had her fortitude wavered. His head fell back against the antimacassar.

"Hard at work?" Robert's voice wafted into the room from the open doorway.

"Always." Gerald managed a smile, but his voice cracked.

His friend entered and took a seat in the chair opposite, the springs squeaking. "Am I disturbing you?"

"No. Too weary to focus my eyes, I'm afraid."

Robert leaned back, his long legs splayed out. "It's been a long week. You've earned a rest."

Gerald sighed. "Week? How about year? I won't be sad to see 1906 go."

"It's only August, but I suppose I agree. A few good things have happened as well." Robert smiled. "And we have a few blessings to look forward to before 1907 arrives."

The fog cleared from Gerald's thoughts, the gleam in his partner's eye catching his attention. "Have you and Abby set a date, finally?"

Robert grinned. "You know, if it had been up to me, we'd have married the week after the quake."

"Abby has always been more pragmatic. What have you decided?" There had already been a record number of post-earthquake nuptials, even among the hospital staff.

"We thought November might be a good time. My family would be able to join us. I suppose I can survive three more months—barely."

"Where are you planning the festivities?"

"That's the thing." Robert glanced down at his lap, smoothing wrinkles from his trousers as he spoke. "Abby wants to have the wedding here."

Gerald yanked off his spectacles. "Here—at the house?"

"Just a small gathering. Her family, and—and mine."

Two families. How bad could it be? "A small family gathering sounds acceptable." Gerald squinted in thought. "Not much different than now, I suppose. A bit fancier. You know my mother and Clara have already discussed cakes. Might be good for them to combine forces on a project beyond fattening us up." Robert's solemn expression gave Gerald pause. "What aren't you telling me?"

Robert cleared his throat. "My mother will be joining us. She'd—she'd need to stay here."

Gerald sank against the padded back. "Of course. Another cook for the kitchen."

"And a few sisters."

He squinted, drumming his fingers against armrest. "How many sisters?"

Robert raked fingers through his dark hair. "You've already met Ruby, and there's five more besides."

Gerald sat forward, sending the book crashing to the floor. "Five more women? In my house?"

"Six, if you count my mother."

A stone the size of Gibraltar settled in Gerald's stomach. *Complications, indeed.*

"Abby was confident you'd approve. I told her I was less certain." Robert stood and strode toward the doorway. "Oh, and maybe a few cousins, too. Did I mention them?" He grimaced before ducking out the door.

Gerald dropped his face into his hands.

12

$\mathcal{R}$uby covered her nose and mouth with a handkerchief as the stench of latrines overcame her senses. The homeless camp stretched across the park, up the hill and out of sight—a sea of identical green wooden shanties set out in a perfect grid, like a battalion of battle-worn soldiers on a well-trampled parade ground. The countless stories from the *Evening Bee* came to life before her eyes. Ruby's heart jumped.

"The facility was built by the army." Abby gestured to the structures. "They've brought some order to the chaos."

"So I see." Ruby lowered the cloth and tried not to wrinkle her nose. "Five months have passed since the earthquake. How many still live here?"

"Countless families. Thousands fled during the original disaster, but the men returned to work in the reconstruction effort and their loved ones followed. Much of the early rebuilding has taken place in the financial district and, of course, homes for the well-to-do. There's still nowhere for these people to go." Abby strode between the clap-board shacks with ease, nodding at women gathered in small groups and pausing as bands of children raced across their path, shrieking voices raised in play.

Ruby hoisted the hem of her skirt out of the mud and struggled to keep pace. If she got turned around in this labyrinth, she'd never find her way home. "What are we here to do?"

"Whatever is necessary." Abby cast a smile over her shoulder as she stepped up onto a wooden boardwalk. "We hand out food, clothes, blankets. The Red Cross organizes the relief supplies, and we try to keep order."

Ruby glanced about at the unkempt children and the women working to maintain some type of households in this grime. The place reeked of need and desperation. Ruby nearly collided with Abby's back when the young woman halted at the end of a lengthy row of shacks. The open area beckoned them out into the sunshine, the brown grass flattened into the mire. A Red Cross flag fluttered in the breeze above a large tent, the fragrance of hot food wafting from the canvas flaps. A restless crowd milled about outside.

"Here we are." Abby took a deep breath and smiled. "Isn't it marvelous?"

The odd assortment of fragrances stung Ruby's sinuses, and she brushed her nose with a handkerchief. The ammonia-scented hospital seemed a million miles from this outdoor arena. "Splendid."

Abby's lips pursed. "I know it probably appears quite shocking, but you should have seen the park during the fires. People camped everywhere, belongings strewn about, children crying."

A thorn pricked Ruby's heart. She'd heard some of Robert and Abby's stories about the terror of those days—who was she to judge? "I'm sorry. I didn't mean to make fun. This is what brought me to San Francisco." She smoothed a hand across her white hospital apron. "What shall we do first?"

"Ah, you're here, then!" A male voice boomed through the yard. A tall, muscular fellow strode from the tent, a grin beaming from his pleasant face. "Good to see you again, Miss Abby. And who might this be?"

Abby smiled and looped her hand through Ruby's elbow, guiding her forward. "Patrick, this is Dr. King's sister—soon to be mine, too, I suppose."

A glimmer danced in the man's eyes. "Well, it's an honor, Miss King. Patrick Allison, at your service." He pulled off his round derby, his red hair catching the sunlight. "You look like a lass from home. Are you Irish, perchance?"

Mr. Allison's brogue tickled Ruby's ears. "It's a pleasure to meet you, Mr. Allison. And it's *Mrs.* Marshall. I'm not from Ireland, I'm afraid, though one of my grandmothers emigrated from Dublin as a child."

Patrick hooked his thumbs inside the armholes of his pin-striped vest. "Disappointed on two counts—married and only a touch of the Irish. More's the pity. I apologize, Mrs. Marshall. I shouldn't have assumed you were single, like our sweet Abigail."

Abby laughed. "Not for much longer. Robert and I will wed in November."

The man's grin widened. "Cause for celebration." He grinned, turning to the milling crowd. "Our own Miss Fischer is about to be married! What do you think, folks? Shall we hoist a bowl of stew in her honor?"

Ruby's heart lifted as the onlookers cheered. She saw no comfortable way to correct Abby's friend about her own status.

She and Abby followed Mr. Allison into the tent and took up stations behind the long table. A heavy-set woman stirred huge cast-iron kettles over a roaring fire, pausing to ladle a sizeable portion into a cook pot before handing it to Ruby.

Ruby grasped the handle with a thin towel. Staggering under the weight, she managed to haul the container a few yards without sloshing its content on the ground. She eyed the table, wondering how she'd hoist the heavy load to its surface.

"Here, allow me." Patrick Allison stooped over and took the handle from Ruby, his large hand closing over hers.

"Thank you." She released her grip and stepped free.

"I don't believe soup would be an appropriate decoration for your lovely feet."

Ruby drew her toe tips under the edge of her skirt and reached for the ladle. A line of people waited, bowls in hand. As they handed small tickets to a woman waiting at the front of the line, Ruby gave the thick stew a quick stir.

A boy stared up at her with sparkling blue eyes, a toothy grin brightening his smudged face.

Warmth spread through Ruby's chest as she watched him juggle a wooden tray, bracing it against his dirty shirtfront. Miriam would be proud. In this city, a sense of purpose called from every needy face, and Ruby's long-dormant heart beat anew.

She cast a glance over her shoulder to where the Irishman washed dishes, shirtsleeves rolled up to his elbows, the linen fabric outlining the muscles of his biceps. He met her gaze with a grin and a quick wink.

Abby balanced a basket of bread rolls on her hip and leaned close to Ruby's ear. "The women here all think he's a handsome devil. Not me, of course." She cleared her throat.

A devil indeed, Ruby hadn't met a man as flirtatious since her school days. Ruby pressed her lips together. She forced her gaze back to the stew. "Mr. Allison seems quite friendly." She couldn't help comparing the charismatic fellow to Gerald Larkspur's refined demeanor.

Abby set a roll on a woman's plate. "It's *Reverend* Allison, actually, but he doesn't like to draw attention to the fact. Patrick prefers to do his charity work on the sly."

Ruby paused, halting the dripping spoon in midair. "A minister? Are you serious?"

"Is it so difficult to believe? Patrick's down here at the camps nearly every day from dawn to dusk. If that doesn't suggest a man of God, I'm not sure what does."

Vegetable-scented steam wafted up to warm Ruby's cheeks. She glanced back at the gentleman with new eyes.

He wiped his hands on a white dishcloth draped from his belt and made his way down the line, greeting the folks with cheerful words and welcoming smiles. Why hadn't she spotted it right away? He resembled a shepherd tending to his flock. *Or Jesus feeding the five thousand.*

Ruby turned back to Abby. "It's not Father Allison? I thought most Irish were Catholic."

Abby shrugged. "Little surprises me in this city anymore. There are people of many nationalities and creeds in this camp." A corner of her mouth lifted. "If you promise not to tell Robert, I'll introduce you to my Chinese friend, Kum Yong. But she doesn't live here."

Ruby cocked her head. "Why keep it from Robert?"

A shadow dropped over the Abby's face, and her gaze lowered to the basket of bread. "He doesn't approve of me spending time with the Chinese mission girls." She glanced back at Ruby from under long lashes. "I was going to ask you if you knew why he had such strong feelings about the Chinese. It's the one area in which we disagree."

Ruby stirred the pot, the ladle sending the broth and vegetables swirling like her thoughts. "I can't imagine. Our father was adamant about treating all patients—all people—equally. I'm surprised Robert would speak otherwise."

Abby sighed. "I know he and Gerald sometimes treat Chinese patients. Perhaps I should ask Gerald about it. Kum Yong is a good friend. I don't understand why Robert doesn't approve."

Ruby continued spooning helpings into the waiting bowls. "Maybe I need to have a word with my brother."

"Oh, no, please don't. I wouldn't want him to think we're forming ranks against him."

Patrick appeared at Ruby's elbow with a second batch of hearty stew. He lowered the kettle into place with a grunt and cast a glowing smile at her, his gaze capturing hers for a moment.

Ruby blushed, moving the ladle to the fresh pot. "Thank you."

"My pleasure." Patrick claimed the empty container and moved away, his gray vest highlighting the width of his shoulders.

Forcing her attention back to Abby's problem, Ruby clucked her tongue. "Forming ranks? My dear, you must learn . . ." She gave Abby's hand a quick squeeze. "It's what sisters do."

❧

"Six sisters?" Dee giggled, a fresh bit of color rising to her pale cheeks. "You're going to have your hands full." Dappled sunlight from the tall window drifted across her bed.

Gerald tucked the pencil into the pocket of his white lab coat. "Yes, well, I'm sure not all of them are coming. I imagine at least a few have other engagements."

The dark-haired woman shifted in the narrow bed. "Engagements—nice choice of words, Doctor. Perhaps we'll see you engaged to one of these sisters before they all pack up and head home. You've been on the shelf too long if you ask me. It's time you found a nice girl." She patted his arm. "Must be lonely for a man like you to go home to an empty house every night."

Gerald snorted. "My house hasn't been empty since the quake, Miss Feinstein. I'm fortunate if I can spend two minutes in my own company before I'm interrupted."

"How many times must I insist you call me Dee?" She pulled herself higher on the pillows. "And houseguests aren't the same as a wife. What's the old saying about fish and guests? They both stink after three days? Sort of like the cannery down at the pier."

"Then it's surprising you can't smell my house from here. Likely the King girls won't want to stay after all."

"You'd better throw open a window or two. Air the place out." Dee leaned back against the pillow and brushed a trembling hand across her brow.

Gerald replaced the clipboard. He shouldn't let her get so worked up, but her jokes brought him a flicker of hope. "I'll do that. For now, you need to rest. We've got another treatment scheduled in a few hours."

She sighed. "I'd rather go sunbathing at the seaside than sit under your machine again. I know the X-rays work miracles, but it's growing a bit tiresome."

"Let's get you healthy, and I'll escort you to the shore, myself."

A faint smile touched the woman's pencil-thin lips. "No, I want you to take the lovely redheaded widow or one of her sisters. Ruby and Robert are both so handsome, it's quite unfair to the rest of us. I'm certain one of the King girls would be an ideal bride for a lonely doctor." She coughed, grimacing. "You make sure and woo one, you hear?"

Gerald pushed away the thought of Ruby in a bathing costume. "They'll be here to see their brother get married, not to snare a bachelor."

"Two birds, one stone. And what's more romantic than a wedding?" She sucked in a short breath, wheezing like a Stanley Steamer. "Timing couldn't be better."

13

*R*uby clamped her fingers on the edge of the wooden bench as the cable car rattled its way down the street toward Gerald's house. She locked her knees, pushing the soles of her shoes against the floorboards to keep herself from swaying with each jolt. After a few weeks in the city, she was finally growing accustomed to the sensation.

"We've only two blocks, and we must be ready to spring out. The car doesn't pause but a moment." Abby slid to the front of the seat, the breeze fluttering the wisps of brown hair along the sides of her face.

Ruby adjusted a single hatpin, her own curls behaving for once, even after a second long day volunteering at the refugee camp. If Abby took a little more care, she wouldn't have to contend with loose strands. Her brown locks would be lovely teased up into a Gibson Girl Psyche knot. *Would she be willing to let me try it?*

A wave of homesickness rippled through Ruby's heart. She never thought she'd miss helping her sisters style their hair. Elizabeth, especially, had the most beautiful blonde tresses. Ruby could still feel the silky strands slipping between her fingers. She pushed away the memory. Other than her family, Sacramento held nothing for her. San Francisco was the city of promise. The time had come to put down roots in this new place.

Ruby grasped the brass pole for balance as the car slowed. "Where will you and Robert live once you are wed?"

Abby stood and whisked into the aisle without even a wobble. "Robert's looking into it. We've seen a few new homes built along Van Ness, not far from here. But the demand is high, as you might imagine. We may need to go farther afield."

Ruby pushed to her feet, her stomach lurching with the car's movement. As the vehicle slowed, she lifted the hem of her walking skirt and followed Abby down the two narrow steps to the cobblestone street. Ruby darted a quick glance both directions, anxious to be out of the road before any automobiles or carriages rolled through. "So you are definitely staying in San Francisco?"

Abby led the way through the sidewalk as the cable car rattled on down the hill. "Oh, yes. Robert's work is here. I don't enjoy the crush of the city, but since the disaster, the people here have become like family."

"Robert told me your family owns an orchard. Is it nearby?" Ruby frowned at the mud on her shoe tips.

"The farm is in San Jose. Papa decided to sell the land after Cecelia passed away—in fact, he was there preparing the orchard for sale when the earthquake struck. It was terrifying being so far away and not knowing how he had fared. With everything that's happened, he hasn't been able to sell the property yet."

"I imagine he was quite frightened for you, as well."

"Your family must have been equally concerned for Robert."

The unwelcome memory washed over Ruby, a familiar knot reforming in her stomach. "We were sick with worry until his telegram arrived."

"I was with him when he sent it." A tiny smile teased at Abby's lips. "He'd just asked me to marry him."

Ruby stepped over some loose cobbles, still shifted from the quake. "I can't believe the rascal never told us about you."

"I suppose he felt you'd already had enough of a shock."

Ruby's heart warmed. Dismayed as she'd been to find her younger brother secretly engaged, this sweet young woman had wasted no time worming her way into Ruby's affections. She could see why

Robert was smitten. She wove her arm through Abby's elbow as they walked. "Yes, but it would have been a pleasant shock. If I'd known he was taken care of, I might not have traipsed off to join him."

Abby's brown eyes glowed. "Then I'm glad he maintained the secret. You've been a welcome addition. Robert is glad you're here. And I haven't seen Gerald smile so much in months. All of us, really."

Ruby swallowed, turning her gaze back to her soiled shoes. "Dr. Larkspur seems quite good-spirited. I don't believe I can claim any of the credit."

Abby squeezed her arm. "Good-spirited, yes. But he'd been growing . . ." she scrunched her freckled nose, "a bit melancholy. I think the research has wearied him. Since you arrived, he's been smiling and laughing again. It does my heart good to see my cousin so cheery." Her pace quickened, as if the idea gave an extra bounce to her step. "Perhaps the four of us could go out to dinner sometime. Get away from the rest of the family for an evening."

A weight descended on Ruby's shoulders as Abby's hints grew more pointed. She searched for a suitable diversion. "Tell me more about Reverend Allison. I'm perplexed as to why he acts like such a jokester when in reality he's a man of God."

Abby reached for the gate, clicking open the path to Gerald's home. "Patrick is a wit, that much is certain. But who's to say a minister must be a dour-faced old man? If he has the joy of Christ in his heart, is it wrong for him to crack a smile?"

Ruby pressed her lips together. "I'm not saying he shouldn't be joyful. But he didn't even introduce himself as a minster. It's as if he's ashamed of the fact."

As they approached the door, Otto's excited bark sounded on the other side. Abby twisted the knob and the dog bounded out about her legs. "It's the welcoming committee." She smiled, reaching down to scratch the dog's ears. Straightening, she turned to Ruby. "Patrick is quite sincere about his work. He feels he can reach people better if they know him as a man first—without all their preconceived suppositions about ministers. He spreads the gospel through serving their needs. He's not there to preach. He's living out God's love."

Ruby followed Abby into the house, sinking down on one knee to greet her dog, smiling as the damp nose pressed into her hand. With a sigh, she swept Otto up into her arms and cuddled him to her chest. Why was she always so quick to judge people? *Living out God's love?* All she'd seen were Patrick's strong shoulders and his outgoing personality. A shiver ran through her. Besides, she had no business looking at a man in such a way—especially a man of the cloth. Next time she'd keep her gaze fixed on those she'd come to serve.

❧

Gerald tapped his fingers on the desk. Ruby's dog barked an alarm any time someone arrived or even walked past the house. With so many of them coming and going all day, they had little need for the turnkey doorbell. The women's voices faded from the front hall.

He closed the notebook containing Robert's most recent article, written for the *California Medical Quarterly.* He'd marked a few passages, adjusting some of the younger man's more optimistic projections. *If my name is going on the piece, I want the claims kept conservative.* He rubbed a hand against the pinching muscles in his neck. The evidence thus far suggested X-rays only delayed the inevitable. Could they do more? He closed his eyes, leaning back in the wooden swivel chair. Dee Feinstein would be the next to die. The knowledge settled like a rock in the pit of his stomach.

He needed a day away from the cancer ward. Next week, he'd drive over and see if Sergeant Tobias needed a hand with the emergency medical center at the Presidio camp. Nothing could cure the malaise of research like rolling up his sleeves and working with the people—illnesses and wounds he could actually hope to treat. Perhaps Ruby would like to accompany him. Unless she'd had her fill of the camps this week.

He ran a hand over his eyes. Why was her name never more than a whisper from his thoughts? He wasn't some young medical student who needed an admiring nurse dogging his footsteps.

But Ruby was smart and capable. He couldn't refute it. She shouldn't be denied the opportunity to put her skills to use simply because he had difficulty controlling his thoughts. He laid Robert's article on the desk blotter. *I'll ask her if she'd like to join me. Who knows—she might refuse.*

※

Ruby wrapped her hand around the teacup, steam curling into the air. She crossed the dew-laden grass to the grape arbor, relishing the morning's damp, earthy fragrance. After several weeks of living in the packed house, she'd learned a few moments of privacy before the day began fulfilled her craving for solitude. The long angled beams of sunshine filtered through the yellow-leafed vines, spilling out over the wrought-iron bench like so much California gold dust.

Loosening her grip on the woolen shawl, she spread the garment over the bench, preferring a dry backside to snug shoulders. Ruby set the cup on the seat and ran her still-warm fingers across weary eyes. She'd fallen into bed last night, her feet aching from a long shift at the hospital. Why had she agreed to accompany Gerald to the Presidio today?

Oh, yes. Because he'd gazed at her with those blue eyes. *Charlie's eyes.* Ruby sighed. She'd planned to assist Robert in the X-ray laboratory, but her brother had been quick to say she'd be of more use to Gerald. Ruby pressed her lips into a firm line. All of her good intentions to come to San Francisco and aid her brother scrambled into disarray the moment she'd stepped off the ferry. She spent more time with Gerald and Abby than Robert. Ruby lifted the teacup, the fragrance awakening her senses. At least her skills were useful here, and it's more than she could say for Sacramento.

Tomorrow she would go downtown and purchase some driving goggles and a duster coat. Between the ash and the demolition, the filth kicked up by the wagons and automobiles was incredible. *Good thing I didn't think about the automobiles before I came to San Francisco.*

She took a sip and gazed across the small yard to the quiet house. If Robert and Abby moved to a new home after their wedding, where would she go? She couldn't stay on with Gerald and his family. People might talk, and she wouldn't wish to be accused of unseemly behavior.

But the newlyweds deserved their privacy. Ruby rolled the warm liquid around in her mouth before swallowing. No, it wouldn't do. She'd need to find another place to live. Half of San Francisco was also searching for housing, unfortunately. If Ruby wasn't careful, she'd be forced to bunk in one of those relief cottages.

The back door opened, and Gerald stepped out to the back porch, his coat pressed and spotless. The man ran a hand across his jaw and wandered across the yard to the rose bushes, a flurry of blooms decorating the thorny canes.

Ruby tucked her braid behind her back, regretting not fixing her hair before coming outside. The arbor hid her from view, but she didn't relish the awkward encounter if he discovered her spying. She stood and shook out her wrap, folding it over one arm and balancing her cup in the other. Stepping out from under the arbor, she crossed the wet patch of grass to join him.

He glanced up, brows raised. "I didn't know you were awake."

"Just enjoying a quiet moment before our day."

"I'm sorry if I disturbed you." Gerald turned back to the roses. "Robert and Abby are mooning at each other across the kitchen table. I decided to make myself scarce."

Ruby ran her finger across the rim of the teacup. "It must be odd for you, having all of these guests in your home."

"I'm growing accustomed to it. There are certain advantages." He pulled a folding knife from his pocket and deadheaded a few of the spent blossoms. "We could get an early start this morning, if you like. Maybe visit the old Civil War post at Fort Point. You can look out across the Golden Gate, see the entrance to the bay." The corner of his mouth lifted. "It's a lovely day for a drive. Usually our summers are foggy. God must be blessing your stay with fine weather."

The teasing lilt in his voice grated at Ruby's ears. *He thinks I'll refuse because of the drive.* She swallowed and lifted her chin. "Sounds delightful. Just let me get a scarf to keep my hat in place. I'd hate to lose another. Perhaps you might give me another lesson while we're there."

Gerald hooked his fingers along the top edge of his vest. "Considering how the road hugs the cliff face, I think it might be best if I stayed in the driver's seat on this trip. But this weekend we could make another attempt.

Ruby bit her lip. In the span of a few minutes, she'd volunteered for two driving outings. Looked like she'd need those goggles for certain. "I'll finish getting ready." She turned toward the house, swigging the last mouthful of tea as she walked, the brew bitter on her tongue.

❧

Gerald swallowed a chuckle, shaking his head.

The woman's braid swung between her shoulder blades as she hurried across the yard. He couldn't help tracing the braid's path down her back with his eyes, settling on the curve of her hips before tearing his gaze away. Such fixations would only get him into trouble.

Of course, if it were only her beauty, he'd have no difficulties. There were plenty of attractive women in San Francisco. But they didn't also have a heart for service, a thirst for medical knowledge, a determined spirit, and a gentle touch with patients. No, Ruby, unfortunately, had it all. She also had a protective brother.

Gerald turned his attention back to the garden. His mother babied the bushes, and she was rewarded with rich blossoms continuing late into the fall. One particular rose garnered his interest, the orange-red petals the same hue as Ruby's hair. Sweet scented and laced with thorns—like every woman he'd known. He cut a single bud and pinched the prickly stem between his fingertips with care.

Gerald returned to the kitchen, placing the bloom in a vase on the windowsill.

"Lovely rose." Abby glanced up from the breakfast table, smiling. "Fortune's Double Yellow, right?"

He chuckled. "It's a rose. You'll have to ask my mother about the variety."

"I'm certain. They're a favorite of mine. Usually the blooms are a little more pink. We had some in San Jose. Papa grew them from a cutting Aunt Mae brought us."

"She had several plants moved when she came to live here. It might have been one of these. You and my mother are two of a kind,

Abby." He strolled to her side, eyeing the pastries on the table. "You inherited her love for growing things."

"From her and from Papa." She dabbed the napkin against her lips.

Robert grinned, leaning back in his chair. "Both sides of the family. That explains it."

She examined her fingers. "Yes, it explains why I always have dirt under my nails."

Robert took her hand, pulling it to the tabletop. "It explains why everything you touch blossoms."

Gerald turned his back so the couple wouldn't see his eyes roll. "I'm on way to the Presidio today, Robert. You're certain you can manage without Ruby? She's agreed to accompany me."

"Yes, fine. I'm going to make some adjustments to the equipment and run a few tests. Nurse Maguire will be covering the patients."

Gerald snagged an apple for his pocket before hurrying to the study for his medical bag. Opening the glass-fronted case, he examined the various medications he kept on-hand for visitations. The army had been proactive in establishing sanitary conditions throughout the refugee camps, but he'd heard rumor of illness spreading. Gerald rifled through his supplies, adding small amounts of various remedies to the leather case in addition to the iodine, bandages, instruments, and antiseptic.

He lifted his head as footsteps sounded on the front stairs.

Ruby appeared in the doorway, her face framed by a silver and blue scarf tied over her head and knotted under her chin.

"What do you think? Will this keep my hat safe?"

Gerald swallowed and managed a nod.

She smiled, one brow lifting. "Is there anything I can help you prepare before we leave?"

He glanced back at the gaping mouth of the medical bag, studying the even row of vials and bandages. What had he been looking for? He ran a hand across the items, checking them off one by one. "No, I believe I have everything. It's difficult to know what we might need. When the quake first happened, we were facing trauma casualties. Now it's anyone's guess. Of course, the clinic is well stocked."

Ruby cocked her head. "I think it's admirable you take time away from your practice to serve in the camps."

Gerald snapped the lid closed. "Everyone's doing what they can. The city could have dissolved into chaos, but I witnessed countless cases of people helping each other survive regardless of their social standing. Did Robert tell you how he and Abby helped deliver a baby the day after the earthquake?"

She settled her hands on her hips. "No. The scamp's hardly told me anything."

He hoisted the bag from the desk. "It was a harrowing week. He was lucky to survive after the ceiling fell in on him at the hospital."

"The ceiling?" Her head jerked upward. "I think my brother has kept quite a bit from us."

"He was one of the lucky ones." Gerald gestured for Ruby to precede him through the door as they moved into the hall. "We witnessed many casualties during those days." He pushed away the horrific images clamoring for attention in his memory. Gerald reached for his brown derby, setting the valise on the Oriental rug. "Serving the displaced is my way of showing gratitude to God for sparing my family and my home."

Ruby tightened her wrap. "I may not have been here during the disaster, but I certainly want to do my part."

14

*R*uby locked her grip on the edge of the automobile's seat, her heart drumming out of control. The wind tugged at her hat's brim, fluttering the scarf's gauzy material like the tail of a kite.

"Isn't the view splendid?" Gerald glanced toward her.

Her stomach tightened. "Watch the road." She licked her lips, the air drying them instantly. "Please?"

He laughed, turning back to face the front. "I promise. But you need to look around. You're missing the glorious scenery. I'll watch our path."

Ruby blinked, unwilling to release her grip even to wipe the dust from her lashes. A few feet to the side, the roadway ended at the edge of a cliff, dropping a sheer distance into the foaming waves below. Her stomach churned with the waves as she scooted closer to Gerald, swinging her attention back to the front. "Must you drive so near to the edge?"

He patted her arm. "For the third time, we're not close. I'm practically driving down the center of the road."

Ruby flung off his hand. "Keep that on the wheel. What if something happens?"

Gerald sighed. "You're not enjoying this. Not even a little bit?" The corners of his mouth drooped, like a child whose gift had been spurned.

A jab pierced her heart. "The view is lovely. I'm just having a little trouble appreciating the landscape at this breakneck pace."

He eased off the throttle, the breeze slackening. "I didn't think it was overly hurried, but I can slow further if you would be more comfortable."

"Yes, thank you." Ruby peeled her fingers from the seat and folded them, clenched, in her lap. Her heart slowing, she allowed her gaze to wander out over the bay, the morning sun glittering along the tops of the waves. Gulls wheeled over the swells, their white, feathered bodies glowing in the light.

"Is this better?"

Ruby reached up to push back the scarf impeding her view of the water. "Much. Thank you."

Gerald guided the car into a turnout and the wheels rolled to a stop, pointing toward the waterway. He climbed out of the vehicle and wandered around to her side. "There's a lovely outlook here. Perhaps you'd enjoy the experience more if your feet were on solid ground." He held out a hand.

Ruby followed Gerald to a grassy bluff overlooking a sprawling brick fortress and the water below. Matching headlands rose on the far shore. Her heart still thrummed, but the vise grip of tension around her chest eased. "Is this the Fort Point you mentioned earlier?"

"Yes. It was built during the Civil War to protect San Francisco. The waterway down there is the Golden Gate, it connects the Bay to the Pacific." He smiled. "It's nice we can see everything this morning. The area's often fogged in."

"It's lovely."

"I'm glad I had the honor of showing it to you."

She turned, studying the man's lanky form as he leaned against an iron bench. He looked more relaxed than any time she'd seen him. "Do you come out here often?"

He tipped his head. "Often enough. It's a nice respite from the hospital. I find the scope of the vista helps me persevere when melancholy threatens."

The wind tugged at her skirt. "What do you mean?"

He reached up and pulled off his derby, the sun illuminating the golden strands in his hair. "When I start asking the unanswerable questions—like after losing a patient, or when I was overwhelmed with the enormity of the disaster." He stared off toward the strait. "The quiet of this place reminds me God is in control. He's more powerful than my problems. I can find rest when I release all my frustrations to Him."

She glanced toward the tumultuous waters—anything but restful. "But you don't receive answers to any of your questions."

Gerald chuckled. "Not usually. But God doesn't owe me answers. My job is to trust. And since I know He's still on the job, I can do so."

A tendril curled around her heart. She'd spent the past year clutching her life together with her fingertips. Trust seemed a foreign concept. "How do you know?" Her voice quavered.

He pushed away from the bench and stepped behind her. "You see how the water rushes past the headlands?" His arm brushed against her shoulder as he pointed to the far side of the strait.

She nodded, staring out at the vista.

"Let's say you're the water. You're rushing back and forth with the tides—from the Bay to the ocean, splashing against the rocks, whipped by the winds, in constant motion and turmoil." He lowered his hand, resting a palm on her shoulder.

The warmth of his fingers sent a rush of shivers through her. "Yes?"

"Some days you're storm-tossed, some days you're quiet and calm. No day is ever exactly the same." Gerald slid his hand down her arm and gave it a quick squeeze before lifting his hand away. "God is the headland. Strong and sturdy. Reliable. Even when the quake shook the ground, the hills didn't fall into the waves. My father used to quote a psalm, "He only is my rock and my salvation; he is my defense; I shall not be greatly moved."

Ruby took a few steps, creating a comfortable distance between them. She crossed both arms in front of her, wrapping them tight around her middle. Gerald may have dealt with loss and grief, but God had never taken his plans and tossed them aside like so much discarded rubbish. She blinked back tears, sudden images of Charlie's broken body lurching into her memory. Ruby's gaze roamed the windswept strait, whitecaps topping each tiny wave. For a brief moment, her stomach lifted, as if tossed on the surf. The past two years of her life had been one unending storm. Gerald could put his trust in the strength of the hills. She intended to build a raft and start paddling.

15

*R*uby ran careful fingers through the girl's hair. No sign of head lice. A stitch of tension loosened from her shoulders. Who knew what kind of vermin ran in these camps?

The child's fine blonde curls surrounded rosy chipmunk cheeks. She swiped a small hand across her runny nose before dissolving into another batch of barky coughs. Poor thing sounded like Otto when the postman arrived.

Gerald finished with his patient, shaking the older man's hand and walking him to the door of the small medical clinic. He wandered over to Ruby's side. "How's our littlest one?"

Ruby's father had always encouraged her to offer opinions, but over the years she'd learned most doctors were too arrogant to accept them. Was Gerald the same? "It doesn't sound like flu or pneumonia." She lifted her chin. "I believe it's more likely she's asthmatic."

Gerald nodded and pulled a stethoscope from his inside pocket. "We've seen quite a bit since the fires." He turned to the young mother. "Have you given her any paregoric?"

The woman shook her head, lifting a squirming baby higher on her hip. "We've come three times, but they've never given her anything."

He pressed the stethoscope bell to the girl's back and lowered himself to her eye level. "Okay, sweetie. Do you know how to blow out a candle?"

The girl nodded, tugging at the fraying hem of her pinafore.

Gerald gestured for Ruby to step closer and reached for her hand.

Ruby's stomach fluttered. *What is he doing?* His warm touch sent shivers up her arm.

He smiled and pressed one of her fingers upward. "I think this will work for a flame, don't you, Nurse?"

"Oh, I see." *Clever.* She kneeled in front of the patient and pointed skyward. "Rosie, pretend my finger is a light. Do you think you could blow it out?"

As the girl screwed up her face and blew across Ruby's fingertip, Gerald lowered his gaze to where the instrument touched the child's back. "Barely a flicker. Take a big breath this time."

Rosie giggled. She puffed up her cheeks and spluttered a long exhale through pursed lips.

Ruby swung her wrist back like a treetop bending in a gale. "There's some wind!"

Gerald smiled, fine lines crinkling about his eyes. "Once more."

Rosie sucked in more air, but gasped into a coughing fit, eyes watering.

Gerald removed the earpieces. "I believe you're right, Nurse Marshall. It does sounds like asthma." He turned to the girl's mother. "Some people have decent luck with the asthma cigarettes from the drug store, but I don't recommend them. Especially for one so young. I'd try the paregoric, but be careful not to give her too much. It contains traces of opium, and it will make her sleepy. You want just enough to ease the paroxysm, no more.

The mother accepted the bottle from Ruby's hand and nodded. "I know, doctor. My auntie used to use it for her coughing spells. I've seen what happens when someone nips too much."

Ruby cleared her throat. "Dr. Larkspur, what about epinephrine?"

He nodded, turning back to the girl's mother. "Nurse Marshall is correct. If your daughter gets into a coughing fit and can't find her breath, bring her to the hospital and ask for an epinephrine injection. It works in mere seconds." Gerald scooped the girl off the table and walked the family toward the door, explaining more about the injections.

Ruby sighed, pushing a stray curl over her ear. Gerald seemed unique among the doctors for whom she'd worked: impartial, kind, and well mannered. And rarely had she seen a doctor—other than her father—with such a tender approach to working with children.

Another woman and a boy waited at the door. Gerald guided them inside, pushing a chair up against the table so the child could clamber up to its surface without being lifted. The grimy hand clamped to his elbow suggested the source of trouble. The youngster plopped onto the tabletop, his red hair flopping over one tear-stained eye as he pinned Ruby with a pointed glare.

"Let's take a look, shall we?" Gerald took the child's arm in his hands.

The boy winced as Gerald palpated the elbow joint. The little fellow blinked several times, his chin quivering.

Gerald released the grubby arm. "How long has it been like this?"

The mother hovered at the doctor's elbow, her fingers plucking at a lace cravat about her neck. "Just since yesterday. Not long. He and his brother play too rough."

The boy pulled the arm back to his chest and tucked a hand under the elbow with a scowl. "He plays rough, I just give it back to him."

Ruby stepped closer, offering the child a smile. "What's your name?"

He chewed on his lip, glancing up at her with red-rimmed eyes. "Henry Rogers."

"And you're what . . ." Ruby studied the youngster. He was probably seven or eight years, but better to guess high. "Nine?"

His frown trembled, chin jerking upward. "Eight."

"Seven." The mother folded her arms across her bosom.

Henry cast his gaze downward before darting a glance back at Gerald. He stuck out his lower lip. "Seven."

Gerald winked. "You want to help me fix your arm so you can get back to roughhousing with your brother?"

A shadow crossed the boy's face. "I'd like to take a lickin' to him."

"Henry!" Mrs. Rogers frowned.

Ruby hid a smile. The boy had spirit. Good. He'd need it for what lay ahead.

Gerald leaned forward. "Pretty tough to do with your arm hurting. So what's say we put it back in fighting condition, eh?"

Henry nodded, his hair—bright as a pumpkin—fluttering in the breeze coming through the open window.

Glancing at the mother, Gerald smiled. "I noticed a delivery of fresh, juicy peaches being delivered to the commissary tent. Perhaps you'd like to step out and claim a few while Mrs. Marshall and I help him with his arm? Tell them I sent you."

The woman hesitated for a moment, glancing down at her son. "Are you certain? Henry?"

"Oh, Ma. I'm not a baby." Henry jutted his chin forward, but his Adam's apple bobbed twice.

Ruby's heart ached for the little fellow—trying so hard to be brave. She longed to sweep the child into her arms, but clearly he desired to be treated like a man. Little did he realize how many men acted like tots when hurt.

Henry's mother pressed a kiss to his forehead before hurrying away.

"Girls aren't strong like us, right, Doctor?" A corner of the boy's mouth lifted as he blew the hair from his eyes.

Gerald leaned forward, cocking a hand around his mouth. "Don't tell anyone, but Nurse Marshall here is tough as nails."

Ruby shot him a glare before turning to Henry. "That's because it takes a strong woman to keep doctors in line."

❧

Gerald grinned, Ruby's tough expression sending a ripple of mirth through his chest. For half a moment, he pictured her face peering over the steering wheel as the automobile hurtled across the cow pasture a few weeks ago. A woman forcing herself to face her worst nightmare? Ruby Marshall contained an inner strength equal to ten men. Hopefully she could give a little of her strength to their patient.

He caught her eye, jerked his chin toward the table, and held out a hand. "I think you know what needs to be done. Do you think you could assist Henry?"

Ruby's gaze softened as she placed her fingers in his grip. "I'd be pleased to, Dr. Larkspur."

The warmth of her palm pressed against his, for the second time in twenty minutes, made Gerald's heart race. He'd worked with female nurses before without ever managing to touch one. How come he kept finding excuses to take her hand? He squeezed her fingers for a moment before helping her up to the tabletop next to their young patient.

"What'cha doing?" Henry scooted away from her, mouth agape.

Ruby settled herself, bracing one high-button shoe on the top of the wooden chair. "Dr. Larkspur is going to fix your elbow by doing something called a reduction. He's going to pop the ligament—the band holding the joint—back into its proper position. You're going to sit on my lap, so I can help you hold the arm still."

The nurse's matter-of-fact tone surprised Gerald. Most female nurses coddled their younger patients. Ruby spoke to him as an equal.

Henry's jaw twitched. "I'm no sissy. I can sit tight." Henry glanced back at Gerald, color fading from his face. "Is it going to hurt bad?"

Gerald folded both arms across his chest, eyeing the boy. He preferred not to lie—even to children. "Does it feel good now?"

"Nuh-uh. Hurts like the devil."

Ruby touched Henry's shoulder, her tone softening. "After Dr. Larkspur is done, it will feel much better. The more you can relax, the faster it'll go."

Henry sighed. "All right. But don't tell no one." He clambered up on her lap, tucking his ruddy head under her chin.

Gerald waited as she moved Henry into position, locking one of her arms around his midsection. With their matching coloring, he could have been Ruby's son. If her husband had lived, she might have a child like this one. Though—knowing Ruby—he'd be a mite cleaner. And better dressed.

She grasped the boy's arm just above the elbow. "I think we're ready. What about you, Henry?"

The boy pressed his lips into a line and managed a curt nod.

Gerald took Henry's wrist in one hand, sliding his other under the boy's forearm. Turning it palm-upward, he eased the limb forward.

Henry whimpered, tucking his face against Ruby's chest, his tough façade dissolving.

"You're doing fine." She murmured, pressing her cheek against his hair.

Gerald tore his gaze from her face and fingered the joint, checking the ligament. He extended the arm further as Henry tensed. With one final tug, the band clicked into place.

Henry gasped, a shudder coursing through his small frame. He lifted his head, eyes wide and glimmering with unshed tears. "Was that it? It don't hurt no more."

Flexing the boy's arm back toward the shoulder, Gerald kept his fingers in place, checking for proper rotation. "All finished. Well done. Are you sure you're not ten?"

Henry grinned and sniffled. "My brother's twelve. He's strong."

Gerald rocked on his heels. "You tell him not to yank on your arm again, or he's going to have to deal with me." He released Henry's hand, patting the boy on the leg.

"No, Doc. He's going to have to deal with me!" Henry hopped off Ruby's lap and held his arm out in front of him. "I didn't think it was ever going to work right again."

Ruby brushed her hands across her apron. "You were brave, Henry. I'm sure your brother couldn't have done better, so let's not see him here next."

Henry bent the elbow and smiled. "He'd have cried like a girl. He's strong, but I'm tough. That's what Papa says."

She touched his chin. "You didn't need my help at all."

The boy smiled. "Nah. But it was nice, anyway." He swiveled his head toward Gerald. "Thanks, Doctor."

"You're welcome, Henry. Be careful with your arm. I don't want to have to do this a second time. Why don't you run along and see if your mother found any of those peaches?"

Ruby slid down from the table as the boy scampered off, bending and flexing his arm.

Gerald folded the stethoscope and laid it atop the medical bag. "Nice kid."

"It's a shame his family has to live here. What about his schooling?"

"They've set up a temporary schoolhouse on the outskirts of the camp. I'm sure he's being looked after."

She turned, a line pinched between her brows. "How long will people be living like this? There's barely room to walk single file between those cottages. This is no place for children."

"They have food, shelter, and medical care. Some folks are saying with all the help, the refugees won't want to leave."

The door burst open, slamming against the wall a few feet away from Gerald's shoulder.

Ruby shrieked, scampering back against the table, eyes rounding.

Gerald spun to face the door, placing himself between Ruby and the entry as two men appeared silhouetted in the doorway, half-dragging a third. Gerald gestured to the table. "Place him up there."

The wounded man's feet scraped along the floorboards as his friends hauled him inside.

Gerald helped them lift the patient to the examination table, and he ran a quick assessment. Blood oozed from an injury above the patient's right eye, his clothes reeking of whiskey. Gerald pressed a rag to the head injury. "What happened to him?"

The red-faced man whisked off his flat cap and bent over, puffing. "Fight. Down on the edge of the camp. We hauled Davis out before the soldiers got there. Didn't want more trouble.

The patient stirred, groaning.

Ruby edged forward. "Can I help?" Her gaze flickered to the open door, as if briefly considering an escape route.

The second fellow stepped into her path, slamming the door shut. "Just patch him up, and we'll go. If the army gets involved, we'll be tossed out on the street." He held a hand outstretched. "Please, ma'am."

Gerald turned to the table as the patient's lids flickered. He checked the man's pulse—strong and steady. "What did you say his name was?"

The man at the door folded both arms across his chest. "Davis. Jeremy Davis."

Lifting one of the lids with a thumb, Gerald leaned down and checked the pupils. "Mr. Davis?"

Davis turned his head away and blinked several times, his forehead rippling into a row of weathered creases. "Gaw." He brought both hands up over his eyes. "What happened?"

His buddy stepped closer. "Mildred's husband's what happened. Took you out with the butt of his gun, though you're a mite lucky he didn't use the other end. What were you thinking?"

"Nurse, will you please hand me some gauze?" Gerald cleared his throat before the story progressed. "We'll get Mr. Davis cleaned up."

Ruby bobbed her head, hurrying for the supply cabinet.

Davis lowered his hand, eyeing the blood smeared on his fingers. "The lout. I didn't expect he'd find out, what with him being gone most of the time. No wonder Millie gets lonely." He struggled up to a sitting position.

Ruby stepped forward with a handful of dressings. "Shall I . . ."

"I'll take care of this one." Gerald frowned, supporting the patient with one arm. "Why don't you step next door and see if there's any coffee left?"

"I'm not leaving." Lines formed around her mouth as her gaze darted between him and the man standing near the door.

Gerald cleared his throat, addressing the men. "I'm sending my nurse over to the supply tent. If it's a problem, perhaps you should take your friend down to the county hospital."

Davis pressed fingers against the bridge of his nose. "No, she can go. I'm sorry if these fellas here frightened you, Miss. We don't want trouble."

The red-faced man wrung his cap. "Davis, you didn't see how steamed up Johnson was. If he turns the army on us, we're history."

"Ruby, go." Gerald gritted his teeth. She'd likely return with a whole garrison, but it wouldn't prevent him from treating his patient. And she'd be safe.

After a moment of hesitation, she nodded and slipped around the men, snatching her hat from the hook. She reached for the knob, but the door flew open a second time.

Gerald's stomach fell as he spotted the Goliath-sized man standing on the threshold, the barrel of a shotgun pointing directly at Ruby.

Ruby backed up, hands held out to each side. "Dr. Larkspur, I believe we have additional company."

16

*H*eart pounding, Ruby edged backward. The small room was not designed for six people—especially when one wielded a shotgun. The sticky smell of sweat hung in the stale air. Did the scent emanate from the hooligans or from her? She pressed her back against the medicine cabinet, reaching behind to grasp the handle. Perhaps if the man were distracted, she could retrieve something of use. *Like what, a wad of bandages?*

Gerald elbowed his way through the men to stand between the newcomer and the patient's bristling companions. "Gentlemen, this isn't the place—"

"Where's Millie?" The intruder's lips pulled back from his teeth, his bulk filling the doorway. He swung the weapon toward the man on the table. "What've you done with my wife?"

The fellow standing closest to Ruby sniggered. "What hasn't he done?"

The thug's eyes narrowed, and he swung the shotgun in a wide swath. "Where is she?"

Davis staggered up behind Gerald, his palm pressed against the oozing scalp wound. "She ain't here. I haven't even spoke to her in a week."

Johnson's brows bunched. "You're lying. She told me you were over last night."

Ruby eased the cabinet open behind her back, hoping for a scalpel or a syringe.

Gerald stood firm. "I won't allow violence in here. Take your disagreement outside. And don't expect me to patch you up when you've finished."

Johnson advanced, eyes locked on his target.

The patient ran a palm across the back of his neck. "I ain't lying to you. If Millie said so, then she's the liar. Perhaps she's entertaining other fellows while you're off working."

Johnson lifted the shotgun and jammed the weapon into the smaller man's chest. "Let me hear you say that again."

Ruby's gaze darted between the figures, her stomach tightening. She dug her hand into the cabinet and rummaged through the supplies, trying to find something more useful than tongue depressors and cotton gauze.

Gerald placed a hand on the gun barrel. "If you commit a murder in front of all these witnesses, what will you gain?"

Sweat dripped down Johnson's brow. "I got nothing left—my house, my business, and now my wife. I got nothing but revenge."

A tapping from the doorframe stilled the room. Patrick Allison stood on the threshold, a round hat clutched to his chest. "Now, Mr. Johnson, is your missus telling tales again?" The reverend strolled inside, the men parting before him like the Red Sea. He nodded to Ruby. "Mrs. Marshall. A pleasure." He turned and faced Johnson, placing his back to Ruby.

The shotgun barrel dipped toward the floorboards as a scowl crept across Johnson's face. "Patrick, this doesn't involve you."

Ruby's hand settled on the smooth, wooden box. Keeping it hidden, she opened the lid and pulled a small pair of shears into her palm. It wouldn't be of much value against a gun, but it felt good to have something in her hand. She slid the cool object up into her cuff.

The Irishman clasped the thug's shoulder. "Johnson, let's take this discussion outside—and away from the lady. We can't have you fellas stinking up the place." He wrinkled his nose. "Your Millie came crying to me, fussing about your brawling and a-fearing you would be arrested or worse. Let's go reassure her you got no holes in your head—besides those the Good Lord put there."

Johnson's expression softened. "She fears for me, does she?"

Patrick placed a hand on the shotgun and pushed the barrel even lower. "She's a scrappy, quick-tempered one—not unlike yourself, eh?"

The big man smirked. "She is. And she knows how to get attention. D'ya know she used to be a dancer over Barbary Coast way?"

The minister gripped Johnson's arm and steered him toward the door. "Truly? Tell me more as we walk. I'm sure she's worked herself up into a full-blown hysteria by now." He moved to follow the large man through the opening, tipping his brown derby to Ruby as they departed. "Pleasure to see you again, Mrs. Marshall."

Davis's two buddies ducked out and hurried in the opposite direction.

Gerald turned to his patient. "I'd advise you to be scarce for a while. Your injury doesn't appear to be serious, but you should avoid any further blows to the head until it's fully healed."

Davis ran a hand through his hair and reached for his derby. "Trust me, Doc, me and my thick skull are going to hightail it over to Oakland until this all blows over. Millie will have to find another fella to play the fool. After surviving the quake and the fires, I don't want to get bashed by a jealous husband." He jammed the hat onto his head with a wince. "Though for a gal like her, it's almost worth it." He disappeared out the door, leaving the room in an eerie silence.

Ruby released the breath she'd been holding, her ribs so tight it felt like her corset was made of rusty metal bands.

Gerald closed the door and leaned against it, leveling a steady gaze at her. "Are you all right?"

Her stomach churned. She cleared her throat and turned her back on the doctor's intense blue eyes. She slid the shears free from her sleeve and returned them to the case. "Well, it certainly made for an interesting afternoon. Thank you, Doctor, for arranging this fascinating look at some of San Francisco's more colorful characters." Ruby's voice shook, but she managed to cover it with a tart tone.

"Our rescuer spoke to you by name. You failed to introduce me."

She gripped her sides. "I saw no opportunity."

Gerald crossed the floor, gathering up the soiled bandages and dropping them in the laundry pile. "So, who was he?"

Ruby's thoughts wandered back to the handsome Irishman, the twinkle of mischief in his eyes. She hadn't failed to notice the man's muscled arms when he'd gripped Johnson's shoulder. Did the Lord's work require such strength? "Abby introduced us at the Golden Gate camp. His name is Patrick Allison. *Reverend* Allison."

"I've heard of the man." Snapping open his medical bag, Gerald nodded. "It explains why Johnson was so quick to listen. I suspected either respect or fear motivated him."

"Fear?"

"I've heard rumors of a criminal element taking control in these camps. I didn't think lawlessness would be a problem here at the Presidio, but you never know." He glanced back at the door. "Allison looks more like a hooligan than a man of the cloth."

Ruby jutted her chin. "I didn't take you for one who judged on appearance."

He gathered his instruments with a grimace. "I don't care to be. But we can't be too careful these days."

Ruby thought back to her first impressions of the minister. She'd also misjudged the man. If she met him again, she'd treat him with a little more respect. Her skin prickled, the idea of a third encounter a tad too intriguing. Ruby ran a quick hand over her arms. No. She'd decided at Charlie's gravesite she wouldn't risk her heart a second time. Not for a kind, good-looking doctor with eyes the color of the California sky, and certainly not for a rather charming supporter of the disenfranchised.

But it didn't hurt to look, now and again, did it? Her gaze flitted back to Gerald as the physician organized the tools in his bag. Sunlight from the window glinted off the golden strands in his hair. Her throat ached. *Yes, it does hurt.*

Gerald folded the stethoscope and put it away. The way Ruby had brightened at the clergyman's smile sent a sickening sensation through his chest. Gerald exhaled, pushing away the odd response. It's not as if he had any claim on the woman. Still, he wouldn't mind seeing a lady's face light up at *his* appearance. He'd never had the effect on anyone except a few elderly female patients.

He shut the clasp on the leather case and hoisted it under his arm. Danger lurked in these camps. Robert and Abby had the disagreement on a weekly basis. Gerald scowled. Bringing Ruby had been a vain attempt to exhibit his talents and good deeds. He'd put her in a perilous position, and Patrick Allison defused the situation with hardly more than a word and a grin. Gerald's shoulders fell. He should be grateful to the man for his assistance. Why did it feel more like a punch to the gut?

℞

When they arrived home, Ruby joined Mrs. Larkspur in the kitchen while Gerald disappeared into his study. Ruby sighed as she sank into a chair near the window. The buttery yellow walls glowed in the late afternoon light, the air scented with fresh-baked rhubarb pie. "You shouldn't cut into it just for me, Mrs. Larkspur. Why don't you save it for supper?"

"Nonsense, child." The lines around her mouth deepened as she smiled and adjusted the gold wire glasses lower on the bridge of her nose. "I made several. And who says I'm cutting it for you? A responsible cook should taste the products of her kitchen and ensure they meet the fine standards of the house."

Ruby pulled the teacup and saucer closer to the table's edge, the bone china rattling in her shaky grip. "I can't argue with such wisdom."

"Nor should you. It's impolite to disagree with your elders." Mrs. Larkspur tempered her curt nod with an impish grin. "After the day you've had, you certainly deserve pie. And ice cream—if we had any. You'll have to settle for tea."

If Ruby stayed at the Larkspur home much longer, her clothes would need to be altered. Her corset lacing already showed signs of strain.

Gerald's mother placed the dessert plates on the table, serving out two generous triangles. "I can't imagine what you must think about our fair city, between seeing it in shambles and having some ruffian point a weapon at you."

Rather than the wild-eyed Mr. Johnson, Ruby found her memory lingering on Gerald's protective stance and Reverend Allison's startling intervention. "The situation alarmed me, but I suppose one must expect such behavior when people are crammed together in less-than-optimal living conditions."

"Yes, our family has been fortunate. Not a day passes I don't thank the Lord we're not staying in one of those ramshackle cabins. I'd already been living here with Gerald a few months before the quake struck. Clara's family was staying in my old house. When we fled the fires, I didn't know what the future held." Mrs. Larkspur sank into the seat opposite Ruby. "My home didn't survive. For years Gerald had urged me to sell, but the house held memories." Her gray eyes shimmered like watered silk. "I'd been dillydallying, I suppose."

"Will you rebuild?"

"I don't believe so." She sniffed, touching a finger to her lashes. "I suppose it was God's way of telling me my son was correct."

Ruby pressed her lips together. The Larkspurs were quick to ascribe God credit for everything. She controlled her own life—not God. He could help, certainly, but she held the reins.

Mrs. Larkspur reached for a fork. "Actually, I wished to get your opinion on something. I've spoken to Gerald about deeding the lot to Abigail and Robert as a wedding present. They wouldn't be prepared to build on it right away, of course. But I'm getting older, and I'd rather see it settled now. You know your brother better than I. Do you think he would welcome such a gift?" She leaned down and slipped a morsel of piecrust to Otto.

The dog circled about the women's shoes, lapping up the crumbs.

Property in San Francisco? Ruby lowered her cup to the saucer before her trembling betrayed her misgivings. Robert was putting down roots here in the city. He had no plans to return home to Sacramento. Hadn't Abby already confirmed as much? Still, the thought echoed around her chest. "What about Abby's parents?"

After a bite of pie, Mrs. Larkspur ran a napkin across her mouth. "They haven't found a buyer for the farm, yet. If you ask me, Herman has no desire to part with it. He's done well for himself working in the reconstruction effort, I'm wondering if he'll earn enough to keep it. Gerald thinks they may decide to move back, in time."

Ruby leaned forward. "Back to the farm? Is Abby aware of this?"

"I don't believe so. And we don't know anything. Herman's been tightlipped since Cecelia's passing. I think he's afraid to disappoint anyone again."

"I'm not sure I understand."

Mrs. Larkspur's chin puckered. "Herman's always had such belief in his own abilities. Even though he started out with nothing, he worked hard with an eye toward progress. When Cecelia took ill, he thought he could fix it. Hire enough doctors, buy all the right medicines—whatever it took. But he was left with nothing but heartache. And bills. We know Cecelia went on to great reward, but her family endures the pain of her absence. Herman learned some things are in God's hands, not our own."

If Ruby could've fought for Charlie's life, she'd have done the same. She blinked back tears, determined to keep her emotions in control.

Mrs. Larkspur fell silent, gazing toward the window. After a long moment, she turned back to Ruby. "What of the house property? Do you believe your brother would accept it?"

Ruby ran a hand around her lace collar. "I'm not certain I understand him as well as I once did. Perhaps Gerald would know better."

Footsteps sounded behind them. "On what topic am I so knowledgeable?" Gerald walked into the room, a grin lighting his face. "Pie? I'm just in time."

His mother rose to retrieve another plate. "We were discussing Robert and Abby's wedding gift."

"Aha." His smile faltered. "Wedding gifts. Not usually a man's arena."

Mrs. Larkspur swatted him on the shoulder. "The property, Gerald. You haven't forgotten already?"

"Of course. I'll try to find a way to broach the subject with Robert." He took a seat at the far end of the table.

His mother set the plate down in front of him. "Please, be circumspect."

"Always, Mother. Always."

Ruby lowered her gaze to the empty plate. She needed to plan her own future before this wedding commenced. Three choices remained—return to Sacramento, search out her own place to live, or find herself as homeless as the San Francisco refugees. The way her face flushed every time Gerald approached, it might be ill-advised to remain under the man's roof a moment longer.

17

Gerald adjusted the Crookes tube and checked the control panel, dropping Robert's evening report to the desk. Tension curled around Gerald's neck, and he rolled his shoulders in an attempt to dislodge it. The figures didn't lie—the radiation readings fluctuated at an alarming rate. He couldn't risk burns and X-ray dermatitis in their already fragile patients. *Why is the equipment malfunctioning?*

Gerald switched on the system. Everything appeared normal, but he'd need to assess the levels before authorizing any further treatments. He laid his arm on the raised table, spreading his fingers in preparation for the test. A thirty-second dose should only make the skin mildly pink, the standard erythema dose. He paused, studying the lesion on his blue-stained palm. A whole month and the methylene blue didn't seem to be making any difference. Would extra X-ray exposure help the healing or worsen it? He switched hands. Why borrow trouble?

An angry buzzing captured his attention. Gerald jumped back just as the tube popped, the flash stinging his eyes. *Not another one.* Spots danced on the insides of his lids as he blinked to clear his vision. Gerald glared at the glass cylinder as the telltale white smoke curled inside its confines. These tubes were too expensive and unpredictable. Robert had a good head for invention, perhaps he could make some modifications. Heat radiated off the glass, so Gerald powered down the machine, waiting for it to cool before changing the part.

His young partner was a fantastic doctor, an astute researcher, and gifted when it came to supervising the technology. What was Gerald? Little more than a simple physician. He sighed. Next time he picked an assistant, he needed to choose someone who wouldn't surpass his abilities in a few short years.

The one advantage of being the senior partner—he could still issue instructions and expect Robert to follow them. Gerald scribbled a note and left it on the table, weighted down with one of the broken coils. He'd leave this mess for the young expert and go check on Miss Feinstein. He'd rather spend his time on a living person than a pile of wires and circuits.

Ruby filled the water glass and held it for Dee. She tried not to favor specific patients, but the woman's droll sense of humor had made her a delight to serve during this past month. Dee's relentless teasing of the doctors brought light to the serious ward. Until this week.

Dee managed a few sips before the liquid dribbled over her cracked lips and onto her chin. She leaned back against the pillow, a puff of air rushing from her lungs. "Thank you."

Ruby dabbed a cloth against the woman's neck, catching the trickle of water before it escaped. "Would you like another pillow? Maybe if we set you up a bit higher, you'd have an easier time?"

A wan smile crossed Dee's face. "No. But could you . . . sit?" The wheezing interrupted her words.

Setting the glass on the bedside table, Ruby sank into the chair beside the bed. Her heart ached for her friend. "Are you in pain?"

In the past week, the woman had faded, her sallow skin drawing paper-thin across her cheekbones, shadows circling her dull eyes. Dee glanced away, her lack of words an answer in itself.

Ruby leaned forward. "Perhaps I could ask Dr. Larkspur for additional morphine."

Dee clutched at the edge of the blanket. "No. Just makes me . . . sleep."

What more could she do? Ruby's gaze traveled the room, settling on the ragged Bible, a regular feature at Dee's bedside. "Would you like me to read to you?"

Dee nodded, her jaw hanging open as she struggled for air.

The black leather cover felt worn and soft in Ruby's hands. She opened to a ribboned bookmark, the onionskin pages crackling as they settled into place. "You're reading in Job?" She ran her finger down the page, stopping at the first available chapter.

Dee shifted under the covers. "Yes."

Ruby resisted the temptation to flip to a more pleasant section of Scripture. Why read about suffering when Dee already endured such pain? Shouldn't she be providing messages of hope? Ruby cleared her throat. "My breath is corrupt, my days are extinct, the graves are ready for me. Are there not mockers with me?" Ruby's heart cringed at the harsh words, her gaze wandering from the page.

Gerald stood in the doorway, his attention traveling the ward. He paused on Ruby and Dee at the end of the long room.

Prickles crept up Ruby's neck. She should be on rounds, not spending her time reading. The other patients needed her, too.

Dee lay still, little more than a lump under the blankets, glazed eyes turned to the window.

Ruby turned her focus back to the book. What could be more important than offering comfort to a dying woman? It seemed more effective than the morphine she'd provided earlier. "My days are past, my purposes are broken off, even the thoughts of my heart. They change the night into day: the light is short because of darkness. If I wait, the grave is mine house: I have made my bed in the darkness." She pulled the Bible to her chest. "Dee, are you sure this is the section you wish to hear? I could read a comforting psalm, or a chapter of Corinthians instead—"

"Allow me." Gerald approached, stopping in front of the bed.

She stared at the doctor's outstretched hand for a moment before passing the Bible to him.

He crossed to Dee's side. "Job understood suffering, didn't he?" Gerald's voice barely stirred the quiet air in the ward. "And God recognized his pain."

Dee offered a faint smile. "God spoke to him. Even when Job questioned."

Ruby leaned back in her seat, her throat dry. Is it why Dee was drawn to the passage? Because she doubted?

"How about I read part of God's response?" Gerald turned the page. "Then the Lord answered Job out of the whirlwind, and said, 'Who is this that darkeneth counsel by words without knowledge? Gird up now thy loins like a man; for I will demand of thee, and answer thou me. Where wast thou when I laid the foundations of the earth? Declare, if thou hast understanding. Who hath laid the measures thereof, if thou knowest? Or who hath stretched the line upon it? Whereupon are the foundations thereof fastened? Or who laid the corner stone thereof; When the morning stars sang together, and all the sons of God shouted for joy?'"

Ruby struggled with the meaning of the words. Job was hurting, and God responded by speaking of His might? Wouldn't it have been better if He'd come with a healing touch?

Dee's lids fell closed as Gerald recited the words, the lines smoothing from her face. "That's my . . ." she struggled to speak, "my God."

Gerald closed the book and touched Dee's arm. "He laid the cornerstones of the world. God knows beginning and the end of every story. He is all-powerful, and He hasn't forgotten you."

The woman nodded. She coughed, clasping a hand to her throat.

Ruby jumped to her feet, reaching for the water glass.

The doctor slid a hand behind the woman's back, helping her to sit forward as Ruby lifted the glass to her lips.

Dee took a small sip, her coughs quieting. "Thank you . . . both."

Gerald eased her back onto the pillow. A furrow crossed his brow as his shoulders rounded. "Rest. Nurse Marshall can read more to you later if you're feeling well enough."

Dee closed her eyes. "No X-rays?" she whispered.

"Not just now, I think."

Ruby stepped back. Gerald's words echoed through her chest, as if a great emptiness resided there. One didn't need to be a doctor to see the woman's struggles would soon pass, X-rays or no.

Gerald turned away, touching Ruby's arm as he passed. "May I speak with you?"

Ruby took a final glance at Dee, but her friend appeared relaxed, perhaps even asleep. "Of course."

Gerald strode to the hall, far too aware of the tapping of Ruby's shoes behind him. He struggled to put Dee's situation from his mind so he could think clearly. Witnessing Ruby's kindness to his patient had sent his emotions into a tailspin. Many nurses disengaged emotionally from their patients when they sensed the end approaching. Ruby did the opposite, moving closer, softening her voice, her presence a balm to Dee's raw nerves. *She's a gift from God.* But was she a gift for the patients—or for him?

He continued walking toward the front doors, picking up the pace. Gerald needed the fresh breeze so he could shake the sensation of the hospital walls closing in about him and sucking the oxygen from his lungs. He regretted beckoning Ruby along. He'd wanted to thank her, but now a thousand prickles ran across his skin, like the X-ray set on high. He should have waited until he'd gathered himself.

"Doctor?" Ruby's voice sounded behind him as his hand settled on the door handle.

He paused, suddenly aware of his own heartbeat. Ruby always called him 'Doctor' at the hospital, but in this moment—his emotions like an open wound—he wanted to hear her say his name. Turning, his pulse increased as he gazed at her. Why did she have this effect on him?

Ruby's brows drew down, as if in question. Tiny wisps of strawberry curls floated around her heart-shaped face. "You wanted to speak to me?"

Gerald swallowed. "Would you like to take some fresh air? We could walk across the street to the park."

"Now?" Her eyes widened.

What was he thinking? Gerald cleared his throat. "Never mind. Just a thought."

She touched his arm, sending a surge of electricity jolting up to his shoulder "I'd love to. I just thought you were completing rounds."

Gerald glanced down at her fingers resting on his gray coat sleeve, each of her smooth fingernails trimmed to the exact same length. "I'm finished for now. I'll need to speak to Robert when he arrives, but it won't be for another forty minutes or so."

A smile hovered around her lips. She unpinned her nurse's cap. "Let me get my coat. I'll meet you on the steps." She hurried away, her feet scurrying across the polished floor.

Gerald leaned against the doorframe, watching her depart. Forty minutes of conversation. He should be able to manage without much difficulty. Gerald opened the door and stepped out into the cool evening. *As long as I keep my eyes down.*

⁂

Ruby wet her fingers and smoothed the hairs back into place. A few pins should keep her unruly locks under control. Now, if only someone would invent such pins for the heart.

Memories of her Scripture-loving father had bubbled to the surface as Gerald read from the Bible. Ruby closed her eyes. *I miss you, Daddy.* Her father would have liked the kind-hearted doctor, similar to him in many ways. Perhaps it's why she found herself so at ease with Gerald. That, and his strong jaw and kind eyes. She placed a palm on her chest, willing her emotions to behave. *No need for such nonsense.*

She pinned her hat into place and smoothed her skirt. A break from the hospital would cause no harm. She deserved a few moments of fresh air and pleasant conversation. And on the arm of a handsome gentleman? Why not?

Ruby hurried down the hall, spotting Gerald through the glass doors.

He stood relaxed, facing into the setting sun, the low-angled light spilling over his shoulders and emphasizing his stature.

She pushed away the tension wedging between her shoulder blades. A *walk. Nothing more.*

Gerald turned and grinned, pulling the door open. "So nice of you to join me." The dark cloud from earlier no longer marred his countenance.

Ruby stepped outside, her heart tripping along like an overexcited child. "I'm pleased you thought to ask me. I'd think you'd be weary of me by now, constantly underfoot."

He touched the brim of his brown derby. "You bring beauty wherever you go. It's a pleasant change from your brother."

"Thank you." A flush climbed her neck. The man did know how to spin a compliment, but she mustn't read too much into the polite words. With downcast eyes, she accepted Gerald's proffered arm.

The sound of carriages and automobiles filled the evening air as they walked down the marble steps. After waiting for several vehicles to pass, Gerald escorted her across the street and into the small, neglected park. An unkempt rose bush straggled over the stone benches, spent pink petals scattering in the breeze.

He chuckled. "Looks like this place could use a little of Abby's gardening touch. I suppose everyone's been otherwise occupied since the quake. Nature has been left to her own devices."

Ruby swept her fingers along the bench, scattering the petals to the wind. "Pruning and weeding must seem frivolous after witnessing the worst the world can offer."

Gerald's smile faded. "The city will come back stronger than ever."

"Some losses cannot be replaced."

"But new life springs up as well." He gestured to the patches of wildflowers sprinkled through the flowerbeds. His lips pulled down. "God provides healing for our losses—if we allow Him. 'Weeping may endure for a night, but joy cometh in the morning.'"

She turned away, Gerald's words ringing in her ears. Was her dead heart reawakening, too? It would explain why the annoying thing refused to obey her commands.

Gerald walked to her side, brushing his elbow against hers. "I appreciate you taking Miss Feinstein under your wing."

"You make me sound like a mother bird. She's the protective one. How could I not love her?" Ruby glanced up, drawn to the intensity in Gerald's eyes. "She speaks of you frequently. I believe she's quite attached."

He pulled off the derby. "Yes, I think she entertains notions of . . . well, for us. She's a romantic. Ever since you arrived last month, it's all she speaks of."

"She's not the only one." Ruby meandered a few steps along the brick walkway. Her conversation with Abby trailed through her memory. Robert's fiancée would love nothing better than to see Gerald married off—preferably to Ruby. And Mrs. Larkspur seemed to use every opportunity to push the two of them together. *Ridiculous.* Of course people talked, but she needed to guard her mind. Her own thoughts were too quick to gallop down the same ruinous path.

Gerald shoved his hands into his pockets. She must share his feelings—those lingering gazes couldn't lie. He trailed behind, the desire to hold her in his arms overwhelming his thoughts. "What do you mean, 'She's not the only one?'" One more hint of acquiescence, and he'd kiss her. His resolve to stay away weakened with each passing moment.

She cast a glance over her shoulder, a tiny frown pinching around her lips. "Of course not. Can't you sense it?"

He grasped her elbow, turning her to face him. "Perhaps I do. But I wasn't certain you felt the same."

Ruby tipped her head to the side, gazing up with round eyes. "How could I not?"

Gerald exhaled. *Finally.* Energy surged through his limbs. He locked an arm about Ruby's waist and drew her close in one fluid motion. Cupping her chin in his palm, he pressed a kiss on those perfect beckoning lips—as he had dreamed of doing for weeks.

She lurched back with a gasp, her hand shoving hard against his chest. "What—what are you doing?" She twisted free from his grasp.

He straightened with a jerk. "I—but, you said—"

"I didn't mean me!" Color rushed to her cheeks. Ruby lifted splayed fingers to her face, her eyes glimmering with tears. "I meant your mother. And Abby. Everyone who joked at our expense. Did you think—" A strangled cry burst from her mouth. She spun away, rushing down the path.

Gerald dropped to the bench, a shower of rose petals cascading over his coat. He pressed a hand against his face, the touch searing his palm.

$\approx$

Ruby's breaths ripped from her lungs in painful gasps. He'd thought she wanted his kiss.

Had she?

A single woman—living in his house, working at his side, practically falling at his feet for the chance of a romantic walk—what excuse did she have? Of course he'd assume her to be in love with him. Everyone must think so. Her cheeks burned as a sob bubbled up from her stomach. She paused in her headlong rush back to the hospital, glaring at the double doors. *The first place he'd look.*

Ruby swiped a hand across her mouth, remembering the touch of his lips against hers. Her heart fluttered a seditious beat. She spun around, skirt swishing, and strode toward the cable car stop. Hopefully she'd determine a destination before she reached the end of the line.

18

Gerald slunk into his narrow office and shut the door without bothering to switch on the lights. Darkness closed in around him. His throat burned, the image of Ruby's stunned expression seared into his memory. This blunder bordered on epic proportions. How could he explain his mistake? His stomach churned. What would he say to Robert?

"Yes, I kissed your sister. A terrible misunderstanding—I thought she wished it."

Gerald groaned. He stumbled through the dark to the desk chair, sinking down into the seat. A sliver of light crept under the door, assuring him the world and all its mistakes remained. Pressing hands across his face, he blocked out the distractions and turned inward. "Lord, what was I thinking?" He sighed, the words rushing between interlaced fingers. It didn't take divine wisdom to see where his desires had led. Gerald slumped forward, resting his head on his arms.

He'd been content before this woman had arrived and set his life careening down a whole new path. Before he'd spent time listening to Dee spin her tales and basking in the presence of Robert and Abby's young love. At nearly thirty, he'd considered himself too old for such diversions. Gerald shuddered. Apparently not.

The door rattled, and he jerked upright.

Light poured in from the hall, a familiar figure silhouetted in the doorway. "Gerald?" Robert pressed the light switch.

Gerald squinted, the sudden glare stabbing at his eyes. He braced an arm across his brow and leaned against the chair back, his thoughts scattering to the wind.

"Were you sleeping?" Robert frowned. "I'm only a few minutes late. I thought you'd be in the laboratory."

Gerald swallowed, his mouth dry as cotton wadding. He shook his head, reaching back through the afternoon to remember why he'd left the lab in the first place. "No. The tube blew again. I figured I'd let you replace it."

Robert leaned on the doorframe and fiddled with an ink pen in his fingers. "Where's Ruby?"

Jumping up from the chair, Gerald gathered a stack of files. "I—I saw her earlier. I'm not certain where she is now." *Or how angry she might be.* He ran a hand through his hair as a lead weight settled in his gut. "I'll make a last sweep through the ward before heading home. If I see her, I'll tell her you're looking for her."

Robert grasped his arm before Gerald could exit. "What's wrong with you? You look like you've lost your best friend."

Swallowing a reply, Gerald shook his head. "I'm weary, nothing more."

"How's the hand?"

Gerald brushed past his partner, escaping the office confines. He pressed the files against his chest. "A little stiff. No need to worry."

Tiny lines formed around his friend's mouth. "I wish you'd let me take another look. Or someone else. Maybe Dr. Dawson?"

"Another time." Right now, Gerald needed to find Ruby and explain. Somehow.

❧

Ruby grasped the brass rail, a tangled knot of emotions wedged under her ribcage making each breath a chore. The cable car glided down the hill toward the bay, the breeze cooling her face. She could escape for a few hours, but eventually she'd need to return to Gerald's house. Ruby closed her eyes, wishing the line went on forever. If only it led all the way back to Sacramento, she could lock herself in her room with her memories, safe from further embarrassment. And hurt.

Her mind made the return journey, hovering over the images of her mother and sisters, their eyes rich with sympathy. And Miriam—how large her belly must be by now. Ruby swallowed the bitter taste creeping up her throat. No, her future lay here in San Francisco.

She opened her eyes, gazing out at the street. Buildings stood in various states of transformation—some in demolition, others stretching up to form a new skyline. In the pocket around Gerald's neighborhood, the homes had escaped major devastation, but here in the financial center, workers were busy putting the city back to rights. *Like me. Forcing my life back on track.*

So why was she running? She had nothing to be ashamed of. Her feelings for Gerald Larkspur were natural, if unwelcomed. She could push them aside, as easily as they had bubbled to the surface. Ruby wrapped her fingers around the railing, the metal cold against her fingers. A few hours walking the waterfront would give her time to lick her wounds. Then she'd return to the house, as if nothing had happened.

Gerald might even be relieved. Certainly he didn't desire a relationship with her. He probably assumed she pined for him—a poor miserable widow seeking love and devotion. A simple mistake, easily rectified.

The brakeman slowed the vehicle as it bumped down the hill, creaking to a stop in front of the Ferry Building. Ruby followed the other riders as they stepped onto the freshly laid cobblestones. She paused, gazing up at the depot clock tower encased in scaffolding. If this city could put itself back together, so could she.

19

*R*uby ran a hand across her forehead, pausing to pinch the bridge of her nose. A throbbing ache settled behind her eyes, the weight of the day pushing down on her shoulders. Lights shone from the windows of each of the narrow, elegant homes lining the road, as if beckoning weary travelers.

She reached Gerald's house and opened the gate, gazing up at the beautiful structure. What would it be like to own such a lovely home, nestled between other distinguished residences? The warmth spilling out the bay windows spoke of family, love, and belonging. Ruby sighed, a lump growing in her throat. In two months Robert and Abby would wed. Children would follow. Ruby would be doomed forever to the role of widowed aunt. No amount of serving mankind could replace the dream of raising her own brood.

Her shoes remained stationary, as if glued to the front walk. The new electric streetlights were coming on in the distance, warning Ruby of the impending darkness. She lifted her fingers to her lips, remembering Gerald's kiss. Sweat broke out along her skin. How could she face him?

She turned to stare at the distant orange streaks of sunset. The door creaked open behind her. Ruby stiffened, waiting.

"I was getting worried." Gerald's voice sounded. "I thought perhaps you'd made a beeline for the ferry."

Ruby gripped the cement column for strength. "It crossed my mind."

Gerald came up beside her, settling his hands on the top of the gate and facing the quiet street. "I'm glad you didn't." He lowered his head. "I owe you an apology."

Ruby dropped her shoulders, releasing the tension trapped in her chest. "You don't. It was a misunderstanding."

"No, I acted irresponsibly. I don't want you to feel ill at ease—either here or at work." He scraped a hand across his chin. "I wish I could go back a few hours and fix everything."

Her heart skipped as he admitted to regretting the kiss. "Just so you know, I didn't come to San Francisco in search of romance. I'm content to serve. I'm not pining away for a man."

Lines formed around his mouth. "I never thought such a thing." He released the gate, his hand moving toward her arm for a moment before he drew it away and hooked his fingers over the top edge of his vest. "I—I just thought . . ." He looked up to the horizon, the sunset's glow emphasizing the firm line of his jaw.

Thought what? She studied Gerald's furrowed brow, a prickle racing up her arms. The man's lips turned downward, like the boy with the dislocated elbow. It didn't take nursing training to recognize his pain. But it's not as if she'd spurned him. The handsome doctor could have his pick of eligible women in San Francisco. He'd be fortunate not to be saddled with one like her. Ruby sighed. "Let's not speak of it anymore. We've spent quite a bit of time together. A few misplaced feelings would be . . ." She searched his face. "It would be expected, I imagine."

His eyes narrowed. "If you feel it's for the best, I won't speak of it again."

She forced a smile. "Did your mother save any pie? I'm starving."

A corner of his mouth lifted. "Of course. Though Davy nearly talked her out of it."

"I suppose I might share a bite or two." Ruby hid a yawn and limped toward the steps, more than ready to put the day behind her. She paused in the doorway, glancing back toward the front walk.

Gerald turned back toward the sunset, his silhouette dark against the bright sky.

She swallowed hard, her heart's yearning producing a hollow pain in her chest.

꩜

Gerald ran a finger along the fine cracks in the painted cement of the gatepost. Today's blunder had sent fissures through him as well. Had his apology helped at all? Or had it simply made him appear more foolish?

Streaks of red darkened the western sky, deepening to purple and blue above. The stench of smoke and dust still clung to the city, noticeable in the dank evening air. He squeezed his eyes closed. *Lord, am I striving after things you don't intend for me?* He glanced over his shoulder at the front window of his home, the warm glow of family beckoning him. Family—and more. His heart quickened. *Please take away these desires, Father. How can I have a beautiful woman under my roof and keep my thoughts pure?*

꩜

The springs squeaked as Ruby settled on the edge of the bed. She pulled off her gloves and laid them in her lap, fighting the urge to throw herself prone on the mattress.

Abby sat on the desk chair, book in hand. "Robert told me about Dee Feinstein. I'm sorry she's not improving."

After the incident with Gerald, her time with Dee seemed like it had happened days before. Ruby stretched and rose. She must put the gloves away properly before she could relax. She tucked them into the top drawer of the bureau and retrieved the porcelain-handled shoe hook from its wooden box. "Dee's struggled for so long. I ache for her." She made quick work of the buttons, freeing her feet from the stiff boots.

"I remember how I felt when Cecelia took her last turn. I had convinced myself the X-rays would cure her." Abby closed her book and laid it on the desk.

Ruby rubbed the bottom of her foot, the arches aching from the day's walk. "Robert's work must be a constant reminder for you."

Abby fiddled with the buttons on her sleeve. "It's important—his calling. He may not have saved my sister, but he may save someone else's. And I know Cecelia is safe in God's arms."

Ruby rubbed a polishing cloth over her boots as Otto padded across the floor to his cushion and plopped down with a sigh.

Abby folded her hands in her lap and leaned forward. "I spoke with Patrick today." The change in topic seemed to bring a new confidence to Abby's voice. "He talked about the incident at the Presidio. He says you were quite brave."

Ruby's stomach tightened, the reverend's kind words pricking at her conscience. "He was the hero. He walked in and took control of the situation in a manner I never expected."

The younger woman leaned an elbow on the desk and lowered her chin to her palm. "People listen to him. He's gained much respect among the city's disenfranchised. I'm certain my cousin was relieved to see him take charge."

Ruby closed the wardrobe and glanced at her dusty frock in the mirror. An afternoon of wandering the streets had left her tired and mussed. What she needed was a hot bath. "I'm sure Gerald could have handled the incident."

Abby shook her head. "I don't know. I don't view him as the heroic type."

A burning sensation tickled Ruby's throat. "He spends days on end working with dying patients—what could be more heroic?"

The young woman blushed. "I meant no disrespect. Kindness and empathy is what originally drew me to your brother as well. But Gerald isn't one to take risks. He's careful and pragmatic, not given to rash decisions."

Ruby kept her gaze lowered. *If only she knew.*

"Robert received a letter from your mother today. Apparently, only she and one of your sisters will be coming to the wedding."

Ruby sank down on the bed, bath forgotten. "Which sister?"

"Elizabeth."

The youngest. Of course. Elizabeth would never miss a wedding. Or a chance to stir up trouble.

"Do you . . ." Abby bit her lower lip. "Do you think they'll approve of me?"

Ruby sighed. In reality, Abby had more in common with Elizabeth and Mother than Ruby did. "They'll adore you." Elizabeth—always determined to right society's wrongs—would be instantly drawn to Abby's unconventional sense of style. *They'll be thick as thieves in no time, much to Robert's dismay.* And it would leave Ruby on the outside. As usual. Ruby moved to the dressing table and began removing pins from her pompadour frame. "Have you decided on a gown for the big day?"

Abby frowned. "No. Mama keeps showing me pattern books, but every dress seems so frivolous, considering what we've all been through."

A quiver raced through Ruby. She'd designed Miriam's dress and two for her sisters. "Let me help. We'll go downtown tomorrow and look at styles. I saw some lovely ensembles in the new shop windows. Wait until you set eyes on them—it'll inspire you." Her imagination sparked with thoughts of ribbons and carved ivory buttons.

Abby's face paled. "Perhaps . . ."

"It'll be fun. You'll see." Ruby turned back to the looking glass and ran the boar-bristle brush through her hair, the day taking shape in her mind. Sure, she'd sworn off weddings, but dressing the bride could be rewarding. Two women on the town perusing elegant silks and fine Irish lace and maybe enjoying lunch at one of the new hotels—it sounded like an ideal day. Besides, Abby needed her guidance. Ruby's spirits lifted. Best of all—she'd stay far away from Gerald Larkspur.

Gerald sat up in bed, a faint glimmer of a moonlight shining through the crack in the curtains. What had disturbed him? A jangling ring broke the stillness, and the dog barked in response. Gerald jumped up and lurched out into the hallway in his pajamas, the floor icy against his bare feet.

Ruby stood outside his door, her white wrapper whispering around her ankles. "Was that the telephone?" The bell jangled again.

He hurried past, the little dog following at his heels. Tromping down the dark stairs, he swept the receiver off the switch hook before it woke anyone else. Gerald sank into the chair and pulled the candlestick telephone close. "Dr. Larkspur speaking, how can I be of assistance?" The words rasped in his throat.

"Gerald, it's Robert."

Gerald rubbed a hand across his eyes, the earpiece cool against his palm. "What time is it? Are you still at the hospital?" He squinted at the clock on the mantle, but the room was too dark.

"Dee Feinstein's heart is weakening. I don't think she's going to last until morning."

Gerald slumped back in the seat, lowering his arm until the receiver bumped his chest. *Not again.*

His partner's tinny voice wafted upward from the cone-shaped device. "She's asking for you."

"I'll be there as soon as I can." Gerald returned the telephone to the desk, closing his eyes for a brief moment. He jumped as Ruby's warm fingers touched his arm.

She clutched her dressing gown about the neck with one hand. "Is it Dee?"

He managed a nod. "I need to go."

"Would you like me to come?"

Gerald closed his fingers over hers, her touch undoing him. The momentary sweetness of the afternoon kiss rushed back. *If only.* He ached to pull her close and bury his face in her hair. He pushed up to his feet. "No. Get some sleep. There's nothing more you can do."

20

$\mathcal{G}$erald finished securing the new tire before standing and brushing dirt from his trouser leg. He resisted the temptation to chuck the shredded one into the gutter and instead dropped the strips of black rubber onto the floorboards beneath the rear seat. Flat tires always occurred at the times of greatest inconvenience. He rubbed his hands together, freeing the last bits of grit and gravel from his palms and rolling his shirtsleeves back in place.

Climbing behind the wheel, he glanced around the dark, empty street. In an hour or two, milk wagons and delivery trucks would be making the rounds, but for now the neighborhood remained deserted. He revved the engine, eliciting a popping cough from the motor before it wheezed and lunged forward. The vehicle's symptoms persisted. If it were a patient, he'd suspect pertussis. Gerald ran a hand across his dry eyes. Perhaps the contraption needed oil. Did petroleum work like cough syrup for an engine?

There was a good reason he worked with the human body rather than machines—he preferred a patient who could tell him what hurt. The same problem kept him far away from the inner workings of the X-ray apparatus.

Gerald drove six more blocks and parked across the street from Lane Hospital, the building still in the renovation process. He shut off the engine, ignoring the faint hiss coming from under the hood, as if the motor sighed in relief. *You may rest, but you'd better still be working when I'm ready to leave.*

He glanced both directions before loping across the cobblestones and charging up the marble steps two at a time. He pulled open the double doors, the familiar hospital scent washing over him. Gerald nodded to the duty nurse as he hurried toward the ward without bothering to stop at his office.

Robert entered the hall, his white coat wrinkled. "There you are. What took you so long?"

Gerald yanked off his hat. "Don't ask. What's her condition?"

"A little better than when I called. Her fever seems to be abating, but her pulse is weakening. Respiration is labored, so I administered epinephrine. It seemed to help."

"If the fever's fallen, there might still be a chance."

Robert pinned him with a dark stare. "I know what you would say if our positions were reversed."

"Let's just see her through the night." Gerald set his jaw. He wasn't ready to let this patient slip away without a fight. Even if it were a battle he couldn't win.

Robert pulled a watch from his coat pocket. "It's morning. But I'll let you assess the situation."

Gerald opened the door, scanning the ward. Most of the patients slept, gentle sighs and snores filling the shadow-filled room. He followed the sound of ragged breathing to Dee's bed, close to the window. A gossamer curtain separated the room from the dark night, not unlike the fine threads tying his patient to the world.

She turned toward him, the bedside lamp reflecting off her dilated pupils. "You made it, Doc."

He laid his fingers over hers. "I could say the same of you, Miss Feinstein . . . Dee. When Dr. King telephoned, I was afraid you wouldn't wait for me."

The corners of her mouth tightened in an almost imperceptible smile. "Was feeling a bit low. Thought the Lord was ready for me."

"And now?" The tension in Gerald's chest eased a stitch. His patients often had an accurate sense of when the fight was over.

She glanced down at her arm, to where Gerald's hand rested. "Dr. King gave me a shot of something . . . helped a bit." Her words, like dripping molasses, could not be rushed between the tortured inhalations.

Gerald hovered beside the bed, content to let Dee take her time. It was hers to spend.

She gazed up at him. "I'm inclined. Today or tomorrow."

He lifted her hand and squeezed her fingers—the bluish cast of the woman's nail beds drawing his eye. *Cyanotic.* He pushed his gaze back to her face. If only he didn't know the truth. The tumors in her lungs no longer allowed oxygen to flow through her bloodstream in sufficient amounts. Robert's injection could only provide temporary relief. And time. *Like everything else we've done.* "It's in God's hands."

"Safe . . . in His hands." Her fingers curled around his. "So why so scared?"

"Are you?" He searched her glassy eyes.

Dee struggled, finally pushing out a single word. "You."

Gerald's throat tightened. "Me? I'm not the one in the bed."

Dee appeared smaller than when she'd first arrived, her dark eyes taking up a larger proportion of her face. She focused on Gerald, as if daring him to argue with a dying woman. "You . . ." she coughed, blinking twice before fixing her stare once more, ". . . might as well be." Her pale lips hung open. "You're afraid to live."

He shifted his weight between his feet. "My job is to help others live."

"Bah." Dee closed her eyes.

"I should let you rest."

Dee's vice-grip tightened. "Love her." Her lids fluttered open, gaze unfocused.

Ruby. Gerald's chest squeezed as if Dee's fingers clamped about his heart. He glanced over one shoulder, but his partner had left the ward. He turned back to his patient and bent close. "I tried, Dee. She doesn't love me." He set his jaw. "And why should she?"

Dee wheezed sharply, the air whistling in her chest.

Gerald slid both arms behind her back, lifting her to a sitting position until she could manage a deep breath. When it ended in a gasping laugh, he frowned. Had she slipped into a delirium?

Dee's fingers grasped his neck, drawing him close until he could hear her whispered words. "She loves you. A woman knows her . . . competition." Dee's chuckle melted into a coughing spasm, jerking against Gerald's arm. "But she's been a dear friend." Her eyes fell closed as her body relaxed.

Gerald remained motionless until he heard Dee's respiration continue. He lowered her onto the pillows, bunching them so they propped her at a more comfortable angle. Gerald stared down at his patient—his friend—for a moment before collapsing into the bedside chair. He pressed both hands against his eyes and tried to pray. The words wouldn't come.

❧

Ruby and Abby sat in silence as the cable car bumped down the line. Ruby chewed her lip. If she hopped off at the next intersection, it would be five short blocks to the hospital. She could be at Dee's side in a matter of minutes.

Why had Gerald told her to stay away? Dee was her friend as well.

Ruby stayed in her seat. Abby needed her help, too. Abby and Robert would make a fine picture—if someone took the girl in hand and made it happen. Ruby's gaze lingered over Abby's simple brown walking skirt and peach jacket. Such an elegant figure deserved a sophisticated wedding gown. At least the task at hand would serve as a distraction. "Have you thought any more about what you'd like?"

Abby tore her gaze from the street scene, lines bunching on her forehead. "I've thought a little about what I don't want."

Ruby frowned. *At least it's something.* "What would that be?"

The cable car slowed to a stop and the women descended the narrow steps. As it rattled away, Abby turned to answer. "I don't want ruffles. Or bows. Or any other frivolity."

Ruby paused midstep. "It's a wedding. Frivolity is expected."

The young woman's shoulders straightened. "I'm marrying your brother because I love him. Not to be dressed up like a china doll in a fancy frock and have everyone gape at me."

"There's nothing wrong with having both. Is there?"

"No. Yes. Let's just go." Abby huffed, hurrying down the sidewalk in the direction of the dress shops.

Ruby's throat tightened. "No, wait." She reached for Abby's arm, slowing her to a stop. "I want to understand."

Abby stared at the ground. People pushed past along the sidewalk, as if the world rushed in circles about them.

Ruby forced herself to wait while Abby gathered her words. In some ways, Robert's fiancée reminded her of Miriam—slow to speak, but every word worth gold.

After a long moment, Abby's eyes filled with tears. "My sister loved fashion. She dreamed of designing her own wedding trousseau."

"Cecelia?"

Abby nodded and dug in her bag. "Why do I never have a handkerchief?"

Ruby drew one from its hiding place in her sleeve and held it out. "Don't you think Cecelia would want you to look beautiful on your wedding day?"

The young woman's chin trembled as she accepted the silk square and dabbed at her massive doe eyes. "She'd insist upon it. But I never dreamed I'd be marrying instead of her. Or without her. Did you know it's been almost a year since she passed away? Sometimes it feels like yesterday."

Ruby's heart softened. She stepped close and wrapped an arm around Abby's waist. "I don't mean to take her place. I know what it is to miss someone you love."

Abby's face crumpled. "Of course you do. I'm being selfish and silly. This must be bringing up all sorts of memories for you, too."

Ruby glanced at her shoe tips. Was it odd how seldom she'd thought of Charlie today? "It does, a little." She squeezed Abby's arm. "But I'd hoped our outing could be fun. A way for us to connect as . . ." Ruby paused—she'd intended to say 'as sisters,' but the word choice seemed callous in Abby's present state of mind. "As friends."

"I'd like that." Abby wiped her eyes a second time. "And I apologize for my outburst. I've just been tied up in knots about all of this and didn't have anyone to confide in."

Ruby tugged on Abby's wrist, moving in the direction of the shops. "I hope you will consider me your new confidante. Besides, Robert has ceased telling me anything. He shares all his concerns with your cousin these days. He doesn't need his older sister's advice."

Abby hurried to keep pace. "He and Gerald are close. I suppose it's to be expected with the hours they spend together at the hospital." She gave Ruby a sideways glance. "I'd rather thought you were growing fond of Gerald, as well."

Ruby pushed down the flutters in her stomach. "He's been kind to take me in. But there's nothing of the sort you're implying." She stopped in front of the new storefront she'd spotted yesterday.

"Too bad. I'd hoped he might persuade you to stay."

The plate glass window shimmered in the morning sun, the white dresses catching the light. "Stay?"

Abby frowned at the sign announcing, "Earthquake brides welcomed here." She turned her eyes to the lace-bedecked bodices and skirts. "Robert feared you might return to Sacramento with your mother after the wedding."

A surge of heat climbed Ruby's spine. Were those her choices? Enter some arrangement with Gerald or go home to Sacramento? "He's mistaken. I intend to continue here. Though I'll need to make different living arrangements." She pushed open the door and stepped into the quiet shop, intent on leaving all talk of Gerald Larkspur outside on the street. "Look at this white crepe. Isn't it divine?"

Abby glanced around the room, her gaze skipping from one dress to another without pause. "Hmm." She faced Ruby. "Then, I have a proposal for you." Her eyes narrowed.

Ruby pursed her lips. Was Abby planning to take Ruby in after the wedding? Like a stray mutt? "The only proposal we should focus on now is which style you will wear on your wedding day."

Abby turned back to the dresses and sighed as a store clerk hurried over. "I will agree to try on any and all gowns you suggest—under one condition."

Ruby raised a brow. "Which is?"

The young woman crossed her arms, a smile brightening her freckled cheeks. "I choose where we take our noon meal. And with whom."

21

*R*uby hobbled out of Taylor's Finery, her feet in utter revolt after the long morning of shopping. After three hours and five shops, she'd not succeeded in convincing her soon-to-be sister to choose a dress pattern, much less fabric or notions. She pressed a gloved hand to her grumbling stomach. "I suppose we could try the shop the seamstress recommended—the new one on Market Street."

Abby closed the door behind her with a loud click. "Perhaps after lunch. Or another day, even." She grimaced. "I know I've been difficult, but I believe our styles differ."

The scent of fresh coffee wafted down the sidewalk. Ruby lifted her head, searching the nearby storefronts. Small tables spilled from a neighboring café, diners enjoying an afternoon repast. "You mentioned choosing our noon meal. What did you have in mind?"

Abby jutted her chin forward with a flash of mischief lighting her eyes. "It's a surprise." She grasped Ruby's elbow and drew her down the busy sidewalk.

With a final yearning glance toward the restaurant, Ruby followed her friend through the crowd. "You will need to choose a gown eventually. Unless . . ." *Could there be another reason she's dragging her feet?*

Robert's fiancée cocked her head as she glanced back at Ruby. "What?"

"Maybe you're having second thoughts." The breeze ruffled the feathered plumes draping over the brim of Ruby's hat. Beside Abby's simple elegance, she felt overdone and pretentious. "I'm told many attractions sparked because of heightened emotions during the calamity. It's not unheard of for a bride to change her mind as life returns to normal."

"Never. Robert was a gift from God. An answered prayer. I wish everyone could find the same love we've discovered—tested by fire, if you will." Abby shook her head. "It's all this hullabaloo I regret. If he and I dashed off and married quietly, I'd be overjoyed."

"I'm glad to hear you still love my brother." Ruby tugged on Abby's arm, intent on slowing her pace. The tight-hemmed skirt prevented long steps. "But what's stopping you from sneaking away if it's what you desire?" She had no particular love for weddings, either. She'd seen enough lately.

"My parents would be distraught. I'm their only daughter now, and they've already claimed Robert as a son. How could we wed without their participation?" Her lip quivered. "But when I stop to consider how many people will be attending—your mother and sister, Aunt Mae's Ladies' Aid friends, and countless doctors from the hospital and their wives—I get dizzy thinking of it." She paused at the corner, glaring at the traffic.

"You're fortunate only one of my sisters is attending."

"I know I should be itching to meet all of them." Abby gestured to an approaching electric streetcar. "This is our ride."

"Some things are best taken in small doses." Ruby waited as the vehicle slowed to a stop. As long as it wasn't an automobile. Gerald had promised another driving lesson, but likely as not, he'd avoid any contact with her now. She picked her way down the crowded aisle, spotting an open seat next to an elderly woman whose voluminous black skirt covered most of the bench. "Is this place taken?" *Other than by your dress?*

The lady blinked, as if she'd just awoken from a nap. "No, of course not. Please, be my guest."

Ruby pushed the overgrown mass of taffeta to one side before sliding in beside her. As the streetcar lurched forward, Ruby rubbed fingertips against the muscles in her already-stiff neck. This day had been a disappointment. She'd intended to bond with her new sister-in-law, but she'd underestimated the challenge of shopping with someone determined not to like anything. She glanced back at Abby, sitting alongside a young mother with a toddler balanced on her lap.

Ruby faced front and closed her eyes, appreciating the moment off her feet. Perhaps after lunch, she could sneak back to the hospital. Gerald had no right to keep her away.

"Are you going to the baths?" Her seatmate's voice contained a slight tremor, indicative of her advanced age.

Ruby opened her eyes and glanced at the silver-haired matron. "The baths?" Did she smell so offensive after a morning of shopping?

The woman smiled, deep lines forming around her mouth, suggesting years of smiles. "I thought perhaps you were taking the street-car to the Sutro Baths."

"No, I'm having lunch with a friend." She cast another glance back at Abby who had taken the tyke onto her own knee. The child's feet drummed against the rear of Ruby's seat. "We didn't bring bathing costumes."

"You must be new to San Francisco, if you are unfamiliar with the Baths." The older woman adjusted her tall hat, peacock feathers drooping off the back and catching the attention of the little boy who batted at them with a chubby fist.

"I've been here almost a month. I came to live with my brother."

"Odd time to move to the city, with everything as it is. I've lived here forty years. My husband and I raised six children here. It's just Matthew and me now. We lost our youngest in the quake. He was about your age."

Ruby's throat tightened. "I'm so sorry. How difficult it must have been for you."

"It was. It is. But I go down to the coastline on occasion to remind myself to be thankful." She glanced out the window with a sigh. "Henry loved the beach when he was small. Now I go to remember him. And to thank the Lord for sweet memories."

Ruby turned away and blinked back tears. *Sweet memories.*

The woman jostled Ruby as she rose. "Excuse me, this is my stop. Enjoy your lunch." Her dress rustled as she pushed past, a waft of honeysuckle scent drifting behind.

As Abby's seatmate followed her down the aisle, Abby stepped forward to claim the elderly woman's spot. "You're going to love where I'm taking you."

Ruby sighed. "Like you loved the dress shopping?"

"Who could love dress shopping?" Abby shuddered. She shot Ruby a sideways glance. "So, you're positive you're not interested in my cousin Gerald, right?"

"Of course not." *Or at least, I shouldn't be.*

"Then lunch might be even more interesting."

Ruby's appetite vanished. "Gerald isn't meeting us, is he?"

The corner of Abby's lip curled upward, the freckles on her cheek dancing. "No. Better. And I'm not saying another word until we arrive."

The pair sat in silence as the streetcar traversed westward. Other passengers disembarked at various stops, jostling past them with arms full of packages. Clouds darkened the sky as they hurtled onward, tiny droplets of rain pattering against the car's top and sprinkling in the open windows.

Abby scooted close to the window and turned her face to the breeze. "Isn't it refreshing? The summer was strangely dry. The roses need the water."

"Yes, but I do not. Will we arrive soon?" Ruby pulled her wrap tight about her shoulders, covering her batiste blouse.

"We're almost there. I regret the view won't be as nice as I'd hoped with this weather rolling in." She stood and stepped into the aisle.

"View?" Ruby followed Abby to the exit. While the younger woman hopped from the conveyance with confidence, Ruby measured her steps so not to turn her ankle stepping into a mud puddle.

The fog drifted amongst the spires of the massive ornate building perched on the edge of an impossible cliff. Down below, waves crashed against the rocks, sending spray high into the misty air. "Where are we? It looks like a palace."

Abby clapped her hands together. "I'd hoped you hadn't heard about it. It's the Cliff House. Isn't it marvelous?" She grasped Ruby's hand, pulling her forward. "We must hurry. They're expecting us at one o'clock."

Ruby hoisted her tight hem once more to keep up with Abby's flying feet. "Is this where we are lunching?" After weeks of staring at damaged or half-finished buildings, the magnificence of the Cliff House stole her imagination. This was the San Francisco of which she'd dreamed.

She followed her friend up the steep staircase, quickly running a hand along her hairline and thankful she'd worn her best hat.

"Patrick!" Abby's voice rang out.

Ruby froze midstep, gazing at the image above her.

The redheaded minister stood at the top of the steps, dressed in a fine suit and sporting an equally proud smile. "Ladies. I am pleased you could join me this foggy September afternoon. Reminds me of home. Except for the company, of course."

Abby gave the man a quick embrace. "Patrick, it's so good of you to meet us like this."

Ruby's stomach dropped as if she'd left it at the bottom of the stairs by mistake. There was no misjudging the mischief in Abby's eyes—she'd planned this encounter with care.

Patrick reached a hand out to Ruby, a wide grin splitting his face. "Mrs. Marshall, an honor to see you again. Miss Fischer has been bending my ear about you. I must say, you're looking even more beautiful today than you did with a soup ladle in your hand, tending to my flock."

Perspiration dampened Ruby's palms, so she swept one across her skirt before accepting the man's offer of assistance. "I am surprised to see you, Reverend. I wasn't aware you'd be joining us." She shot Abby a reproachful glance.

"Call me Patrick, please. Everyone does. Even Miss Fischer and her fortunate Dr. King."

Abby grasped Ruby's arm. "Please forgive me, Ruby. I wanted our outing to be a surprise. Robert thought you would be pleased to dine at the Cliff House. Your idea of dress shopping just made it all the simpler to arrange."

Ruby tore her gaze from the handsome minister and surveyed the fine building. "Of course I'm pleased. It's a glorious treat." She patted Abby's sleeve. *Except for the obvious attempt at matchmaking.*

Abby sighed, returning her hands to her sides. "Robert was to join us, of course, but he was all night at the hospital with a patient."

Dee. Ruby blinked back tears.

Patrick grinned. "You might need to accustom yourself to odd hours, my dear. Doctors are on duty at all times—not unlike men of the cloth. I'm more than honored to escort two lovely ladies to lunch." He stuck out both elbows. "Perhaps it's why the Lord gave me two good arms."

Ruby gingerly looped a wrist around the man's elbow, swallowing the bitterness creeping up her throat. Abby had meant well and nothing would be served by grousing. An afternoon at a fine restaurant with interesting companions was nothing to shirk—even if her heart remained solidly lodged at Lane Hospital with a quick-witted woman and an attractive doctor.

❧

Gerald lowered Dee's cool hand to the sheet, his chest aching. *She's home.*

His partner spoke from the far end of the bed. "I'm sorry, Gerald."

Gerald didn't move his gaze from Dee's face, as if by some miracle her heart would beat anew. "We all knew this was coming." The words tasted flat and stale, like crackers left in the cupboard too long.

Robert's voice remained low and quiet. "I'm sorry I ever dragged you into this X-ray project."

Gerald turned away and leaned against the wall. "My own silly pride is to blame. Don't forget, our first cancer patient was my cousin." And each subsequent patient had somehow become family. Why couldn't he keep them at arm's length? The room fell silent, the deafening quiet pressing against Gerald's ears. "Go on home, Robert—you must be exhausted. I'll finish here."

Robert dropped his gaze to the patient with a sigh and a quick nod. The indigo circles beneath his eyes offered testimony to too many sleepless nights.

"Would you inform Ruby? She cared deeply for Dee."

Robert raked a hand through his dark hair. "She and Abby are out for the day. Something about dress shopping and lunch."

Gerald grunted. "Good. She needed an afternoon diversion." And he'd require time to put his heart back together—not much luck there.

"You could use some entertainment as well. Perhaps we should plan another picnic. Get away from the city for a day." Robert tucked his hands into his coat pockets.

Dee's pallid face sent a quiver through Gerald's stomach. He drew the sheet over her head with a sigh. Her words floated in his memory. *"She loves you."* If so, why had Ruby pushed him away? He glanced at Robert. "Yes. Perhaps."

As Robert walked away, Gerald stared at the white sheet. *Dee's seeing Christ's face. What could be more wondrous?* She wouldn't wish him to grieve, but Gerald had little control over his heart. Mourning had become like a second skin.

Likely as not, she'd tell him to get busy. He turned away, scrubbing a hand across his face. A fresh start might be in order. Maybe Dee was correct about Ruby. As long as he didn't throw himself at her like a romance-addled youth, he might eventually earn Ruby's affections. He thought back to their kiss, and the look of horror on the woman's face. Perhaps, with patience, she'd be willing to give him a second chance.

22

$\mathcal{R}$uby slipped her fingers from the white gloves before reaching for her cup of tea. The steamy fragrance of lemon bathed her face as she sipped, glancing across the gold rim toward the clergyman sitting opposite.

Patrick leaned back in his chair, gazing out the spacious window at the fog, his green eyes sparkling like the crystal-laden chandelier above his head. He seemed equally at ease in both the squalor of the refugee camp and the grandeur of the Cliff House. A refined gentleman with a heart for the people—Ruby never realized such a man existed outside of novels. So why could she think of nothing but a certain doctor?

Tea dribbled from the cup to Ruby's chin. She started, clattering the teacup down against the saucer. She swept the napkin to her face before the amber liquid could stain her shirtwaist.

Abby cleared her throat. "Patrick, do you believe the weather will clear and give us a view of the ocean?"

"I'll take it up with the Almighty."

Ruby tucked her gloves into the crocheted purse she'd hooked to the chatelaine clip on her waist. "With all the suffering in the world—and this city, specifically—don't you imagine the Lord has more important matters to tend to?"

Patrick grinned, revealing a dimple in one cheek. "You must think our God very small indeed, Mrs. Marshall. He loves to give good gifts to His children, not just serve their basic needs."

Abby added a cube of sugar to her tea, her brown eyes shining. "Isn't it amazing how He reaches out to us in both the good and the bad times? I'd never truly experienced God's presence until those horrible days of fire following the earthquake. Now I see His hand in all things."

Ruby's thoughts turned back to her last encounter with Dee. "*That's my God.*" Everyone seemed to have a better grasp on faith than Ruby. What was she missing? She stared out the window, blinking against tears. How selfish of her to sit surrounded by opulence while Dee passed from this life. The dismal fog creeping along the coastline seemed altogether appropriate.

Her friend touched Ruby's wrist. "Are you listening? Patrick asked about your preferred dish."

Ruby glanced up, startled to see her companions' attention fixed on her. "I'm sorry. My mind was elsewhere."

The minister frowned. "I hope my teasing didn't upset you."

"No, it simply brought back some unwanted memories." Ruby reached for the menu, determined to change the subject before further questions arrived. "I love fresh seafood. Do they serve crab?"

"This is San Francisco, my dear." Patrick spoke in a hushed voice. "Of course the restaurant prepares crab and every other type of seafood you can imagine."

Abby's nose wrinkled under her freckles. "I never learned to like shellfish, or any other fish, for that matter. If it doesn't walk, fly, or grow from a plant, I'm not interested."

Ruby studied the *cartes du jour* as Abby and Patrick discussed the merits of different cuisines. Noticing a brown splatter on her cuff, she scowled. Perhaps she'd better not choose something she'd have to coax from a shell with a miniature fork. She'd be liable to send it flying over the minister's head.

By the time the waiter arrived, she'd already eliminated most of the menu offerings. A flicker of panic grew in her chest as she scrutinized the entrees.

Patrick's brows knit. "Would you care for me to order, ladies, or would you prefer to do it yourselves?"

Abby smiled at the tuxedoed server. "I'll have the rosemary chicken and the string beans." She shrugged at Ruby. "You can take the woman off the farm—but you can't teach her to eat like a city girl."

"A mixed salad and . . ." Ruby bit her lip, scanning the list once more, ". . . the salmon." Simple fare seemed the wisest option.

Patrick nodded. "Fine choice. I'd like the same." He turned to the ladies as the waiter departed. "Now, I apologize again for being so callous, Mrs. Marshall. I have a tendency to tease. You mustn't put much stock in my words."

Abby shook her head. "You're a flirt, Patrick. An unusual trait considering your calling."

His eyes widened, but his lips curved. "Miss Fischer—I'm shocked to hear you speak so. I am only trying to bring smiles to your lovely faces."

Ruby stared out at the clouds, a spot of light glaring through the mist. "You needn't apologize. I'm afraid I'm not the best company, a fact to which Abby can attest. One of my favorite patients is not expected to survive the day. My heart is not completely here." *And Gerald didn't want me there.*

The man's brows drew together. "Oh, my dear, I'm so sorry. I've heard a little about the research conducted by your brother and Dr. Larkspur. Incredible innovations. I can't imagine being party to such glorious discoveries." He leaned back, eyes intense. "But the work must be heartrending at times. How do you bear up under it?"

Ruby twisted the napkin in her lap. *I don't.* "I could ask you the same question, working among the displaced."

"My answer is simple. Trust."

Ruby frowned. "Trust?" From what she'd seen at the camps, few people there seemed trustworthy.

"When God asks me to serve, I trust He will provide the strength I need. I'm not in the business of saving the city, I leave that to Him." He lifted the crystal water goblet. "I allow Him to bear the weight, for I am no more capable of saving anyone than these drops of condensation have of entering the glass to which they cling. I trust God's leading."

Abby smiled. "Beautiful, Patrick. Well said."

Ruby frowned. Had God ever proven worthy of her trust?

The server arrived with platters of steaming food, placing them atop the table with a flourish. The fragrance of the pink flaky salmon, usually her favorite, turned Ruby's stomach. How could she hope in a God who took everyone she loved—Papa, Charlie, and now Dee?

"Oh—look!" The glare from the window lit up Abby's face.

Ruby turned to gaze out the glass, the fog thinning until a peek-a-boo glimpse of the ocean beckoned, the powerful waves crashing against the rocks.

"And that's our Holy God, ladies. A mighty rescuer and a tender gift-giver." Patrick folded his hands. "Shall I bless our meal?"

Ruby's heart tripped as she pulled her gaze from the view and focused on the man's bowed head. He witnessed the day-to-day cruelties of life, yet never seemed to doubt God's goodness. *Could I ever be capable of the same?*

ॐ

Gerald flopped backward onto his bed, staring at the dust motes dancing in the low-angled afternoon sunbeam. A knot formed somewhere around each temple. He rubbed fingers across his forehead, trying to chase away the image of Dee's empty eyes. *Lord, how many? How many patients—friends—do we lose before admitting this isn't working like we'd hoped?*

Dampness against his cheek caught his attention. He lifted his hand and glared at the oozing sore on his palm. He rolled from the mattress and pushed up to his feet. Crossing the room, he poured water from the pitcher into the waiting basin. He swirled the cool liquid through his fingers. If only he could wash away the day's despair with such ease.

He lifted the rose-scented soap to his nose, the fragrance reminding him of Ruby. The cleanser at work smelled of iodine—perhaps contributing to his skin irritation? Gerald rolled the cake between his palms, attempting to distract his thoughts from the captivating redhead. He plunged his hands back under the water, rinsing the suds from his skin.

Gerald studied the abrasion as the drips trickled down his arm. Thankfully the blue tinge had faded with time, but the spot had enlarged. What had previously been the size of a nickel now covered half of his palm. What in the world was this? Some odd infection?

A wave of exhaustion crept up from his feet, pulling at his spine. He wrapped his hand in a towel and headed back to the bed. Whatever it was, he'd deal with it later.

By the time Gerald opened his eyes again, the sunlight had long disappeared from the window. He stretched, rolled to his back, and blinked at the silver clock ticking on the bedside table. Eleven o'clock? His mind struggled against the fog of confusion accompanying the odd hour. What time had he fallen asleep? His rumpled shirt and unbuttoned vest suggested he'd been there for hours. He shook himself and rose. He might as well dress for bed, even if was after the fact.

Gerald shrugged off the vest and laid it over a chair, adding his shirt to the pile before tying a linen handkerchief around his hand. He paused, standing in his trousers, white union suit, and bare feet, stomach growling. Had he eaten today? It seemed odd no one had roused him for supper. Robert must have explained the situation. The house sounded quiet, so he lit a candle and padded into the hall and down to the kitchen. A turkey sandwich and bowl of cold stew waited for him in the icebox. Gerald bolted down the food while standing at the sink, refusing to glance at the apple pie. He gazed out the window into the darkness of the garden.

Something stirred in the shadows.

He leaned forward, cupping a hand to the glass for a clearer view, but the motion stopped. Animal or a prowler? Lean times led to desperate acts. Gerald glanced around the kitchen for something to use for protection, his gaze skirting over the knife block and the frying pan. He kept his dad's pistol in a box in the attic. Unlike his father, target practice never seemed an intriguing pastime to Gerald. *Where is the silly dog, anyway?* Why keep a dog if it couldn't be bothered to bark at prowlers?

With a shrug, he grabbed the wooden pastry roller, relishing the hefty weight in his grip. He'd probably be more effective with this, anyway.

Slipping into the quiet yard, he picked his way barefoot over the uneven ground.

A ghostly figure rose up from the bench and a soft voice spoke from the gloom. "A little late for baking, isn't it?" Ruby stepped into dim moonlight, the glow casting a silver sheen over loose curls.

Otto sniffed around at the edge of the rose garden, turning his head to glance dismissively at Gerald before returning to his investigation.

Gerald lowered his arm, stashing the roller behind his back. "I—I wasn't sure who was out here so late."

"Robert told me about Dee." She gazed at him, eyes glimmering. "I should have been there."

His gut twisted. "I thought I'd spare you the pain of watching. I'm sorry."

She turned away, stepping back to the shadows of the arbor and sinking onto the bench. "Don't do it again." Her voice trembled.

Gerald hesitated, glancing down at his rumpled attire before joining her on the icy iron seat. He searched for words, but came up empty.

Tiny streams of dim light filtered through the vines like stars, dancing across Ruby's silk gown.

He couldn't resist touching her hand, the warmth of her skin a stark contrast against the cool air. "She spoke of you. It was selfish of me not to ask you to be there."

Ruby lifted her chin, the faint glow illuminating damp cheeks. "I never got to say good-bye. Not to my father, not to . . ." She placed a hand over her lips as if to stifle the words.

A stab of pain cut through Gerald's chest. *Not to her husband.* "Dee knew you'd be concerned."

"What did she say?"

He swallowed hard. *You loved me.* "She called you a 'dear friend.'" He ran a fingertip across the back of her hand. Only a cad would take advantage of grief, but he couldn't help imagining her head resting against his shoulder, her curls tickling his cheek. Was it only yesterday she'd shoved him away after a kiss? How quickly his heart returned to its longings.

Fresh tears shone in her eyes, each droplet reflecting the moonlight like a fine gem. "Sometimes it feels as if everyone I love leaves. I can't trust anyone to stay with me. I need to guard my heart, take care of myself."

No longer resisting, he reached an arm over her shoulders and drew her close. "I'm not going anywhere."

She hiccupped a sob and leaned against him. "You can't know for certain."

Gerald shifted, claiming her free hand and twining their fingers. "Are you kidding? I'm the most steady and predictable man you'll ever find." He grimaced. *Now that's attractive.*

She lowered her ear to his shoulder, burrowing her face against his neck. "And you could be gone in a heartbeat."

The weight of her body made his heart pound faster, her hair scented like a rose garden on a warm day. *Steady.* "And so could you. But the future's in God's hands, not ours."

Ruby lifted her head, a cold draft stealing the warmth she'd provided. "And therein lies the problem." She stood with a sigh, her ivory gown catching the shimmers of light like angel wings. "Good night, Gerald."

He kept hold of her hand, not releasing it until she stepped away.

She seemed to float up the path to the house, her footfalls imperceptible in the still night air.

The small hound leapt up from the shrubs and dashed after her.

Gerald gazed up at the vine-strewn arbor, the cool metal seat like a block of ice against his back. *How does one answer that, Lord?*

23

Gerald tucked the clipboard under his arm, his footfalls echoing through the hospital's long corridor. A final check through the ward, and he would turn things over to Robert for the afternoon. The fitful night's sleep hung heavy on his shoulders.

One of the student nurses strolled in the opposite direction, brightening as she caught his eye. She dipped her head, the white cap bobbing atop her high-piled hair. "Good afternoon, Dr. Larkspur."

He nodded, scrambling to put a name to the face. "Afternoon . . . um, Nurse." He pulled the board to his chest, wishing he had a better memory for names.

The young woman didn't seem to mind, beaming a smile. "I'm not an official nurse yet. It's still Miss Fitzpatrick, I'm afraid. Dr. Lawrence told me you were assisting in the surgery today."

Gerald paused. "Surgery? Which surgery?"

The door to the stairwell swung open, Dr. Lawrence hurrying into the hall. "Dr. Larkspur, there you are. I've been searching everywhere."

Gerald's shoulders tightened. So much for an early day. He should have stayed sequestered in the lab.

Lawrence grasped his elbow and steered him away from the young nurse. "Look, Gerald—Dr. Dawson is performing a hysterectomy this afternoon on a patient with endometrial cancer."

"I didn't realize Dawson took on cancer patients. He seems to think there's so little hope for them."

Lawrence ran a hand across his chin. "I encouraged him to refer the woman to you and Dr. King, but he's determined to handle it himself. He'd like you to assist in the surgery."

Gerald cocked his head. "Did he say that?"

The younger doctor scuffed his shoe across the tile floor. "I may have suggested the idea."

"Dawson doesn't require my help. He could perform a hysterectomy blindfolded. And besides—he has you."

Lawrence raked fingers through his hair. "I'm not certain the patient even requires an operation in this case. I've been reading your studies—"

Gerald held up a hand. "I'm not interfering with one of Dawson's patients."

"You don't need to intervene, just observe. It's all I ask. You could send Dr. King, if you prefer."

The last thing Gerald needed was a direct confrontation with Emil, but he certainly couldn't allow Robert to go in his stead. His impulsive partner would likely get them both banned from the hospital. "Fine, I'll observe." Gerald let his head fall back, gazing up at the ceiling. "When?"

"He's already begun, I'm afraid. I'd hoped to find you earlier. It's in the surgical amphitheater, I'm heading over there now if you'd care to accompany me."

Gerald jerked back to attention. "The amphitheater? I didn't know repairs had been completed." The cavernous surgical hall had taken the brunt of the damage during the earthquake.

"It's better than ever. And almost every medical student will be in attendance."

Gerald's stomach fell to his knees. Dr. Dawson with an audience? Suddenly the earthquake seemed like a walk in the park. He fell silent as he followed Lawrence down two floors to the surgical wing.

The double doors opened into an expansive space. Dawson stood center stage, wielding the scalpel, several nurses at the ready. The pungent scent of ether permeated the room as the anesthetist administered drops to the cone covering the patient's nose and mouth. Students lined the gleaming wooden risers, leaning over the rails with attention focused on the scene below. Light poured in through the glass atrium, rendering the central pendulum light practically unnecessary.

Gerald swallowed. He'd never liked performing surgery in front of a crowd.

Dawson glanced up, his hands obscured within the patient's abdomen. "So nice of you gentlemen to join us." His bushy brows pulled low over his spectacles. "I informed the students," he lifted his voice until it boomed through the open hall, "we would have a premier cancer specialist gracing our presence. I'm glad to see you didn't disappoint."

The hairs on Gerald's arms rose as his gaze roamed the upper reaches of the surgical theater, every chair occupied. The energy in the room seemed akin to a prizefight.

Dawson cleared his throat. "I was just saying how *some* doctors prefer using energy and radiation to treat their patients." He chuckled. "They don't like getting their hands messy." He lifted his blood-stained hands into view. "Isn't that right, Dr. Larkspur?"

Acid boiled in Gerald's stomach. "Not at all, Dr. Dawson." He stepped to the washbasin. "X-ray technology doesn't replace surgery. But when surgery and radiation are used in cooperation, it may prove to be the best treatment for many types of cancer. X-rays can reach into the depths of the human tissues and cells—where cancer begins."

Gerald turned his back and ran the cake of soap between his fingers, the lesion stinging like he'd driven a needle through his palm. He gritted his jaw, swiping suds up both wrists.

Dawson's voice echoed through the room, bouncing off the atrium above. "The only cure for cancer is to cut it out. Every time. You can't cure cancer with X-rays any more than you can clean a muddy floor by shining a light on it."

As Dawson continued his lecture, the young Miss Fitzpatrick appeared at Gerald's elbow, a clean surgical apron in her hands. She leaned forward, her voice soft. "Isn't this exciting? I can't believe I'm assisting in the first amphitheater operation since the quake. And with Dr. Dawson, too."

Gerald ducked so she could pull the apron over his head. "You must have impressed him. He doesn't often invite student nurses."

Her cheeks flushed. "My instructor said so, too. I hope it's not because of my father."

Dr. Lawrence came up beside Gerald and held out his arms for an apron. He leaned close to Gerald's ear. "She's Dr. Fitzpatrick's daughter." He turned, allowing the young woman to fasten the garment behind his back. "Quite capable."

Fitzpatrick—head of the hospital finance committee. Sweat broke out along Gerald's back. *God, I'm certain You know what You're doing, but I'm at a loss.* He dried his hands on the clean apron.

The gallery buzzed with conversations. Several students clutched cigars and pipes, elbows propped on the rails, smoke curling up toward the windows.

Dr. Dawson leaned over his patient, clamping the round ligament in preparation to sever its hold on the offending organ. He lifted his voice. "Dr. Larkspur, why don't you come and join me? How long has it been since you've done one of these?"

Gerald pushed down his irritation. Dawson knew surgery wasn't his specialty. He'd done his share, regardless. He stepped to the doctor's side.

"Do you want the scalpel?" Dawson smirked. "Or would you prefer to hold the clamps?"

The room rippled with soft laughter.

"I didn't come to steal your thunder, Dr. Dawson. Why don't you let your talented protégé take point on this one? I'm comfortable observing and offering advice, should you require it."

The man huffed, his white whiskers pulled downward into a scowl. "Unlikely." He cast a dismissive glance at Lawrence. "You don't mind if Larkspur takes over, do you?"

The younger doctor glanced up, his eyes widening. "No, sir. Of course not. I'd be pleased to watch Dr. Larkspur work."

Dawson's lip curled. He slammed the metal tool down against the tray and stepped back. "Larkspur, you heard the man. Impress us with your expertise. Dr. Lawrence will assist you."

Cold fingers clambered up Gerald's spine. He stepped forward and surveyed the surgery in process. *Lord, guide my hands.* Thankfully, much of the work was already complete. He swiveled toward the tray.

"I'll get it for you, Doctor." Miss Fitzpatrick bobbed her head.

"Of course." Gerald waved Lawrence closer. "Doctor, will you take the clamps?"

Dr. Lawrence nodded, beads of sweat already appearing on his lined brow. He grasped the instruments with a grimace. "Ready."

Gerald's mouth dried as the student placed the scalpel in his right palm. Within a few minutes, the room seemed to fade, the students vanishing in the background as Gerald focused on the surgical procedure. He and Lawrence worked in concert, few words passing between them.

Dr. Dawson cleared his throat. "Gentlemen, may I remind you this is a teaching institution? Our future physicians will not learn unless you explain and demonstrate your glorious technique."

Gerald tipped his head back, eyeing the lines of students peering down at him like rows upon rows of hungry pigeons. Had he been like them? He wiped his hands on a towel and gestured to the open cavity. "As you can see, Dr. Lawrence is securing the posterior artery." The students scribbled in tiny notepads as he explained the past few steps of the procedure in detail. He lifted a hand, using his spread fingers and palm as a demonstration on how to locate the artery.

Emil's eyes narrowed as he stared at Gerald's extended hand.

A prickle raced down Gerald's neck. He clamped his palm shut and drew it to his chest. "I—I think we can continue now." He selected a scalpel without waiting for Miss Fitzpatrick, the cool metal handle pressing against the tender skin.

Dawson folded both arms across his chest, a smile toying at his lips. "Would you like me to take over, Dr. Larkspur?"

24

*F*or the fourth night in a row Ruby stared at the ceiling, her mind consumed by images of Gerald at the hospital—treating his patients, comforting the families, supporting her brother. She stirred, the weight of the blankets pressing her into the mattress. *How can I be falling in love again? I didn't want this, God.* She tossed the covers off, a chill rushing to take their place. She preferred the cold to the stifling bulk.

During the weeks since Dee passed, each day blurred into the next. Avoiding Gerald had become Ruby's primary occupation—an impossible task, considering they shared both a home and a workplace. During the daytime hours, she occupied herself serving at either the hospital or with Abby at the refugee camps. At night, she fell into bed so exhausted, her thoughts should have been unable to disturb her sleep.

In the next bed, Abby breathed slowly, the quiet rhythm of uninterrupted sleep.

Ruby rolled to her side, pulling both knees up to her chest and studying the single beam of moonlight piercing through the narrow opening in the draperies. Dee's death left a similar gap in Ruby's heart. Was she cut out for this line of work? Papa's practice had been all about fractures and colds, gout and rheumatism. Her brother's ambitions had taken them places their father never dreamed possible.

Ruby swung her feet to the floor and stood. She gathered her dressing gown, draping it around her shoulders. Sleep wasn't coming anytime soon, and she didn't want to spend another moment analyzing her life. Tiptoeing to the shelf, Ruby retrieved the portable writing desk and pushed the drapes back far enough to flood a corner of the room with moonlight.

Otto lifted his head from the basket and yawned. The dog thumped his tail three times before lowering his chin to the cushion.

A book rested on the wine-colored chair by the window. Ruby picked up the novel before sitting. *Jack London, again.* Abby's devotion to adventure stories amused her. Ruby's sisters had always read romances, and Ruby preferred classic literature. She flipped through the pages, pausing on an illustration of a snow-covered forest. She slid her finger down the lines of a particularly lovely tree.

Ruby set the opened book on top of her lap desk and rested her head against the wingback chair. The whole Larkspur/Fischer family reminded her of trees—standing tall in the face of storms and adversity. Their shared experiences of pain and loss in the past year drew them closer together. Her mind wandered over each member of the family—Clara, Herman, Mae, Abby—even little Davy. Strong trees bending in the wind, but not breaking under the strain. And Gerald stood tall, the heart of the forest around which the others gathered.

She touched her lips, the memory of his kiss flooding back. Only a fool would deny herself the love of such a man—one who made her weak in the knees and also demonstrated enduring strength. Ruby pushed a hand against her chest as memories of Charlie drifted through her thoughts. Gerald might be the epitome of steadfastness, but he couldn't offer her guarantees about the future. She wouldn't survive losing love a second time.

Abby stirred under the covers, murmuring in her sleep.

Ruby gazed at the picture of the tree, an idea tickling in the back of her mind. She set the book to one side and drew out a sheet of stationery and a pencil. For a moment, she touched the writing instrument to her chin, staring at the white page and letting her imagination run wild.

She lowered the lead to the paper and sketched out a basic form of a wedding gown with simple, long lines. She added flowing sleeves dropping to a point well below the figure's hands. Imagination drove her fingers—vines winding around the waist and lifting leaves up over the bodice, clusters of grapes peeking out from under the foliage. Her heart skipped. The petticoat could be done in lace—tatted with a leaf design. She'd leave an open front panel so the underskirt would show through, emphasizing Abby's lovely figure.

Ruby paused, holding the drawing at arm's length and admiring it. The first rays of dawn filtered in the window, as if radiating its approval.

❧

Gerald flipped the book's page, grimacing at a graphic description of the war-torn scene, thankful he'd never been forced to serve on a battlefield. The surgeon in the story, stymied by the lack of medicines and tools, too frequently resorted to the bone saw. A cold sweat washed over Gerald, remembering an amputation he'd performed in the chaos following the earthquake. His hand trembled, eyes no longer able to focus on the words. He'd never seen the patient again, didn't know whether he'd lived or died. With a grunt, Gerald tossed the book to the bedspread and wiped the perspiration from his forehead.

He glanced at the window, the growing light a relief. He climbed from bed and dressed quickly. Hurrying down the steps, he greeted his mother and Clara in the kitchen, the heady smells of breakfast tempting his stomach.

His mother smiled, patting his arm. "We have hardly seen you in days, Gerald. I hope you can sit and visit with the family this morning—Robert and Herman are already in the dining room."

He paused, enticed by the platter of fried eggs and shoestring potatoes. "Actually, I planned to sneak one of your donuts and dash over to the hospital. I need to get an early start."

Clara frowned. "Honestly, Gerald. I don't know how you stay in such good health always eating on the run like you do. It can't be beneficial for your digestion."

His mother's eyes narrowed. "Of course it isn't." She handed him the serving dish and jerked her chin toward the dining room. "Now go sit down, Gerald. Clara and Herman are leaving for San Jose tomorrow. We need to enjoy their company while we can."

A cloud settled over him as he frowned at the womenfolk cluttering his kitchen. Whose house was this, anyway? Shouldn't a man be allowed to eat as he chose? He stared at his mother's back searching for an appropriate reply, but the tidy bow on her apron rendered no clues.

Footsteps on the rear stairs drew his attention.

Ruby descended into the room, a light dancing in her blue eyes.

Gerald's mind went blank, all words vanishing. A wave of warmth rushed over him as he felt again the touch of her head against his shoulder from the evening in the garden. He'd had trouble forgetting the sensation.

She blushed, as if able to read his thoughts. "Good morning." She hurried to join the other women. "I'm afraid I overslept. What can I do to help?"

Gerald swallowed. Before he could clear his mind, his imagination latched onto the image of Ruby's red hair spilling over a pillow.

"Gerald." His mother pursed her lips. "The tray?"

He glanced down to the forgotten food. "Oh, yes." He turned, momentarily at a loss as to where the dining room lay. Fortunately, his feet remembered.

Robert nodded at Gerald as he entered. "You look well this morning. And it appears you've been put to work."

Herman lowered the newspaper until his bushy chin came into view.

Gerald set the platter on the table. "I informed the ladies I needed to get straight to the hospital, but apparently I've been overruled."

Robert chuckled. "There's no need, anyhow. Dr. Lawrence is covering for us today. Or have you forgotten?"

Sinking into a chair, Gerald scowled. "I don't want Lawrence tampering with my work."

His partner leaned forward. "We agreed, yesterday. We're taking Abby and Ruby out driving."

Gerald's stomach sank. "No—did I say that?"

Robert grinned. "You did. An afternoon diversion."

"I didn't mean today. I just meant—"

"Driving? Today?" Ruby stood in the doorway, clutching a plate heaped with biscuits. Her face paled.

Robert nodded. "We all need a rest. And I should get my country girl out to the fresh air before she rethinks accepting my proposal and follows her family back to the farm."

"I'm not rethinking anything, silly." Abby stepped into the room with a laugh. "But a day out sounds heavenly. Let's do it. Please, Ruby."

"Gerald, I spoke to Lawrence before leaving last night. You don't need to return until the board meeting Monday morning." Robert adjusted his tie, pulling at the stiff collar. "I'll cover rounds this evening. I'm growing accustomed to the night shift, anyway."

Gerald leaned back against the chair. "The board meeting. I'd forgotten." Too many distractions lately.

Ruby placed the biscuits by his plate, the warm fragrance filling the air. "If you need to prepare—"

"No." Robert lifted his hand. "He's already prepared. The notes have sat on his desk for a week. He's not weaseling out of this, Ruby."

A burning sensation tickled at Gerald's throat. As Ruby took the seat across from him, he softened. Why fight it? A day out with Ruby *would* be the perfect diversion. Just because she'd refused him didn't mean he couldn't admire her from afar. His heart refused to be diverted no matter his best effort. He reached for the newspaper Herman had set aside.

Abby pulled a piece of stationery from her pocket. "Ruby, did you draw this?"

A shy smile graced the young widow's face. "It depends. Do you like it?"

Abby sank into the chair beside Gerald, her brown eyes round. "I adore it. I've never seen anything more beautiful."

Ruby clasped her hands together. "I'm so glad. I was thinking about your gown last night and it came to me—you need something that speaks of your heart."

Robert craned his neck. "Do we get to see this amazing Ruby original?"

Abby returned the drawing to her pocket. "Of course not. The menfolk cannot view the gown before the wedding."

Robert unfolded his napkin. "It's not a gown, it's a sketch." He glanced at Gerald. "Help me out."

As Mother and Clara joined them, Gerald shook his head. "Don't look to me for assistance, Robert. I don't make any decisions around here. But your sister has a gift for beauty . . ." he paused, his mouth dry, ". . . for style. I mean style. So, I would—I would trust her."

Ruby's eyes widened as his words came to a stumbling halt.

Gerald hoisted the newspaper in front of his face, locking his gaze on the headlines. *I need coffee before I say anything more ridiculous.*

The hush lasted until Herman cleared his throat. "Perhaps I should ask the blessing, *ja?*"

Folding the paper in his lap, Gerald glanced at Ruby, trying to read her expression before she bowed her head. *What is she thinking?* Her brother might know. Gerald's gaze shifted across the table.

Robert stared back, brows drawn low over his dark eyes.

Gerald ducked his head to join the prayer. He owed Robert a confession, but a little heavenly supplication might clear the path. Considering the expression on his friend's face, Gerald would need all the help he could muster.

25

Ruby clutched the steering wheel with one hand, the other on the gearshift. The car trundled along the dirt lane no faster than a lame mule. "There's a curve up ahead."

Gerald chuckled. "You know what to do."

"Panic?"

"Turn the wheel gently in the direction you want to go. You act as if you haven't done this before."

"Should I slow down?" Ruby darted a quick look at her instructor, thankful Robert and Abby had stayed behind in the meadow. She didn't need the humiliation of an audience. Obviously, she was a slow learner.

He grinned. "If you slacken the pace any further, we'll stop."

Ruby faced forward, her elbows jutting to each side like a tightrope walker gripping a balance pole. "How do I know what's beyond the bend?"

"We never do. You're doing fine."

The car motored around the curve, a flock of sparrows rising from the dust and chattering in protest. Ruby relaxed, the tension easing from her arms and shoulders. "Not too bad."

"And a straight path before you." Gerald leaned back in the seat and braced one foot up on the rail. "Mrs. Ruby Marshall, lady motorist."

Ruby allowed a small smile to creep to her lips. "If only my sister Elizabeth could see me now. She's the forward-thinking one of the family—a suffragist."

"She'll be here in November, or so Robert tells me."

Ruby loosened her grip on the wooden circle. "I can't imagine what your house will be like with three extra women underfoot."

Gerald shrugged his shoulders. "What's a few more? We'll shuffle the bedrooms again. Robert is moving into the room Abby's parents were using. I'll bunk in the study, perhaps. Your sister and cousin can share my room, and we'll place your mother with mine." He winked. "Could be interesting."

Ruby eyed the hill looming ahead. "And after the ceremony?"

"I imagine Robert and Abby will plan a wedding trip." He tipped his derby back along his head. "We'll readjust when they return. I suppose the newlyweds can have my room, and I can take the small spare room. Assuming the guests have departed by then."

Ruby sighed. "It seems a shame to push you out of your bedroom—you own the house, after all."

"Next thing you know, I'll be sleeping under the grape arbor."

"I should begin looking for my own place." She glanced at the controls.

He turned to her, brows ruffled. "I didn't mean that."

"No one expects you to house your partner's sister forever."

"You're much more than that." His fingers brushed her knee.

The sensation jolted through her like electricity. "I—I know. Hence the difficulty." The auto slowed as it climbed the steep grade. Ruby opened the throttle further to compensate.

"I'm not sure I understand."

Ruby chewed on her lower lip, fighting to concentrate on the vehicle's speed. "It isn't proper for us to continue sharing a home when we're both unmarried." A wave of heat climbed her neck.

He scooted closer along the seat. "Tell it to Robert and Abby."

She shot him a dirty look. "I have. But at least they're rectifying the situation."

His eyes widened.

Ruby's stomach churned. She shouldn't have said such a thing—it implied far more than she intended. The engine sputtered, the pace falling off. She frowned. "What's happening?"

He braced a hand against the seat. "Give it more gasoline."

"I am." She pressed hard against the pedal. The engine wheezed and fell silent. The car rolled to a standstill on the steep incline before easing backward. "No!"

"Brake!" Gerald jerked forward, gesturing to the controls. "Use the brake!"

After a moment of indecision, she pressed her boot down on the pedal, halting their descent. "Why did the motor stop?"

"It's gravity. Sometimes on steep hills the engine starves for fuel."

She clutched the wheel, her foot still jamming the pedal to the floor. "What do we do?"

"Back down the road, turn around, and take the hill in reverse."

"Back down—reverse up? Are you jesting?"

"Would you rather I take over?"

Ruby gritted her teeth. "I'd rather walk." As Gerald moved to get out, she grasped his arm. "No. I'll do it." She blew out a long, shaky breath. "Horses don't have to back up steep inclines."

Gerald chuckled. "Good luck getting one to try."

She pursed her lips. "San Francisco is all hills. Why does this never happen to you?"

He leaned against the seat, hooking an elbow across the back. "It did at first. I learned to keep the tank full. But it was a long drive out here. I brought an extra gas can, but it's in the meadow with our other things. I didn't think we'd need it until the return trip. Now, ease off the brake."

She glanced over her shoulder. "Sure. Roll down a hill backward. Why not?"

Gerald chuckled. "There's your sense of adventure. It'll be fun."

The vehicle crept backward, the brakes squealing like a snared rabbit. Keeping her chin on her right shoulder, she gazed behind them, thankful for quiet, country roads. *What if this had happened in town?*

"Ease off the brake a little more. Let's not wear them out."

Ruby did as she was told, jerking the wheel side to side as she acclimated to the reverse steering. The tires zigzagged, jostling over the rutted dirt path.

"Steady now." He added his hand to the wheel, on top of hers.

The car rolled to a stop at the bottom of the hill. She faced forward. "Thank God."

"Yes, indeed. And you did pretty well yourself." He released the steering and grinned.

Ruby couldn't help but smile. "I did, didn't I? I kept it under control."

"Certainly. Unfortunately, it's only half the battle. Do you want to take it up?" He jerked a thumb toward the waiting grade.

No, not really. She straightened the scarf she'd tied over her hat. "What do I do?"

Gerald guided her through the motions of turning the Ford around and lining up with the back bumper to the hill. "Now pull forward a ways, you'll need momentum. You don't want to start climbing from a standstill."

"I don't wish to start at all, but whatever you say, Doctor." Ruby ignored his chortling as she revved the motor and depressed the Ford's reverse pedal. The automobile crept backward.

He frowned. "You'll need more velocity, or we'll just sail down again."

Ruby moistened her lips. She didn't like driving fast in the forward direction. Now he wanted her to speed in reverse? And uphill? She pressed on the throttle. The breeze whipped the ends of her scarf across the rail as they careened up the road. After a few yards, the pace slowed and no matter how hard she pushed the pedal, the car crept along. She clutched the controls. "Come on, sweetie. You can do it."

Gerald leaned against the seat, an insufferable smirk on his face as the automobile teetered to a halt. "I warned you, you need more forward momentum."

"Don't you mean backward momentum?" She brushed the gauzy fabric back into place and eased down the hill a second time, almost relieved to be facing forward, though traveling the wrong direction.

"Had enough?"

"Absolutely not." Steam built in Ruby's chest. She would get this automobile up this rise, even if she were forced to hop out and push. She rolled farther along the flat ground to allow for a better run and raced the motor. Bracing one arm over the seat, she half-turned and glared at her earthen nemesis. "We will ascend the mountain or perish in the attempt."

Gerald laughed. "I hope we have some fuel left when you're finished conquering the topography."

Ruby set her jaw and jammed the automobile into gear. The car lurched, gravel scattering in all directions. The Ford surged up the incline as she kept a stranglehold on the wheel. Though the pace diminished as the engine struggled, this time the vehicle reached the top. She stopped at the summit and grinned. "I did it. I backed up a hill."

"And what a view." Gerald gazed across the valley. "Was it worth the effort?"

She stared out at the scenery, heart taking flight. The green hills dotted with farms and meadows stole her imagination. "It's lovely."

"Lovely." He smiled her direction. "You're a skilled driver now. You can do everything but change a tire."

Ruby swallowed, resisting his compliments. "Perhaps we should save the tire lesson for another day? Robert and Abby will be getting worried. We left them by the pond over an hour ago."

"I daresay they can entertain themselves."

"Yes." She shook her head. "Exactly my fear."

"You seem so determined to maintain their honor. I think you underestimate their self-control. Robert and Abby have behaved admirably under the circumstances."

"I've been married before. I know what they're facing. I want them to begin this marriage on the right foot."

He raised his hands, clad in leather driving gloves. "I have nothing on you there."

Ruby ducked her chin. Why did she keep stumbling into awkward conversations with this man? No sense in pointing out the obvious. Not to mention reminding him of what they both lacked. Her heart skipped as she remembered seeing him in the garden in thin cotton union suit and trousers, suspenders hanging loose at his sides. Ruby gripped the wheel. There was more than one reason to hasten back to the others. Perhaps they weren't the only ones requiring a chaperone. "Which way to the pond?"

"You're not going to like the answer."

She shot him a withering glance. "Down the hill?"

He nodded, a dimple showing in one cheek. "But aren't you glad you learned out here instead of in the city?"

Ruby shifted the car into gear and bumped back down the slope as scattered thoughts bounced through her mind. Why did she keep pushing Gerald away? She'd managed to take control of her fear of automobiles, couldn't she do the same with love? She darted another glance at him, his shoulders back and arms folded across his ribs. Her heart bobbled. How she would like to run a hand along his shoulder, touch her cheek to his. Ruby swung her face forward, reminding herself to keep her eyes on the road. She needed to make some decisions, but perhaps it would be best to do so when she wasn't behind the wheel of an unpredictable automobile.

&

Gerald forced himself back against the upholstered seat, fighting to keep his proud grin under wraps. He'd known what she would face on the steep grade, but hadn't expected her to dig in and master the skill so quickly. The first time he'd stalled on a hill, it'd felt as if Mexican jumping beans had taken up residency in his stomach. And he hadn't been saddled with Ruby's inordinate fear of automobiles.

The breeze toyed with the tails of Ruby's scarf, sending them fluttering like fall leaves. She'd finally gained enough courage to drive at a decent speed. They were probably even pushing twenty-five miles per hour.

He leaned back. "I could get used to having my own chauffeur."

She laughed, the sound carrying above the clattering engine. "I doubt there are many female chauffeurs."

"Much more enjoyable this way, I do believe." He stopped short of complimenting her again. *Mustn't look like a drooling fool.*

She shifted her eyes forward, lifting one hand from the wheel to shade her brow. "I see Robert over by the edge of the wood, but where's Abby?"

He gestured to the trees as Ruby parked the car. "I believe she's climbed up one of those."

Ruby's jaw dropped. "In her best skirt? Whatever for?"

Gerald jumped out and circled around to her side. "Perhaps they're reenacting their first meeting."

Ruby stepped out of the automobile, shaking out her long duster coat. "I can't say as I quite understand her, though I am trying. She's a lovely girl, if a mite unconventional."

"That's my cousin, all right."

"She was tree-climbing when they met?" Ruby's nose wrinkled.

Gerald leaned against the vehicle. "There are probably more memorable first meetings." He ran a hand across his chin. "How did you meet your husband?"

She unfastened her coat and slid her arms free, folding it over her elbow. "In grammar school."

"So young?" No wonder she wasn't eager to begin again.

"I suppose it was no more dignified than Abby's tree climbing." Ruby smiled. "Charlie insulted my cousin, so I cuffed him across the cheek and told him to straighten up."

Gerald stepped back. "Remind me never to get on your bad side. Did he do as you commanded?"

She met his gaze, her blue eyes distant. "Charlie always did what I asked." Her lips turned downward. "Even when I insisted he propose. The only time he didn't was when he bought that crazy horse."

Gerald hesitated for a moment before wrapping an arm around her back and drawing her close. Perhaps his actions would drive away her sad memories.

Ruby laid her head against his chest. Her warm breath teased his neck, her voice soft. "What about you? Would you always say yes to me?"

Gerald paused, sensing the test in her words. *Could he?* He shook his head, her hat's feathered plume tickling his nose. "Sorry, dear. I only do as God commands."

26

Gerald closed the study door, resting his hand against the oak panel. He stared at the swirls in the grain, not wishing to confront the scowl on his friend's face.

"I think you owe me an explanation." Robert's deep voice echoed from across the room. "Is there something going on between you and my sister? At first, I told Abby she was imagining things. After today, I'm less certain. Not only the bizarre comment at breakfast, but you were an hour late coming back from your driving lesson."

Gerald edged to the right, putting the desk between them. As the senior partner, he was unaccustomed to justifying his actions to the younger man. "I didn't intend for anything—I mean, I never planned . . ."

Robert raised a brow.

Gerald pressed knuckles to his forehead to steady his thoughts. "When your sister arrived in San Francisco, I didn't anticipate anything developing between us."

Flattening his palms on the desktop, Robert leaned forward. "When did it change?"

Gerald sank into the swivel chair. "I'm not certain."

"Does she feel the same toward you?"

"Again, I'm not certain. At times she seems to." Gerald's skin crawled. He'd never been comfortable discussing his personal life, and now he was doing it with Ruby's brother. "But I think something is preventing her."

"I can imagine several 'somethings.'" Robert narrowed his eyes. "Shall I list them for you?"

Gerald rose from the seat and wandered to the window. "I realize she's uncomfortable with our housing situation."

"You are slow-witted about these things, aren't you? Small wonder you're still a bachelor." Robert ran a hand through his dark hair. "You never knew Charlie Marshall, but he was practically an older brother to me. A big, quiet fellow who followed Ruby around like Otto does now."

Gerald gazed through the glass to the back yard. Ruby crouched next to Abby, working in the garden, a giant sun hat obscuring her face. "I don't wish to replace Charlie."

"Not much chance—you're nothing like him. Let's see, what else? You're her boss. You're *my* partner, not to mention my friend." Robert crossed the room, dropping into an upholstered chair. "Highly unprofessional. She's also a guest in your home. And did I fail to point out—my sister? Those should be enough reasons to stay clear."

Gerald set his jaw. "I seem to remember having a similar conversation with you a few months back about Abby. What I don't remember is you abiding by my wishes."

"God had other ideas."

"Have you considered this might be His will, as well?"

"His will or yours?" Robert clamped both hands on the armrests.

Heat gathered under Gerald's collar. "I've done nothing untoward in regard to Ruby. I have no regrets beyond failing to conduct this conversation with you beforehand. As I said, it's taken me as much by surprise as it has you." He leaned back against the windowsill. "Robert, this may all come to naught. I might be smitten—honestly, who wouldn't be? Ruby is beautiful, intelligent, cultured, and compassionate. But she obviously has too many barriers in place to entertain the notion. And frankly even if she hadn't, I can't imagine she'd choose me. I promise you—I will stand aside, unless she requests otherwise."

Robert's nose wrinkled. "I suppose she could do worse than you."

"Thanks a lot."

His friend joined him at the window. "I was so consumed with myself, I didn't even see what was happening. I haven't been a good brother." He cast a sideways glance at Gerald. "Or friend."

Gerald jammed hands into his pockets. "No one can blame you. I never realized how much a woman could occupy one's thoughts."

Robert cleared his throat, a low growling sound. "Until I get used to the concept, you might be advised to keep those thoughts under lock and key."

Gerald's gaze remained fixed on Ruby as she straightened and brushed both hands down her skirt. He grunted. "You have no idea."

A wrinkle wandered across his friend's brow. "I might. That's what bothers me."

❧

The earthy scent of turned soil tickled Ruby's sinuses. She pressed the back of her hand against her nose. "Your talent for gardening is far beyond mine."

Abby kneeled on the ground, elbow-deep in the muck as she settled the roots in their new home. "Plants are straightforward—you meet their basic needs and they flourish. I only wish people were as simple."

"But people can express their needs. Talk out their problems." Ruby eyed the dirt under her fingernails. "Plants just droop and wither."

The younger woman pressed the loam into place. "I've never been skilled at conversation. It's my greatest weakness."

Ruby reached for the gardening fork. "You observe. Nothing escapes you."

"But you can put people at ease with a word. Everyone you meet becomes an admirer." Abby scooped up the trowel and bucket, moving along the bedding row to another hole. "My sister had the gift as well." She shooed Otto away from where he helped with the digging, his paddle paws working overtime.

Ruby trailed behind, admiring Abby's tender treatment of the vegetation. She'd rather dig her hands into a pile of silk brocade. "I think my forward manner is disconcerting to some."

"Not true. My friend Patrick is quite taken with you. He asked if I might arrange for him to see you again."

"Patrick?" Ruby stiffened. "Why?" The word escaped like a strangled yelp.

"Why do you think?" Abby smiled, sweeping a lock of hair from her eyes with the back of her hand.

"I've never—I've never given him any reason to believe I'd be interested."

"You didn't need to. He took one look at you and fell in love."

"Don't jest about such things. He couldn't possibly be in love with me." Ruby swallowed, her mouth suddenly as dry as day-old toast.

Abby glanced up, squinting into the sunlight. "And why ever not? You're lovely, accomplished, caring. You gave up your comfortable life in Sacramento to come work in a disaster area. You spend countless hours in the hospital with Robert and Gerald and their patients. You're exactly the kind of woman Patrick admires."

Ruby clenched her dirt-stained hands. "Tell him no. Absolutely not. I'm far too busy for social calls."

"He's not some social climber, you know. He's a minister, and he's devoted to the city's disenfranchised. I know he appears a bit silly sometimes, but he's a good man."

"I've already had a good man. I'm not seeking a replacement." Ruby glanced toward the house. *And if I were, Patrick's not the one I'd choose.*

Abby stood, casting her tools aside. "I'm sorry—I didn't mean to suggest you were. If you want me to dissuade him, I will. But won't you at least consider it?"

Ruby twisted the hem of her apron. "It would be dishonest to encourage his advances. My heart belongs to another."

"Your late husband." Abby nodded and touched Ruby's sleeve. "I understand. He'd be honored by your devotion. If something happened to Robert, I'm certain I'd feel the same."

Ruby stepped back. *Yes, my husband.* A chill raced across her skin. She swallowed. "I'm going inside to clean up. I'd like to start piecing your gown today while daylight remains."

Her friend sighed. "Sewing—an additional area where I'm lacking in skills. If you don't mind, I'll stay out here and keep working."

Ruby nodded and turned toward the house. A few moments to gather her thoughts would be welcome.

A familiar figure darkened one of the windows.

A fresh wave of prickles lifted the hairs on her neck. She hurried through the back door and paused at the sink to wash the dirt from her hands. Tremors tortured her insides. Why did she postpone making a decision about Gerald? She needed to either discourage him or choose to set aside her misgivings. She could no longer deny her feelings toward the man. Love had blossomed, like one of Abby's roses. But, was it enough?

Ruby returned to the room she shared with Abby, retrieved the parcel of fabric from the wardrobe, and sank down on the edge of the bed. She ran her fingers across the smooth silk. Should she risk her heart again? God wouldn't take a second husband from her. Would He? Ruby pressed the delicate fabric to her chest.

She closed her eyes and pictured herself in the automobile, her hands gripping the wooden wheel—a fork in the road ahead. If she turned to the right, Gerald waited, a tender smile and arms outstretched. If she steered to the left, a deserted lane stretched into the distance. Her heart pounded as she slowed to a stop between the two choices.

Right: Gerald, love, future.

Left: Alone and empty, forever.

The choice seemed obvious, so why did her stomach tighten every time she considered it? Ruby stood and shook out the long strip of fabric, laying it across the bed. She retrieved the lace and added the layer atop the silk, relishing the beautiful combination of textures. Such a perfect image for a wedding—two different people joined together, creating something altogether new. The blending provided layers of depth and feeling never existing before. Ruby gathered the material into her arms, the silk spilling down her legs like a heavenly raiment.

She needed to overcome this fear, because her heart had already made its choice.

27

$\mathcal{L}$ate afternoon sunlight drifted in the long dining room windows, illuminating the chandelier's crystal prisms and bouncing along the table's surface. Ruby's hand trembled as she guided the shears through the fine silk. Cutting was always the most frightening part of sewing—no going back. She brushed away a loose thread. *But what good is uncut cloth?*

The light shimmered against the glossy material. Ruby leaned forward and repositioned her hand to make the second cut, her shadow falling across the table. She kept her focus even as soft footfalls sounded in the doorway.

"Well, look at you." Mae's voice broke the stillness. "Hard at work, as always. Don't you ever sit down?"

Ruby tried to smile—a dangerous venture with her lips clamped around three straight pins. She laid down the cutting implement and removed the pointed objects, jabbing them into the cushion. "You've heard what they say about idle hands."

A faint smile rearranged the lines surrounding the older woman's mouth. "The devil's workshop, yes. Not exactly how the Bible puts it, but probably true nonetheless." Mae wandered to Ruby's side, reaching out a hand to stroke the fabric. "Lovely silk. Where did you come by it?"

"Waterston Dressmakers over on Market Street. They had a nice selection—much better than we find in Sacramento. We stopped on the way home. Abby's chosen a design, now I'm eager to get started."

The older woman clucked her tongue. "So many new shops. It's as if the fires wiped the slate clean and everything is beginning anew."

"I suppose. Life returns—rises from the ashes."

Mae circled around to join Ruby, lifting the bundle of lace from where it lay draped across a chair. "Like in Isaiah, 'To give unto them beauty for ashes, the oil of joy for mourning, the garment of praise for the spirit of heaviness.' A perfect description for what has happened in our city—and in our family—during this past year. We still mourn, but this wedding brings great joy. And now you're making a garment of praise."

Ruby retrieved the shears, driving them through the delicate material, turning over Mae's words in her mind. "It seems odd sometimes how the two emotions—mourning and joy—can abide together."

Mae reached for a handful of pins. "God created us to be complex beings, made in His image. Our hearts are like a pantry overflowing with spices, ready to season our lives. Imagine how bland life would be minus their flavor."

"I could do without a few of the more bitter ones."

The elderly woman spread the lace, tracing its pattern with knobby fingertips. "Without the bitter, we wouldn't appreciate the sweet." She smiled. "And we'd all have tummy aches, like overindulgent toddlers."

Is that what I've done? Removed the flavor from my life? Ruby took a final snip and lifted the bodice section free, placing it with the other pieces. "I'm almost ready to begin stitching. I can't wait to see it finished."

"My treadle machine's a bit outdated, but it still manages even rows of stitches. Mrs. Fulsom of my quilting club has a new electric one." Mae helped her gather the scraps.

"I prefer the treadle. Thank you."

The study door swung open, Robert and Gerald chuckling together as they came her direction. Ruby smiled, their mirth a pleasant change from the tension she'd sensed sparking between the two men earlier.

Robert's attention settled on the fabric-strewn table. "Abby's dress?"

Ruby stepped in front of him. "She doesn't want you to see it. And the first rule of marriage is always honor your wife's wishes."

He lifted his hands. "I was only inquiring. Where is she?"

Mae smiled. "Where do you think?" She hitched a thumb over her shoulder, gesturing to the backyard.

"Well, since I can't see the gown, I suppose I'll go see the bride-to-be." Robert grinned and headed for the door.

Ruby fit her shears back into the sewing basket, nestling the pincushion among the scraps of leftover silk. Try as she might, she couldn't prevent her gaze from returning to Gerald. It seemed her stubborn heart was determined to move forward, whether or not she felt ready.

He leaned on one of the end chairs. "I don't imagine I should follow him, somehow."

"A wise choice, dear. Young couples need their space." Mae handed Ruby the lace bundle, her gaze jumping from Ruby's face to her son's. "In fact, I think it's high time I go as well. I must start dinner."

Warmth rushed to Ruby's cheeks. "Would you like any help?"

"No, no, dear. You have your hands full." She grinned at her son as she hurried past, her skirt rustling through the narrow doorway.

Gerald ran a hand over the back of his neck as the room fell silent. "Was it just me, or did that sound a little pointed?"

Ruby's hands trembled as she gathered the lace into her basket. "Perhaps." Now she'd decided to face her fears, she found herself at a loss. How did one express her desires to a man? She'd never faced this with Charlie. He'd just always been there, waiting. She glanced up from her sewing supplies, stunned to see Gerald's penetrating gaze upon her. Her mind raced, but her mouth refused to speak.

"I think I'll take a short walk before supper." He withdrew a step, his eyes questioning.

Otto stood and shook himself, hurrying over to Gerald's feet.

Ruby struggled to swallow, blocked by a lump in her throat. "I . . ." *Say it—"I'd like to join you."* Her knees quivered. As much as they were shaking, she wouldn't make it around the block. He'd be forced to carry her home. Her palms grew damp. "I'd better get started on this." She hoisted the basket to her hip. "Would you mind taking Otto with you?"

He nodded and disappeared down the hall.

The dog whined, looking up at Ruby with brown eyes. After a long moment, he turned and scampered after Gerald.

Ruby closed her eyes. She'd conquered her fear of automobiles by getting behind the wheel. Maybe she needed a few lessons in love. She'd corner Abby this evening.

⟞⟍

Gerald rubbed two fingers against his rough chin. He'd thought for a moment . . . *No, don't be ridiculous.* Her attention centered on her sewing project—not on him. He buttoned his jacket and headed down the hall to retrieve his hat. A change of scenery would help him mull over Robert's concerns.

The dog's toenails scrabbled against the wood floor as it followed at Gerald's heels.

Gerald retrieved his derby and slipped the lead around the dog's stocky neck, pausing to rub its soft ears before heading out the front door. He usually preferred to exit through the back and walk down the alley, but with Robert and Abby making moon-eyes at each other, he wasn't sure he could stand the envy eating at his insides.

He closed the gate and paced down the street, turning toward town. He'd honor the request not to go to the hospital today, but he hadn't agreed to stay at home either. Cold fingers wrapped around his heart. Since when did he feel uncomfortable in his own house?

He ran a hand across his vest front, twiddling the silver buttons between his finger and thumb. The discussion with Robert continued to bounce around in his thoughts. Every reason his friend had flung at him was valid. Gerald had no business pursuing Ruby. What had he told Robert all those months ago about love and professional decorum? He'd been such a pillar of wisdom before a certain redhead walked into his life. Now he was ready to cast every bit of his worldly knowledge to the wind. If God wanted him to be with Ruby, He'd clear the way. And if He didn't . . .

The dachshund tugged at the leash and whined. Gerald shook himself and picked up the pace. He wasn't prepared to entertain such an outcome. He turned on O'Farrell Street and headed downtown. The pounding of hammers rang through the air, like a relentless army of woodpeckers. He paused before the skeleton of a new office building and watched as a group of men unloaded a wagon filled with bricks. It never failed to astonish him how fast builders were assembling these structures. Just a few months ago, this part of the city had been a smoldering ruin.

"Quite a sight, isn't it?" A familiar voice drew Gerald's attention. Patrick Allison strode up the street toward him. "Dr. Larkspur, right?" The man shoved back a brown derby and grinned, light dancing in his green eyes.

Otto strained against the lead, craning his neck to sniff the newcomer.

"Yes." Gerald shook the reverend's hand. "And you're Reverend Allison, Abby's friend from the camps."

"Patrick—call me Patrick, please. I apologize for not introducing myself back at the Presidio, but it seemed more important to focus on calming Johnson and getting him out of your way."

Gerald tugged Otto back. "Yes, I appreciated your help with the situation."

Patrick glanced over the building site. "I came to check on some of my neighbors. The boss here has been hiring men as fast as I can send them down."

"It's good news. Maybe if we get them all working, the camps will empty out."

Patrick tipped his head back, gazing up at the ten-story structure, new windows glinting in the late afternoon sun. "As long as there's a place to go. Housing's as much of a problem as the jobs."

Gerald ran a hand along the lapel of his coat. "I'm disturbed about sanitation issues in those camps. We could end up with a major disease outbreak if people remain in such squalor."

The reverend shrugged, the shoulders of his brown jacket bouncing. "It's better conditions than many parts of the world. Or even some of the bigger cities. And the military is cracking down on cleanliness—at least in the camps they maintain. But if you have any suggestions for improvements, I'd be willing to help."

"I'm most concerned about Golden Gate Park and some of the smaller sites."

The clergyman folded his arms. "Red Cross is doing what they can, but I'm certain your expertise would be welcome. I could meet you over at Golden Gate on Monday if you'd like to look around. I have a few folks who would appreciate a medical visit, if you could spare the time."

Gerald contemplated the workload at the hospital. "I could come in the afternoon. Say two o'clock?"

A grin sprouted on the man's face, and he took a step closer. "Thank you." He grasped Gerald's hand and shook it with strength more akin to a bricklayer than a man of the cloth.

Gerald winced and tucked his hand into his pocket, fighting an urge to glance at his palm. Checking the status of the lesion had become an obsession.

Patrick clapped Gerald on the arm. "And will you be bringing your lovely nurse? Did she tell you about our visit to the Cliff House? I've never had as mesmerizing a dining companion."

"Mrs. Marshall? You dined with Ruby?" Gerald's chest tightened.

"Your cousin, Miss Fischer, invited me. I didn't think she'd agree to see me alone." He leaned his head toward Gerald and hitched his brow up a quarter inch. "But I've got young Abby putting in a kind word for me."

A rock wedged in Gerald's gut. He jerked back a step, overwhelmed by the urge to put some distance between this man and himself. "Mrs. Marshall is terribly busy." His voice lowered to a near growl on the last two words. "I don't believe she has much interest in social calls."

Patrick's smile didn't waver. "Doesn't hurt to ask, though. I'm certain she has plenty of demands on her time. I couldn't resist putting my bid in, if you know what I'm saying."

All too well. "I should return home."

Patrick glanced at the group of men cleaning up the worksite for the evening. "It must be nearly supper time."

This is your cue. Run. Gerald balled his fist, hidden in his pocket. He took two steps, and the dog jumped to its feet, tail wagging. "Reverend," Gerald swallowed, pushing down the internal argument raging in his gut, "why don't you come eat with us? We've got a houseful, but my mother always makes a copious amount of food."

"It wouldn't be proper to drop in unexpected on the ladies. But thanks for the offer. And please, call me Patrick."

A weight lifted from Gerald's shoulders. At least he'd done the right thing. "If you're certain."

"I don't wish to be any trouble. I'll just head back to the camp and see what I've got in the cabin."

Gerald's mouth dried. "*You're* staying in one of those shacks? Doesn't the church provide you with housing?"

Otto plopped back to the ground with a huff.

Patrick hooked his thumbs in the armholes of his vest. "There were two ministers at our church before the fires. It took quite a load of dynamite to bring the old building down. The firefighters told us it was necessary to protect the big homes on Van Ness." He tipped back his derby, his jaw twitching. "The elders—the same men who own those homes—they informed me they'd be keeping the senior pastor, only."

Gerald searched the man's face. *My house was spared. Two blocks from Van Ness.*

Patrick cleared his throat, glancing at the men removing the last of the bricks from the wagon. "I've got my own flock now. Ones who need more than a fancy building." His brows drew down, casting deep shadows around his eyes. "I decided it would be best to live amongst the people I serve."

A cool breeze swept down the cobblestone street, a crumpled newspaper bouncing along with the dead leaves. Gerald sighed. "You must come to dinner. Abby would never forgive me if I let you return to the camp without a decent meal."

"I eat fine, Doc. Half the time, those Red Cross ladies are hand delivering soup to my door. I keep telling them I require no special treatment."

Gerald grasped the man's shoulder. "Come along. I won't accept no for an answer." *I wish I could.*

"If you insist." A grin lit Patrick's face. "And will Mrs. Marshall be joining us?"

Gerald blew air out between his teeth. "I imagine so."

❧

The smell of roasting chicken and fresh-baked rolls permeated the farthest reaches of the house. Ruby turned from her discussion with Abby and hung the pinned-together skirt in the wardrobe, careful to brush out any wrinkles.

Abby plopped down on the edge of the bed. "You've changed your mind, then?"

Ruby lifted her sewing basket to the shelf. "I'm trying to keep myself open to the possibilities. But if I decide I'm ready to begin seeing someone, I need to know what to say—how to act. Charlie and I had been acquaintances since we were children. I never had to pretend with him."

Abby's brow wrinkled. "You shouldn't have to pretend with anyone."

Ruby closed the cabinet and strode to the dressing table, intent on fixing her hair before supper. Gerald wouldn't give her a second glance if she looked like yesterday's weed pile. "I don't mean 'pretend,' exactly. I wish to be interesting, entertaining. Not make a fool of myself."

A smile spread across Abby's freckled face. "Then you're speaking to the wrong person. I'm the queen of fools. I've never known what to say to anyone, much less to a man."

Ruby stared into the mirror, catching Abby's reflection over her own shoulder. "You do fine with Robert."

The young woman blushed. "I didn't do well at first—I lived in a perpetual state of tongue-tiedness."

Ruby reached for the hair oil and dribbled a few drops into her palms. "When did it change?"

Abby clutched a book to her chest. "It took a while. Eventually we'd both embarrassed ourselves enough times, and we got past the silliness." The corner of her mouth twitched. "I also learned he loved me as I already was—not for who I was trying to be."

Ruby ran the oil through her curls, smoothing the loose ones back into place, and teasing the style to new heights, eyeing the Gibson Girl portrait she'd propped up against her powder bowl. Gerald had already seen her worst. Maybe it was time to show him her best.

Abby kicked back onto the bed and flipped open her book. "I think Robert is free this weekend. Perhaps he and Patrick could escort us to the new art exhibit."

Ruby froze, her hands buried in her hair. *Patrick?* Her stomach dropped. Her mind had been so focused on Gerald, she'd completely forgotten about Patrick's request. She pulled her fingers free, knocking the pompadour frame askew. "Let's not rush, Abby. I—I just wanted to ask your opinion. I didn't mean to suggest I was prepared to begin entertaining callers."

Abby spoke from behind the covers of the book. "My opinion is—you're ready. And Patrick is perfect for you."

Ruby stared at her reflection, the curls springing up like the fur of a frightened alley cat. "Please, don't say anything to encourage him."

"I won't. But it won't stop me from encouraging you."

28

Gerald glanced around the hall, conscious of Patrick lingering in the doorway behind him. "Come on in. Let me take your hat."

Patrick swept off his derby and clutched it to his stomach. "Are you sure the family won't mind me showing up like this?"

"Positive. They'll be delighted." Gerald ignored the heaviness in his chest at the thought of Ruby greeting the eager Irishman.

The dog rushed up the stairs, likely in search of Ruby. Gerald wished he could follow.

His mother approached from the kitchen. "Supper will be on the table in a heartbeat. I'm just dishing out the vegetables." Her eyes widened at the sight of their guest. She quickly undid the strings of her soiled apron.

"Mother, I hope you don't mind, but I ran into a . . . a friend." He settled a hand on the man's shoulder. "This is—"

"Goodness, Gerald, I know who he is. Patrick Allison—the hero of the refugee camps. The women from the Ladies' Aid never cease singing his praises." She ran quick fingers across her hair and collar. "We're honored to welcome you to our home, Reverend Allison." Her cheeks pinked.

Was his mother *primping*? Gerald tilted his head, his jaw falling open.

"Mrs. Larkspur." Patrick smiled and accepted her offered hand. "I apologize for dropping in unannounced. Your son is quite generous."

"Nonsense." Gerald's mother frowned. "I'd have been vexed with him if he didn't invite you. I always cook plenty. With all the work you've done on behalf of this city, I would never forgive myself if I knew you were going hungry."

Patrick laughed and patted his vest front. "I rarely go without. Your Ladies' Aid always ensures I'm well cared for." He glanced around the hall. "Fine home, Dr. Larkspur."

Gerald jerked back to attention. "Thank you. Come in, come in. Sorry to leave you standing in the entry." He waved Patrick through to the parlor as his mother rushed back to the kitchen, chirruping like an excited hen.

The front room, which had always seemed conservative, suddenly felt opulent and overdone. Gerald gestured for the clergyman to sit. "I am saddened to hear of your situation. I assumed the church took better care of their shepherds."

Patrick claimed a seat by the window. "Best thing to ever happen to me. I was far too comfortable being a junior minister for a large congregation. It's a simple matter to lose track of the Great Commission when you're feeding off the fat of the land."

Gerald glanced about at the plush furniture and heavy draperies, the comfort tangling his spirits like a snare. "I suppose you're right."

Voices sounded on the stairs. Gerald held his breath. Would Ruby be pleased to see Patrick?

His cousin arrived first, Abby's smile bringing new energy to the room. "Patrick! What are you doing here? We were just speaking of you!"

Ruby's face appeared over Abby's left shoulder, her mouth falling open as blooming circles of pink rose in each cheek.

Patrick sprang to his feet. "Abby, Mrs. Marshall, what a treat to see you both again."

Abby grabbed Ruby's elbow and pulled her into the parlor. "Isn't it wonderful, Ruby?"

Ruby smiled. "Yes, of course."

Gerald shook off the sense of cold fingers creeping up his spine. Ruby could make her own decisions. She'd made her position painfully clear. "Abby, Ruby, would you entertain our guest for a moment? I need to check on a few things before supper." He nodded to Patrick. "If you'll excuse me?"

"You're leaving me in fine company, Doctor. I'll be perfectly content."

I can imagine. Gerald strode out of the room, hurrying down the hall to his study and closing the door behind him. He sank into the swivel chair with a groan. "God, what are you doing?" He turned to face out the window. The light hung low in the sky, the days growing shorter as winter approached. Birds flitted through the shrubs, as if concerned time was somehow running out.

Gerald let his head fall forward, the image of Ruby's excited flush filling his mind. She'd said she wasn't ready to move on from the loss of her husband. *Perhaps it had been a convenient excuse until the right man came along.* He lifted his hands and pressed them against his temples. He'd been foolish to think she'd be interested in him. She was his partner's sister and a houseguest. Nothing more.

The sound of laughter crept in under the door.

Father, give me the grace to survive this meal.

⁐

Ruby led the way to the table, the sensation of a hundred tiny needles prickling across her skin. Just as she'd always suspected, God had a bizarre sense of humor. As soon as she decided to speak to Gerald about her deepening feelings, God cast an unwelcomed suitor in her path. No matter how attractive Patrick Allison might be, her heart didn't thrum like an automobile engine when he entered the room.

Mae had already arranged heaping platters of food, adding a bouquet of late-blooming roses, and exchanged the everyday napkins for a batch of finer quality.

Ruby hovered behind her chair, the rich smells of the evening meal no longer tempting her appetite.

Mae carried in one last dish. "Patrick, why don't you take this seat? My niece Clara and her husband are away this week. It will just be the six of us. Where's Robert?"

"I'm here." Robert hurried in, crossing to Abby's side and placing a peck on her cheek in greeting. "But I need to rush off right after the meal. I'm on rounds this evening." He beamed at the newcomer. "Patrick, how nice of you to join us."

Gerald joined the group, his face unreadable.

Ruby's throat tightened. Did he know of Abby's matchmaking? Had he invited Patrick here on purpose?

Everyone took seats around the table. Patrick beamed, gazing at the variety of dishes spread on the tablecloth. "Mrs. Larkspur, I haven't seen a bounty this magnificent since before the quake."

Mae smiled. "We share what we can with those less fortunate, but with two doctors under this roof, I feel it's important to ensure they are well fed."

Gerald whipped the napkin out from under his silverware and tucked the cloth into his lap. "My mother is one of the best cooks in San Francisco. She even hosted Mrs. Leland Stanford, once."

"Oh, it was nothing." Mae blushed. "Jane came seeking extra funds for the university. We all tried to do our part."

Patrick accepted a steaming bowl of creamed corn from Abby. "Mrs. Stanford—raising money? I thought the Stanfords were richer than Solomon."

Ruby ran a finger around the edge of her water glass, the conversation fading into the background of her mind. Gerald's eyes remained fixed on his plate, as if the topic caused him discomfort. Or was it the guest?

Mae refilled Patrick's glass. "Perhaps. But after her Leland passed away, there was some kerfuffle with the estate—probate and so forth. She feared they might lose the school. Matters were settled a few years later."

"I believe the Stanford mansion burned in the fires, along with the rest of Nob Hill." The Irishman took a bite of the chicken. "There's one interesting turn from the disaster. Rich and poor walked side by side during those terrifying days. We still have a few well-to-do folks in the camps. Some lost everything."

Gerald poked a fork into his salad. "Thankfully, the city's on the mend."

Robert passed around a basket of rolls. "And looking better all the time. I think it will be quite the showcase, once everything is rebuilt."

Patrick handed the bread to Ruby, catching her eye. "Yes, the city grows more lovely every day."

Her fingers closed over the edge of the wicker bowl, and she darted a glance at Gerald.

The doctor scooped food into his mouth as if he'd not eaten for months. The man had kissed her just a few weeks before, and now he couldn't be bothered to meet her eyes. She claimed a roll before passing the basket back to Mae. Ruby swallowed and offered a hesitant smile to Patrick. "How are things in the camps this week? Is the situation improving?"

"Day by day, yes. The government cut off rations for many of the able-bodied men and women, so most folks are working. I imagine they'll close completely by early next year. There's plenty of jobs to be had, just few places to call home."

Abby turned to Ruby. "Margie from the Ladies' Aid showed me the new sewing center at the Golden Gate Camp. The women are supplied with machines and material. They're busy stitching garments to replace what's been lost."

Ruby straightened in her seat. "What a wonderful idea."

Patrick leaned toward her. "I'd be pleased to give you a tour. Dr. Larkspur is stopping by Monday to see to a few of my friends. Perhaps you'd like to join us."

She faced Gerald. "I thought you had a board meeting."

His gaze flickered for a moment, but he continued pushing food around his plate. "Meeting's in the morning. I'll go to the camp in the afternoon. You don't need to come along. I can handle things on my own."

Heat seared her throat. Not only did he refuse to meet her eyes, now he'd toss her aside as a nurse as well? She turned to Patrick and lifted her chin. "I'll accompany Dr. Larkspur. If he doesn't require my assistance with patients, I'd be honored if you would show me the sewing facilities."

A smile spread across the minister's face. "Wonderful. I'll look forward to it."

❧

Gerald's chair squeaked as he pushed it back, the walls crushing in against him. "If everyone will excuse me, I think I'll refill the water carafe."

His mother glanced up, a fork dangling in her grip. "I can do it."

"Sit, Mother. You've been cooking all afternoon. I believe I can handle this." He marched from the room, his thigh catching the corner of the table and setting the glasses rattling.

The kitchen door swung closed behind him, and Gerald took several deep breaths to clear his head. He leaned against the counter and rubbed the sore spot on his leg. Clearly God was getting a hold of his desires, but he hadn't expected it to come in such a painful manner.

The door opened, Ruby's recognizable footfalls breaking the stillness. She strode to his side. "How dare you embarrass me like this. You don't need me?" Her voice cracked. "Or is it because you've lost interest, you no longer want my services as a nurse?"

Gerald dropped the pitcher into the sink and spun around to face her. "Lost interest? Are you mad?" He jerked his head toward the dining room. "I'm not the one escorting you to fancy meals at the Cliff House or walks along the shore—apparently I'm only useful for providing a roof over your head and teaching you to drive."

Ruby clutched the empty breadbasket to her midsection. "The Cliff House? You can blame your cousin for that." She slapped the container on the counter and hooked her hands on her hips. "Are you accusing me of seeing Patrick behind your back? I'm not sure it's any of your concern."

Gerald glanced toward the door, the distant murmuring voices falling silent. He set his jaw before returning his attention to the spitfire in front of him, her nostrils flared like a bull ready to charge. If they were going to have this discussion, they required privacy. He grasped her arm and steered her out the back door, their feet pounding down the steps into the dark garden.

She yanked her hand free. "Let me go. What do you think you're doing? You have a guest—or have you forgotten?"

"I wish I could." He blew out air through clenched teeth. "And I'm not accusing you of anything. If you desire to see Patrick Allison, I won't stand in your way. He's obviously a better man than I— dedicating his life to serving the poor while I wallow here in comfort."

Creases formed on either side of Ruby's mouth as the corners of her lips turned downward. "Better—what are you talking about?" Her voice shook. "There could never be a better man than you."

Her words hit him like a blow to the chest, knocking the air from his lungs.

She tipped her head back for a moment, as if staring up at the first stars twinkling in the night sky. Ruby lowered her chin, her pale blue eyes filling with tears. "You are the most wonderful, most handsome, most—remarkable man I have ever known. How could you think for a heartbeat I would choose Patrick over you?"

The garden seemed to spin as the crisp night air sent chills racing across his arms. "What do you mean?"

A tear trickled down her cheek. "Don't make me say it. I'm afraid my heart would unravel into a pile of loose thread."

Gerald grasped Ruby's elbows and pulled her close, his heart pounding. He ran a thumb across her cheek, pushing away the lone droplet. "Ruby, I don't want to make the same mistake twice, so this time I'll ask—may I kiss you?"

She circled her arms behind his back, the warmth radiating into his spine. "Yes. Please. Now."

He bent down and pressed his mouth to hers, blood humming in his veins like the Crookes tube at full power. When their lips separated, he kept his cheek pressed to hers, relishing the rose-scented fragrance of her hair. "I can't tell you how long I've waited for a second chance to do that."

Her gentle breath tickled his skin. "I'm glad you've been patient. I know I haven't made it easy."

He cupped a hand under her jaw. "You have no idea. But I would have waited a lifetime for a kiss so sweet."

"I'd rather spend a lifetime enjoying those kisses."

Gerald pulled her close and claimed another. Nuzzling along her temple, he whispered in her ear. "If I have any say in it—"

"Ahem." Robert's voice sounded from the porch. "I think you two may have forgotten something. There's a fairly decent view of the garden from the dining room windows."

Ruby gasped and ducked behind Gerald.

Amusement colored her brother's voice. "Any chance you'll be joining us for dessert?"

Gerald turned his back to the house. "In a moment, Robert." He waited until the door clicked shut, the sound of distant laughter turning his stomach.

Ruby buried her face in his shoulder. "How mortifying."

"We could run away, right now. Disappear into the night and never face them." At the moment, he could think of nothing he desired more.

She lifted her chin, staring into his eyes. "At least Patrick knows where he stands."

Gerald chuckled. "Yes—in there. And I'm standing out here with the beautiful woman." He bent down to claim a final kiss, no longer caring who watched.

29

*R*uby guided the silk under the presser foot, using the toes of her shoes to rock the treadle like a seesaw. The whirring needle matched rhythm with the precipitous beat of her heart. She pressed her lips tight to prevent the silly smile plaguing her all morning.

Nothing had changed. So, she kissed Gerald. What difference did it make? She shook her head in defiance. Her spirit didn't seem to understand—it pranced and sang like a girl in a field of wildflowers.

As she reached the edge of the fabric, she grasped the balance wheel to stop the needle, carefully turning the fabric and lining up the next row of stitches. Seamstress work made sense. Cutting, pinning, stitching—creating something new with practiced hands. She could do the same with the blossoming relationship. She just needed to guide and direct her emotions—ensure they didn't wander off-course or become hopelessly tangled like an out-of-control bobbin thread.

What happened with Charlie wouldn't repeat itself.

Ruby slowed the rhythm, eyeing the even line of stitches. If only everything in her life could be so ordered.

Abby's voice sounded from behind her. "It's beautiful."

Ruby lifted her head. "You startled me. I didn't hear you come in."

Her friend peered over her shoulder. "You've been working for hours. I don't know how you can stay at it so long."

Ruby placed her feet on the floor and stretched her stiff back muscles. "I get weary, but then I imagine finishing just one more piece and I can't help myself."

"It's how I am with a book."

"And I with your aunt's molasses cookies." Ruby snipped a loose thread and held the skirt up. "I think this is coming along nicely. I'll be able to add the bodice tomorrow."

Abby ran her hand along the smooth fabric. "It's lovely, Ruby. You are talented."

"Every woman should have a beautiful dress for her wedding." Ruby bundled the skirt into her sewing basket.

Abby sat down in the wingback chair. "Did you?"

Ruby gazed at the silk. "Yes. I made it myself. Acres of satin, ruffles, bows, and sleeves so wide I could barely fit through the door. Ridiculous." Her gaze wandered over the elegant lace spread across the sewing chest. "I was young. I thought I needed such frivolity, somehow."

The young woman smiled. "You are so much like my sister. She would have wanted such a dress, too."

"Somewhere along the line, I discovered marriage isn't about the dress. It's about the people. Their future together." The image of a handsome doctor sprang to her thoughts. Could they reach such a point? Ruby blushed. One kiss and her thoughts rushed to matrimony. *Well, a few kisses.*

Abby slid forward and perched on the seat's edge. "The future has been on my mind of late."

Ruby eyed the young woman's pensive face. "I can imagine it might."

Abby pursed her lips, tucking her chin toward her chest. "I don't think one should go into marriage with secrets." Her friend jumped up from the seat and paced around the chair, stopping to brace herself against its high back.

Ruby's throat tightened. Her brother's fiancée seemed innocent enough—what kind of mysteries could she harbor? "Abby, if there's something wrong, perhaps you should discuss it with Robert. I don't want to come between you."

"It's difficult. I'm certain he wouldn't approve."

Ruby set the basket on the floor and rose, stepping to Abby's side. "My brother is quite reasonable. What could be so loathsome?"

Abby moved away, crossing to the window and gazing down at the street. "I've gone against his wishes. I'm not accustomed to receiving directions—demands." Her fingers curled into her palms, her voice rising. "In fact, if he continues, I'm not certain . . . I'm not . . ." She choked off her words, covering her mouth with trembling fingers.

A chill swept through Ruby. "What are you talking about? What kind of demands?" Her mind rushed to all sorts of uncomfortable places.

Abby faced Ruby, blinking hard. "I told you about Kum Yong, my Chinese friend. Months ago, Robert forbade me to visit her. We quarreled about it but never came to a resolution. Since then we've avoided the topic."

The stitch of tension in Ruby's neck loosened. *Of course.* "And you've seen her?"

Abby pulled her lower lip between her teeth. "Not yet. The mission relocated to Oakland after the quake. But we've exchanged letters."

Ruby ran a hand across her brown skirt, picking at some stray threads left behind by her afternoon's work. "You and Robert live under the same roof. How did you manage to keep the correspondence a secret?"

"Kum Yong passed the letters through her minister. He delivered them to the camp kitchen."

"This is silly. My brother shouldn't choose your companions."

"I agree." Abby shrugged. "I don't understand—he's an angel about everything else. But Kum Yong is dear to me. I refuse to cast her off like so much discarded laundry." She twisted the cuff on her sleeve. "Next week Miss Cameron is bringing one of the mission girls to testify in court, and Kum Yong will interpret. I won't miss this opportunity to see her, if only for a few minutes."

"Perhaps if he accompanied you, he'd see there's nothing to fear."

Abby's face pinched. "If I tell him, we'll end up arguing."

"If you hide it and are discovered, it will result in a bigger quarrel. It's not wise to leave a disagreement unsettled. They have a way of sneaking back to bite you."

"I don't know what to do." Abby sank back into the waiting chair.

Ruby paced the floor. "I'll speak to him. He's always been the even-tempered one of the family." She paused, hitching her chin in the air. "He had me for a sister, after all."

Abby flew out of her seat and threw her arms around Ruby. "Thank you. I knew you could fix this."

"I hope I can." She glanced back at the sewing machine. *I'd hate to be doing all this work for naught.*

&

Gerald's celluloid collar rubbed at his throat like a noose, the air heavy with the stench of Dawson's Cuban cigar. Gerald glanced down at his folded hands and grimaced at the sweat dampening his gloves. *They'll think I'm a dandy.* Better to suffer raised brows than expose his bandaged palm to the board. They didn't need more reasons to question his research.

Emil leaned back against his seat at the far end of the expansive table, the long silver hairs of his waxed mustache almost compensating for a nonexistent hairline.

He can't wait to send me packing. Gerald swiped the back of his hand across his forehead, the fabric grazing his skin.

Robert fidgeted as the men rustled through the stacks of papers.

Emil cast a dismissive glance around the table as if the other board members were inconsequential. "Dr. Larkspur, I expect you understand why we are here."

Gerald set his jaw. "We're here because you summoned us, Dr. Dawson."

"Three months have passed since our last meeting. I've kept a close eye on your reports, and my grave concerns have been verified."

"Three months means little to a long-term research project."

The man's moustache twitched as his lips parted. He lifted a cigar from the polished ashtray and clamped it between his yellowed teeth. "How many patients have you lost now, Larkspur? Ten? Eleven?" A smile toyed at his lips.

A sour taste sprang to Gerald's mouth. Dawson already knew the number. "Thirteen."

Robert straightened his shoulders. "We prolonged their lives."

Gerald shot his partner a warning glance.

The old doctor lifted a bushy brow, ready to pounce. "And what of your two remission patients?"

The trap had been set. No escape. "Twelve and thirteen."

Silence descended on the room like a death shroud.

Dr. Lawrence leaned forward, his prematurely graying hair providing him a distinguished appearance, despite his young age. "My apologies, Dr. Larkspur, but I've heard rumors of ill effects from the treatment. Have you experienced any negative repercussions from the prolonged use of X-rays?"

Gerald tucked his hands under the table. "It's laid out in the report, Dr. Lawrence. We've seen some minor burns, malaise, nausea, and so forth. Nothing out of the ordinary."

"What of the newspaper accounts of Edison's assistant, Clarence Dally? He died four years ago, after losing both arms to carcinoma. It's said the cancer resulted from burns he'd sustained working with the X-ray equipment." Lawrence reached for his water glass. "Edison abandoned all X-ray research. Have you addressed his safety concerns?"

"X-rays are safe." Robert snapped. "You can see from the files the incredible progress our patients have made. These are all patients you and other doctors cast aside as terminal cases. We gave them hope."

"False hope, Dr. King." Emil barked his response like a sea lion. "You and your colleague are making a mockery of science. And if Dr. Lawrence is correct, you could be putting the entire hospital at risk."

Robert stood and jabbed a finger toward his former professor. "And you, sir, are an ostrich, trying to bury its head in the sand!"

Gerald grabbed Robert's elbow and yanked him back to his seat. "Robert, be silent or get out."

Emil cackled. "Your assistant has more fervor than you, Gerald. Could it be you are beginning to see the light?" He leaned back in his chair and folded his arms across his bulging pin-striped vest.

Gerald dug his fingers into his upper leg for control. "Give us six months, gentlemen. If I cannot show you solid results by then, Dr. King and I will shut down the X-ray project and you can settle back into your comfortable bubble of paregoric and mustard plasters. In the meantime, let us finish our research without being dragged before the board every time someone so much as sneezes."

The room buzzed as the group of men muttered to each other. Robert wove his fingers together as if in prayer and pressed them to his mouth. He turned to Gerald. "Six months?" His faint whisper remained hidden among the murmurs.

After a few moments the room hushed, and all heads swiveled toward Emil Dawson.

Dawson leaned back in his seat, cigar dangling from his lips. "I've seen your injured hand, Larkspur. I'm not certain you've *got* six months."

30

Gerald strode down the busy sidewalk, dodging businessmen and paper-hawking newsboys, determined to avoid his partner's attempts at conversation. A dense fog draped over the half-finished buildings, concentrating the mingled odors of exhaust and manure.

"What did Dawson mean—you might not have six months?" Robert's ruddy face and crooked tie spoke of the rushed pace.

Gerald paused, letting a few well-dressed young women pass, their high-pitched voices grating against his raw nerves. As soon as their skirts cleared his path, he bolted again, the brisk walk doing little to chase off the whispering doubts clamoring in his head. "He's sowing seeds of doubt among our supporters on the board."

Robert stepped up the pace, his long legs pushing him in front. He threw an arm across Gerald's chest. "Wait a moment—tell me what's going on. He mentioned your hand. Is he speaking of the radiation burns? Are they still troubling you?"

Gerald balled his fists, shoving them under his arms. "I assisted in a surgery last week with Dawson and Lawrence."

His partner's face darkened. "And?"

"Emil must've spotted the scars."

"Dr. Dawson wouldn't throw you to the wolves over a scar." Robert thrust his chin forward. "Let me see."

Gerald stumbled back. "Here? Don't be ridiculous."

"I'm not asking you to disrobe. Show me your palms."

"When did you become so bossy?"

Robert scowled. "When you started courting my sister."

Gerald glanced to the left and right, the sights and sounds of Market Street not serving as a suitable distraction from his nosy friend. He jerked his head toward a quiet storefront, stacks of books on display in the long front window.

Robert followed him, the derby casting shadows around his dark eyes.

Gerald leaned against the brick façade, his heart pounding from the exercise. He stripped off the glove. "Be quick. I don't wish to be late."

Robert frowned, hunching his tall frame over Gerald's hand. "From this, Dawson assumes you're in your death throes?" He grasped Gerald's wrist and drew it upward for a closer inspection.

"I told you, he's grasping at straws. Anything to shut us down." Pain lanced through his lower arm, his elbow jerking in response.

"What was that?" Robert's eyes caught his.

Gerald yanked his hand away. "Nothing. Joints have been a little achy. I'm probably coming down with a cold."

"It'd explain why you've been such a grouch." Robert stepped back. "You're certain Dawson isn't onto something?"

"Positive."

Robert pressed his hat back and shrugged. "I'd feel better if I could get a tissue sample to examine under the microscope."

Gerald tucked the gloves into his pocket. "I already did. Probably the least interesting slide I've seen all year."

"Doctors make the worst patients." His friend leaned against the storefront and crossed one ankle over the other. "If we answered Dawson's concerns about your health, the board might ease up."

"You think if we prove Dawson wrong, he'll happily acquiesce? You don't know him at all."

"He's a scientist. He can't deny the truth."

Gerald scoffed. "Emil Dawson's a figurehead. His job is to keep the hospital financially stable."

"You'd think he'd be more supportive of our research. If we are successful, it'll bring acclaim to this second-rate institution."

"And if we fail, the board bears the disgrace. Not to mention the cost. How many of those Crookes tubes have we burned through?"

Robert pushed away from the brick building. "I've got a few ideas to help them last longer."

Gerald checked his pocket watch as he fell in beside his friend. He'd agreed to visit the camp in an hour—so much for lunch. Exhaustion dogged his steps. "Make it a priority, Robert. Our funds are drying up. The board won't pay for many more unless we start showing some results."

❧

The scent of fish stew lingered in the misty rain drifting about the refugee camp. Ruby lifted her feet high with each step, the mud clinging to the soles of her second-best shoes. "How much further?"

Patrick chuckled, lifting the umbrella high above Ruby's head. "Not far now." His white shirt gleamed under his tailored coat.

Ruby wrinkled her nose. How did the man stay so clean, living in these conditions? She stepped onto the wooden boards laid as a pathway between the buildings. "Gerald is meeting us at the medical center at two-thirty. I don't want to be late."

The minister checked his timepiece. "Then we have thirty minutes to view the sewing facilities before we meet with your Dr. Larkspur."

"He's not *my* Dr. Larkspur."

The corner of Patrick's lip twisted. "Could've fooled me. The family cheered when he planted the kiss on you the other night."

Heat rushed to Ruby's cheeks. "Please, don't speak of such things. It isn't decent." Had they clustered around the windows, watching?

The clergyman halted. "I've no pretense in me, Ruby. I believe in speaking the truth. Too many hide behind the veil of manners and good breeding." He caught her hand and pressed it in his own. "If you're not keen on the man, I wish you'd speak plainly. My heart can't take it."

His wide-eyed expression tore at her spirit. She pulled her fingers away. "I respect you and your work, Patrick, but my affections belong elsewhere."

He managed a curt nod. "With Larkspur."

"Yes." She swallowed hard. As much as she loved Gerald, she hated disappointing this kindhearted fellow. "I never dreamed I would find love after I lost my first husband. I'm not quite certain how to react."

Patrick exhaled. "Our Lord has a way of surprising us when we're least expecting it. And we know 'All things work together for good to them that love God, to them who are the called according to his purpose.'"

"I don't imagine God had much to do with this."

A grin played around his lips. "Our lives boast His fingerprints, Ruby. He cares about each of us, intimately. He knows the number of hairs on your ginger head." He gazed into her face and heaved a second sigh. "Oh, the lovely redheaded brood we'd have had, you and I." He shrugged as if dismissing the errant thought. "But there I go again. As I said, never been one for manners."

Ruby tugged the brim of her hat to shield her eyes. If God cared so much, she'd already have a life full of children, instead of fading dreams.

Patrick gestured to a cottage at the end of the wooden path. "Shall we?"

She wove her hand through his offered arm as he led the way to one of the obscure green shacks and pushed the door wide.

Peals of laughter rang out as Ruby stepped over the threshold. Six women sat at treadle machines, the whirring contraptions clicking along at a rapid clip. Their voices rose above the din, like a flock of cackling hens on nests.

"Good afternoon, ladies." Patrick's voice cut through the noise as all eyes turned toward the doorway.

"Patrick, how good of you to stop by!" A younger woman— probably not even eighteen—bounded from her place and hurried to his side. She clutched his sleeve. "Let me show you what I'm making."

The machines slowed to a stop as the workers gave Patrick their attention.

Patrick freed his arm from her grip. "In a moment, Miss Howard. Allow me to introduce you to our honored guest."

The girl stepped back, mouth puckering. "I'm sorry. I didn't notice your companion."

Ruby glanced around the room. *Of course she didn't.* All of the ladies gazed at Patrick with eyes agog. Likely as not, none of the women had noticed her presence. At Patrick's words, their curious gazes focused on her.

He cleared his throat and held a hand toward Ruby. "May I introduce Mrs. Ruby Marshall? Mrs. Marshall heard of the excellent work you ladies have been doing and asked to see it firsthand."

Ruby pasted a smile on her face, the women's eyes studying her like a crooked bit of stitching. "Patrick—I mean Reverend Allison—speaks quite highly of your industrious efforts on behalf of the camp." She glanced around the room, bolts of fabric lining the walls and stacks of finished garments laid out on a long table in the rear. "I'm impressed."

Miss Howard bobbed her head. "Patrick says busy hands prevent gossiping tongues."

A dark-haired woman chuckled. "Little does he know, you put a bunch of women together, we'll whip up all sorts of wicked thoughts."

Patrick made quick work of the introductions, the six names rolling off his tongue so fast Ruby struggled to match them with their owners.

The young Miss Howard tugged his arm anew. "Come and see. It's a surprise."

Patrick and Ruby followed her to the machine set up in the far corner, a white shirt bunched under the presser foot. Miss Howard loosed the garment from the grips of the contrivance. "It's for you. Look, I embroidered green shamrocks on the neckline. Of course, they'll be hidden by your collar—but I thought they'd remind you of me." Her freckled face colored. "I mean, of us. Of how much we appreciate you."

Ruby examined the tiny clovers. Patrick had clearly made an impression. Perhaps not the one he'd hoped.

His smile shone as he patted the girl's arm. "It's mighty kind of you. I'll wear it with pride. There's a rough and tumble lad over in cabin six who's put a hole in the seat of his short pants. Do you suppose you might work up something for him next?"

Miss Howard clutched the shirt to her bosom. "Of course, Patrick. I'd do anything for you." Her breathless voice matched the intensity of her words.

Ruby wandered the rows of machines, studying the sturdy garments. She paused to admire a dress being stitched by a dark-haired woman. "It's lovely. Is it for a friend?"

The woman guided the midnight blue fabric in a straight line as her feet rocked the treadle in an even rhythm. "It's for one of the other working girls. She don't have much 'cept her old saloon clothes." She glanced up at Ruby. "I thought if she had something more serviceable, it might help her stay on the straight and narrow. Like Patrick's teaching us."

Ruby bit her lip and nodded. "Good idea. Are there many . . . um . . . working girls here?"

Patrick appeared at her elbow. "We'd best be moving along, Mrs. Marshall, if we're to meet Dr. Larkspur." He cast a pointed glance at the older woman.

"Just a moment, Patrick." Ruby crouched down, studying the machine. "It might go faster if you ease the tension a bit." She fiddled with the controls. "Do you have difficulty with your thread breaking?"

The woman rolled her eyes. "You have no idea. Seems like I'm always rethreading the blamed thing."

Ruby twisted the wheel forward, squinting as the needle bounced like a nervous jackrabbit. "The mechanism needs adjusting. How old is it, anyway? I've not seen one like it."

She huffed. "As old as Methuselah, likely. But we're mighty glad to have it." She lowered her voice, for Ruby's ears, only. "I let the other gals have the nicer ones. I know I'm here on Patrick's good word—or on God's grace, as he says. No idea why the good Lord would give it, but I don't want to push me luck." Her wrinkled hand hovered over the fabric. "If you know how to help me work it better, I'd be mighty grateful."

"Of course." Ruby tinkered with the controls. "It needs a few drops of oil. I'll bring some tomorrow. We'll get it working smooth as silk in no time."

A smile spread across the woman's lips, wiping years from her face. "Thank you, Miss. I could sew for more of the gals if the pesky bobbin thread didn't keep snapping."

Ruby stood, her heart warming. She might not be worth much in the soup kitchen, but she knew her way around a sewing machine. "I'll return tomorrow with my sewing tool kit."

Patrick glanced up from a gaggle of bright-eyed admirers. "Ready now?"

Ruby inhaled deeply, the energy in the room flowing through her. "I am."

◈

Gerald frowned as the odor of outdoor latrines accosted his nose. The military had done much to enforce sanitation rules in the camp, but the sheer numbers of people hampered their best efforts. *Lord, be merciful.* Not even the five-cent bounty on dead rats could prevent the looming health catastrophe if God wasn't on their side.

He hurried toward the medical center, arriving just as Ruby and Patrick rounded the corner, deep in conversation. Ruby's wide smile sent a complex flood of conflicting emotions through Gerald's chest. His arms longed to pull her close—and away from Patrick.

Ruby turned her gaze on him. "I met some of the seamstresses Patrick told us about." She glanced down at the muddy path, as if searching for words. "Interesting women. Industrious."

Patrick beamed. "I believe you made quite an impression on them."

Gerald fought the urge to step between them. The last thing he needed was to come off as a jealous suitor. He focused on the minister instead. "You said you had some people you wanted me to see." His voice graveled deep in his chest. He coughed into his glove.

Ruby frowned. "Are you all right?"

He nodded, clearing his throat. "Long morning with the board."

She tucked a hand into the crook of his arm, warmth spreading from her fingers up through his veins.

Patrick gestured down the plank path. "A few more are suffering today, I fear. I'm glad you could come."

31

Gerald knelt by the small child curled on a makeshift pallet. Hardly more than a babe, the toddler's chest caved as he tried to draw in breath, the lymph nodes bulging around his neck. Gerald propped the fellow up and motioned for Ruby to cradle him. "How long has he been like this?"

The mother wiped her brow, stringy blonde hair hanging from her bun. "Two days, though he's getting worse by the hour. It's not the influenza, is it?"

The child's cheeks glowed with fever. Ruby curled her legs under her as she grasped the tiny shoulders and head, easing the airway. "Poor little mite."

"Tip him back a notch. I'd like to examine his throat." Gerald lowered the boy's jaw and inserted a tongue depressor while Ruby placed a hand on the child's forehead, resting him on her forearm. The limp form didn't struggle as Gerald pressed the wooden stick against his tongue.

A cold sweat seeped down Gerald's back, despite the sweltering heat in the room. "Can you see this, Ruby?" The swollen tonsils nearly filled the patient's trachea, a sickly gray coating clinging to every surface.

Ruby stooped forward. "What in the world?" She lowered her voice to a whisper. "It's a wonder he can breathe at all. Is it . . ." Her rounded eyes confirmed she recognized the problem. *Diphtheria.*

Four more children huddled in the opposite corner of the cottage. Ruby's gaze swept the room, her cheeks paling.

Gerald rocked back on his heels, keeping his head down. "Patrick, is this how all the patients are presenting?"

Patrick lingered in the doorway, the fresh breeze from outside a welcome addition to the room. "Very similar, yes."

"How many?"

He pursed his lips, as if mentally counting. "Perhaps a dozen now? There may be more today. Mostly young'uns."

The mother stepped closer. "What's wrong? Will he recover?"

Gerald's hand wavered as he unsnapped the latch on his leather bag and withdrew the stethoscope. He cupped the bell-shaped device against his palm to chase the chill from the metal. "It's diphtheria, I'm afraid. Are any of your other children suffering from sore throats, Mrs. Ives?"

She sank down in a wooden chair, covering her mouth with her hands. "Di-diphtheria? My little cousin, she died of—"

"The others. Do they complain of trouble swallowing?" Gerald pressed the scope to the child's chest, watching as the boy's skin pulled against his straining ribs. The heartbeat swished in the ear-pieces, racing.

The woman's eyes filled with moisture. "Two of them, yes." She lifted her gaze to the cluster of children on the far side of the room.

Three out of five. How long before the other two succumbed? "Let's hope for the best."

Ruby bit her lip. "Antitoxin?"

Gerald's throat ached, as if in sympathy for the toddler. He rubbed a hand over the child's sandy hair, smoothing it back from the damp forehead. He lowered his voice. "Let's examine the others first."

He turned to the children. Their fear radiated across the floor-boards, but he didn't have time for tenderness. "Sore throats, over here. The others need to wait outside."

The siblings scrambled to their feet, the younger two hiding behind the skirts of the oldest. She spoke out. "Doctor, my little sister and I are the ones. But Jess and Michael—they don't have it yet." She shoved the two boys toward the door.

Gerald gestured for her to come closer. "What's your name? How old are you?"

She swallowed, obviously with some effort. "My name's Myrtle, I'm thirteen. This is Birdie. She's eight." The little girl wrapped her arms around Myrtle's waist, peeping out around her side.

After a quick check, Gerald's heart sunk lower. Both girls had grayish-yellow patches of pseudomembrane on their tonsils, though neither as severe as the youngest. He turned to the mother. "Put these two to bed. Nurse Marshall and I will examine the rest of the patients, and then we'll return."

The woman nodded, wringing her soiled apron in her fists. "My boys?"

"I'll assess them on my way out. If they exhibit any symptoms, I'll send them in here. Otherwise, they'll need to stay elsewhere."

"My sister lives next door."

Ruby reached for the bag. "Any sickness there?"

"No. She has no children, and she hasn't said anything about feeling poorly."

Patrick rubbed a hand across his chin. "I'll go over and explain, Mrs. Ives."

Gerald took the case from Ruby and gestured for her to exit first. Following in her wake, the fresh air cooled his raw nerves, the day's worries sitting like a lead weight on his chest. After checking the other two children and sending them off with Patrick, he turned to Ruby. "I'm glad you're here. Today's shaping up to be a long day. You're the only bright spot I've seen."

She offered a weak smile and laid a hand on his arm. "I'm sorry the circumstances aren't better."

He leaned close, dying for a whiff of her rose-scented hair. "We'll make up for it this evening. What say you to a moonlit walk?"

Ruby squeezed his wrist. "Sounds delightful. But will our families approve?"

"Little point in hiding now." He claimed her hand and drew her a step closer. "I plan on kissing you in front of the dining room window every evening. I don't care who watches."

She blushed, but the bright smile was his reward. "Now, who will require a chaperone?"

Patrick reappeared a few minutes later, his shoulders hunched. "I suppose this confirms your fears, Dr. Larkspur. How bad is the situation?"

"I'll need to evaluate the rest of the patients. We'll move some of them to the County Hospital and treat them there."

Ruby's head jerked upward. "Why not our hospital?"

Gerald raked fingers through his hair before replacing his derby. "County handles most infectious disease cases. We may receive some at Lane if things get desperate. The patients will need to be isolated during treatment. Any affected cottages need to be under quarantine. We can't allow this to spread." He glanced around at the rows upon rows of tiny green cabins, barely three feet between each—like lines of dominoes. "An epidemic would be disastrous."

"What is the treatment?" Patrick's brow wrinkled.

"An injection of antitoxin. I've one dose in my case, another in my home office, and I'll put a call in to see how much more we can get our hands on."

Ruby's lips pursed. "Two doses won't even treat *this* family."

Gerald shook his head, the enormity of the situation pressing against his shoulders. "I pray we find enough for everyone." He glanced back toward the cottage. "I'll give my dose to the Ives baby. It may be too late, however. His heart's already weakening—myocarditis. He's not likely to survive the night, but it'll give him a chance."

Patrick pressed a hand to his brow. "I had no idea."

"I should've come earlier, when you first mentioned illness in the camp. This is what I've been dreading."

"Can we prevent the spread?"

Gerald searched for encouraging words, but came up empty. "It'll be tough. I'll inform the health department. We'll post quarantine notices on the affected cabins. I'm not certain what else we can do."

Ruby stared out across the dark camp as she waited, dim lights flickering in a few of the postage stamp windows. She ran a hand over the back of her neck, muscles protesting the long day. She and Gerald had checked every last patient in the camp, diagnosing four-teen sick children and two adults. Her heart ached nearly as badly as her feet.

Gerald had administered his single dose of antitoxin and raced back to the house for the second. Robert arrived with two more from the hospital. Only four children treated in the whole camp.

She watched the late evening sun paint the sky with broad strokes of violet and pink. Ruby pressed an embroidered handkerchief against her eyes, determined not to submit to tears. Hopefully they'd be able to procure additional vials tomorrow. God willing, as Gerald said. She turned from the sunset in time to see Robert and Gerald closing the door to the cottage behind her.

Her brother's face grim, he shook his head. "This is the last thing the city needs."

Gerald nodded, his mouth twisted into a scowl. "We need more doses. We should check with the General Hospital at the Presidio. They might keep some stocked. If they don't, they'll know where to locate it."

Robert shrugged into his jacket. "I'll go over there and see what I can find."

Tucking the medical bag under his arm, Gerald blew a slow breath between his lips. "If the Ives baby isn't responding to the antitoxin, Ruby and I will take him over to County. We could try intubating him. I need some bit of good news, today."

A chill laced the evening air, and Ruby shivered. "I've never seen anyone intubate a child before."

"And I've never done one." Gerald grimaced. "But I'm willing to give it a go. It would be preferable to a tracheotomy."

She nodded. The idea of cutting into a child's throat set Ruby's stomach aflutter.

"It won't be necessary." Patrick's voice echoed out of the darkness a moment before he appeared at Ruby's elbow. "I'm afraid it's too late."

Ruby covered her mouth with her fingers. "So soon? Why didn't you come find us?"

Gerald took her hand. "The baby's heart was already damaged, Ruby."

She sank against his shoulder, thinking of all the sweet children they'd seen today. *How many more?*

"I'll take you home. There's nothing else we can do tonight."

"What about the additional doses?" Ruby lifted her head.

"If Robert locates some, he'll administer them. Otherwise, we'll search for more first thing in the morning."

Ruby chewed the inside of her cheek. She battled between the idea of returning to the house and hiding from this disaster or pounding on each hospital's door and demanding every unit of antitoxin in the city.

Gerald wove his arm around her waist, drawing her close. "We'll return at dawn, but the doctors from County are on their way. They can watch over things tonight." His brow furrowed. "Ever been exposed to diphtheria?"

"Robert and I both had mild cases as children. My mother always said Papa brought home every illness he encountered."

He squeezed her arm. "Good. One less worry."

"And you?"

"I believe so. But I never catch anything—healthy as a horse." He thumped a fist against his chest and uttered a mock-cough. "Diphtheria mostly affects children, anyhow."

"You gave away your only dose."

"Good thing we have no youngsters at home. I'm glad Davy returned to San Jose with Clara and Herman."

They walked toward the automobile parked at the edge of the camp. Her heart gave its normal kick as she gazed at the metal frame, gleaming under the glow of the electric streetlight. She shook her head, brushing away the misgivings. Why fear such a contraption, when a simple bacterium could steal life every bit as easily?

When they arrived at the house, Gerald opened the auto door for Ruby, casting a quick glance at the light spilling out the windows—a welcome sight after the military-style barracks at Golden Gate Park.

He took her hand, wincing at the cold skin. He tucked it between his palms. "Chilled? Or nervous about my driving?"

She ducked her head, but didn't pull away. "A little of both, I'm afraid."

"I hope you're still up for our moonlight walk." He tried to keep the excitement from lining his voice, but failed.

Her smile lit the night. "I'd love to. After supper."

"I'm not hungry, are you? Let's sneak away now, before anyone realizes we're home."

"We shouldn't be selfish. I'm certain your mother and Abby held the meal for us. Besides, I'd like to find a warmer wrap."

He pulled her into his arms, tucking her between his body and the automobile. "I can keep you warm."

Ruby laughed. "I'm sure you can, Dr. Larkspur. But let's take things slow, shall we?"

He let her wriggle from his grasp, suddenly understanding Robert's ongoing dilemma of having Abby under the same roof. *Lord, I asked for this—but I may require Your strength to survive it.*

He followed Ruby up the front walk, hurrying ahead to open the door. As his fingers closed over the icy knob, a sharp pain lanced up his forearm, like the sting of an angry scorpion. Gerald hopped backward, clamping his jaw shut before a yelp could escape. He shook his hand, willing feeling back into his quivering fingertips.

Ruby paused, head cocked. "What's wrong?" She reached for his arm.

"Nothing." He tucked his palm behind him, grasping the knob with the opposite hand. "Just a sore spot. Nicked myself with the scalpel."

She frowned, her eyes narrowing. "You were at a board meeting this morning and at the camp all afternoon. When were you handling a scalpel?"

He swung the door wide and gestured for her to enter. Ruby's dog spilled out the open door and circled around their legs, its tail beating out a steady rhythm.

Ruby planted her feet. "Robert mentioned your hand to me earlier. He said you refused to let him examine it."

"He looked at it—I only prevented him from turning me into a ridiculous laboratory experiment. Allow me a scrap of dignity?" Gerald squeezed his fist, pressing it to his chest. "And your brother talks too much."

Ruby blew a noisy exhale through her lips and crossed the threshold with her shoulders pressed back. "I've seen the condition of the camps. You might have picked up a nasty fungal infection. If you intend to allow something to fester through your system, you can forget about coming anywhere near me—with either hand." She glanced back over her shoulder at him, chin raised.

Gerald pushed the door closed behind him and leaned upon the oak panel. "You, my dear, are not playing fair. Robert put you up to this, didn't he?"

Her brows lifted. "I'm not playing at all. I've never been more serious."

32

The walls of the tiny cottage pressed inward as Ruby tapped the glass syringe with her fingernail, double-checking the measurement.

A pair of massive brown eyes stared up at her from the bed. Not yet six years old, Myrna Walker likely had never seen a hypodermic needle.

Ruby crouched beside her and forced a big smile. "This will only hurt for a moment and probably much less than your throat does right now."

Myrna's older brother sat at the girl's head, stroking her hair. "It's nothing, Sis. I took mine like a man, didn't I, Nurse?"

The robust thirteen-year-old reminded Ruby of Robert at a similar age—man and child, all at the same time. "Yes, you did, but your sister might appreciate a little privacy for hers, I think."

The boy nodded and turned his back.

The girl shifted onto one side and yanked at her nightdress, a shiver coursing through her body as she exposed her backside to the air.

Ruby bit her lip, plunging the needle into the girl's pale skin before the child had time to reconsider her cooperative attitude.

Myrna gasped, but only a meager whimper escaped her mouth.

The hairs on the back of Ruby's neck prickled as she withdrew the syringe and pressed a piece of gauze to the wound. How many would they have lost, if not for the army's supply of antitoxin? Without treatment, the death rate from diphtheria could rise as high as fifty percent of those infected. As it stood, she, Gerald, Robert, and Dr. Jones from the health department had treated twenty-two patients over the past week and the only fatality had been the Ives baby. Most saw remarkable improvement within twenty-four hours. She tucked the covers around her shivering patient. "All done, sweetheart. You'll need to stay in bed for a few weeks, but I think you'll start feeling better by tomorrow."

"Thank you, Nurse." The boy returned to his spot at his sister's head. "Ma will be relieved. She had to stay with the baby. He's never got it, not yet, anyhow. We've been staying away so he won't."

Patrick loomed in the doorway. His voice echoed off the thin walls. "You're a good lad, Jonathan. Your mother is lucky to have you. And with Nurse Marshall's help, she'll have both of you around for years to come."

Ruby tucked the needle back into the silver case and snapped the lid closed. She followed Patrick out into the fresh air.

The man took the medical bag from her hand, hoisting it up under his elbow. "I think that's the last of them for today. Will you be going home now?"

"After a quick stop at the sewing center. I told Mrs. Williams I'd repair her machine."

"I'll walk you there." His ran a finger under his collar as if the slender bow tie squeezed his throat. "I'm mighty beholden to you and Dr. Larkspur for all you've done."

She smoothed the wrinkles from her apron, Patrick's pensive expression causing her to tense. "You are well, aren't you?"

He glanced up. "Aye . . . well, no, but I'm not here as a patient. I'm just feeling a little down in the mouth." A smile glittered his eyes, though it didn't change the fine lines gathering on his forehead. "Not down in the throat."

Ruby cocked her head to the side. "Why? What's bothering you?"

He ran a hand down the front of his pin-striped vest. "Are you counseling now, in addition to your nursing duties?"

"I'm speaking as a friend."

He ducked his head. "Ah. Of course." Patrick glanced each direction down the mud-splattered board path. "I've been pondering my future. The camps are emptying, little by little. It's time I faced facts." He shrugged. "I'm a shepherd without a flock. I've got no church to return to."

Ruby dug her hands into her pockets. "Couldn't you find a new congregation?"

"I'm not sure I have the heart for it. Or the calling. I know the Lord has something in mind for me, but I don't think it's working in the hallowed halls of some dusty building." He lifted a hand, gesturing to their surroundings. "I've never felt so alive as I do walking the camps. It's like I'm journeying with the Lord through the streets of Jerusalem—walking a few miles in his sandals."

Ruby stepped over a slick-looking spot on the pathway. "You've found purpose."

His eyes lit up. "Yes."

"I came to San Francisco in search of significance. I was wasting away in my grief back home. I needed to find a reason to continue."

"Did you discover one?"

Ruby thought through the past months—sitting at Dee's side, rocking the feverish baby, and nursing the sick in the camp. And then there was the time spent with Robert, and getting to know the young woman who'd captured her brother's heart. And Gerald . . . Her pulse skipped along faster, like the needle flying on the sewing machine. "I believe so." She couldn't hide the smile rushing to her face. "More reasons than I could have imagined." She paused before the door to the sewing cottage.

"I'm glad. If the Father could show you how to go on, I've got to trust He will point me in the right direction as well." Patrick cocked his head to the side, his green eyes gleaming. "Will you pray for me, Mrs. Marshall?"

A stitch caught in her throat. Pray for Patrick? Had she even prayed about her own situation? She swallowed. "Of course."

The chill in the office matched Gerald's mood. He pushed back the load of papers cluttering the blotter and placed his hand palm up on the hard surface. A bitter taste settled in his mouth, as if he'd consumed a headache powder with no water. "Let's get this over with, shall we?" He'd postponed the procedure twice already. Ruby was unlikely to tolerate another delay.

Robert hovered over his shoulder. "Won't it be better to know the truth—one way or the other?"

It's not your life we're deciding. Gerald shot a silent glare at his partner, not trusting his tongue to remain civil.

"I think you'll be relieved when this is complete." Robert placed the tray on the table. "We should have done this in one of the examination rooms."

"I didn't want to take the chance of Emil walking in on us. He's already turned both you and Ruby into anxious mother hens." Gerald moistened his lips, the walls of the small office suddenly feeling closer than usual. He picked up the vial of Novocaine and ran it between his fingers.

"Give it to me." Robert grasped the syringe and reached for the anesthetic. "There's no way I'm letting you do this yourself." He pressed the needle into the bottle and measured the dosage. "You relax."

Unlikely. Gerald leaned back in the office chair, his knees bouncing an unsteady rhythm. "I'm taking your sister to lunch when we've finished here. She's put in too many hours at the camp. She deserves some time away."

"As do you." Robert pulled his stool closer to the table and motioned for Gerald to flatten his palm. Placing the needle, he injected the drug just under the skin.

Gerald flinched. "I don't think that's even necessary." Cool tingles spread across his skin, moving up along his knuckles. "How am I supposed to drive with a numb hand?"

Robert huffed. "Let Ruby take the wheel. She's getting pretty skilled."

"She's not prepared for city traffic." Gerald shook his wrist, the creeping cold unnerving, as if Marley's ghost had taken him by the fingers and was luring him off to the grave.

"Never underestimate her, my friend. If she set her heart on it, she would be driving circles around you. Ruby is the definition of determination."

"I don't doubt it. It seems to be the primary trait in your family. I wouldn't be subjecting myself to this if it weren't true."

"And since you admit it, I'm going to do a more thorough examination than you agreed to. And you will submit with no complaints."

Gerald's stomach tightened. "I will? See here—"

"Starting with the lymph nodes." He reached for Gerald's throat, his warm hands closing on either side of his jaw.

Gerald jerked back in his chair, grasping Robert's wrist with his good hand. "This is completely unnecessary."

"We have a few minutes before the anesthetic finishes taking effect. Humor me and pretend to be an adult."

Gerald grunted, releasing his grip.

Robert probed the nodules above Gerald's collar. His brows crumpled as he ran a thumb along Gerald's neck a second time, fingers tracing a path on the opposite side.

Gerald's mouth dried. "You have a lousy poker face." He brushed his friend away, checking for himself. The nodes seemed enlarged.

Robert frowned. "Have you been unwell? Besides the burn, I mean?"

"Only a little tired. But with the hours . . ." Gerald swallowed, pressing his fingers against the glands. Swollen. Not necessarily alarming. *On its own.* He glanced down at his palm, numb and lifeless. A prickle wandered up his arm, like a spider climbing a silken thread.

"Let me check the ones under your arms." Robert's voice grew husky.

"Not now." Gerald pushed him away. "Ruby's expecting me. Just do the biopsy. If you find something, then we'll talk."

Robert reached for the scalpel. "You can bet we will."

Ruby sat perched on the iron bench, gazing out over the water of the Golden Gate. The gusting winds caught loose tendrils of hair and blew them across her face. She captured the strands with quick fingers and tucked them behind her ear, not wishing to miss the glorious view.

Gerald stood behind her, one hand shielding his eyes from the sun. "Quite different than the last time we were here."

She glanced up at him, her hat's silk draping fluttering in the breeze. "I agree. Come down here so I can see you."

He sat, resting an arm behind her shoulders. "I've been anticipating this moment all day."

Ruby ducked her chin, suddenly self-conscious. "How did things go with Robert?" She touched the gauze swathing his palm. "Did you find anything? Was it a fungal infection, like he guessed?"

He drew the hand back, tucking it under his coat, and stared out toward the waterway. "We won't know for a while. He'll be running tests on the tissue samples."

Ruby gazed at him, memorizing every nuance of the man's face. His eyes shone in the late afternoon light, but tiny lines gathered around them, like threatening storm clouds. Life had been hard for so many weeks. Surely they'd earned a moment of peace. If she could just accept it.

He tightened his arm about her shoulders, drawing her closer. "What was it we discussed last time we were here?"

The day remained etched in her memory. "You spoke of your faith. How this place always reminded you God's in control."

The corner of his mouth hitched upward. "You sound as if the topic's been heavy on your mind."

"Perhaps. Yes." Ruby traced a finger up his wrist and let it settle on the bend of his arm. "I've never been good at trusting. In anyone." She closed her eyes for a moment, her throat thickening with the emotion of the words. "It was hard to give in to Him. To you."

Gerald cupped her cheek, the sensation sending a fluttering of wings through her insides. "So, I wasn't the only one seeking your heart?"

She let her mind wander over the past months. Had God been trying to get her attention? Even before she came to San Francisco? "I think God has been calling to me, too. Asking for control over my life." She shivered, the sea air tugging the ends of her scarf.

Gerald stroked her jaw line with his thumb. "He's not content to be a genie in the sky, granting a few wishes now and then. He wants to be Lord in our lives. Placed first in our hearts, above all else."

"I can put Him first."

"I know you can."

"But, if I do, will He protect me this time?" She swallowed hard. *I hate sounding so weak.*

Gerald's hand stilled, his eyes searching hers. "Not necessarily. God doesn't always choose the easy road for us. But He always chooses the best path."

"I hope He's a better driver than you."

Gerald pulled back, his face aghast. "You still think I'm a wild driver?"

She gripped the lapels of his coat and tugged him close. "I think it's a wild existence. It's like we're all driving automobiles with no brakes. We're careening through life trying not to hit anything."

He touched his bandaged hand to her chin. "I can't think of anyone I'd rather go crashing through life with than you."

Ruby leaned into his shoulder. "Let's skip the crashing part." For now, she wanted to believe everything would be all right. *If just for this one moment.*

33

Gerald tugged at the feather pillow until it nestled perfectly under his neck. Sleep eluded him, the day's thoughts and worries spilling over into the night, as if he'd not given them enough focus during waking hours. He rolled to his back, staring up at the ceiling. A sliver of light from the streetlamp illuminated the fine web of cracks— reminders of the earthquake. He passed a hand along his throat, fingers stopping at the lump on the left side. It could mean anything. Or nothing. He clenched his fist, the pressure driving away the nagging ache in the base of his palm. What if Emil was right?

He'd spent the last two weeks basking in the glow of Ruby's attention. Since the evening in the garden, he'd walked around with a permanent smile etched on his face. Being constantly surrounded by chaperones provided a rare challenge, but Gerald had managed to claim a few more kisses since the fateful night. One at their picnic yesterday and three more in the shadows of the grape arbor after supper. This morning, Ruby had waited until Robert was busy with rounds before she casually visited the office to inquire about a new patient. At this rate, they should marry before Robert and Abby. *Not a bad idea.* Unless . . .

He rose from the bed and retrieved his trousers from the wardrobe. Perhaps a glass of water would wash away the tight feeling in his throat. It was senseless to sit here stewing. Better to wait until Robert had the results.

Gerald pulled the door open as Ruby emerged from the bathroom, a towel wrapped about her head like an elaborate Turkish headdress. His anxious thoughts scattered to the winds. "Sort of late for a bath, isn't it?"

A flush of red trailed upward to her ears. "A lady appreciates a little privacy, at least until she's put up her hair."

Gerald leaned against the doorframe. "It's my house. I'm obliged to know who's roaming the halls at such a late hour. You could be a burglar."

"An unwanted houseguest, perhaps, but not a burglar." She tightened the belt on her housecoat.

"I'd hardly call you unwanted." Gerald swallowed, the scratchy dryness in his mouth reminding him why he'd risen in the first place.

As she moved to pass him, Gerald grasped her wrist. "I'm in earnest, Ruby. I'll always thank God for sending you here." The touch of the silky gown against his knuckles sent an unexpected tremble up his arm.

Ruby's eyes trailed up to meet his gaze. "This isn't how I expected things to turn out, that much is certain." She stood still, not pulling away from his grasp.

He ran his fingers up her arm, the fabric doing little to dispel the warmth radiating from her skin. Gerald cupped a hand behind Ruby's elbow and drew her a step closer. The curve of her neck beckoned, and he longed to bury his face there and not emerge for hours. His heart hammered in his chest. *Don't be a fool.* "I shouldn't detain you. You must be chilled, fresh out of a hot bath."

Her gaze darted down the deserted hall before a smile claimed her lips. She stepped into his arms. "Not so much. I just . . . what if someone wakes up?"

Gerald settled his hands on the small of her back. "You're probably right. One kiss." He lowered his head until his lips brushed her cheek.

She turned in to meet him, her soft mouth pressing against his, her hand catching the side of his face.

A jolt of electricity shot through him. He pulled her up to her toes, the kiss deepening. Ruby's sigh sent his thoughts spinning. He kissed her again, his lips wandering down to her jaw line as he wound a hand behind her neck, under her damp hair.

She exhaled with a shudder. "I need to go."

"I know." He breathed the words into her ear, pulling her into a long embrace. "Because if you kiss me like that again, I'll never—"

A sound from downstairs sent Ruby jerking back as if she'd touched a live wire. She stumbled into the hall table, sending a glass vase rocking.

Gerald snatched up the vase, grabbed Ruby's hand, and pulled them both into the shadows.

Her fingers dug into his arm. "Someone's downstairs. Who could be awake at such an hour?"

Faint sounds drifted up the stair. A door clicked shut and footsteps sounded in the entry.

"It's Robert. He's just getting home from the hospital."

She covered her mouth with a trembling hand. "He can't find me here. He's already sensitive about us." She glanced back toward the room she shared with Abby, but it was at the far end of the hall.

"Come with me." He pulled her into his room and closed the door, holding the knob so the latch wouldn't click.

She tugged at his elbow, her large eyes glimmering in the darkness. "If he finds—"

"Shh." He leaned against the wooden panel, wishing he were on the other side. The ache in his throat intensified. What was he thinking, bringing her in here? He glanced across the room at the tousled bedcovers. *Robert's going to hang me.* "Where's your dog?"

"With Abby. She let him sleep on the end of her bed once, and now he thinks he owns it."

The soft knock caused his heart to wedge somewhere below his Adam's apple. Discovered already?

Ruby's eyes widened as her hands clutched at the neckline of her gown. Her mouth fell open as she mouthed the words: "What do we do?"

He motioned her to the corner.

The tap sounded again. "Gerald? Are you awake?"

Gerald swallowed, his chest afire. He darted a final glance at Ruby, pressing herself against the wall, before he opened the door a crack.

Robert stood in the hall, his derby still upon his head, dark circles around his eyes. "I need to speak to you."

Gerald coughed twice, hoping Robert couldn't hear Ruby's rapid breathing. He searched his friend's face. "Now?"

Robert took a step closer, gripping the doorframe with one hand. "Can I come in? I don't want to wake anyone."

Gerald stepped into the doorway, blocking Robert's path. "Perhaps we should go down to the study. I believe Ruby left the bath a few minutes ago." *Left the bath and came into my room.*

Robert's eyes narrowed. "And you're arranging flowers?"

The glass slithered around in his sweaty palm. Gerald pulled the door shut behind him and thrust the vase back onto the table. "I noticed someone had moved this into my room. I was just returning it."

The image of Ruby crouched in the darkness sent a quiver through Gerald's stomach. What if they'd been trapped in there together? How long before he made a mistake they'd both regret? Once he drew Robert downstairs, she'd escape back to her own room. No one would be the wiser. *And we'll both be more careful from here on out.* No more midnight rendezvous. Not until he could put a ring on her finger.

Gerald shook himself, pushing away the enticing thought. Such a day was still a long way off, no matter what he desired. He followed Robert toward the stairs, the floor icy against his bare feet.

❧

Ruby pressed herself against the wall until the men's footsteps receded. The glow from the streetlamp cast ghostly shadows on the drapes. A stack of books sat on the bedside table, perhaps selected from the tall bookshelf lining the far wall. *What was she doing here?* She brushed fingertips across her lips, still warm from Gerald's kiss. Ruby pulled her gaze from the unmade bed.

Cinching her dressing gown tight around her waist, Ruby pressed an ear to the door before grasping the knob. What if Gerald's mother or Abby were awake? What would they think seeing her emerge from his room in such a disheveled condition? She held her breath and ducked her head through the opening.

Ruby hurried down the empty hall on tiptoes, ducking into the room she shared with Abby. Darkness enveloped her as her feet sank into the plush rug next to her bed.

The bedclothes rustled, Abby's sleep-slurred voice echoing in the stillness. "Ruby? What's wrong?"

Otto's head popped up from the foot of Abby's bed.

"Nothing. I—I didn't want anyone to see me in my nightclothes." Ruby tried to keep her voice light. The chill of standing around in her damp hair and dressing gown finally touched her, a shiver racing along her spine. She plaited the unruly curls with trembling fingers and covered her head with a sleep cap before jumping into bed and drawing the covers to her chin.

Otto jumped down from Abby's bed and hopped up to Ruby's. Padding down to her feet, he turned several times before collapsing with a sigh.

Cuddling with the soft quilt, Ruby closed her eyes. She could still feel the sensation of Gerald's strong arms around her waist. They'd almost been caught. As mortifying as the idea seemed, it also brought a rush of warmth.

☙

Gerald studied Robert's hunched shoulders. Which of their patients had made a turn for the worse tonight? Another loss would only cause Emil and the others to cast further doubt on their research. His stomach soured. When had he begun thinking of the board over his patients?

Robert plopped into the upholstered chair in the corner of the study without bothering with the lamp.

Gerald pressed the switch, the brilliant light driving the shadows into hiding. "Who is it? Mr. Thurber?"

His partner's attention remained riveted on the floor. "No."

"Miss Gaines?" Gerald paused. "You couldn't have tangled with Dr. Dawson at this late hour. He's prefers early rounds."

An explosive exhale burst from Robert's lips. "Why do you suppose I prefer working nights?"

Gerald hurried to his friend's side. "Then what's wrong?"

Robert lifted his gaze, his brown eyes piercing.

The walls seemed to press inward, the oxygen rushing from the room. Gerald sank into the chair, his heartbeat sounding in his ears. "The tissue sample?"

Robert finally pulled off the black derby, dropping it on his knee. His hair lay plastered in a ring around his head, as if he'd spent hours walking the streets before returning home. He raked fingers through the strands. "I'm not positive yet, but . . ."

Gerald leaned forward, lowering his face into both hands. The gauze scraped against his cheek. "What is it?"

Robert's voice cracked. "Carcinoma."

The word hung in the air like poisonous gas. Gerald fell back against the chair, his lungs refusing to function for a moment. He blinked, hoping he'd awaken and find himself back in his room.

"I'd like to bring Dr. Dawson in to confirm. If I'm correct, he can advise—"

"Advise?" Gerald sprang to his feet, his legs jellylike. "He's the last person on earth I'd want treating any . . ." The words turned to ashes in his mouth, nausea roiling his gut. He pressed a palm to his brow, his arm trembling. "You and I know more about—about . . ." He choked, unable to say the word.

Robert stood and grasped his elbow. "Gerald, sit down."

The floor seemed to gyrate, reminding him of the earthquake. Gerald locked his knees. "I won't have Emil on this." He glanced down at his clenched fist. Cancer? He sank down onto the seat, not trusting his legs.

"I could be wrong." Robert strode across the floor to a pitcher of water in the corner and poured a glassful. He returned and handed it to Gerald. "The sample wasn't completely consistent. We should take another."

Gerald took a gulp of the tepid drink, the glass shaking in his grip. He plunked it down on the table. "Take the whole blasted lesion. I've got instruments in the cabinet. We'll do it right now."

Robert splayed his feet, folding both arms across his chest. "We'll do it tomorrow at the hospital. But I want a second set of—of hands." He glanced down at Gerald's bandaged palm. "We need to bring someone else in. I'm your friend—I don't want to be your physician."

Perspiration dampened Gerald's shirt, his throat closing. It couldn't be cancer. "Say nothing to Emil, Robert." The words hissed from his mouth. "It'd be all over the hospital by afternoon."

"Lawrence, then. From his questions at the meeting, he's obviously been researching X-ray-related injuries."

Gerald rested his head against the curved back of the chair. "He's little more than Dawson's toady." He sighed. "But I suppose he'll do, as long as you swear him to secrecy."

"Lawrence is a good man. He hasn't had the benefit of a great mentor, like mine." Robert managed a grim nod. "If you'd rather, I could ask Ruby to assist and wait to bring in Dr. Lawrence until we confirm the results."

Ruby. Gerald closed his eyes once more, the glare from the overhead bulb unbearable. "No. She must know nothing of this."

"I agree—for now. But if it's positive, she deserves to know the truth."

A throbbing pain took up residence behind Gerald's temples. *If it's true, I'll buy her passage on the next ferry. I won't let her face another loss.*

34

$\mathcal{G}$erald rose before first light, the weight of the evening's news pulling at his frame. He sat on the edge of the bed, head throbbing. He ran a hand along his throat, the glands even more swollen today. He coughed, the scratching deep in his throat, like he'd swallowed shards of glass. A quick gulp of water from the glass resting on the bedside table did little to soothe. He lowered his head into his hands, a shiver racing through his body. *Compose yourself. Do you want everyone to see you like this?*

He pulled on some clothes and headed for the door. Perhaps he could get out of the house before anyone awakened. As he neared the door, a knee buckled and he caught himself on the edge of the dresser. A quiver raced through his stomach. This wasn't skin cancer—he was coming down with something. He glanced down at his hand, the skin red and puffy. An infection. It was the only logical explanation. The swollen glands, the sore throat, the shakes—a simple infection, not cancer. In spite of the discomfort, his heart lifted.

Gerald pushed his arms into the sleeves of his jacket. He'd like nothing better than to crawl back into bed and give in to the malaise, but he needed to put Robert's mind at ease. He'd let Robert wield the scalpel and remove as much tissue as he desired—whatever it took to put this nonsense to rest. He stepped out into the hall and glanced toward Ruby's bedroom door. The future held great promise, and he was determined not to let it slip away.

꒰ꙮ꒱

Brilliant sunshine poured over the garden as Ruby gazed out the kitchen window. The blue sky and sunshine lifted her weariness. How Gerald had managed to rise and be gone before she awoke, she didn't understand. She turned back to the table where Robert sat eating his morning meal. "Have you thought about what I said?"

Robert took the fork from his mouth and swallowed. "This isn't your concern."

Ruby took the seat next to him. "You and Abby are my concern. Your wedding is next month—I don't want see a wedge driven between the two of you."

Her brother reached for the platter of sausages, rolling two onto his plate.

Otto sat up on his hind legs, tail thumping the kitchen floor.

Robert grunted, breaking off a small chunk of meat for the dog. "You don't understand, Ruby. The feelings against the Chinese run deep in this community. If Abby is seen consorting with—"

"Consorting?" Ruby choked on the word. "Kum Yong is Abby's friend. You make it sound sordid. Father welcomed patients of all races. He'd be ashamed to hear you speak so."

He jabbed the sausage with a fork. "She's not a patient. I've treated patients in Chinatown. Those girls that end up in the mission houses are—they're . . ."

Ruby hitched an eyebrow. "Yes?"

He grunted. "Not the type of women I want my wife to befriend."

Ruby pushed away from the table and mustered her sternest sisterly glare. "You'd rather she hobnobbed with San Francisco socialites? Women who care about nothing but the length of the feathers on their Parisian hats?" She pushed to her feet and folded her arms. "I haven't met Kum Yong, but if Abby's willing to marry my numbskull brother, I'd say she's capable of judging character. And if you push this too far, she may change her mind. I didn't think you were the type of man who'd demand to choose a lady's friends."

Robert lowered his eyes. "Fine. I don't care to argue about this. I didn't forbid her to see the woman, I only tried to dissuade her. I want to protect her. There is a dark side to this city. She experienced enough of it in the days after the earthquake, she doesn't need to expose herself further." He ran a hand over his eyes. "Of course, she may go see her friend. Just do me a favor and go along, would you? I need to meet Gerald at the hospital, or I'd go myself."

With a quick sweep of her hands, Ruby began clearing the table. "I thought Gerald was staying home today." She swallowed her disappointment. She'd hoped to have a frank conversation about last night and ensure it never happened again.

Her brother averted his gaze. "Something came up. He left early this morning. I needed him to—to see a new patient."

Ruby frowned, placing the plates in the sink. "Is that what you discussed last night?" She froze, her hands in the soapy water.

Robert locked his gaze on her. "Last night?"

She sucked in her lower lip, clenching it between her teeth. *Stupid girl.* "I heard you come in. I was up late."

"Did you hear anything else?" Robert's face took on a strange hue.

"No. I assumed you were consulting about a patient." She rinsed the plate and reached for the towel. "Would you like me to come in and assist?"

His chair screeched as he pushed back from the table and stood. "No. You attend to Abby." Robert brushed loose crumbs from his shirt. "We're evaluating this patient to see if . . . if he needs further treatment."

Ruby shrugged. It had been four days since she'd been in the cancer ward, spending most of her time at the refugee camp with the diphtheria victims. Perhaps she would stop by after she and Abby finished with their outing. She missed seeing the patients. "As you wish."

Robert cocked a brow. "I *wish* you and Abby were going elsewhere today."

Ruby smiled, flicking the towel in his direction. "Your future wife has wishes of her own."

Gerald stared through the brass microscope, squinting with first one eye and then the other. He pulled up a tall chair, his back aching from leaning over the table. He turned the knobs on the instrument, tightening the focus on the stained cells. The light glowed through the glass slide.

"Not liking what you see?"

Gerald started as Robert's voice interrupted his concentration. He glanced up, blinking to clear his gaze of the one-eyed blurriness caused by the microscope.

Robert crossed to the table, the breeze from the open door fluttering the corners of the papers strewn across the desk and table. Dark circles dragged at his lower lids.

"I'm not certain what I'm seeing."

Robert shrugged one shoulder. "Nor am I. But you must concur it looks suspicious."

Gerald peered through the lens. The clusters of odd-looking cells clumped in strange configurations, as if drawn by a clumsy child. "Yes. Something's not right. Could it be sample contamination?"

"That's what I'd like to rule out."

Gerald lifted his head from the scope. "I'd prefer it to be the case, if you don't mind."

"Of course."

Gerald dropped back onto the stool, exhaustion pulling at his frame. If he told Robert about the fever, his partner would demand to postpone the procedure. *I can't wait another day.*

His friend shuffled his feet. "Gerald, I know you wanted to keep this private."

The air turned cold. "You didn't." *Not Ruby, please.*

"Dr. Lawrence is waiting in the hall. I asked if he'd assist me—I didn't tell him you were the patient."

The tension in Gerald's back eased. "I imagine he'll figure it out pretty quickly when you start cutting on me." He returned the microscope to its wooden crate, tucking his slides into a separate box. The label curled slightly until he ran a fingertip across it. *Patient #24.* His stomach curdled. He followed Robert out to the hall.

Lawrence leaned against the wall, thumbing through a stack of files. "I see I'm working with both of you today. I've been reading up on your latest results. Impressive."

"I've put everything we need in room thirty-two." Robert gestured to the stairwell.

"That's pretty out-of-the-way. Why so clandestine?" Lawrence jammed the files under his arm. "The surgical amphitheater is unscheduled. I could put your name on it. The students would benefit from seeing the famous Drs. Larkspur and King in action."

Gerald ran his palm down his white coat. Just what he needed—his situation on display in front of the entire medical school. "Our patient prefers anonymity during a sensitive procedure."

Lawrence fell in beside him as they ascended the stairwell. "Who is this fellow? Politician? Businessman?" His brows lifted. "There's been rumor of the governor being ill."

Gerald pushed through the doorway of the quiet examination room. The air smelled sterile and cold, like a tomb. He turned and faced Lawrence. "It's not the governor."

Robert shut the door behind them without saying a word.

Dr. Lawrence glanced around. "Where is the mystery patient?"

Gerald shrugged off his coat. "You're looking at him."

"You?" The younger man frowned. "Is this about what Dr. Dawson said at the meeting? You said his concerns were unfounded."

Robert laid the tools out on the table. "We should use ether this time, Gerald."

"No. Just the local anesthesia. I don't want to be knocked out and have Dawson walk in."

Lawrence backed up against the door. "You can't be serious. Are you saying you've come down with the very disease you're trying to cure? Does Dr. Dawson know?"

"We don't know anything yet." Gerald bumped the small table, sending a pair of forceps sliding across its surface. "And you'll not say a word to him. He's already determined to run us out of this hospital. I will not add fuel to his arguments."

Lawrence jammed fingers through his hair. "I knew these X-rays were dangerous. After what I read—"

"Let's just get started. Shall we?" Gerald rolled up his sleeve. "I want to get this over with. I have patients to see at Golden Gate Park."

Robert flattened his lips. "I told you, we need a deeper sample this time. You won't be in any condition—"

"Let me be the judge of that." Gerald pulled the stool up to the table and laid his arm flat. "Now are you going to handle the injection, or shall I?"

Dr. Lawrence glanced back and forth between the two men. "Dr. Larkspur, if cancer is growing in that hand, you realize what will have to be done."

Robert grasped the hypodermic needle and jabbed it into a vial of Novocaine. "Let's not get ahead of ourselves. I'm sure my partner would prefer to keep his hand—at least until we can confirm the diagnosis."

"Or deny it." Gerald wriggled his fingers, glancing down at the digits. How would he live without them? Perform surgery? Hold Ruby's hand? A deep ache settled in his stomach. He brushed away the unsettling thoughts. He'd counsel a patient to sacrifice the appendage in order to preserve his life. The idea didn't settle well. What would be next? The whole arm? Hack him into pieces in a vain attempt to prevent the inevitable? Could X-rays cure the disease they created?

He closed his eyes for a long moment, the image of Ruby's face floating in his imagination. She'd already buried one man, she'd never choose to endure the pain again.

A hand braced his arm as the needle pressed into his flesh. Gerald gritted his teeth. *This test has to be negative, Lord. Because if it isn't, I'll put her on the ferry, myself.*

Ruby followed Abby up the marble stairs leading to the courthouse, dodging workmen as they hauled loads of materials and tools up and down the steps. She lifted the hem of her dress, thankful she'd chosen to leave the hobble skirt at home.

Abby grasped Ruby's arm, her face pale. "I wonder if she's as eager to see me as I am to see her?"

Ruby patted her friend's hand. "She wouldn't have invited you if she felt otherwise."

A man standing nearby pulled open the tall door for them, nodding to the women with a smile and a tip of his hat. "Ladies."

Ruby ushered a trembling Abby through the doorway and into the massive hall beyond. Sounds of voices and footsteps echoed around the cavernous hall. She stiffened her back, determined to be strong for her friend's sake. Though Abby dragged her feet, Ruby pressed forward, centering on a help desk in the front of the hall.

A hulking man sat at the tiny desk, crouched on a chair much too small for his bulky frame. "Can I help you, Miss?"

Ruby lifted her chin. "We're looking for the Occidental Mission case. We were told there would be a hearing on it today."

The man flipped through a series of papers, running a meaty thumb along the lines of print. "Occidental . . . Miss Cameron, ain't it?"

Abby's head bobbed. "Do you know her?"

A grin sprouted just above the man's whiskery chin. "Everyone here knows Miss Cameron. She's the angry angel of Chinatown. Every time she walks in here with one of those little gals, sparks fly." He leaned across the desk, bracing himself on his arms. "The judges are a-feared of her. And rightly so. Those gray eyes can see right through to the darkness of a man's soul—or so the district attorney told me. Who else would dare take on those Tongs?"

Ruby glanced at her friend. "This is the missionary of whom you spoke?"

Abby nodded. "I met her when she brought one of the girls to the hospital, even though they're not supposed to admit Chinese. She convinced Robert to break the rules."

"She must be persuasive. My brother can be a stubborn mule at times."

The security guard pointed them in the direction of the courtroom, and the women hurried through the crowded hall to the open door.

The long courtroom overflowed with milling spectators, including a handful of Chinese. Up near the front of the room, an elegant silver-haired woman conversed with a man in a black suit. She gestured at the paper in the man's hand with a pointing finger. Two Chinese women stood by her side, one sheltering the other with a protective arm.

Abby lit up. "There's Kum Yong." She edged into the room, careful not to disturb any of the people waiting near the doorway.

Ruby followed, studying the room. The only open seats were in the third row, near the far aisle. Abby grasped her hand and tugged her toward the openings.

As they approached the front, Miss Cameron glanced up from her discussion and a flicker of emotion crossed her face. She tapped one of the women on the arm and gestured toward Abby.

A broad smile erupted on the young woman's face, her sleek dark hair gleaming in the light from the large windows. She guided her companion to a stool behind the long table. With a quick word to Miss Cameron, Abby's friend hurried toward them on slippered feet. "You came!"

Abby spread her arms, and the woman fell into them.

The interaction created a stir in the crowd, people whispering and pointing fingers. Ruby straightened her posture, thankful Abby and her friend seemed too focused on their reunion to care about the rude stares.

Abby grasped Ruby's hand, pulling her close to her side. "Ruby, this is my dear friend, Kum Yong—the one I've been telling you about." Her eyes shone. "Kum Yong, this is Robert's sister, Mrs. Ruby Marshall."

Ruby pressed a smile to her face, the best she could do with so many people watching. "It's a pleasure to meet you, Miss Yong. Abby has told me about your experiences after the earthquake."

The young woman bobbed her head. "I am honored, Mrs. Marshall. Please, call me Kum Yong. Our names in Chinese are different than yours."

"Certainly." Warmth rushed to Ruby's face. Had she made a mistake already? Perhaps she should have asked Abby for hints on Chinese culture. "I'm sorry. And you must call me Ruby."

A smile played around her lips. "A beautiful name." She turned back to Abby. "I am so glad you came. I have enjoyed reading your letters. My class begs me to read them my letters from Earthquake Abby, too."

Abby's eyes widened. "Is that what they call me?"

Kum Yong giggled, covering her mouth with a hand. "The little ones. They remember you from earthquake day. They like me to tell them the story of how we rushed through the flames with Miss Cameron to save the documents from the Mission house while they slept."

Abby cocked her head with a smile. "It sounds even more exciting than I remember."

Her eyes glinted. "The girls embellish a little."

"Kum Yong," Miss Cameron gestured from the front. "It's time." She smiled and waved to Abby.

Kum Yong grasped Abby's hand. "You'll stay, won't you? Miss Cameron will want to greet you."

Abby nodded. "Of course."

Ruby and Abby took seats in the fourth row between two elderly women. The woman next to Ruby smelled of lemons, her round face crisscrossed with laugh lines. She smiled at Ruby and leaned toward her. "I'm so excited to see Miss Cameron at work. She spoke at my church back before the earthquake. Brought some of the sweet little children to sing for us. So inspiring."

Ruby nodded and leaned back against the hard bench, enamored by the energy in the courtroom.

The trial rushed by in less than thirty minutes. Miss Cameron petitioned for custody of the young woman, a fourteen-year-old girl named Ah Chin. The judge questioned Ah Chin, with Kum Yong translating. In halting words Ah Chin described the past year of brothel life in heartbreaking detail.

Ruby dug in her purse for a handkerchief as tears stung her eyes. No child should be exposed to the depravity Ah Chin had witnessed, and what the poor girl had endured at the hands of her captors broke Ruby's heart. How could this be happening, right here in San Francisco? Ruby closed her eyes, fighting the urge to flee the room. Abby's fidgeting jostled her back to attention.

Ruby darted a glance at Abby, noting her friend's damp face. She pulled an extra handkerchief from her bag and pressed it into Abby's hand. "Did you know?" She mouthed the words.

Abby shrugged one shoulder. "A little," she whispered.

The woman beside Ruby blew her nose into a large handkerchief.

Ruby directed her eyes at Kum Yong, unable to face Ah Chin's pain. Abby's friend set her jaw, translating the young woman's words with clarity. *Is this Kum Yong's history as well?* Robert's fears suddenly seemed all too real.

No one protested Miss Cameron's petition. The tall missionary seemed to relax, her shoulders lowering a few inches. A tentative smile crossed Kum Yong's face, and she nodded to the trembling girl. The pair returned to the front table as the judge stamped the paperwork and passed it to Miss Cameron's lawyer, dismissing the courtroom.

Ruby studied the young attorney. He barely appeared old enough to have finished law school. The wide grin lit his face, a dimple showing on one cheek. The man stuffed the paperwork into a leather valise before turning to congratulate his clients.

People rose from their seats, and the sounds of murmured conversations filled the room. Kum Yong waved at Abby, beckoning her to the front.

Abby hurried to join the group while Ruby hung back. What could she say to these women? Her sheltered life provided no suitable words. A bitter taste filled her mouth as she pushed herself forward.

Abby introduced Ruby, and Miss Cameron grasped her hand with a welcoming smile. "What an introduction to our work you've had." She lifted the precious papers and drew them close to her shirtwaist. "Ah Chin's story is particularly heartrending. I'm relieved her captors didn't contest our case. She'd have had much more difficulty testifying if she'd been forced to face them. Many of our girls cave under such pressure."

Ruby glanced about the austere room. She couldn't imagine living such a story, much less telling a room filled with strangers.

Abby's face darkened. "Did you have to do this when you were rescued?"

The Chinese woman nodded. "I was younger than Ah Chin, so I had not faced some of the same—" she glanced down at the young woman shrinking into her wooden chair, "—the same struggles."

Abby grasped her friend's hand. "I am overjoyed to see you again. It's been so long. When will you return to San Francisco for good?"

Kum Yong sighed. "I'm not certain. But Miss Cameron says gifts are arriving from all over the country to pay for a new mission home. I don't understand why so many wish to help us, but I am grateful."

Ruby fiddled with her earbob. "San Francisco is rebuilding so quickly, soon you won't even be able to tell anything happened. Perhaps as the city recovers, some of this vice will be cleaned up."

Kum Yong blinked. "Do new clothes change a person's heart? Evil is not so easily cast aside. But we pray things will improve."

Ruby swallowed, her thoughtless remark sticking in her throat. "You're right. Of course."

Miss Cameron turned back to them, taking Ah Chin's hand. "Kum Yong, we need to be leaving. We should get Ah Chin back to Oakland before there's any trouble."

Abby bit her lip. "I'd hoped maybe I could buy you lunch."

Kum Yong wrapped an arm around her, resting a head against Abby's shoulder. "I wish we could, but it's not safe for Ah Chin."

Ruby's heart pounded as she watched Abby struggle against tears. How long she'd waited for her friend, only for a few stolen moments. "We're staying with Dr. Larkspur and his family. I'm certain they would welcome you to their home for a meal. You would be safe there."

Miss Cameron smiled. "It's a generous offer, but we have a long ferry ride back to Oakland. It would be best if we returned before dark."

Abby embraced Kum Yong. "Next time, perhaps? Or . . . you could both come to the wedding. I'd love to have you there."

The young Chinese woman smiled, her hands fluttering to her mouth. "Yes? I would be overjoyed!"

With the attorney leading the way, Miss Cameron and Kum Yong surrounded Ah Chin and guided her from the courtroom with hurried steps.

Abby sighed. "Robert will never approve."

"He loves you." Ruby wove an arm around her friend's waist. "He'll come around."

35

*G*erald cradled his arm against his chest, swaying as he stared out across the camp. After four hours, the effect of the anesthetic had waned. *I should have accepted the morphine.* He straightened his shoulders as Patrick approached. "Afternoon, Reverend. How's the flock today?"

Patrick ran a hand across his forehead before jamming his hat lower over his eyes. "A few new cases, I believe. But we've turned the corner. Most of the children are getting fractious and trying their mothers' patience."

"They'll need a few more days of isolation before we can lift the quarantine." Gerald squeezed his medical bag under his good arm. "I'm down to a handful of doses. It's good we caught this before things got out of hand."

"I appreciate your swift response, Doctor. I hate to think of what might have happened if you and Ruby hadn't discovered it in time."

The mention of Ruby's name brought heat to Gerald's neck. The touch of her lips, the feel of her damp hair under his fingers. He shook off the memory. No more midnight meetings—it wouldn't be safe for either of them.

Patrick lifted a brow, his gaze searching Gerald's face. "Will Nurse Marshall be joining us today?"

"Yes. She said she'd meet us at two o'clock."

"Good, because you look a mite peaked, yourself." Patrick glanced down to Gerald's bandaged hand. "Trouble?"

Gerald tucked the hand inside his jacket. "Just a little run-in with a scalpel."

The clergyman chuckled. "A hazard of the business, I suppose. I'm glad the most dangerous weapon I wield is the word of God—sharper than any two-edged sword."

"And far more powerful than a surgeon's blade." Gerald adjusted his arm, the throbbing reaching his elbow.

"Well said, my friend." Patrick clasped Gerald's shoulder. "Now, who would you prefer to see first—the newest patients or the ones on the mend?"

"Let's begin with the Farley family. We'll see the new cases when Ruby arrives." Better let her handle the needle today. He'd rather not tackle it with his left hand.

Two hours later, Gerald cradled a one-year-old in his arms, jabs of pain shooting through his hand in protest.

The weak child barely uttered a cry as Ruby dosed him with the life-saving serum. She murmured to the baby, running gentle fingers over the flushed cheeks.

Gerald pushed away his own pain, focusing on the kindness in Ruby's eyes. She deserved children of her own. The idea sent a shiver through his stomach. If Robert was correct . . . *God, she's already lost so much. Please, don't take this from her.* The pressure of the child in his arms brought a lump to his throat. He tucked the baby up to his shoulder, wedging the fuzzy head under his chin and rubbing circles on the warm back.

The child's mother hovered two steps away. "And this will help him, like it did for my Liza?"

Ruby replaced the cap on the needle. "It should. But you will want to keep him warm and quiet for a few weeks. He might need another injection tomorrow if he doesn't improve."

Gerald placed the baby back in his mother's arms and beckoned Ruby outside. "Hopefully this is the last new case. After today, we've only three doses left. Once they're gone, we'll be back to more traditional—and far less effective—treatment methods."

Ruby frowned, touching his arm. "Surely we can locate more."

"The county health department is working on it, but we've already brought doses in from far and wide. The country has been hard hit by diphtheria this year. We're not the only ones."

She took his arm, touching his bandaged hand. "You left early this morning." Her voice trailed upward on the last word, as if in question.

He glanced around to assure their privacy. "I had to . . . see a patient."

Ruby pursed her lips. "I could have come along."

A wave of longing gripped his chest. He stepped closer, touching the underside of her chin with a bent finger. "You were up late last night. I thought you might need the rest."

A twinkle appeared in her eyes. "About that . . ."

He lifted both hands, stepping back. "I know what you're going to say. I was foolish. I apologize."

"I'm not saying I didn't enjoy it." Her lips curved upward. She grasped his fingers and pulled him close. "But we need to be cautious."

The jab of pain in his hand didn't distract him from the hunger in her face. He felt anything but cautious at this moment. He settled his arm behind her back, planting a brief kiss on her lips. "Yes, cautious."

She snuggled into his arms with a laugh. After standing there for a long moment, she lifted her head. "By the way, how did it go this morning?"

A wave of cold gripped him. "What do you mean?"

"Your new patient? Is he a good candidate?" She squeezed his waist with her arms.

A patient. He didn't like thinking of himself in those terms. Gerald tucked his hand under his coat, pressing it to his quivering stomach. "The tests were inconclusive. Robert took a second biopsy. We'll know more in a few days."

Ruby cocked her head, studying him with narrowed eyes. "Are you feeling all right? You look so pale." She lifted a hand to his cheek, running it along his jaw line. "You feel warm."

Gerald captured her hand and kissed her fingers. "I'm tired. Late night, long day."

"It's only five o'clock."

He stretched his arms. "Feels like midnight to me. Come on, let's head home."

"Let me say good-bye to Patrick, and I'll meet you at the automobile."

He gripped the medical bag as she hurried off. Normally he'd escort her, having no desire to leave her side, but it consumed most of his remaining energy to plod back to the car. He set the bag in the back seat and plopped behind the wheel, shoulders sagging. One more day gone. Perhaps Robert would have good news tomorrow, and he could put all this nonsense behind him.

Gerald laid his head back against the seat and closed his eyes, remembering the brush of Ruby's skin and the touch of her lips. The past few days had given him a glimpse of Heaven here on Earth. He squeezed his hand closed. Now if he could trust God not to pull her away.

⁂

After visiting with Patrick for a few minutes, Ruby hurried toward the car, pausing to gaze at Gerald slumped behind the wheel. He looked so haggard and weary, as if the strain of their relationship dragged on his shoulders. A familiar prickle raced down her spine. She shook herself, forcing her muscles to relax. *I'm trusting God to be in control, remember?*

Of course, she needed to be responsible, too. The first step would be to avoid traipsing half-dressed through the halls at night. Like a finely sewn garment, she'd make sure this relationship didn't unravel because of poor choices. She walked the last few steps and brushed her fingers against his arm. "Are you sleeping?"

Gerald blinked several times before his eyes seemed to focus. A smile toyed at the corners of his mouth. "Dreaming of a beautiful girl."

"Then I'm sorry to have woken you." She stepped back as he exited the automobile.

"Am I awake?" Gerald escorted Ruby around to her side, covering a yawn.

Ruby slid onto the bench seat as she eyed his complexion. The man didn't look at ease—his face pale and his arm clutched awkwardly to his chest. "Are you certain you're well? You've been working so hard."

He leaned against the edge of the seat, staring at her. "Does lovesick count?"

She shook her head. "Now you're toying with me. Don't expect me to fall for such frippery."

"You deserve as much frippery and frivolity as I can muster." He covered a second yawn. "Unfortunately, it's about as much as I'm capable of today."

She patted his hand where it rested atop the cushion. "Let's go home. You look like you're asleep on your feet."

He smiled before leaning over and pressing a kiss against her hand. "I'm just thankful it doesn't mean good-bye."

Ruby shifted on the seat. "Yes, well. About that." She waited as he hurried around the car and cranked the engine to life. "I think we need to tell someone about our incident last night."

He climbed in, eyes wide. "You're jesting. Why would we do such a thing?"

She pulled the veil around her hat and tied it under her chin. "We need a chaperone even more than Robert and Abby, Gerald. You must realize that."

He frowned as he shifted the automobile into gear. "We're older and wiser than those two."

"And more experienced." Her cheeks burned in response to her indiscreet words.

Gerald's brows shot upward, disappearing under the brim of his derby. "And all along I thought you were afraid of my lack of self-control."

Ruby's stomach twisted as she fought against the urge to crawl under the car seat and hide. What must he think of her? "Women are not immune to such . . ." she swallowed. Why did she ever start this conversation? Oh, yes. *Last night.* "We're not immune to such desires."

He grinned. "I'm glad to hear it."

"You are?"

"Of course. I'd hate to think I'm alone in this burning furnace."

Ruby pulled at her lace cravat, heat crawling up the inside of her corset and her chest. Furnace was an apt description.

Gerald's fingers tapped out a rhythm on the wooden wheel. "So, who do you propose we bring into our confidence? Not your brother, I hope."

She choked back a laugh. "No. He's still adjusting to the idea."

His lips drew back from his teeth. "And not my mother."

"Leaving Abby."

Gerald ran a hand across his jaw. "My cousin? I still think of her as a little girl."

"She'll be a married woman in a little more than a month."

He sighed, slowing the automobile as vehicles stacked up behind a delivery wagon loaded with bricks. "And to my best friend, none the less."

She turned, gazing at his troubled face. "You and Robert are two of a kind. You claim to be friends, but neither of you fully trusts the other."

His gaze remained fixed on the road, furrows forming in his brow. "I don't think it's a matter of trust, exactly. There's just an uncomfortable line between colleagues and friends. Friends and family. What if everything falls apart? Then you've lost all three."

"My father used to quote a proverb: 'A friend loveth at all times, and a brother is born for adversity.' Isn't it good God gave you a friend who could be as close as a brother?" Ruby touched Gerald's sleeve. "When he marries Abby, he'll join your family. But, if *we* were to marry, you would join ours—you two would be brothers by law and by God."

Gerald's gaze turned to meet hers, a darkness appearing in the depths of his eyes. The car rolled to a stop, traffic moving around them. "If we were to . . . marry?"

A horn blast behind them shocked them both into reality. Gerald jerked his gaze forward and steered the automobile through traffic. His lips formed a thin line, and the muscle above his jaw twitched.

Ruby shrank in the seat, pulling her hands to her lap. She'd said too much. What was she thinking? A few kisses did not mean a wedding. She turned her face to the far side, her heart lodging in her throat. But, did Gerald believe she'd simply kiss him in the hall—hide in the shadows of his bedroom and not expect to wear a wedding gown? Her vision blurred. She needed to finish Abby's gown. The silk and lace sat forgotten in her sewing chest, waiting as Ruby fantasized about a second chance at love.

She risked a quick glance in Gerald's direction, his eyes fixed on the road ahead. *I've been a fool.*

36

Gerald swung the front door open, standing aside to allow Ruby to precede him. The lump in his throat clogged his windpipe like a cork in a champagne bottle. *If we married.* The words echoed in her tender voice, the light dancing in her eyes. If only she knew how much he desired the same. *Lord, Your hand cleared this path through her suffering. You wouldn't deny us now—would You?*

Voices echoed through the house. Otto bounded to meet them, dancing around his mistress's shoes. Gerald prayed for strength. He ached to scale the stairs and fall into bed. He and Ruby had finished the drive in silence, the lack of conversation weighing the evening air like an approaching storm front.

Ruby stepped inside, shrugging her wrap from her shoulders.

He caught the shawl as it swung down her back, draping the silk across his bandaged hand.

Her eyes caught his as she turned, pulling the fabric from his grip. "I have it." She gestured toward the parlor. "It sounds as if you have guests." She paused, her head tipping slightly to the side. "In fact, it sounds like . . ." Her lips parted. She scampered toward the front room, Otto at her heels.

Gerald followed, tossing his hat atop the coat tree as he passed.

"Mother—" Ruby gasped. "You're here, already?"

Gerald froze, taking a quick step in reverse. *Mother?*

A diminutive woman stepped into his line of sight, her wide skirt filling the space between the sofa and the low table. "Ruby, there you are." She pulled Ruby into a quick embrace. "Mrs. Larkspur was just informing me how hard you've been working." She clucked her tongue. "You'll drive yourself to an early grave, just like your poor father. What is it with Kings and hospitals?"

Ruby's shoulders drew inward as if she'd determined to fold herself lengthwise. "We go where we can serve. Father taught us well."

Gerald brushed his hand against the small of Ruby's back, where it would be hidden from view. "And fine work they do, too."

Gerald's mother stepped forward, freeing herself from the shadow of Mrs. King's skirt. "Mrs. King, may I introduce my son, Dr. Gerald Larkspur."

The woman's eyes traveled up Gerald's frame as if he were a specimen under a microscope. "Yes, my son has mentioned you in his letters. His infrequent letters." She tipped her head in Gerald's direction and extended her hand. "It's a joy to meet you at last, Dr. Larkspur. I appreciate the care you've taken with my children." Her gaze turned toward Ruby. "Both of them."

Gerald took her hand and gave it a quick squeeze, the woman's skin cool against his fingers.

Ruby's posture seemed to stiffen further. "Dr. Larkspur has been generous to take us in. I didn't realize when I arrived, Robert was living with another family."

A chill shook Gerald. If she'd known, they wouldn't be standing here now.

His mother took Ruby's arm, her eyes twinkling. "And I have thanked the Lord every day for sending you to us, Ruby. You've brought light and life into this house—you and Robert, both. We've seen our share of tragedy in the past year. I'm filled with joy that the Lord has seen fit to bless us with your presence."

Leave it to his mother to find the appropriate words for every moment. As she excused herself to the kitchen, Gerald dug into his vest pocket after his watch. "When did you arrive, Mrs. King? If we'd known, Robert or I would have met you at the Ferry Building with the car."

She waved a hand, flicking her stubby fingers through the air. "The girls and I hired a cab. I didn't wish to cause a disturbance." She glanced around the room. "But I'm not certain about the accommodations. Perhaps we should have let a room at the Palace Hotel?"

Gerald shook his head. "I'm afraid the fires decimated the Palace. The Fairmont, too. And every other room is likely full."

Ruby unpinned her hat. "We weren't expecting you for weeks, yet. The wedding is still a month away. Why are you so early?"

The older woman lifted her chin, her presence in the room much larger than her diminutive height. "I had to meet this girl who's stealing my Robert away."

Gerald leaned on the back of the closest chair, his legs growing unsteady. The women moved to sit, their conversation flowing unhindered. He sagged into the cushioned seat, fighting the urge to slip away to his study. If it were anyone other than Ruby's mother, he'd sneak off without guilt.

As if sensing his thoughts, Otto hopped up from his spot and padded over to plop on Gerald's shoe tips.

"Where are Elizabeth and Miriam?" Ruby perched on a chair, her hat resting on her knees.

"Mrs. Larkspur was kind enough to let them rest in your room, my dear. Or should I call it Miss Fischer's room?" She tittered, her laugh ringing off the walls. "Goodness, this is confusing. All in one house." She glanced around the parlor, her lips pursed. "How cozy. You should have informed me, Ruby. I would have made other arrangements."

Ruby fingers clenched and unclenched. "There are no other arrangements to be had, Mother."

"And when will Robert and Miss Fischer be returning?" Her eyes spoke volumes.

"They're not here?" Gerald jerked back to attention. "I thought Robert would be home from the hospital hours ago."

Gerald's mother returned, setting a teapot on the low table. "He telephoned earlier. He met Abby downtown, and they were picking up a few items for the wedding. They will be late for supper."

Mrs. King sniffed. "I guess I will be forced to wait before meeting my soon-to-be daughter-in-law."

Gerald leaned back against the seat, his energy draining away through the floorboards.

"Gerald, are you all right?" His mother's voice cut through the din of conversation.

Gerald's eyes popped open. He hadn't even realized he'd closed them. He jerked to his feet. "Yes, yes, fine. If you ladies will excuse me, I'm going to clean up before supper." He might as well disappear, it couldn't make a worse impression than falling asleep.

"Of course." Ruby's soft voice broke through his weary thoughts. "You've had a trying day."

Her emotion-laden words tugged at his heart, but he managed to nod and leave the room without further embarrassment. She didn't know the half of it—and never would, if he had his way.

Gerald dragged up the stairs to his room, his hand aching as he tugged off his tie. How much tissue did Robert remove? He'd willingly accept the morphine shot now if it wouldn't put him under the table at supper. How would he survive meal conversation in this condition? Gerald reached for the knob and swung the door open, ready to fall into the bed.

The bedcovers stirred.

Gerald froze with one foot over the threshold, his heart leaping to his throat. Did Mrs. King say the girls were in Ruby's room or in his?

A young woman sat up, her face appearing in the shaft of light, long blonde hair cascading over one shoulder. "Hello?" She pulled the covers up to her throat.

"I'm sorry. I didn't realize anyone was in here." Gerald retreated to the hall only to back into another woman, her hand sliding along the paneling.

Beneath dark glasses, a cautious smile lit the woman's face, her reaching fingers traveling up his arm. "You're not Robert. I'd recognize his voice."

"Uh, no—I—" He pushed his back against the wall for support as his breathing settled ragged in his chest.

The young woman from the bedroom appeared in the doorway, dress rumpled. "You must be Dr. Larkspur." She tucked her hair behind her. "I'm sorry we surprised you. I'm Elizabeth King, and this is my cousin, Miriam."

Gerald edged sideways, the blind woman's hand still resting on his bicep. "I didn't intend to disturb you. My apologies, ladies." He glanced back and forth between the two women, the house suddenly feeling very small.

Miriam smiled, her face pointed in Gerald's general direction. "I believe we're the ones who have disturbed you, Doctor. It's so kind of you to take us in."

The younger girl piped up. "And to give us your room, too. Your mother said she'd moved your things to the study with Robert."

Gerald dug into his pocket for a handkerchief to mop his brow. Robert's family was multiplying like rabbits. He removed the woman's grip from his arm, passing her to Elizabeth. "It's a pleasure to meet you, ladies. I look forward to seeing you both at supper. Now, if you'll excuse me . . ." He turned on his heel, the floor rocking like a boat deck. Gerald caught himself on the hall table, sending the Bristol vase rocking. He waited for his equilibrium to settle before plodding down the back stairs, through the kitchen, and into the study.

Gerald pulled the door shut behind him and leaned against it. Sweat dampened his shirt. He unfastened his collar and gulped air, the room settling into a slow spin. He'd dreamed of filling the rooms with family, but in the fantasies it had always been his own family. *A few weeks—that's all it will be.*

He fought the urge to slide down the door and collapse on the rug, instead managing a few stumbling steps to the divan. Gerald landed on his sore arm with a groan. He pulled himself over to his back, tucking the hand into the hollow of his stomach. Chills raced across his skin, but he couldn't summon the energy to reach for the wool blanket folded on the far end. He curled into a fetal position and closed his eyes. A few minutes rest and he'd be fine.

Ruby gritted her teeth and tucked both hands under her knees. Mae had excused herself to make final preparations for the meal. "I'm pleased to see you, Mother, but you haven't answered my question. Why are you here so early?"

Her mother sighed. "I told you, darling, I wanted to meet Robert's bride before the festivities begin."

While there's still time to interfere. "You're going to love Abby. She's the perfect match for Robert."

Her mother's brows drew together. "One who's traipsing through the city unescorted? I hope she understand what it takes to be the wife of an esteemed physician. She should be here, preparing a comfortable home for her husband."

Ruby balled her fist under her leg. "It could be a little difficult, considering this isn't their home." She reached for her teacup. "Abby's quite talented with plants and flowers. Have you seen the garden, yet?"

"One can hire a gardener for such work."

Had Ruby been this hard on Abby when they first met? A wave of self-loathing swept over her. "Trust me. Robert adores her, and it's what counts."

The front door rattled, sending Ruby's stomach into a dive. If only she could warn the happy pair before they stepped into the lion's den. She hopped up from her seat. "Excuse me a moment. I'll see who it is."

Mother rose unsteadily, leaning on her cane. "Are you expecting guests?"

Ruby dashed to the front hall, intercepting Robert and Abby as they walked through the door. "Mother is here."

Their smiles froze, the color draining from Abby's face.

Robert cupped both hands under Abby's elbows. "Don't worry, sweetheart. She's going to love you. Just like I do."

Ruby pushed down the panic rising in her chest. Was her brother really so naïve? Their mother would never convince him to revoke his proposal, but she could make life miserable for Abby in the meantime. No woman would ever be good enough for her only son.

She flanked Abby's other side, weaving a hand through her arm for extra support. Perhaps if Mother saw their united front, she'd back down.

Robert glanced around the hall. "Is Elizabeth here, too?"

"Upstairs in our room, sleeping. I haven't seen her or Miriam, yet. Gerald and I just arrived fifteen minutes ago."

Robert's brow creased. "How is he?"

"Gerald?" Ruby paused. "He seemed tired. He went up to his room. Why do you ask?"

Her brother glanced away. "No reason." He gestured toward the parlor. "We'd best get this over with."

Abby gazed up at him, her eyes rounding.

"I mean, it'll be fine." He patted her hand as he steered her toward the front room. "Mother. Such a surprise." Robert placed a quick kiss on his mother's cheek.

She placed both hands on either side of Robert's face. "If you would write home once in a while, we wouldn't have to drop in unexpected to discover news of you. It took Ruby's arrival to entice you into telling us of your engagement."

"With the disaster and my work, there simply wasn't time." Robert stood upright, freeing his face from her grip.

"No time to write your family? Tsk." She stood on tiptoe and straightened his tie. She glanced around his side. "Aren't you going to introduce me?"

"Of course." Robert reached back for Abby's hand, tugging her forward. "Mother, this is Miss Abigail Fischer, my fiancée. Abby, my mother, Mrs. Hetty King."

The older woman glanced up and down the girl's slight frame. "A pleasure, my dear. You two met during the quake?"

Abby pulled off her straw boater and clutched it before her like a shield. "No, Mrs. King. Months before, actually. He and Gerald were treating my sister."

Robert cleared his throat. "I explained everything in my last letter, remember? Abby is Gerald's cousin—second cousin."

"Oh, yes. Dr. Larkspur. The pale young man who was just here."

Ruby bristled. Her mother wrapped every statement with a thin insult. "Perhaps I should check on Elizabeth and Miriam. They'll want time to freshen up before supper. You said they were in my room?"

"No." Her mother tapped her mouth with a well-manicured fingertip. "As I think about it, I believe Mrs. Larkspur said she was placing them in Dr. Larkspur's room."

Ruby's stomach tightened. Hadn't Gerald gone up? She excused herself and hurried up the stairs. Giggles echoed down the hall as she approached. She tapped on Gerald's door.

Elizabeth pulled the door open wide and flung herself into Ruby's arms. "Ruby! You're here."

Ruby hugged her younger sister, surprised by the emotion washing over her. She pulled back and gazed into Elizabeth's face, as if reminding herself of each sweet feature. Ruby released her and stepped into the room to grab Miriam, pulling her into a tight embrace. "I'm so glad you're both here. I've missed you. I hadn't even realized how much until now." She pressed her palms to her own cheeks. "So much has happened since I left."

A smile lit Miriam's face, her face pointed toward the door. "I knew it. I knew God had big things in store for you here." She squeezed Ruby's arm. "I can't wait to hear all about it."

Ruby sighed. "Did you meet Gerald? He was coming up here."

Elizabeth giggled. "Is he the owl-eyed fellow who ducked out of here twenty minutes ago? I believe we gave him quite a fright."

"Oh, dear. He's going to regret ever having any of our family to his home." Ruby covered Miriam's hand with her own. "Do you know where he went?"

"I heard his footsteps going down the back stairs." A stitch formed between Miriam's brows. "His gait seemed unsteady. I thought perhaps he'd been drinking, but I didn't smell anything."

Ruby's throat tightened. Something was wrong—Miriam always seemed to know these things. "He was acting a little strange. I'll go check on him."

Miriam caught her hand on the way out. "Is he part of the 'so much' that's happened?"

A wave of heat prickled up Ruby's neck. She leaned in close to whisper in her cousin's ear. "Maybe."

A trickle of girlish laughter followed her into the hall. Where would he have gone? It was dark in the garden, so likely he headed for the study. She pattered down the back stairs. The study door was closed, but no light shone under the door. Ruby turned the latch, peeking inside.

Gerald lay sprawled over the divan, face flushed and eyes closed.

Ruby hurried over and knelt at his side. "Gerald?" She placed a hand on his cheek, the heat from his skin making her draw back. "Gerald?" She gave his shoulders a gentle shake, and his bandaged hand tumbled to his side, catching her arm on the way down toward the floor. Ruby gathered it into her own, turning his palm upward. A spot of fresh blood showed in the center of the gauze.

She tucked it close to his side and reached for the blanket, drawing it over him.

His lids flickered open, eyes glazed. "Ruby?"

"Shh. You're not well. Why didn't you say something?"

He groaned, shifting on the cushion. "Robert said he wouldn't tell you."

A hot poker lodged in her throat. Her brother knew? "Lie still. I'll get you some water. You're feverish."

He gripped her forearm for a moment before wincing and dropping the wounded hand back to his chest. "No. No one must know."

She pushed to her feet. *Why do doctors believe they should be immortal?* Ruby tucked the blanket around his chest, but stopped short of kissing his forehead, memories of their last conversation flooding her mind. She hurried to the parlor.

Entering the room, she spied her mother grilling Abby with questions, Robert hovering nearby. Ruby grasped his arm and pulled him to the hall.

"Ruby, I'm not certain I should leave them alone. Mother is acting like a lioness on the prowl."

She shook his arm, a storm brewing in her chest. For the moment, she didn't care what Mother said to Abby. "What's this about Gerald being ill, and you not telling me?"

His jaw dropped. "What?"

She clamped hands on her hips, squeezing until she could feel the corset boning under her fingers. "He's in the study, burning up with fever."

Robert took two quick steps. He cast a quick glance at Abby before turning and dashing toward the study.

⚬

Gerald gripped the edges of the cushion as the room swayed. Another earthquake? He pushed his eyes open and tried to rise, but a hand met his chest, pressing him back into the soft surface. He squinted against the dim light.

Robert stared back, his face blurred by the shadows.

"What's—" Gerald paused, clearing the rasp from his throat. "What's wrong?"

"I'm trying to figure it out." Robert's mouth pulled down into a pinched frown. He pressed the back of his hand to Gerald's forehead.

Gerald tried to swipe away Robert's touch, but his arm refused to cooperate. "I'm just overly tired."

"Tired doesn't cause fever." Robert stood and turned on the floor lamp above the divan. "What else is going on?"

Robert's voice faded to a hum as Gerald closed his eyes against the bright light. Too tired. Too heavy. A second voice tickled at his consciousness. Ruby? He forced his eyes back open, the light stinging at his pupils. The resemblance between brother and sister blurred together for an uncomfortable moment. Gerald turned his face from the light. "Why's everyone in my room?"

Robert leaned forward, his head framed by the lamp's glowing corona. "Were you ill this morning? When did this start?"

How was he supposed to answer questions when the man never paused for two seconds in a row? A dense fog settled over Gerald. "Don't know. Go away."

"Not a chance. How's your throat?" He gripped Gerald's chin, pulling it downward and to the side.

Gerald managed to grip Robert's wrist, but the pain in his palm jerked him back with a groan. He closed his eyes and let his arm fall back to his chest. Let Robert do as he wished. Then maybe he'd leave.

&

Ruby's heart thrummed as she shook her hands loose. *There's no need to panic over a minor fever.* Bad timing, sure. She glanced over her shoulder. How many guests?

The curve of Robert's spine as he perched on the edge of the sofa sent a second wave of flutters through her chest. "It's not serious, right?" She edged closer, gazing over his shoulder. Gerald's eyes rolled shut, strands of damp hair sticking to his forehead. Her throat tightened.

"Can you find me a better light? I want to look at his throat."

Ruby strode to the desk and lifted the lamp, but the cord wouldn't reach. She found a small oil lamp on the shelf with a book of matches. She lit the lamp, replaced the chimney, and brought it to Robert's side.

"Hold it steady." Robert tipped Gerald's head back and lowered his chin. Gerald groaned and turned away, but Robert held him firm. He glanced at Ruby. "Can you locate a tongue depressor as well?"

She nodded, hurrying to the glass-fronted cabinet where Gerald kept his supplies. She extracted a wooden stick from the box and delivered it to Robert. She passed the lamp to her other hand, holding it high.

Robert pulled open Gerald's jaw and twisted his head a little further toward the light. With a sigh he released his friend and sat back on his heels.

Ruby set the lamp on the desk. She braced herself against the wooden surface, watching as Robert pressed his face into his hands. Her stomach churned. "It's diphtheria then?"

Without looking up, Robert nodded.

"He said he'd already had it."

"There are certain instances . . ." Robert broke off, dropping his hands to his knees. "How much antitoxin do we have left?"

A chill swept over Ruby. "Two vials. But they're intended for children at the camp."

A shadow passed over her brother's face. "We'll give him one tonight. I'll drive over to the Presidio in the morning and shake down the military doctors until they produce more. I can't believe they haven't stockpiled extra."

Ruby's shoulders felt tight, like her shirtwaist had shrunk a few inches. "But the illness is less dangerous in adults—right? He could fight it off. The children—"

"Are you the doctor?" Robert pushed to his feet, his dark eyes sparking. "I'm in charge here. Get the dose *now*."

Ruby stumbled back, unaccustomed to harsh words from her brother. She turned and raced from the room. Where had Gerald left his bag? Normally he walked it straight into the study and placed it by the ornate cabinet. The front hall remained strangely quiet, the voices from the parlor now hushed.

The black bag sat under the coat tree. Ruby picked up the heavy leather tote. Clutching it under her arm, she glanced into the front room.

Her mother and Abby sat side-by-side on the sofa, their quiet conversation stiff. Otto lay sprawled on the rug at Abby's feet, his chin on the toe of her shoe. He glanced toward Ruby with large eyes, but didn't move from his position.

Footfalls on the stair pulled her gaze upward. Elizabeth and Miriam descended, the baby cradled in her cousin's arm.

She opened her mouth to tell them she'd be late to supper, but as her eyes rested on Miriam, all words rushed from her head. *Baby.* Her throat squeezed. "Go back upstairs and stay there."

The women stopped. Elizabeth's eyes widened. "What's wrong?"

"I can't explain just now. I'll come up in a minute." Crushing the bag against her ribs, Ruby dashed for the study and slammed the door behind her. "Robert—what will we do? The house is full of people. What of Miriam's baby son?"

Her brother bent over Gerald, unfastening his shirt. "We'll isolate Gerald here in the study, but it would be best if they left immediately." Robert straightened. "They've been in his room all this time?"

"I believe so."

Robert blew out a noisy exhale. "I wish he'd told us he was unwell. I wouldn't have . . ." His gaze shifted downward.

Ruby shook the senseless words from her ears and imagined pulling on her hospital apron and cap. Calm action saved patients, guilt would only be wasted effort. She pressed the glass vial of antitoxin into Robert's palm. "Here, you do this. I'll inform Mae and see what we can do about the family."

Robert closed his fingers around hers. "Ruby—" His brown eyes filled with emotion that traveled through his touch. "I'm sorry for yelling before."

She managed a brisk nod. "I understand. He's your friend." She retrieved her hand and hurried from the room. *And my future.*

37

Gerald stirred, the weight of the blanket pressing him into the drowning blackness. He pushed against it, heat burning in his throat and chest. He lifted a hand up to his neck, opening his eyes.

Robert sat beside him on the cushion, a syringe lifted upright as he tapped it with a fingernail.

"Wha—" Gerald's voice cracked. He coughed twice into his hand. "What is that? The morphine?"

His friend met his gaze. "We're far past morphine. It's antitoxin."

Gerald mustered his energy, thrusting away the smothering exhaustion. He braced his elbows on the divan and pressed up. A tight strap squeezed his bare arm. "No. We're almost out. The children need it."

Robert placed a hand on Gerald's sternum. "You need it more. You're not going to be able to fight this off without help."

A tightness settled in Gerald's chest, and he fell back against the pillow. His tongue grew thick, a bitter taste filling his mouth. "The biopsy?"

His friend lowered the syringe, lines deepening around his eyes. He nodded. "Cancer. No question."

The darkness beckoned. Gerald eased back against the pillow. A cold touch on his arm, and his lids popped open. The acrid scent of isopropyl alcohol burned his nose.

Robert swiped the swab across Gerald's arm, light reflecting off the needle. He tightened the strap around Gerald's bicep. "Hold still. I'm going to do this intravenously."

"Don't waste the medicine on me." Gerald's voice rattled.

After a quick glare, Robert jabbed the needle into his vein. "Listen to your doctor, will you? We're fighting this. The diphtheria first, then the cancer."

"I'm not ignorant like most of—" His throat constricted, choking off his response.

Robert's attention never wavered from the needle. After the dose emptied, he withdrew the needle and pressed a wad of cotton to the site. "You, better than anyone, know there are many treatments available. I'll try every single one."

Gerald pressed his bandaged hand over his arm as Robert removed the strap. "I also know how the story ends."

"Look, you're not only my friend, but—against my wishes—my sister's fallen in love with you. That's two good reasons for you to fight this."

A throbbing ache pulled at Gerald's head and heart. "You—you haven't told her."

"No. But I should."

Gerald squeezed his eyes shut and turned toward the wall, pulling the blanket with him. He pressed the quilt to his chin. "Let me deal with this."

"I won't say anything to the family until you've recovered from this." The springs creaked as his friend stood and walked across the floor. "But you can't keep everyone in the dark."

The void called to Gerald, pulling at every limb as if it could suck him through the divan and down into the earth. He imagined Ruby's hand reaching through the blackness. His stomach twisted, coiling like a snake waiting in the gloom. "No. I can't."

Ruby cradled the tiny infant, sighing as the baby crammed a tiny fist into his round mouth. She touched the little bud of a nose with her clean fingertip, warm and pink from the scalding wash.

Elizabeth helped Miriam stack clothes in their trunk. Ruby's younger sister frowned. "We only just arrived. This is ridiculous. It's not like we haven't already had every illness under the sun."

Ruby turned away, stepping up to the long window and relishing the sunlight dappling on baby Jackson's rose-petal skin. "Yes, but this sweet treasure hasn't. We can't risk his safety." She pulled the newborn close, rubbing her face against the top of his fuzzy head. "We lost an infant in the camp last week from diphtheria. I'd never forgive myself if something happened to him."

Miriam swept up a handful of cotton diapers and thrust them toward Elizabeth. "Has he already been exposed? I don't mean to be heartless, Ruby, but isn't this the doctor's room?"

"I think he'll be fine if we move you now."

Elizabeth closed the lid with a snap and swept a loose strand of blonde hair from her face. "Where will we go? Mother said there were no hotels."

"Mrs. Larkspur has found a place for you with one of her friends." Ruby placed Jackson in his mother's arms. "I wish it were different. I wish you could stay."

Miriam touched Ruby's sleeve. "Will we be able to see you? What about the wedding?"

"I don't know. Let's see how Gerald responds to the antitoxin." She pulled her friend close, the touch of her hand crumbling every wall around her heart. "I hope so. We have so much to talk about."

Miriam lifted Jackson to her shoulder and pulled Ruby close. "We'll pray for Dr. Larkspur." A smile curled at the corners of her lips, and she tipped her head close. "Gerald."

"I'll pray, too." *Prayer would have been Gerald's first response.* Ruby rested her head against Miriam's, watching Elizabeth make final preparations. Why had she always felt closer to her cousin than to her baby sister? Elizabeth had always been the rough-and-tumble little girl, so young when their father died. Ruby still remembered the rosy, tear-stained cheeks as Elizabeth cupped an abandoned kitten or an injured bird—as if the child's heart was too big for her chest.

The young woman straightened, willowy and beautiful. Not a child, anymore. "I think we're ready. Mama said Abby would be joining us."

Ruby sighed. "Poor Abby. Meets her future mother-in-law and moves in with her, all in one day."

Miriam squeezed her hand. "Don't worry, I'll look after her. And God will watch over you and Gerald." She smiled. "Even though I can't see Jackson with my eyes, I can feel when he relaxes in sleep against me. It's your turn to rest in God's arms—trust in His plan."

Ruby laid a hand on Jackson's back, as if she could absorb the baby's peace through the thin blanket. "I'll try, Miriam. I'll try."

Gerald coughed and gagged, waking himself from a fitful sleep. A dim light filtered through the study windows, casting eerie shadows across the room. He struggled to swallow, his throat swollen and raw. He choked a second time and pushed up on his elbows, gravity assisting functions he'd long taken for granted.

As the blanket fell to the side, a burst of cold swept over his damp skin. Gerald reached for his shirt to fasten the buttons, only to discover it missing. He yanked up the blanket and clutched it to his thin white union suit, shivers coursing through his frame. A fire roared in the small fireplace, but the heat didn't seem to reach the divan.

A faint murmur drew his attention. Ruby slept in the wingback chair, her legs tucked underneath her, and the dog nestled on her lap. The firelight flickered on her face, accentuating the curve of her cheek. Her hair hung in a loose rope over one shoulder, the curls spiraling into a joyous riot of freedom.

Gerald lowered his head to the pillow, a tender ache wedging itself between his ribs. What had he done to earn the love of such a woman? He would do anything to stay at her side for a lifetime, but it was not to be. *God, I thought this was Your plan.* He ran his fingers up his arm to where Robert had injected the antitoxin. The serum would battle this infection, but what then? Cancer would eat away at his body until he ended up like one of their patients—wasting away in a hospital bed until the end.

"*If we married.*" Her words echoed in his mind. He swallowed hard, the pain like a hole in his chest. *You'd bury a second husband.*

⁂

Ruby stirred, opening her eyes to the early morning light filtering through the window. The fire had burned down to ash, the sooty smell permeating the closed room. She stretched her arms over her head, sending Otto slithering to the floor. He landed on his paws with a whimper.

Gerald's pillow had escaped off the side of the divan. He lay curled on his stomach, the quilt hanging loose around his chest.

Ruby fell to her knees beside him, checking his temperature with a kiss to the forehead. She still remembered her portly nursing instructor's dimpled smile and laughing voice. "*The lips are more sensitive than the hand, dearie, but save it for children. Male patients might get the wrong idea.*" Gerald might not be a child, but Ruby didn't mind giving him a few ideas or, at least, pleasant dreams.

She pushed fingertips through his damp hair, smoothing the lines on his forehead. Yesterday her heaviest concern had been assuring she didn't spend time alone with the man. A few hours later, she'd slept in the same room. She tugged the blanket over his shoulder. *I'd spend every night by your side, if you'd have me.*

Gerald shivered and pulled the covers closer, drawing his knees into a gentle curve.

Ruby stood and hurried to the fire, lifting the poker and stirring the ashes before adding a small pile of kindling. The antitoxin would work soon. It had to. She glanced over her shoulder. Gerald would tell her to pray. How long before prayer became a habit?

The fire crackled, the embers catching the slivers of wood. Ruby blew against the sparks, encouraging them to flicker to life. *As this family's done for me.* Ruby closed her eyes, sensing God's presence only a heartbeat away. *Lord, thank You for bringing me here. Miriam said You had a plan greater than what I'd choose for myself.* Her spirit jumped and spun like the flames, dancing upward on the wings of her prayer.

Ruby sank back onto her heels, gazing into the twisting orange and gold light. *I know Charlie is safe in Your hands.* Her heart squeezed at the memory. The words of the verse Mae often quoted floated through Ruby's mind. *For I know the thoughts that I think toward you, saith the Lord, thoughts of peace, and not of evil, to give you an expected end.* She glanced back to where Gerald slept. *God had thoughts for me. For us both.*

She added a small log to the fire before pacing back to her chair. Ruby dropped into the seat and pulled the shawl into her lap as she gazed at the sleeping man. *Help him, Lord.*

38

*R*uby stepped into the hall, leaving the study door open a slight crack. The cooler air swept down the corridor, teasing her cheeks with its refreshing sweetness. Voices in the kitchen drew her forward.

Mae dealt plates out onto the table as Robert leaned against the stove, cradling a mug of coffee. He straightened as Ruby entered. "How's the patient?"

Ruby pressed fingertips to her lips as a yawn stalled her words. "About the same, I believe."

Mae hurried to her side, guiding Ruby to a chair. "I peeked in earlier, and you were both sleeping. I feel so much better having you and Robert here." Lines around the older woman's mouth spoke to her fears. She turned to Robert. "I've always worried for you boys, working around such horrible disease. It's a wonder you're not sick more often."

Casting table manners aside, Ruby propped her elbows on the table as a brace for her chin. "Gerald told me he was never ill."

Mae placed a cup of coffee in front of Ruby, its pungent fragrance filling the air. "I can hardly remember the last time. But I do remember him having diphtheria as a toddler. My sister Margaret's girls—Clara and her sister—were living with us at the time, helping with the mercantile. All three of them had it. Thankfully, we didn't lose any of them, but I was so frightened."

Ruby took a sip, the bitter brew scalding its way down her throat. "My father said you could only get it once. I don't understand why Gerald contracted it a second time."

Robert set his mug in the sink with a clatter. "Now that Gerald's room is empty, I think we should move him."

"Do you think it's wise?" Mae pressed hands to her apron front.

"Trust me, I've slept on the divan for months. He'll be more comfortable in his own bed."

Ruby reached for a piece of toast. Perhaps she'd feel more alert if she ate something. "Can he make it up the stairs, do you think?"

"I'll help him." He swiped a hand over his eyes. "Then I'll drive over to the Presidio and ask about additional antitoxin."

Mae's lips turned downward. "I thought you already gave Gerald a dose."

Ruby touched Mae's arm, unaccustomed to seeing the woman so ruffled. "We did. But if he doesn't improve, he may need another. Plus, the vial we administered was intended for a patient at the camp."

Her brother stood, his back to her, shoulders hunched as he gazed out the small window. "He tried to refuse it. A doctor is no good to his patients if—"

"Is it so serious?" Mae sank into the chair beside Ruby.

Ruby wrapped an arm around Mae's shoulders. "The antitoxin should help." She nodded encouragement to the worried mother. "And he has an in-house doctor at his beck and call."

Robert chuckled. "Not to mention a nurse willing to sit up all night."

She shot him a warning glance. "As I would with any patient."

"I'm glad you kept an eye on him. I haven't had a decent night's sleep in weeks. Once I return, I'll take a watch, so you can rest."

Mae frowned up at him. "I may not be trained, but I am his mother. I'll sit with him. I won't have you two taking ill as well."

Robert straightened his tie. "Gerald's fortunate to have two devoted ladies at his side. I leave him in good hands."

Ruby stood, walking to her brother's side. "What of the hospital?"

"I'll ask Dr. Lawrence to assist me. If Gerald approves, I might ask him to come on the project full-time. It might take months before Gerald feels up to going back to the hospital." Robert glanced out the window, his eyebrows drawing together.

Ruby's throat tightened. There was something her brother wasn't saying. "Why so long?"

He paused, opening his mouth and closing it again. "It can take longer for adults to recover."

Mae lifted her head. "What of the wedding?"

Robert lowered his head. "We'll know more in a few days."

❧

Gerald sank onto the bed, sweat beading along his brow. He'd never known a trip up the stairs to require such exertion. Even leaning on Robert's shoulder and gripping Ruby's arm did little to stabilize his wobbly legs. His stomach roiled as another set of chills raced across his skin. The pinched expression on Ruby's face made him curl inward.

Ruby plumped the pillow and eased him back.

Gerald tucked his hand under the sheet. The last thing he needed was for Ruby to offer to change the bandages. The charade had gone on long enough. He needed to either tell her the truth or assure she'd never ask the question. A coughing fit rattled his chest, tearing upward through his raw throat. Gerald turned and covered his mouth with his good hand.

Robert stood at the end of the bed, deep creases forming on either side of his mouth.

Gerald swallowed, with effort. "Pseudomembrane?"

His friend nodded. "And spreading. You're going to need more antitoxin. It's a severe case. We need to arrest the progress before you end up with heart damage."

"No."

Ruby perched on the edge of the mattress, the springs squeaking. "Don't argue with your doctor." She slid a cool hand along his bare arm. "But you'll get your way for now. We don't have any doses to spare."

Gerald turned his face away, her touch sending prickles through his body. He closed his eyes, letting the malaise carry him away. The deadly words waited in the back of his throat, like the infection ripping through his system. *I don't love you. Go home.*

Quiet footsteps sounded as Robert moved around to the side of the bed. "I'm going to head over to County and see what they have on hand. I can't believe there's none left in the city."

Ruby stood, the pressure easing on the bed. "Thank you, Robert."

"Be sure to—" Gerald attempted to clear his throat, but the blockage remained. Pretty soon he'd have no voice. "Be sure to check on Mr. Guinness."

Robert nodded. "I'll swing by on my way. Get some rest. The only patient I want you worrying about today is you."

"Who's worried?" Gerald coughed several more times, pressing a handkerchief against his lips.

Robert smiled. "Not me." Shadows around his eyes spoke otherwise. He pressed a hand to his sister's shoulder before he left the room.

Gerald shifted in the bed, tensing as Ruby straightened the covers. "You don't need to hover. It doesn't help."

She pulled her hands back and reached for the book on his bedside table. "I could read to you, if you like."

Gerald rolled to his side and tugged the quilt to his chin. Perhaps she'd get the idea if he didn't bother to answer. The room grew quiet, except for the sound of the rocking chair being drawn up. *Lord, I'm not ready to do this yet.*

Head down, she spread the white dress across her lap and took up a needle.

Gerald propped an arm under his cheek and watched until his weary eyes glazed over. The serenity of her presence lulled him to a fitful sleep, shadows chasing him through his dreams. By the time his lids eased open the light had dimmed.

Ruby remained fixed in the chair. Her attention flitted up from her work. "You're awake."

He grunted, not trusting his crusty voice to cooperate. He glanced toward the windows, assessing the angle of the sun to determine how long he'd slept. The dog lay curled against his leg, like a hot water bottle. Gerald frowned. *How did it get up there?*

"Can I get you anything? Water? Soup?" Ruby bundled up the dress and set it on the rug, scooting to the edge of the seat.

"No." Gerald coughed out the word, lifting a hand to his throat. His neck felt foreign to his hand, swollen. He shifted, a jab of pain lancing through his arm and chest.

Ruby jumped forward. "What's wrong? Why did you make that face?"

The pulsing ache settled between his ribs. "No-nothing." He pressed his wrist against his chest.

Ruby sat down on the edge of the mattress, sending a second twinge down his arm. "I don't like your color."

"Off the bed." His words came out in a wheezing gasp.

She hopped up, her hands fluttering about her middle. "Let me get you some water."

Anything to have her out of his way for a moment. Gerald nodded, eyes watering, as she sprinted from the room. The pain softened, allowing his lungs to pull in a decent breath. He pressed his head back against the pillow, fingers of cold creeping along his arms.

Scurrying footsteps sounded from the doorway. Ruby appeared at his side, a glass clutched in her hand, droplets of water clinging to the outside. "Can I help you sit up?"

"No, just put it down."

"Gerald you need—"

"Put it down."

She set the cup on the table with a sigh. "You're not going to make this easy, are you?"

Get it over with quickly. Like removing a bandage. Gerald pushed up on his elbows. Ruby moved to help, but a quick glare sent her into reverse. Gerald shimmied up to a near-sitting position, unable to ignore the hollow pain in the center of his chest.

Ruby pulled the chair closer and sat. "Better?"

He managed a nod, lie that it was.

She lifted the dress from the basket and spread it on her lap. "I'm almost finished. I think Abby will be pleased." She ran her finger along the leaf designs decorating the skirt. "I've grown quite fond of your cousin. My future sister." Her lashes fluttered as she glanced up at him. "I guess it almost makes us family, so to speak."

His mouth dried as he gazed at Ruby, her beautiful face showing signs of strain from the past two days. *Imagine what the next few months could bring.* He reached for the glass, his hand trembling.

She twisted her fingers in the glossy fabric. Probably the effort of not assisting him.

Gerald took a sip, the liquid doing little to soothe the burning in his throat and chest. He lowered the glass to the table without causing a spill. "I need to . . . to tell you something."

She drew the fabric tight against her lap and slid forward, the rocker tipping with her motion.

He lowered his gaze, the brilliance of her eyes tempting him to surrender the battle before it had begun. "I've been thinking." Gerald pressed his arm harder against his chest, as if it could obliterate the gnawing ache. "I made a mistake. I shouldn't have . . ." He dared a glance in her direction, but pulled his attention away in the next beat. "We're not right together."

Ruby froze, half off the chair. Her face faded to an ashen color. "What do you mean?"

"I don't love you." The words tore at his throat. "I won't marry you."

Ruby clutched the silk to her stomach. "This is the fever talking."

What could he say to make her believe? "I need to be truthful, in case I don't recover." He coughed into the handkerchief, determined to finish the relationship before his resolve wavered. "I thought with you being married before, and with us living in the same household, I might be able to convince you to . . ." His throat closed, refusing to cooperate. He choked the words out. ". . . *reward* my hospitality. Why do you think I pulled you in my room the other night?"

The wedding dress rippled to the floor in a glossy heap. "Why— why are you saying this?"

"I won't die with it on my conscience."

She shook her head slowly, lips parted. "I don't believe you."

The room spun. *Finish it.* "Are you really so naïve?"

A long moment passed before a strangled sound emanated from Ruby's throat. She pushed to her feet, swaying as she swiped a knuckle under one eye. "You—you're . . ." Her fingers curled into fists. Her shoe slid on the discarded garment as she fled the room.

Gerald closed his eyes as the door slammed. He pulled his shoulders inward, trying to ease the clawing ache in his ribs.

⤸⤵

Ruby pounded down the narrow stairs and dashed through the back door, gulping back sobs. The grape arbor beckoned like the arms of an old friend. She sank down on the wet bench, her thoughts tangling like so many unraveling stitches. *I knew it. Too good to be true.* Ruby dropped her head into her hands, her stomach quivering. How could this have happened? How could she have let herself be deceived?

Ruby lifted her head, staring up through the dripping vines to the gray sky. Hot tears burned her eyes. "Can I go home now, God?"

"Ruby?" Mae's voice echoed in the distance. "Are you out there?"

Ruby swiped at her eyes with the heel of her hand. "Y-yes." She stood, peering toward the house.

Mae stood in the doorway, one foot on the back step. "Goodness, I've been looking all over for you. Robert is on the telephone. He says it's urgent."

A drip from the vines caught the back of Ruby's neck. She gathered her skirt and hurried Mae's direction.

Mae retreated inside, twin creases forming between her eyes as she scanned Ruby's appearance. "Why ever were you outside in the rain? Don't we have enough sickness at present?"

At least Gerald's mother would disregard any tears as stray raindrops. She dabbed a handkerchief at the tip of her nose and sniffled. "Robert's on the line?"

"Oh, yes." Mae waved her hand toward the study. "He's phoning from the hospital, I believe."

Ruby shivered, the damp soaking through her shirtwaist and chilling her skin. She strode through the house until she reached the study, grasped the receiver, and pressed it to her ear. She lowered her damp backside into the seat, not caring whether she ruined Gerald's fine chair. "Robert? Are you still there?"

The telephone crackled to life. "Ruby, there you are. I need a favor."

She glanced around the study, her woolen cloak still resting on the side of the divan where she'd nursed Gerald the night before. A lump rose in her throat. "What is it?"

"I'm over at County Hospital. They only had two doses of anti-toxin left. I'm going to deliver them to the camp right away. But we won't have any left for Gerald. How is he?"

Ruby pushed a hand up through the strands of hair, the curls loosening each time she touched them. How was he? A cad. A scoundrel. Her throat tightened as new tears sprang to her eyes. *Think like a nurse. How is the patient?* She straightened her shoulders and took a mental assessment. "Not improved, I fear. He's feverish, weak. His cough has worsened, I believe. Breathing is labored."

"Listen, Ruby," Robert's voice lowered. "Is he complaining of any chest pain?"

"No." She frowned. Had he? "But he clutched his chest oddly at one point. And I thought his color was off."

"Off how?"

She bit her lip. "He seemed a little gray, almost. I'm sorry, it's not a clinical description."

"No, it's what I feared. If we don't get this in hand, the toxins will travel his bloodstream and damage his heart."

Ruby closed her eyes.

"Ruby, are you still there?" Robert's voice sounded tinny and distant.

She swallowed. "Yes. What do I do? Can you come?"

"I need to go to the camp first." The line crackled as Robert paused. "Doctor Jones from County said he sent three doses over to Lane yesterday. Why don't you go over and see if they still have any? Ask for Dr. Lawrence."

She glanced over at the clock. The cable car would be passing as they spoke. She'd never catch it. "It might take me a while to get there and back."

The telephone crackled. "Take Gerald's car."

Her stomach twisted. "I can't."

"Yes, you can. You must."

"Robert," her voice tightened. "I can't drive—no, I won't drive. I'll run, I'll catch the cable car . . ."

"If Gerald's showing signs of cardiac involvement, Ruby, there isn't time. You need to go now. I'll meet you at home as soon as I can get away." The line went dead.

Ruby clutched the receiver in her clammy palm. She settled the receiver onto the hook with trembling fingers. Her heartbeat sounded in her ears. She glanced up at the ceiling, imagining Gerald clinging to life, waiting for the lifesaving medicine.

Had he clutched at his chest, or had she just imagined it? His fever wasn't raging out of control. He'd already had the infection as a child. Surely, it couldn't have traveled to his heart in a few hours. A tremor raced through her shoulders. And if it had?

"Why do you think I pulled you into my room the other night?"

It hadn't taken much pulling. She'd practically thrown herself into his arms. Prickly heat crawled up her neck. Did this man deserve her care?

Yes. Her heart whispered the word before her brain had a chance to consider the question. She pushed up from the chair and walked to the glass-fronted cabinet. Unlatching the door, she retrieved the stethoscope. Ruby's eyes blurred. She strode from the study and scaled the stairs. Pushing open the door to his room, Ruby glanced inside.

Gerald lay on his side, brows pulled low over closed eyes, forearm braced against his chest, the bandaged hand nestled under his chin.

Otto lifted his head, as if keeping watch, and thumped his tail against the mattress.

Ruby bit her lip, praying the man was sound asleep. She rubbed the cold metal on her cheek to warm it as she crept forward, falling to her knees beside the bed.

He didn't move.

She grasped Gerald's wrist and slid it out of the way. "*Are you really so naïve?*" His words echoed in her mind.

He stirred, the lines on his brow deepening, but his eyes remained closed.

Ruby situated the earpieces. Her fingers trembled as she maneuvered the chest piece inside the yoke of Gerald's shirt and pressed the diaphragm to his skin. Closing her eyes, she focused on the swishing sounds. She lowered her head, moving the bell to the left to improve the clarity. Was the heartbeat abnormal, or was Robert's prediction coloring her observations? Ruby leaned closer, as if it would help the sound come clear. An extra swish sent a tremor through her fingertips. *Not right. It's not right.*

She opened her eyes to see Gerald gazing back at her. "Problem?" His voice cracked. He caught her hand as she withdrew it from his chest. "What were you doing?"

"I—nothing. Everything's fine." She put on her best nursing face as she pulled her fingers free. "Just checking." She slid the blanket back up to his shoulder and gave him a gentle pat. "Go back to sleep."

"Why . . ." He struggled to form the word, but with a grunt, he pulled his wrist back to his chest and closed his mouth.

"I'm your nurse, remember? That's enough."

⁂

Gerald blew a long exhale through his lips as the door clicked shut. Ruby might be harder to run off than he'd estimated. He wrenched his eyes shut as another wave of pain arrived. Much more of that and it might be out of his hands. He considered calling her back.

Dying with a clear conscience? Hardly.

Ruby had patted him like a cosseted child. At least she treated him as a nurse, not as a woman in love. Gerald rolled over in the bed, staring up at the ceiling. Not good enough. He needed to drive her away completely. *I won't allow her to stay and watch me die—whether from diphtheria or cancer.*

Gerald's gaze wandered the cracks in the ceiling left from the April earthquake. He'd thought he'd come close to understanding

God's motives behind everything that had happened over the past year, but now he was as lost as ever. *God, You need to help me, here. Obviously, You don't want us together. But I beg of You—draw her close to Your side.*

❧

Ruby climbed into the automobile's seat, her heart beating out a bizarre rhythm in her chest, like the feet of the Chinese dragon dancers she'd seen as a girl. She pulled Gerald's driving gloves over her fingers, the leather sticking to her damp palms. "I can do this."

She reached for the wheel, her mind suddenly going blank. She closed her eyes and went back through her memories. "Switch. Lever. Crank." Her eyes fluttered open, and she scanned the controls. She switched on the ignition and pushed the lever into place. Everything looked ready. Everything except her instructor.

Ruby clambered back out of the seat and hurried to the crank. Eyeing the handle, she set her jaw and gave the lever a timid turn. The cold metal slipped from her grip before it went a quarter turn. Didn't Gerald give some warning about it jerking back? She steeled her nerves. This had to be done. Ruby grasped the crank with both hands and gave it a hard yank.

The motor coughed twice and then caught, sputtering and growling to a nice cadence. Ruby patted the hood. "Thank you." She paused, her hand still on the vibrating hood, and glanced upward. "Or thank You. Whichever."

Ruby hoisted herself back into the seat, taking a quick moment to adjust her hat. The straw boater bobbed on its single hatpin. With a groan, she yanked the pin and tossed the hat into the rear compartment. She'd also forgotten to retrieve her driving veil. On a day like today, who cared?

Ruby adjusted the controls, stepped on the reverse pedal, and eased the automobile out into the alley, the tires crunching over the loose stones. After a false start, she managed to shift the vehicle back to forward and roll toward the main street, her heart climbing further up her throat with every inch. She slowed to a stop at the end of the alley, peering across the main street as automobiles, delivery wagons, horses, and buggies rattled past in both directions. *I can't do this, God.*

A man rode by astride a tall, black horse. The animal tossed its head, rolling its eyes and dancing sideways. Ruby's stomach soured, a familiar metallic taste rising on her tongue.

She lowered her forehead to the wooden wheel, closing her eyes as the wood vibrated against her skull. *Lord, everyone tells me You have a plan for me. I hope they're right, because I can't control this part. I need You.*

Sweat trickled down her back, dampening her corset. She lifted her head and glanced both ways. Traffic slowed and Ruby fumbled for the pedals. The automobile lunged forward, bouncing into the street like a spirited colt let out into spring pasture. With a cry, she eased off the throttle and jammed her foot on the brake to avoid colliding with the back of a farm wagon. The driver turned and scowled before tossing his burning cigar down onto the road. He muttered some unintelligible words and slapped the traces along his horses' backs.

Heart pounding, Ruby guided the auto along the rough cobblestones, keeping a large cushion between herself and the wagon, crawling along at a snail's pace until he waved her around. Swallowing hard, she steered to the left and swerved wide around the slower vehicle, darting back in before another automobile approached in the opposite direction.

She gritted her teeth and scooted up along the seat cushion for a better angle on the pedals. The wind tugged at her curls, more popping loose by the second. By the time she arrived at Lane Hospital, she'd look like a wooly mammoth. She didn't dare lift a finger, her hands busy wringing the life out of the steering wheel.

After a few more blocks, the tension tapered from her arms, her elbows lowering a few inches. It wasn't so different from driving on a deserted country road. As long as she ignored the other vehicles and the—she jammed her foot down on the brake pedal as a newspaper boy dashed across the street, his short pant legs flapping.

Ten minutes later, Ruby slowed to a stop in front of the hospital, parking the automobile behind a white delivery truck. She shook out her arms and climbed down to the sidewalk, knees quivering. Ruby dashed up the stairs and pulled open the double doors.

The hospital lobby yawned in front of her, the expanse of black and white tile flooring exaggerating the lengthy path to the front desk. The duty nurse glanced up, her lips pulling into a tight frown. "Nurse Marshall—we just heard the news. How is Dr. Larkspur faring?"

Ruby gripped the edge of the counter with Gerald's gloves. "Not well, I'm afraid. My brother—Dr. King sent me. He said to ask for Dr. Lawrence."

The nurse glanced down at the roster sheet open on the desk. "Drs. Dawson and Lawrence are in surgery in the amphitheater. He should be done in an hour or so." She leaned closer to Ruby. "I hear the patient isn't expected to survive. More of a spectacle for the medical students, if you ask me."

Ruby didn't have time for chitchat. She spun on her heel and raced down the hall, dodging patients and equipment until she stood at the surgery door. Glancing past the No Admittance sign, Ruby yanked at the door handle.

The cavernous amphitheater extended upward, the gallery seats filled with murmuring medical students. Ruby stepped through the dark entrance hall into the bright light spilling from the glass atrium above.

Dr. Dawson's head jerked up, his long silver whiskers bristling as his lips pulled back from his teeth. "What are you doing in here?"

After maneuvering through San Francisco traffic, Ruby wasn't about to be intimidated by a barking physician. "I need to speak to Dr. Lawrence. It's urgent."

Dr. Lawrence glanced up from his work. His red-stained hands hovered over an open cavity in the patient's chest. "Nurse Marshall? I'll be with you in a moment." He pushed back a strand of hair with the back of his wrist. He turned to the pink-cheeked woman beside him. "Could you get me towel?"

The older doctor sputtered. "Lawrence, what is the meaning of this?" A snicker traveled through the crowd of spectators, a few rising to their feet.

"I apologize, sir. But I believe this may be a life-and-death situation." He glanced toward Ruby.

She nodded, taking a step back toward the exit.

"And this is not?" Dr. Dawson gestured to the motionless form on the table.

"Of course, sir. I won't be but a minute." Dr. Lawrence wiped his fingers on the white towel and shoved it back at the nurse, hurrying to join Ruby in the doorway.

She followed him into the hall, practically tripping on the man's heels.

"I hope this is serious, because I probably just cost myself a month of surgeries." Dr. Lawrence lowered his voice as they stepped out into the busy corridor.

"My brother—Dr. King, sent me. He said you might know where we could get some additional doses of antitoxin."

Dr. Lawrence rubbed his eyebrow, his shoulders rounding. "For Dr. Larkspur? We just heard this morning. Is he worse?"

"I'm afraid so." Ruby lifted her chin and kept her eyes focused on the young doctor. "Did you receive the vials from County?"

He managed a curt nod, shadows drawing close around his eyes. "But we administered them immediately. We have several cases—it's why we requested the serum in the first place. It's in short supply."

Ruby's composure collapsed, her knees threatening to join it.

The doctor took two steps closer and grasped her elbow, as if aware of her crumbling spirits. "If I'd known Gerald was ill, I'd have held one for him—somehow. He and Dr. King only brought me in on the carcinoma a few days ago. I'm still reeling from the news. I can't imagine how you are feeling. It's little wonder he succumbed to the infection so quickly."

Ruby shook her head, the conversations of dozens of people in the hall filling her ears. "Carcinoma? You mean their new patient?"

"I had no idea when they requested my help with the procedure we'd be operating on one of our own. I knew Gerald had suffered a nasty X-ray burn, but I had no idea it had progressed to cancer."

Ruby stumbled backward, her lungs clamping down. *Cancer?* She pressed fingernails into her palm to steady herself. "I'm concerned about the diphtheria right now. We can deal with the . . . the other, later."

"Right, right." The doctor glanced back toward the surgery door. "I need to get back. You might try the General Hospital at the Presidio. The military doctors often keep stockpiles beyond what they tell us about. I believe Dr. King procured some from there before. I don't know if they'll release it to you, though."

"I'll try. Thank you." She pressed a hand against her lace cravat, hoping to slow the bouncing of her heart.

Dr. Lawrence gripped the brass door handle. "Wish me luck."

Ruby stared at the wooden door as it swung shut. Someone bumped her elbow in passing, but she didn't bother to lift her gaze. She gulped stale hospital air, ribs aching. Breaking from her trance, Ruby ducked through the busy hallway, weaving past patients and doctors until she slid across the black and white tiles and slammed though the front door.

Gerald has cancer.

39

Gerald paddled through the waves, pushing his head through the sea foam. Darkness reigned both above and below the surface, but breathing seemed easier up here. The swells lifted and dropped him at their whim, like a carousel ride at the carnival. Gerald didn't know how he'd gotten into the water, but he'd think of it later. Right now, he needed to focus on staying alive.

Spray caught him in the face, tumbling him backward and filling his lungs. He pushed upward, coughing and gagging, but firm hands grasped his forearms and thrust him back under. He sagged down, drawn into the depths.

"Gerald, wake up." A voice sounded out of the gloom.

Gerald's eyes flew open, even as the pressure of the deep water crushed against his chest.

Robert's face loomed before his eyes. "You're going to throw your-self off the bed."

"Can't . . . breathe." Gerald coughed out the words.

Robert reversed the pressure and yanked Gerald forward, pulling him to a sitting position.

A deep gulp of air rushed into Gerald's lungs, an agonizing burn as it burrowed through his chest. He gasped and choked, the jolting pain demanding a second and third inhalation. After a few excruciating minutes, the spell passed. The pressure eased, air pushing in and out of his chest with less effort. Gerald's racing pulse slowed, the ravening waves fading into his memory. He leaned on his friend's arm, focusing on little more than staying conscious. Sweat trickled down his back.

"Better?" Robert tipped his head.

Gerald managed a weak nod.

Robert released his grip. He gestured to the dachshund pacing the floorboards near the bed. "Otto was downstairs raising a ruckus. When I got up here and found you, you were hardly breathing." He balled up a pillow and forced it behind Gerald's back, adding two more for good measure. "Let's keep you upright. Chest pain, yes?" He retrieved the water glass from the bedside table and pressed it into his friend's hand. Not waiting for an answer, he pulled a stethoscope from the bag.

"Myo—myocarditis." Gerald leaned against the feathery pile, fighting the sensation of falling back into the sea.

"Yes, Dr. Larkspur. I'm not your student anymore."

"Sorry. Habit."

Robert settled the stethoscope bell against Gerald's chest, the metal like a sliver of ice against his skin.

"At least Ruby stopped to warm it."

Robert glanced up from under his dark brows. "Was she in here? Very long ago?"

Gerald shrugged, the action jolting his ribs. He pressed an arm against his side—the action becoming habit. "Asleep. Remember?" A wave of exhaustion swept over him, traveling upward from his legs. He closed his eyes.

His friend sighed and folded the instrument in his palm. "Your heartbeat is irregular."

Gerald grunted. "Could've told you."

"Gerald . . ."

At the touch of Robert's hand, Gerald opened his eyes.

"We're out of antitoxin." Lines gathered around his friend's mouth, visible through the day's growth of beard. Robert raked a hand through his dark hair, spiking it like a boar bristle brush. "I could use your advice."

Gerald moistened his chapped lips. "Talk through it." His partner might not be a student anymore, but sometimes he still needed a cold dose of reality.

Otto scrambled up into Robert's lap and leaped across to the foot of the bed. He sniffed Gerald several times before curling up beside his leg.

Robert sat back in the chair. "Male patient, age thirty-one. Mid-stage carcinoma on left palm, nodes potentially involved."

"They're involved."

Robert's lips thinned. "You don't know for certain. They could be enlarged due to the infection." He cleared his throat. "Presenting with diphtheria—pseudomembrane partially obstructing throat and tonsils, progressing to myocarditis after single dose of antitoxin."

"Why?" How easily he slipped back into instructor mode. Perhaps he should seek a teaching post at the medical college. *Assuming I live.*

Robert cleared his throat, leaning forward and bracing his elbow on his knees. "The toxin spreads through the blood and causes inflammation of the heart muscle and valves."

"Prognosis?"

Robert hesitated. "If it's slight, patient might see a complete recovery." Silence fell over the room, broken only by the sound of rain dripping from the roof. "If it's severe . . ." Robert lowered his gaze, "the patient could endure years of chronic heart disease."

Assuming he had years. Gerald turned his head away from the light. "Or?"

Robert jumped from the chair, sending it skittering back across the floor. "Why are you doing this? You know the prognosis. Paralysis. Congestive heart failure. Do you need me to say it?"

The dog lifted his head, his gaze darting between the two men.

Gerald took a deep breath, ignoring the rattle in his chest. "I want you to face facts. If I survive this—what do I have to look forward to? Carcinoma. Amputation. Prolonged illness. Death."

Robert spun around to meet his gaze, fire in his eyes. "You can't predict the future. You don't know how far the cancer's progressed.

Give yourself a chance to survive. Please. For your family's sake. For my sake."

A weak laugh gurgled in Gerald's stomach. "You've always been the dreamer. I'm the pragmatist."

Robert sank back into the chair. "It's why we make a good team." He leaned forward, bracing an elbow on each knee, his energy feeding into Gerald. "Let my dreams carry you, for once. You're the one who led me to faith—what if God wants you to live?"

Gerald studied his young partner, his shoulders hunched forward. "Then He's not making it easy."

Ruby pulled onto the bluff overlooking the water, the rocks crunching under the automobile's tires. The misty rain stung at her cheeks, her throat squeezing until she allowed a frustrated cry to thrust its way up from her stomach. She slammed both palms against the wooden wheel. "How dare they not tell me?" She dug the heel of her hand against her eyes to wipe away the stinging tears.

The wind tugged at Ruby's curls. The hat was lost under the seat after her hair-raising drive through the city. She didn't bother to retrieve it as she stepped out of the car.

Ruby stomped over to the bench where she and Gerald had sat together just a few weeks ago. His gentle kiss lingered in her memory. Had he known then? She stood and glared at the bench as if Gerald sat waiting. "You let me fall in love with you. You spoke of God and trust and life." Her stomach curdled. "You never mentioned cancer or—or death." She crouched and swept up a handful of pebbles and flung them at the imagined apparition.

His hoarse voice from earlier today echoed in her thoughts. "*I don't love you . . . I won't die with it on my conscience.*"

It was a lie—at least in part. He didn't want to die with *her* on his conscience.

Ruby stumbled forward, gazing out over the fog-strewn waterway. *I was content alone. I didn't need him, God.* Another sob tugged at her chest. She pressed both hands against her lace blouse, pushing away the ache growing there.

The chilly breeze pulled at Ruby's sleeves, so she wrapped her arms around her middle, tucking her hands under her elbows. Wisps of fog crept up over the bluff. Except for the temperature, it reminded Ruby of steam from an overheated kettle. An unwanted tear spilled down her cheek, tickling the edge of her lip. *I didn't need him, did I, God? I needed You.* The new idea curled its way through her heart. Warmth flooded through her frame, beginning in the center of her back and working its way to her fingertips. She swallowed a sob inching its way up her throat. *I needed You.*

The wind lifted her hair, blowing it back from her face. Ruby closed her eyes, letting the damp air wash over her. *I need You.*

Gerald lay in the quiet room, glancing across at his mother dozing in the chair. He pulled his eyes away. She'd endured too much already. What would she do if he died? Gerald grimaced. *When I die.*

Robert's words continued to echo through his thoughts. *"What if God wants you to live?"*

Gerald lifted himself a few inches to get more air past the membrane obstructing his throat. *Do You, Lord?* Was this just another challenge to face—a trial to build his faith? Gerald pulled his hand out from under the quilt and stared down at the bandages. He flexed it, wiggling his fingers. Fingers he might never see again.

He closed his eyes, Ruby's face never more than a whisper away from his thoughts. For the first time all day, he allowed her image to flood his mind. *Lord, even if I decide to fight this, I can't ask her to do the same.* A dull ache settled in his stomach. Life without her would be gray and empty, but at least he wouldn't be risking her heart as well.

Gerald pushed up to a sitting position, the quilt falling to his waist. He reached for the water glass, his arm trembling with the simple exertion. A sip of the tepid liquid cooled his throat, and he returned the glass to the table. Red light streaked the sky outside the window, the rain-soaked afternoon giving way to a quiet evening.

Gerald shivered in the silence, but he didn't reach for the blanket. He gazed out through the pane at the setting sun. *Your will, Lord. Not mine. If You want me to live, I'll do my best. Just You and me.*

❧

Ruby pushed through the doors of the Presidio hospital, glancing down the long hall.

A nurse approached from the left. "Can I help you, ma'am? Visiting hours are long over." As her gaze traveled over Ruby's unkempt appearance, her upper lip twitched.

Ruby ran a quick hand through her curls. They likely resembled the frizzy-topped marigolds in her mother's flower box by now. "I'm Nurse Marshall from Lane Hospital. We have a desperate need for diphtheria antitoxin."

The nurse frowned. "Most of the doctors have gone home. Major O'Connor is on call. Would you like me to contact him?"

Ruby pushed down the scream building in her chest. "How long will it take? I have a patient in severe distress. He can't wait."

The woman pursed her lips. "Come with me. The pharmacist owes me a favor." She flashed a crooked smile. "A few, in fact."

Ruby scurried after the woman as she marched down the long corridor. "I don't want to get you in trouble." She choked off the words. *What am I saying?* Ruby cleared her throat and began anew. "I appreciate your help. I wouldn't ask if it wasn't urgent."

The nurse touched her white cap. "I know, honey. Nurses must join forces, right?"

Ruby's heart lifted. "Yes, we do. Oh, thank you!"

"Don't thank me yet. Pharmacists are a different ilk." The woman turned the corner and approached a long desk where a white-coated man worked, head down. "Henry?" Her voice carried a teasing lilt.

The man lifted his head, his brows pulled together. "Margie— don't call me—I mean, Nurse Jones . . ." He sputtered the words, face flushing.

She placed both hands on the desk and fixed him with a stare. "There's no one here but me—and my friend, Nurse Marshall from Lane.

He jerked to attention and nodded at Ruby. "Ma'am."

Nurse Jones explained the situation, laying it out better than Ruby, in her exhaustion, had managed.

The pharmacist scowled, clamping both hands on his hips. "We can't release medication without a doctor's order."

Ruby lifted her chin, matching Nurse Jones's strong countenance. "Do you have a telephone? Contact Dr. Lawrence at Lane Hospital. He sent me. The patient is another doctor."

The man paled. "Dr. Lawrence? He works with Dr. Emil Dawson, doesn't he?"

Ruby nodded, folding her arms across her sodden shirtwaist. "And I don't believe either like to be kept waiting."

The pharmacist swallowed, his Adam's apple prominent in his narrow neck. "No, ma'am." He glanced at the telephone on the desk. "I'd heard rumor a doctor had taken ill. Didn't know it was him."

Ruby opened her mouth, but the words died in her throat as he spun toward the long line of shelves.

"I've got twelve vials. How many do you need?"

40

$\mathcal{G}$erald leaned on the cane, regretting his stubborn desire to stand for the entire ceremony. Two weeks out of bed, a man should be able to be on his feet for ten minutes. Or so he thought.

Abby's smile brought a lump to his throat. She clutched her father's arm, her freckles fading behind a rosy blush.

Herman Fischer's eyes brimmed with tears as he bent down and kissed his daughter's forehead. "*Meine Prinzessin.*"

She touched his cheek. "Always, Papa."

Gerald ignored the tightness in his chest, probably nothing more than fingers of joy spreading through his body. His family had long anticipated this day. He scanned the room. His mother sat in a chair to the left, her silver hair pulled up in a tortoiseshell comb—Clara's doing, most likely. She'd pulled little Davy onto her lap, where he sat with two fingers jammed into his mouth, his eyes wide. Tiny lines crinkled at the corners of Clara's eyes. This past year had aged her, but the smile playing at her lips added a fresh vitality he hadn't seen in years.

The parlor overflowed with visitors, even more crowding in the entryway, craning their necks to see. Hospital staff, women from the Red Cross and Ladies' Aid, family from near and far—everywhere he looked, he spotted more familiar faces. Robert's mother, his sister

Elizabeth, and Miriam sat perched on folding chairs near the front window.

Robert's back was turned toward Gerald as he took his bride's hands, but the younger man's shoulders rose and fell as if the wonder of the moment had swept away the year's trials.

Gerald pushed down the jealousy coiling around his insides. *God, You're all I need. Don't let me forget.* He squeezed the cane's handle, glad for its support. The ceremony hadn't even begun, and his knees wobbled.

As Abby turned to face her groom, Gerald's eyes met Ruby's on the far side. Gerald blinked hard, unable to break his gaze. Ruby's curls had been drawn back, as usual, but she'd left a few straggling around her ears, like the coiled tendrils of the grapevines in the backyard. He longed to gently tug on one and watch it spring back into place.

A tiny smile curved about her lips. She'd never asked him about the things he'd said to her that horrible day, even after appearing at his bedside with the lifesaving vials. She'd been kind and concerned, but distant.

When he'd announced his diagnosis to the family, she was the only one who didn't respond with shock, though Robert insisted he'd never spoken a word of it. The family had pulled together, as always. This time around him. The idea tore at his spirit.

Ruby turned her attention to the ceremony, her eyes blinking back moisture.

Is she thinking of Charlie? Or of me? His heart ached with longing, but things could never be as they had before. He tore his gaze away, turning to face Patrick as the clergyman opened the Scriptures.

Sweat dampened Gerald's collar. *Speak fast, man. Or they'll be picking me up off the floor before the lucky couple gets to kiss.*

◆

Ruby chewed on her cheek as she gazed at the beads of sweat on Gerald's brow. She should have insisted on bringing the man a chair. There was no rule requiring the best man to stand. His pride would be his downfall.

She glanced at her dress. The aquamarine silk puckered where it drew snug over Ruby's hips. She ran a quick hand along her side to smooth the glossy fabric. Mrs. Larkspur and Mrs. Fischer had been at it again—pies, cakes, cinnamon buns, cookies. How was a woman to resist such temptations? She risked a quick glance at Gerald. *Or other temptations?*

Abby, on the other hand, had barely eaten a bite in days. The poor girl complained of fluttering nerves, but Ruby sensed it was more in regard to the presence of Ruby and Robert's mother than the wedding itself. Ruby ran a critical eye down the embroidered leaves on her friend's gown. Was the third one crooked? She'd whispered a prayer as she embroidered each leaf. She prayed for God's protection over Abby and Robert. She asked God to heal her heart and to turn her focus to serving Him. She begged Him to save Gerald's life, even though they'd never be together. And she'd prayed God would show her His perfect plan.

Ruby pressed the bouquet to her midsection and tried to focus on Patrick's words. The guests had laughed several times, thoroughly entertained by his banter. The sparkle in his green eyes danced as he spoke of Robert, Abby, and of the great God who'd brought them together in the midst of chaos.

Thank you, Lord, for bringing me here. And for my brother's happiness. Robert's eyes remained fixed on his beautiful bride. Even the presence of Abby's surprise guests—Kum Yong and Miss Cameron—hadn't cast a shadow over his enthusiasm for the day or his love for her.

Before she knew what was happening, the vows were complete, and Robert leaned forward to claim a kiss from his bride. He held her face in his hands and whispered something into her ear bringing a smile and a blush.

Ruby's throat tightened. Had she looked as happy when she'd wed Charlie? She used the thumb of her lace glove to wipe an errant tear from the edge of her lashes.

The visitors clapped and cheered, rushing forward to congratulate the bride and groom before they had an opportunity to depart. Ruby retreated two quick steps to avoid the surging crowd.

She backed straight into Patrick, who put a hand on her arm to steady her. "Steady, Mrs. Marshall. No escaping so easily."

She cast a quick glance toward Gerald to be certain he moved toward a seat before someone jostled into him by mistake. She turned back to Patrick. "It was kind of you to do this for Robert and Abby. Thank you."

He smiled. "The joy was mine. I've performed quite a few earthquake weddings in the camp, you know, but this one 'takes the cake,' as they say."

Ruby laughed. "And cake there will be. Mrs. Larkspur and Mrs. Fischer have been planning it for weeks."

"Then I'm in the right place." His smile flashed for a brief moment before his eyes narrowed and voice lowered. "Are you well, my dear? I observed you and the good doctor are not . . . as you were. If I might say so."

The crowd moved in step with Robert and Abby as they edged toward the door. As the far end of the parlor cleared, Ruby managed to take a step back from Patrick without tromping on someone's shoe. "Yes, be that as it may—"

He lifted a quick hand to stop her words. "I didn't mean to imply anything. Only, I count you among my friends—both of you. It troubles me to see you in pain."

Across the room, Gerald pushed to his feet with the help of the cane. He followed the crowd as they mingled in the hall and dining room.

Perhaps he's going to his room. I wonder if he needs help. Ruby placed a hand on Patrick's arm. "I appreciate your concern, Patrick. I think God had other plans for us."

Patrick lifted a brow. "I've rarely heard you speak of the Almighty in such welcoming tones."

"We've come to an understanding. Gerald helped me learn to trust God with my future." She glanced over to where he stood at the far side of the room, conversing with a few guests. "Even when life seems unbearable." Ruby turned her eyes back to Patrick. "I don't think I'd seen much need for faith before coming here. I thought I could take care of everything by myself."

The reverend smiled and clucked his tongue. "Sometimes He allows us to wander for a time, but eventually we reach the end of our own strength. We must learn to let Him take the reins."

"Or the steering wheel." Ruby watched as Gerald paused at the door, bracing a hand on the frame. She touched Patrick's sleeve. "Would you excuse me?"

He touched fingers to his forehead as if tipping an invisible hat. "I'll go find the cake of which you spoke so highly."

Ruby hurried across the room to Gerald's side. "Can I give you a hand?"

"Under normal circumstances, I'd be embarrassed to accept such an offer."

She wove an arm under his. "How about you pretend to escort me? Then no one will suspect I'm offering assistance."

"Clever." He took two steps from the doorframe and paused to catch his breath. "I can't believe I'm done in already."

"You're barely out of bed. Robert should have pushed the wedding back a month or two."

Gerald frowned. "I wouldn't allow it. Today is about Robert and Abby. It's been a relief to have a full day where no one's concerned with me." He started toward the kitchen. "Let's take the rear stairs. I don't want an audience for my humiliation."

Ruby laughed. "You never have been one for the spotlight. Neither you, nor Abby."

"Must be a family curse."

She squeezed his arm. "Or a family strength."

Abby's surprised squeal drew their attention toward the front door. Robert scooped her up in his arms and carried her across the threshold, much to the delight of those watching.

Ruby sighed. "My brother, on the other hand, doesn't seem to mind the attention. Doesn't he know you're supposed to carry the bride *in* over the threshold?"

"Does it matter?"

"I suppose not. It's not like they have a home of their own yet."

Gerald sighed, shuffling on toward the kitchen. "There's no hurry. My home is theirs, as long as they'd like to stay."

"Do you ever long to have your house to yourself again?"

He shook his head. "Never. My dream was always to fill this house with family. Of course," his voice cracked, "I thought it would be my own." Gerald's hold on her arm faltered.

Ruby repositioned her grip, adding a little extra strength underneath his elbow. "Maybe it will. Someday."

"I believe that ship has sailed."

She swallowed down the lump in her throat and stepped into the kitchen, giving Gerald a tug to keep him moving. "Want to sit for a moment?"

Patrick leaned against the kitchen counter. "May I be of assistance?" He raised his brows. "Or should I give you two some privacy?"

Gerald grunted. "No need for privacy, Reverend. If you wouldn't mind offering a strong arm, perhaps you can spare Ruby the effort of hauling me up the stairs. She seems to think I need to rest."

"I'd say it's always wise to listen to a lady. A rest it is. My arm is at your service, Doctor. Unless you'd rather I hoist you over my shoulder like a sack of potatoes?" The man chuckled.

Gerald's muscles tightened in Ruby's hand. "An arm will be sufficient. Thank you, anyway."

Ruby moved to follow, but Gerald pressed her back. "I think I can make do with Patrick's help, Ruby. Go join the others. You should be wishing the happy couple good-bye, not dragging this broken body around." He leaned on the cane.

"They're only sneaking away for one night. Hardly a long trip. But I will leave you two to tackle the ascent." She patted Gerald's hand. "Get some rest. I'll save you a piece of cake."

Ruby bit her lip as the pair disappeared up the narrow stairway, their arms around each other's shoulders. One would think they were old school chums—not one-time rivals. She sighed. Probably best she didn't return to the man's room just now, anyway. His sad words about family had triggered a similar longing in her heart. Two lonely people would not be good company for each other after such a blessed event. She closed her eyes for a moment, drawing on a host of pleasant memories to give her strength for the rest of the afternoon and evening. No more weddings after today. At least this much was certain.

Gerald sagged onto the mattress, the ache in his chest radiating through his shoulder. He clamped an arm against his ribs until the pain eased. His heart had been much improved since the additional injection of antitoxin and the occasional dose of digitalis, but every once in a while he still received twinges as if in reminder of what he'd lost.

Patrick gestured to the chair parked near the foot of the bed. "May I? Or do you need to sleep?"

"Please do." Gerald loosened his tie and collar. "Do you mind if I take this off?"

"No, sir. Hate those celluloid things, myself." Patrick dropped onto the seat, leaning back with a sigh. "Wonderful day. Your family must be bursting with joy."

"After this past year, I think we've earned some high spirits." Gerald yanked the collar free and set it on the bedside table. He'd put it away later. He kicked his feet up onto the mattress and leaned back on the mound of pillows the womenfolk had arranged for him. Every day he seemed to find one more. Soon there'd be no space for him on the bed. "I discouraged the relationship back when Robert and Abby first met. My friend courting my cousin? She was also sister to his patient. There were so many barriers to them ever being together."

Patrick propped a heel up on the bed frame. "Seems God had other plans."

Gerald pulled off his shoes. "He does sometimes, I'm learning."

"Are you speaking of them or of you and Ruby?"

Gerald cleared his throat, eyeing the clergyman. Not a discussion he wanted to have with someone who had declared his intentions toward Ruby months ago. "Perhaps both."

The man leaned forward, supporting his chin with a hand. "She tells me you led her to God's fold."

"She said that?"

"Something akin to it. Perhaps you missed your calling."

Gerald exhaled slowly. "I'm glad to hear she's choosing to trust Him. I was afraid with everything happening—"

"You mean with you pushing her away because of your illness?"

A familiar ache settled in Gerald's chest. "Not any of your business, is it?"

Patrick chuckled, cocking his head. "Of course not. But it leaves me in prime position to pick up the pieces."

Gerald sat forward, "Now, see here—"

"I'm jesting, doctor." He lifted both hands, palms outstretched. "The woman made her choice plain. She's not interested in me. I pale in comparison to the heroic doctor."

Gerald ran a hand through his hair, leaning back. A chill washed over him. Wouldn't he wish her all the happiness in the world?

"So, your fervor for the woman hasn't waned." Patrick's mouth lifted into a smile. "Why are you refusing her love?"

The sound of an automobile horn blasted out front, people cheering in response. One happy couple, heading out to face the world together. A sick feeling sank into the pit of Gerald's stomach. Rice flew, but never for him. "God doesn't intend for me to have such a life."

Patrick tapped two fingers against his chin. "You claim to know God's will?"

"The woman of my dreams stepped into my life—into my arms. Now I'm losing one of those arms to cancer. I might die. I can't ask Ruby to share an uncertain future."

"She already buried one husband."

"Exactly." Gerald pressed back against the wall of cushions as the man fell silent.

Patrick stood and paced to the window. "I can see her down there, waving at the bride and groom. She looks content." He turned and faced Gerald. "She shouldn't have married Charlie Marshall. After all, he was going to die and leave her childless and alone."

"They didn't know what the future held."

Patrick folded both arms across his chest. "Robert tells me, after the—the surgery, you have a good chance at living a normal life."

"I'll have *a* chance. And only one arm."

"One strong arm to hold her. It's better than she has now."

Gerald lowered his gaze.

Patrick held out his hands, wiggling his fingers. "Of course, I have two arms. Perhaps she'd rather take her chances on a bloke like me. I've got two hands to hold and a long life ahead of me." He cleared his throat. "Unless I fall under a streetcar. Or take a bullet in a camp brawl. Or contract the plague." Patrick walked to the doorway. "'Course, she doesn't love me. But what's love worth, anyway?" He waved both hands before walking out of the room.

Gerald leaned his head back, staring at the ceiling as Patrick's footsteps clattered down the stairs. She could do worse than Patrick. *"'Course, she doesn't love me."*

Would she love again? What kind of man would she choose? Gerald closed his eyes. A two-armed one, most likely.

Ruby leaned against the fence and stared down the street, the guests' mingling conversations humming in her ears. A long afternoon of feasting lay ahead, but a wave of weariness descended on her. Robert and Abby had been wise to escape while they could.

She turned and gazed up at Gerald's house, her eyes settling on his bedroom window. *I hope he's resting.* The memory of his face as he'd watched the wedding tickled at her thoughts. Her stomach quivered. *If only.*

Miriam came up beside Ruby, lacing a wrist through her arm and resting her chin on Ruby's arm as if she too stared upward.

Ruby squeezed her hand. "How did you know where I was?"

"I could hear you sighing from across the lawn."

"I wasn't sighing."

Miriam's mouth lifted into a faint smile. "Yes, you were. Like a girl who has lost her true love. I'm quite accustomed to hearing you sigh."

Ruby's shoulders drooped. "You always see right through me."

"And you're going to let him get away?"

"I can't force him to love me." Ruby picked at the lace on her sleeve.

Miriam patted her hand. "He loves you. I hear it in his voice. The question is—can you still love him, knowing his time might be short? It's a lot to ask of anyone. Even more so for you, after what you've endured."

The soft afternoon breeze fluttered the loose curls around Ruby's face. "I've placed my trust in God. I know His way is best, and I won't turn away now, no matter how much it frightens me. Gerald's illness doesn't change my love for him. But if he's chosen to walk this path alone, what more can I do?"

Miriam cocked her head and touched Ruby's cheek with her fingertips. "Have you asked God?"

"I've asked God to show me His will."

"Just because you're asking God to take control of your life doesn't mean He doesn't want you to ask for things you desire."

A lump rose in Ruby's throat. "Like Gerald?"

Miriam pulled her into a hug. "Like Gerald. I'll ask, too. Let's see what He says."

Ruby glanced up at the windows. *Lord, please.*

41

*G*erald woke early the next morning, the bright sunlight pouring in his bedroom windows. He'd been too exhausted to draw the drapes. He stretched, accidentally knocking half the pillows off the bed. Every sound seemed magnified as he rummaged about the room, pulling on clean clothes and retrieving the Bible from the bedside table. The morning was too inviting to spend it lounging in bed. He'd had enough of sick beds for a lifetime—however long it might be.

Gerald padded down the stairs and out the back door, inching it closed behind him. He listened until the latch clicked into place. The sun's rays did little to warm the dawn air, but the day promised to be pleasant. He tossed a burlap bag from the garden shed across the iron bench, settling down onto its hard surface and letting the Bible fall open on his lap.

His bookmark noted the psalm Dee had requested for her funeral. He ran a finger over the words, reading them to the gnarled trunks of the grapevines. "Lord, make me to know mine end, and the measure of my days, what it is: that I may know how frail I am." Gerald's voice cracked, the words rattling his soul, much like they had the day he read them over Dee's grave. "Behold, thou hast made my days as an handbreadth; and mine age is as nothing before thee: verily every man at his best state is altogether vanity." He pressed his lips together, scanning the next few sentences until his eyes settled on the seventh verse. *And now, Lord, what wait I for? My hope is in thee.*

He closed the Bible, leaving his bandaged hand inside to hold the page. *I place my hope in Your plan, Lord. I only wish I knew what it entailed.*

Otto appeared, as if out of nowhere, placing cold paws against Gerald's legs and looking up at him with a doggy smile.

Gerald jerked his head up, scanning the yard.

Ruby balanced a tray on one arm as she trailed down the porch steps and across the brick path toward him.

Gerald stood. "I didn't mean to wake anyone." He reached a hand out to help her with the tray. She'd made little effort to spend time with him, outside of nursing, since he'd recovered from diphtheria. Seeing her here, within arm's reach, tortured his resolve.

She pulled the tray close. "No, I have it. You relax. No lifting until your doctor approves."

He grunted. "My doctor is a fussbudget. And he's somewhere in the redwoods, deliriously happy."

Ruby's cheeks pinked. She placed the items between them on the bench while Otto wandered off to explore the garden.

He stared down at the plates. "Wedding cake? For breakfast?"

She shrugged. "Let Robert and Abby enjoy their happiness. We'll enjoy their cake."

A laugh bubbled up from his chest, her presence a tonic to his tattered spirits. "I like the way you think." He claimed a fork and passed a second one to her.

She took a large bite, a smear of buttercream icing clinging to her lip. "Oh, tell me this is what Heaven will be like."

He chuckled, fighting the urge to brush the sweet crumbs from her chin. "Better." After a few bites of cake, he cradled a cup of tea in his bandaged palm, wisps of fragrant steam lifting into the chilled air.

She picked a few last crumbs from her dish and lowered the plate to her lap. "Do you think of it often?"

He glanced up, an eyebrow cocked. "Of what, exactly? Heaven?"

"No." She nodded to where he gripped the cup. "What life will be like, after your surgery? It must be difficult to imagine."

Gerald shifted the cup back to the tray and laid the hand in his lap. "It's been with me my whole life." He flexed a finger each in turn. "I've performed amputations on others. I never considered . . ." He curled the fingers toward his palm.

"But it means you can live?"

He met her gaze for a moment before looking away, gauging his words. "There's a decent chance. Robert believes the cancer is contained in the hand."

"Then why are you having part of the arm . . ." She paused.

"Say it." His stomach churned. "If no one else can say it, how can I?"

"Why are you having so much of the arm amputated?"

He lowered his gaze. "To be safe. There are a few suspicious spots on the wrist as well. The burn covered the skin up to here." He rolled back his sleeve, exposing a stretch of puckered skin along the inside of his wrist. "Better to get ahead of the cancer."

Ruby's eyes glistened. "All because of the X-rays?"

"Ironic, isn't it? My reward for trying to help people."

Ruby grasped the tray and lowered it to the ground.

Gerald tensed as she slid closer along the bench.

With a fingertip, she traced the skin on his exposed wrist. Like butterfly wings, she ran her touch along the heel of his hand and across the bandages to his fingers.

Gerald's pulse hammered. He tore his gaze from her touch and glanced at her face.

A single tear glistened on her cheek. "They would thank you—all those people you've helped." She lifted her chin, her blue-eyed gaze holding his captive. "And the people who will learn from what you've done. There may still be a valid treatment in this."

He closed his fingers over hers, the sweetness of her touch too enticing. "If someone can make it safe."

"Will you and Robert continue the study?"

"I'm done with it. I can't speak for Robert. I'll hand my responsibilities over to Dr. Lawrence." He reveled in the warmth of her skin, unable to convince himself to pull away. "I'm not the only one to suffer ill effects. Robert's found other cases in the literature. Lawrence is looking into safety protocols."

"Robert worked with the same equipment. Will he have problems, too?"

"We have no way of knowing." He shook his head. "It's in God's hands."

She pulled her lower lip in for a brief moment as she gazed into his eyes. "So are we."

His stomach tightened and he dropped her grip like a live wire. "Ruby, no. We can't—"

"Are you one to argue with the Lord?"

A lump grew in his throat. "Of course not."

Ruby reached for his hand a second time, pulling it to her lap and opening his grasp. "A gypsy woman once told me she could read my palm."

"You know better."

"Listen to me." She tugged on the bandage, unwinding it until his disfigured palm lay exposed. "You told me to trust God." She ran a finger along the ragged edges of the wound. "If your life's plans are not written here, in these scars, where are they?"

Pain filtered through his chest, his heart beating like a prisoner rattling the bars of his cell. He couldn't let her hope—it wasn't fair. "In God's hands."

"So are mine." She curled his fingers over his palm and drew the hand up to her cheek. "Why can't we live those plans together? Unless God tells us otherwise?"

"Ruby—you've already lost one man."

The hint of a smile toyed around her lips. "And you think I'm not strong enough to live through a second?" She kissed his knuckles, rubbing her cheek against the back of his fingers. "You might be right. But, as my Scripture-quoting father used to say whenever things got tough—'I can do all things through Christ which strengtheneth me.'"

He touched her jaw. "I can't ask you to."

"You're not asking. I am."

His hand paused, midstroke. "You are . . . what?"

Ruby leaned forward and pressed a kiss on his lips before a smile spread across her own. She touched her forehead to his. "Asking you to marry me."

Gerald pulled back, even as his lips hungered for more. "No." He sprang up from the bench, the toe of his shoe catching the tray and sending dishes scattering across the brick path.

She rose, slowly. "I want to marry you. One arm, two arms, I don't care. A month, a year?" Her eyes filled with tears. "How long is a lifetime? None of us knows. I'll cherish every minute with you."

He turned away, his heart pounding. *Lord, is this Your answer?* A rush of energy spread through his fingers, creeping up his arms and flooding his lungs. He blinked back hot tears. Gerald swung back around, grasped Ruby's shoulders, and pulled her to his chest. "Every minute—even if they're few?"

"Each one will be precious."

He kissed her, the warmth of her lips sending tremors through his soul. Gerald brushed his cheek along hers, his hands sweeping up the curve of her spine. "I love you. You know that?"

"I hope so after such a kiss."

He chuckled, the sound unfamiliar and rusty. "I'd best be careful. Too many of those could be dangerous." He smiled, drawing her in for another kiss. "But worth it."

She ran her lips along his jaw, before nuzzling her head between his chin and shoulder. "Let's stay like this, always."

"We can't."

She sighed. "Why not?"

"We're not married. Eventually someone will talk."

She laughed, a musical sound lifting into the cool morning air.

"But we can rectify the situation." He stepped back and gestured for her to sit.

"What are you doing?"

Gerald balled his fists, the weariness settling in before he was ready. *Just one more minute, Lord.* He lowered himself to a kneeling position before Ruby, bracing himself with one hand against the iron bench.

Her eyes widened. She gripped his shoulders as if to provide extra stability.

God's strength flowed into his bent knees. "Ruby King Marshall, will you marry this . . . this broken man?"

Ruby grinned, wiping tears with the back of her hand. "I'd have none other." She tugged on his arm. "Now get up off the ground while you still can. I can't believe you managed it." She laughed as he fell back on the seat.

He stroked the back of her head, the texture of her hair tempting him to pull a few hairpins and see what happened. "I can't believe I did, either." He pressed his lips to hers again, as if her kisses renewed his energy. "Let's make the wedding soon."

"Very soon." Ruby squeezed his arm.

A squeal from the house froze them both. The back door creaked open. The dog yipped from the rose garden, streaking across the yard to the porch.

"Abby and Robert are back already?" Ruby lowered her chin, resting her forehead against his jaw.

Gerald nodded. "Sounds like it. They must have spotted us."

Ruby pressed a hand to her temple. "Window."

"We'll get draperies. Heavy draperies."

"I'll sew them myself."

Movement from the house suggested they'd soon be joined by well-wishers. Gerald lifted Ruby's chin, determined to claim a final kiss before they were interrupted. Whether they had a few months or a lifetime, he was determined not to waste a single God-given moment.

Group Discussion Guide

1. Ruby is terrified of automobiles. Do you struggle with irrational fears? How far out of the way do you go to avoid these triggers? Have you ever been tempted to face them head-on, like Ruby does when she learns to drive?

2. Ruby is afraid to love again because she fears grieving a second time. What frightens you the most about love?

3. Gerald tells Ruby he goes to the Golden Gate vista when he's feeling discouraged. What do you like to do when you're feeling overwhelmed?

4. Gerald uses the image of the water flowing between the headlands as a way to describe a life of trusting in yourself and a life focused on trusting in God. Are you currently paddling in the tumultuous waters, or are you secure in knowing God as your rock? Has it always been like this for you? How has it changed your outlook on life's events?

5. Ruby views marriage as a blending of two fabrics, creating "layers of depth and feeling never existing before."

   If you are married—how have you seen this blending at work? How are you and your spouse different? How are you similar? Do you balance each other, or do the seams sometimes feel strained?

   If you're single, how do you imagine this would work? What qualities would you seek in a spouse? What qualities do you bring to the table?

6. Mae Larkspur quotes part of Isaiah 61:3: "To give unto them beauty for ashes, the oil of joy for mourning, the garment of praise for the spirit of heaviness." What have been the "ashes" in your life? Have you seen God working beauty, joy, or praise into these situations? (Don't be discouraged, He may not have done it yet.)

7. Mae also says, "God created us to be complex beings, made in His image. Our hearts are like a pantry overflowing with

spices, ready to season our lives. Imagine how bland life would be minus their flavor." Which of life's flavors (emotions) would you be tempted to leave out of your recipe?

8. Gerald Larkspur reminds us, "God doesn't always choose the easy road for us. But He always chooses the best path." Has God ever led you down a difficult road? How did you respond at the time?

9. Gerald and Robert have developed such a deep friendship, Ruby says they are closer than brothers. Do you have a friend who is like a brother or a sister to you? How long has it taken you to develop that level of friendship?

10. Ruby makes a difficult choice near the end of the book—choosing to marry Gerald even though he's fighting cancer. Did you agree with her choice? Would you have done the same? What do you think the future holds for them?

Want to learn more about Karen Barnett
and check out other great fiction from
Abingdon Press?

Visit our website at
www.AbingdonPress.com
to read interviews with your favorite authors,
find tips for starting a reading group,
and stay posted on what new titles are on the horizon.

Be sure to visit Karen online!

www.karenbarnettbooks.com

We hope you've enjoyed Karen Barnett's *Beyond the Ashes*, and that you'll continue to read her Golden Gate Chronicles. Here's a brief excerpt from book 3 of the series, *Through the Shadows*.

Sacramento, California
June 1908

Elizabeth King held her fingers against the ivory keys, refusing to stir as the final chord rang through the stillness of the parlor. Were God ever to speak to her, Elizabeth imagined it would be in the precious instant after a last note died away and before an audience responded. The moment preserved a holy space, as if the breath of divinity hung in the air.

No voice arrived today, but there was no audience either. She ran her fingertips silently along the cool surface, the black and white pattern softening as her eyes blurred with tears. As if God would converse with the likes of her, anyway.

After three years of intense instruction, every note conjured Tobias's memory—his touch. She sprang from the stool and stalked to the window, staring out at the darkening clouds. She couldn't let her mind travel to those memories. Before she knew it, she'd be at his door.

"Turn your back on me, and you're finished. You'll never perform again."

She'd done the right thing. So why did the shame still cling, like a vine curling around her soul?

Her mother swept into the room, a cream-colored apron tied over her flowered dress. "Elizabeth—you aren't dressed yet?"

Elizabeth pulled her gaze from the window. "Dressed?"

"Have you forgotten? Mr. McKinley is joining us for supper. I've been trying to get the attorney to come here from San Francisco for months."

The man's name sent a shiver along Elizabeth's skin, like a discordant note in the middle of a Bach concerto. Of course, she'd forgotten—if she'd remembered, she'd have left earlier. "I promised Lillian I would attend the suffrage meeting with her this evening."

"You attend too many of those silly political gatherings. They've ruined you for polite society."

"Mother, you know I've never been much good at 'polite society.' That's your arena."

"Your father spoiled all of you children. I thought you, being the youngest, might turn out all right."

A lump formed in Elizabeth's throat. Even though she'd been young when he passed away, her father's determination and generous nature shaped her heart. *"Your talent is a gift from God, Elizabeth. It brings Him glory."* Not anymore.

"Hurry, now. Mr. McKinley will be here soon."

No escape. Perhaps she could make excuses after supper. Elizabeth climbed the stairs to her room and dug through the wardrobe for a suitable dress. She couldn't choose anything too nice for the cantankerous old lawyer.

Her fingers lingered on her favorite silk gown. The navy blue had gleamed under the auditorium's electric lights as she'd curtsied to a large crowd. Elizabeth shoved it back and pulled out a russet wool skirt and matching vest, instead. Her stage days were past. All she had to look forward to were dull evenings in the company of stodgy attorneys. She might as well dress the part.

Her sister, Ruby, had once described Silas McKinley as being akin to a moray eel, and the image cemented itself in Elizabeth's mind. They hadn't seen him in over a year—not since he divulged that most of her late father's assets had been lost in the fires following the San Francisco earthquake.

With her musical dreams crumbling about her ears and the family in financial crisis, Elizabeth needed a new direction for her life—and fast. Perhaps this evening's suffrage meeting would give her some ideas.